Adriana Herrera was born and raised in the Caribbean, but for the last fifteen years has let her job (and her spouse) take her all over the world. She loves writing stories about people who look and sound like her people, getting unapologetic happy endings. Her Dreamers series has received starred reviews from *Publishers Weekly* and *Booklist* and has been featured by the *Today* show on NBC, *Entertainment Weekly*, *O Magazine*, NPR, *Library Journal*, the *New York Times* and the *Washington Post*. She's a trauma therapist in New York City, working with survivors of domestic and sexual violence.

Joanne Rock credits her decision to write romance after a book she picked up during a flight delay engrossed her so thoroughly that she didn't mind at all when her flight was delayed two more times. Giving her readers the chance to escape into another world has motivated her to write over eighty books for a variety of Mills & Boon series.

Discover more at millsandboon.co.uk

JUST FOR THE HOLIDAYS...

ADRIANA HERRERA

THE STAKES OF FAKING IT

JOANNE ROCK

MILLS & BOON

First Published in Great Britain 2021
by Mills & Boon, an imprint of HarperCollins*Publishers* Ltd
1 London Bridge Street, London, SE1 9GF

www.harpercollins.co.uk

HarperCollins*Publishers*
1st Floor, Watermarque Building,
Ringsend Road, Dublin 4, Ireland

Just for the Holidays... © 2021 Adriana Herrera
The Stakes of Faking It © 2021 Joanne Rock

ISBN: 978-0-263-28308-2

1021

JUST FOR THE HOLIDAYS…

ADRIANA HERRERA

One

"I'm bored of playing the same character," Gael Montez muttered as he flipped through the pages of the script Manolo, his manager—and uncle—had asked him to review. "Is there nothing else I can do than play the 'ambiguously ethnic guy' in superhero ensembles?"

"*Ambiguously ethnic guy* parts in billion-dollar franchises make for a very good living," his uncle responded in that lecturing tone that put Gael's teeth on edge. "Space Squadron money is nothing to lift your nose at, mijo," Manolo continued, offering more unsolicited advice. "And this role has you as the lead, plus you'd get a producer credit. You're just in a mood this time of the year." The older man lifted his champagne flute, signaling to the private jet's flight attendant. Gael glanced away, annoyed that his uncle was right on both counts. His current gig as part of the cast of one of the most popular movie franchises ever was a dream job for anyone, *and* he hated Christmas.

Well, he didn't hate it exactly; it just brought back memories he'd rather forget. And he'd have to put his most cheerful face on by the time they landed, because there was no way he was going to put a damper on his mother's favorite holiday. Not after the year she'd had.

"I'm not in a mood." That got him a scoff from his sister, Gabi.

"You're always in a funk in December, Señor Grinch."

Gael bared his teeth at his sister, who loved to comment about his less than festive disposition around the holidays and every other "attitude" of Gael's she found lacking. Gabi lived to bust his balls. "I'm just tired," he sighed, and he felt it. Bone tired and depleted in a way that was starting to worry him. It was like in the past year he'd become completely numb. He did his work, and he did it well—Gael had high standards for himself and he never gave anything less than one hundred percent to any of his performances. He just couldn't get excited about *anything* lately. Maybe he was burnt out. Since his breakout role in an acclaimed cable series five years ago, he'd been working constantly. Offers just started coming in, and they never stopped. And having been raised by a single mom, who at times struggled to put food on the table, didn't let Gael even consider turning work down. He couldn't even remember the last time he'd taken more than a few days off to just do nothing. Maybe he needed a break.

He had the next ten days, at least.

The production schedule for the most recent installment of the Space Squadron—in which Gael played the brown guy with superpowers—allowed for time off from the press tours for the cast and crew for the holidays. Which was why Gael, Gabi and his uncle were on their way from LA to his house in the Hamptons, where his mother and the rest of their family would be spending Christmas. He was looking forward to not having to be "on" for the cameras 24/7.

He wasn't an ungrateful ass. He knew how lucky he was to have made it as far as he had. You didn't have to be in Hollywood too long as a Latinx actor to notice there weren't many others around. Never mind being cast for one of the most profitable movie franchises in the industry. On paper, he was living the dream. His profile was growing with every one of the movies he was in, and what was more, he was able to provide for his entire family. Hell, it seemed he employed half of them.

But five years into what seemed like movie after movie where his culture had no bearing—where his roots were some muddled inconsequential footnote—he yearned to take on a project that would show a different side to him. He had a couple of co-stars from Squadron—Tanusha, a Malaysian actress who was his love interest in the movies, and Kwaw, a Ghanaian actor who was his friend off- and on-screen—who had warned Gael about that, to not let himself get pigeonholed as the "hot ethnic guy" in all his projects. Kwaw already had indie projects lined up before filming for the next Squadron, and Tanusha was directing a documentary about the effects of climate change in her country.

Meanwhile, Gael was reading scripts for more movies that only required him to flex his muscles and look pretty. He tossed the script on the table and took a swig of his own glass of champagne. "I'm not interested in this, Manolo."

"Did you even read what the starting offer is? It's more than what you're making with the Space Squadron movies and you would have *the leading role and an executive producer credit*. That's a great opportunity."

"I've never heard of this production company, anyone in this writer's room or the director. Looks like it's a bunch of frat bros trying to make a buck off the popularity of the Marvel franchises." That came from Gabi, who for the past three years had been working as Gael's publicist. It was a bit of Latinx cliché to have his family working for him, but his sister was excellent at what she did, and had a keen eye for what was a good use of his time and what wasn't.

"Gabi, I appreciate your opinion, but I've been doing this a bit longer than you have. I've been with your brother from the time that no one gave him an audition."

Gael scowled at Manolo's harsh tone. He loved his uncle and he was grateful for the support he'd given him over the years. It was true that he'd helped him get to where he was. That he'd been there every step of the way. But sometimes Manolo acted like Gael's abilities and talents were incidental. Like it hadn't been Gael busting his ass working two jobs while going to drama school. Or it wasn't Gael who ran from audition to audition from the time he was eighteen until he finally caught a break that last year of college. And he didn't owe that break to Manolo; that had been because of...well, that wasn't anything Gael would be rehashing, not if he wanted to show up at his mother's in a better frame of mind. None of it mattered anymore. What did matter was Manolo's high-handedness.

Gael turned to his sister, ignoring the glares she and Manolo were directing at each other, and pointed to the stack of screenplays he was supposed to look over. "What project do you think I should do next?"

"Nothing in that pile," Gabi replied, clearly ready for the question. "Gael, you're in a good place in your career. Money-and work-wise. You *can* afford to take on a passion project, bro." That earned her a sneer from Manolo, which Gabi completely ignored.

She was in more casual attire today, her usual designer power suits replaced by Gucci sneakers and a tracksuit—*a*

Prada tracksuit, but nonetheless, it was dressing down for her. They may have been twins, but Gabi took more after their mother. She was short and very curvy, while Gael was tall and brawny. He'd inherited his father's bronzed skin and green eyes, as well as his height. Gael was well over six feet tall and made sure he stayed in Hollywood Heartthrob shape. It was part of his job to look the part, after all. Like his mother said, if the acting gig hadn't worked out he could've been right at home in an NFL defensive line.

What Gabi lacked in stature she made up by being a total hard-ass, and his sister was rarely wrong when it came to the moves that would push his career in the right direction. Whether Manolo liked it or not, Gabi had an instinct for this stuff.

In the family they'd always joked that Gabi had been born clutching her planner and with her iPhone to her ear. His sister worked hard and kept her finger on the pulse of what was happening in the industry. Manolo was more focused on the money side, on what kept the family financially secure. They both loved their jobs, and frankly, their jobs depended on Gael's staying employed.

That meant that when it came down to it, he always made the choice that guaranteed him—and all of them—security. That particular approach had cost him dearly through the years, but he was a realist, and when you had people depending on you like he did, you didn't always get what you wanted. Gael thought he'd made peace with that, but in the past year he'd started losing his drive. Taking every lucrative offer that came along was killing his passion for the craft. He needed something to rekindle the fire he'd always felt for acting. In theory, he had everything any Latinx actor at this stage in their career could ask for, and still he felt...dissatisfied.

And yet...there had been a time not too long ago when

nothing and no one felt more important than career success. A time where he'd made choices that might've seemed heartless to some in order to stay on the path he'd set for himself.

"Did you hear me, Gael?" His sister's voice snatched him back from his thoughts.

"Sorry, what did you say?"

She sucked her teeth at him for daring to ignore her, but soon was talking excitedly. "Word is Violeta Torrejos just signed on to direct a period series about Francisco Rios and his wife. It's about their time at Harvard." Gael perked up immediately at the mention of the Puerto Rican freedom fighter who was one of his heroes. "They're still looking for an actor to play the lead." Gabi smiled knowingly as he sat up in his chair. That last morsel of information jolting him out of the ennui he'd been steeped in a second ago.

"No eso, no. I already told them this part's not right for you and—" Manolo protested, but Gael held his hand up, annoyed that Manolo had passed on a project like that without running it by him first.

"Tio, esperate," he interrupted and turned to his twin. "Tell me."

Gabi grinned icily at their uncle, then bent her head to scroll on her phone, presumably looking for the information she had on the project. "It's called *The Liberator and His Love*. The showrunner is Pedro Galvañes."

That was a good sign. Galvañes's name attached to a project usually meant there would be a lot of buzz for the show. "They've cast Jasmin Lin Rodriguez as Claudia Mieses," Gabi informed him, eyes still on her phone screen. Also a good sign, Gael thought, excitement already coursing through him. He knew Jasmin and she didn't sign on to just any project.

Gael leaned back, considering the information his sister

had just given him. It was exciting to think about. A series about Francisco Rios, the leader of the Puerto Rican independence movement, was a dream project. The man had led an extraordinary life. He'd graduated from Harvard Law School in 1921—the first Puerto Rican to do so. While studying there he'd met Claudia Mieses, a Peruvian biochemist—and the first Latina to be accepted to Radcliffe College—who was remarkable in her own right. Gael had always thought their love story was a romance for the ages. And that Rios's life story deserved to be told. Being a part of bringing something like *this* to the big screen was more than a dream…it was the kind of opportunity that had drawn him to be an actor in the first place.

"I want it," he said with finality, feeling a buzz of excitement he hadn't felt in months. "Who do we talk to?" he asked. Hell, he'd probably be willing to do the part for free. But his sister frowned at his question, her expression almost reluctant. When he looked at Manolo, Gael noticed the man looked smug. Clearly, the other shoe was about to drop.

"The studio producing the series is Sambrano," Gabi blurted out, as if trying to quiet their uncle before he could get the first word in. No wonder the older man was smiling. What felt like a ball of lead sank through Gael. The skin on his face felt hot. He shouldn't be surprised that the mention of the Sambrano name still had this effect on him after all these years, but it did.

"Tell him who's in charge of casting, Gabriela." His uncle sounded a little bit too pleased with himself for that nugget to be anything other than the person Gael suspected.

Gabi fidgeted, her eyes everywhere but on Gael. "Perla Sambrano's doing the casting." Unsurprisingly, he felt the blood at his temples at the mere mention of his ex-girlfriend.

Perla Sambrano was someone he took pains not to dwell on. "She's working for the studios now," Gabi added, pulling him from his thoughts. "She's their new VP of global casting and talent acquisitions." His sister's tone was sharp, laced with recrimination. Perla Sambrano had been the reason for the one and only time his twin had stopped speaking to him.

"I don't know if this is the right project," he said, ruthlessly tamping down the pang of discomfort that flashed in his chest. He stared at his sister, expecting her to rehash old arguments. But she just stared at him, disappointment written all over her face. He knew enough not to take the bait. That conversation was over and done with. He would not apologize for making the choices that had them all sitting in a private jet heading to the ten-million-dollar mansion his money had bought.

"This is not going to work, Gabi," he told his sister, before turning away from her withering glare. He looked at his uncle and felt a surge of irritation at the pleased little smirk on his face. He was not some damn toy for Manolo and Gabi to compete over. "These aren't going to work, either," Gael quickly added, gesturing to his uncle's pile of scripts. "Let's keep looking." That made Manolo's smile flag, but he wasn't here to save anyone's feelings. This was his career, and family or not, they worked for him.

Gabi nodded tersely. She opened her mouth as if to say something, but then seemed to let it go. Gael focused on the book he'd been reading on his phone and tried very hard not to think about Perla or the project.

Dwelling on ancient history was not a habit he indulged in.

"You really don't mind doing this?" Perla's older sister asked. Esmeralda's warm smile always seemed to calm her even when she could only see it through the screen of her monitor.

"Of course I don't mind," Perla said, honestly. She couldn't exactly blame Esmeralda for looking a little doubtful. A year ago no one, Perla included, would've believed that she'd be ready for a conference call at 7:00 a.m. on a Saturday two days before Christmas, but here she was.

To be fair, a lot had happened in the past twelve months. First, her half sister, Esmeralda, had taken up the helm as president of Sambrano Studios, the television empire their father, Patricio Sambrano, had built. The same television empire everyone expected to be passed to Perla and her brother—Patricio's "legitimate" children. Instead, the Sambrano patriarch had surprised everyone by expressing his last wish was to see Esmeralda, the child he'd fathered out of wedlock, lead the billion-dollar studios into the future. In the aftermath, Perla had gained a relationship with Esmeralda after years of estrangement.

Unlike her mother and brother, Perla didn't begrudge her sister the position. She'd never wanted that kind of responsibility. In truth, until ten months ago, when Esmeralda had reached out to her, hoping to mend their relationship, Perla thought she would never set foot in the company's offices again. She'd even sold her shares to make sure she never had to sit in a board meeting for the rest of her life. But Esmeralda's warmth and passion for keeping their family legacy alive had lit a fire under Perla. And now here she was, the new VP of global casting and talent acquisitions for Sambrano Studios. As her sister said, "putting to good use all that fancy schooling" their father had paid for.

"Perlita?" Her sister's soothing voice pulled Perla out of her musings, and when she looked at the screen, she saw that Esmeralda's fiancé and the CEO of Sambrano

Studios, Rodrigo Almanzar, had joined her. They sat side by side, shoulders and arms pressed together. Completely comfortable with each other. They made quite the power couple, but their chemistry was not reserved just for the boardroom. Esmeralda and Rodrigo were the very definition of *soul mates*. You only had to see them together to know they were perfect for each other. Even when they had been at each other's throats competing for the top spot at Sambrano, they could not stay away from each other. And although Perla would never be jealous of what her sister had, she did feel a pang of longing for that kind of connection.

"I'm ready," Perla assured her sister.

"And after this, no more working," Esme chastised, making Perla smile. "We've all been working nonstop."

Perla would never admit it to anyone, but it felt good to finally have this, family who cared about her without making her feel like a child. Family that didn't make her feel expendable.

Her mother, Carmelina, had always been overbearing and the worst kind of helicopter mom. She constantly made Perla feel like she was useless. But Esmeralda treated her like an adult. Like a competent, trustworthy adult capable of taking on responsibilities. And more than that, Esmeralda made Perla feel like her presence mattered, like she valued her opinion.

"Let's get on with this meeting, then." Perla nodded, getting herself in order. They would be doing a virtual conference call with the producer and director of an upcoming series project.

The conversation with the show producers started well, and before she knew it, it was Perla's turn to ask some questions about casting. "Pedro, I know you have such deep connections with some of the best Latinx actors,"

Perla spoke truthfully. Pedro Galvañes was a legend, and was also infamously vain, which was confirmed when he smiled widely at her compliment.

"We know who we want," Galvañes confirmed. "Violeta has pretty much confirmed Jasmin Lin Rodriguez to play the part of Claudia Mieses." Perla, Esmeralda and Rodrigo all nodded enthusiastically at that. The Puerto Rican actress was a rising star, especially coming out of her huge success with the *Carmen in Charge* series.

"That's wonderful. She's perfect for that role," Perla said, grinning, not even trying to hold back her excitement.

"Yes, she is," Violeta chimed in. "And we need someone who can really hold his own with her. Francisco Rios was such a presence, larger than life. We need an actor who exudes that charisma and power, but who can also play the part of romantic heartthrob. This is a romance, after all." She winked, eliciting a smile from Perla and the other faces on the screen.

"Yes, we need a powerhouse to play Mr. Rios," Perla agreed. She'd been reading up on Francisco Rios since Esmeralda announced Sambrano would be making *The Liberator and His Love*. The man was a legend, and they needed an actor with a lot of depth to do him justice.

"Who did you have in mind?" Rodrigo asked, not one to beat around the bush.

"We want Gael Montez," Violeta announced, and Perla's heart skittered in her chest like a caged bird. As if the very mention of the man aggrieved the organ he had so badly battered.

"Montez," Esmeralda said, and Perla could hear her sister's effort to sound neutral. One night after one too many glasses of champagne, Perla had confessed the entire sordid story about her college boyfriend and her first—only, if she was honest—love.

A story she tried extremely hard to never think about, and now it seemed she would be tasked with securing him for a role.

"He's perfect for the part. Strapping like Rios was, and compelling on-screen," Pedro said, before Esme could finish what she was about to say. "But we have not been able to get so much as a call back from his people. The man's manager is a real piece of work. He flat-out refused to pass on the script to Montez."

Over the thumping of her heart and rushing of blood between her temples, Perla was able to process the mention of Manolo Montez, Gael's uncle and manager. She'd never liked Manolo and had always suspected he'd had a hand in how things had ended between her and Gael six years earlier. She wasn't at all surprised to hear he was still running interference. Manolo was never shy about the intensely specific vision he had for Gael's career. And the plan seemed to be very much about keeping Gael's status as the family's golden goose by encouraging him to take whatever role paid the most money.

He was ruthless, too. If Manolo thought this wasn't the right kind of project for Gael, he'd do whatever it took to keep it off his nephew's radar. And the truth was this was a passion project for everyone involved. They wouldn't tolerate egos in this production. The hope was that the expected accolades and critical acclaim would be an incentive for the bigger Hollywood names they were attempting to sign on—Manolo would never see it that way.

And Perla should be glad for Manolo's shitty ways because that meant she wouldn't have to deal with Gael. Except the more she thought about it, the more she agreed with Pedro and Violeta's assessment that he was the right actor for the part. What was more, she knew this was the kind of project Gael would've loved to be a part of. In col-

lege, when he'd been the darling of the drama school, this
would've been a dream for Gael. Being Puerto Rican, he
longed to play the kinds of roles that allowed him to rep-
resent his roots, even if he'd decidedly strayed from that
as his career took off. And like the fool she had always
been when it came to that man, the words were out of her
mouth before she could stop them. "Gael's a friend. I bet
I can talk him into taking the part. I'll give him a call."

Esmeralda and Rodrigo's stunned silence was somehow louder than the delighted cheers coming from Pedro
and Violeta.

Once the call was done Perla's pulse still raced as she
reckoned with what she'd done. She'd practically assured
them she could secure Gael. She hadn't seen or talked to
the man in six years. Since he'd come to her apartment
on Christmas Eve and told her he'd finish the last semes-
ter of school online because he'd gotten a role in a new
show. Then he'd dumped her with the excuse of needing
to focus on his career. Even after all this time, she could
barely recall the details of what he'd said. The pain of
his betrayal still fogging her recollection of that horrible
night. She sometimes wished the same fog would blur the
two years before that. That she could forget how happy
she'd been with him. But the memories of what she'd lost
were still intact, and just as insidious as the pain of losing Gael had been.

"You don't have to do this, hermana." Esmeralda's un-
certain tone shook Perla out of her thoughts. "I'll call Violeta and Pedro myself and tell them they need to go with
someone else." Perla felt queasy and furious at herself for
still letting the mere thought of him get to her like this.

God, she could not believe she'd put herself in this situation. But this was just like her, to try and please people,
even if it came at the cost of her own peace of mind. Still,

this was her job. She oversaw the casting of this project, a show she knew could be the talk of the awards season next year if they cast it well. She wanted them to have the best possible actors, not just for the sake of popularity, but because Francisco Rios deserved to have someone in that role who understood the man they were playing. Who got the size of the shoes they were attempting to fill.

Perla smiled at her sister through the tightness in her throat, trying to express as much gratitude as she could for Esmeralda's wanting to make this easier. "It's okay, Esme. I can do this. I shouldn't have said I could talk Gael into taking the role," she admitted. "But I can give him a call." *Or give someone in his camp a call, because I don't know if I can handle hearing his voice. Or maybe I'll just dial up my old college roommate, who I iced out without explanation after her twin brother broke up with me.*

"If you're sure," Esme said, the concern coming through in her voice.

"I am." Perla attempted to infuse her voice with confidence, trying to reassure her sister and herself. "Honestly, it's not a big deal. Gael and I are not super close anymore, but we're not enemies." Friends didn't exactly go six years without speaking a word to each other, but Perla hoped her sister didn't know her well enough to tell she was lying through her teeth.

"Okay," Esme relented, but Perla clearly saw the concern on her sister's face. "But if you change your mind, call me." She waved a hand then, her eyes widening as if remembering something important. "Or better yet, you can tell me in person when you're here."

Perla's mouth tugged up at that. Last year had been the worst Christmas of her life—well, the second worst. Her mother and brother had shunned her after she'd gone against them by selling her shares to the studio. The decision had thwarted their plans to destroy her father's legacy, and they'd stopped speaking to her after that. She'd ended up spending the holidays completely alone—in a Swiss chalet in the Alps, but still, alone. But this year she was going to Punta Cana with Rodrigo and Esmeralda. Esme's mother and aunties would be there, too. Perla had been looking forward to it for months. The idea of being around people who actually wanted her there, with people who liked being around *each other*, made her chest radiate with warmth.

"By the time you wake up tomorrow, I'll be there. I'm taking the jet out of Westchester. We leave at 11:00 p.m." She couldn't wait to be on the beach, even though she'd miss the snow. She was a New York girl, after all, and loved seeing a white Christmas morning. But this year the blanket of white would have to come from the sandy beaches of the Dominican Republic.

She said her goodbyes and sat there for another minute, considering her options. She didn't know what prospect would be worse, to call and have Manolo send some lackey to rebuff her, or actually get a response from Gael. Just the possibility of hearing his voice made her nauseated. She breathed through the jittery energy that was threatening to overwhelm her. There were no two ways about it—and the more she delayed it, the worse she would look when she had to break it to the production team that she had not in fact been able to secure Gael Montez for the project. She grabbed her phone and stared at it for a long moment, considering what to say on the off chance she got ahold of Gael himself. Maybe it wouldn't be that bad? It was business, after all. Gael could not begrudge her trying to woo him to the project. It *was* her job. Yeah…it would be fine. She'd call, put forth the offer and hope they accepted.

Maybe if she kept telling herself that, she'd start believing the lie.

She tapped on her phone and the screen came to life with an image of Perla and Esmeralda with their arms around each other at the studio's holiday party just a week earlier. She had to do this. For her sister, and for herself. This was her job now. And dammit, she would do it. Gael would understand that better than anyone. How could *he* judge *her* for putting her job ahead of personal feelings after the way he'd treated her? Still, she couldn't help but send a prayer up asking for a Christmas miracle.

Just as she was about to search in her contacts for Gael's old number, the screen of her phone lit up with a phone number she never thought she would see again.

Two

"Gabi?" Perla asked, scarcely able to believe Gael's sister was calling her. Had she summoned her with all her fretting?

"Hey, Perla. Do you have a minute?" Gabi sounded more than a little apprehensive, and knowing that her old friend wasn't unaffected by reaching out after so much time eased Perla's nerves. The two of them had only spoken a few times since she and Gael split. The last time it had been when Perla found out Gael's mother was sick. Perla had loved Gael, but she'd adored his mother, too. Veronica was always good to Perla and when she'd heard the older woman had fallen ill, she'd called Gabi to ask if she could come see Veronica at the hospital. Gabi had been grateful for her concern and told Perla she could come whenever she liked, but other than that, she'd kept her distance. So yeah, this call was a surprise.

"Hey, how's your mom doing?"

"She's good. Much better, thanks for asking."

Perla could hear the smile in Gabi's voice. Both she and Gael were devoted to their mother. If there was a pang of longing tugging at her heart for the warmth and joy she'd experienced with the Montez family, Perla would ignore it. There was nothing for her there. Gael had made that very clear six years ago.

"How can I help you, Gabi?" She tried to sound nonchalant, but even she could hear she failed.

"I've been told you're in charge of casting for the Francisco Rios series." Gabi was nothing if not direct.

"I am," Perla answered, stretching out the words.

"Between you and me, Gael may be interested in the role." Perla's pulse kicked up like she'd been given a shot of adrenaline, and she could not for the life of her tell if it was because she was happy or terrified about what this could potentially mean. She didn't have time to dwell on it; Gabi's urgent tone brought her back to the conversation. "The issue's Manolo. He's hell-bent on passing up on it. Saying it's not going to be good for his image," she scoffed. "Whatever the hell that means. And like always, my brother listened to him."

Perla knew that it was a lot more than just Gael's listening to Manolo, his uncle. She knew Manolo had stepped in to care for their family when Gael's dad abandoned them, leaving his wife with ten-year-old twins to support on her own. Veronica, who had been a stay-at-home mom until then, had been forced to go to work. In a gesture of solidarity, her brother-in-law Manolo had packed up from Puerto Rico and helped raise the twins. Gael felt like he owed his uncle, and that was not something he took lightly.

But Gabi had also confirmed what she'd suspected: Gael wanted this role. And unless he was a completely different man than he'd been six years ago, she knew he would likely take it.

Gael listened to Manolo because as long as his uncle took care of the "business side" he could focus on the only thing he really cared about—his craft. Success was never really about the money for him; it was about mastering what he did, about reaching the very top of his field. The possibility of being a contender for a best actor nomination with a role playing a Puerto Rican legend would be too tempting for Gael, even if it went against his uncle's advice. More than anything, Gael wanted a legacy, and he had to know that superhero movies could only take him so far when it came to claiming his star on the Walk of Fame.

"What do we do to convince him?" Perla heard herself ask.

"We can figure this out!" Gabi responded, clearly excited. Her old college roommate had always been a little too willing to get up to mischief to get her way. "I think it won't take much, to be honest. He's intrigued by the part. Rios is one of his idols." Perla remembered that, like she remembered every detail about Gael Montez like they were burned into her brain. "Timing is the key here," Gabi said, bringing Perla's focus back to the task at hand. "He's got the next week off before he goes on the Asian press tour for Space Squadron. We're at the new house in Sagaponack. We got in last night with Tio Manolo, but he took off for the city first thing this morning and won't be back until Nochebuena."

Perla hummed in acknowledgment, her matte, blood-red gel tips tapping on the desk as she thought. She'd seen a spread in some magazine about the enormous ten-million-dollar Hamptons mansion Gael had bought for his mother. Not surprising they'd all be there for the holidays.

"What if you call him?" Gabi suggested cautiously. "I know it's a big ask, but he always trusted your advice when it came to his career." Perla could practically taste the bitterness that statement brought up. Gael *had* listened to her, until he didn't. And despite what she'd told herself a minute ago, she didn't think she could handle being rebuffed by some assistant. No, Gael owed her this, and if he was going to tell her no, he'd have to do it to her face.

"Why don't I bring him the script," she heard herself say, feeling a little floaty from the barrage of feelings the prospect of seeing Gael brought on. "I can tell him in more detail what we're envisioning for the show. We could even do a reading."

"Okay, if you're sure." Gabi sounded unsure.

"It will be harder for him to turn me down in person," Perla said, now sounding a bit more sure of herself. More committed to the plan.

"I like it," Gabi finally answered. "Having you here will force him to consider the role seriously." Perla's pulse quickened as blood rushed through her veins. Seeing Gael was not a good idea. But she knew this was the right call. Once he read it, he would want it.

As if she could sense where Perla's thoughts were heading, Gabi piped up again. "Didn't Caballero-Mendez write the script?" Gabi asked, prompting a quick yes from Perla.

"Gael's been wanting to work on something by him for years." The Puerto Rican playwright had risen to supernova levels of fame after his musical based on the life of one of the US founding fathers had become the Broadway hit of the decade. Everyone wanted to work with him, but he only took on very selected projects.

"He *offered* to write the script for us," Perla clarified for Gabi, who crowed in response.

"Excelente. Wait to tell him that until he's got it in his hands," Gael's sister suggested with glee. "You're coming with an offer he can't refuse."

Perla had to breathe through the thumping in her chest

as she prepared to speak. "Would lunchtime today be too soon?" Perla was already mentally listing what she needed to do before she got on the road. "I'm planning to fly out to Punta Cana late tonight, from Westchester. I can drive out to you before that and be back on the road with plenty of time to catch my flight at 11:00 p.m."

"Yes! I can make that work," Gabi was yelling into the phone. "You know he's a workaholic and already bored to tears with nothing to do. Send the script over now, and I'll print it out and give it to him. He has all morning to read it." She made another celebratory sound on the phone and Perla wished she could get some contact giddiness; alas, all she felt was nausea. "I have a good feeling about this, and Mami will be so thrilled to see you. We've all missed you." Gabi said that part in a more subdued—but no less genuine—tone. And maybe this would be a way to prove to herself she was past this. That the heartbreak from years ago was ancient history.

"I look forward to seeing her, too," Perla said sincerely, and after hammering out a couple more details they disconnected. Perla tried to push down the blizzard of emotions that seemed to hit her all at once. She was nervous. No. She was terrified of seeing Gael again. Not just because of how things had ended, but because she had no idea how she would react to having him in front of her. She wondered if it would still feel like the sun, the moon and the stars were encompassed in his green eyes. If it would still seem like he was the only person in the world who could make her fill up with light.

She reminded herself that she wasn't that lost girl, who in Gael had finally found someone who could see her. That she had people in her life now, and more important, she'd been working hard on loving herself. And she did; she'd felt more confident in this past year than she could remember. And despite all that being true, the longing she felt for what Gael had been to her was a yawning, undeniable void.

Seeing him was a risk; there was no use in denying it.

This was dangerous, treacherous territory she was threading into. But she *would* do this. If the old Perla would've cowered at the possibility of seeing the man who had broken her heart, this one would toss all that useless sentimentality aside and do her job.

Gael was going to kill his sister. He was at least going to have decidedly strong words with her. The fresca had barreled into his bedroom at barely 9:00 a.m. in the morning with a ream of papers and announced that no one other than Perla Sambrano was coming to talk to him about taking the lead role in the Rios series. Only the most brazen and fearless of people would dare talk to Gael before he'd had his coffee, especially with news he would not be happy about. But Gabi had always lacked a healthy sense of self-preservation. It was the only reasonable explanation as to why, without consulting anyone, his sister contacted his ex-girlfriend and invited her to his house.

And now here he was, standing in his driveway, waiting for the woman whose heart he'd trampled. Gael made no apologies for his choices. He was ruthless in his dedication and ambition—mercenary, his mother would say—and he had no regrets. The only way that a kid from Bridgeport, Connecticut, had been able to achieve what he had in such a short time was because he never let his emotions get the best of him. Even if that meant breaking the heart of someone he'd loved.

Perla had been his sister's roommate freshman year at Yale. And then she'd become much more than that. In the summer between sophomore and junior year, Perla and Gael had started dating. She'd been the first girl he'd fallen head over heels for. They'd had two almost perfect years. She'd been more than his girlfriend; she was his best friend, his confidante. The person he came to for everything. And when his career started taking off and he'd been overwhelmed and intimidated by the entertainment business, she helped him navigate the new world he'd been thrust into.

It was her playground, after all. Perla had grown up in the lap of luxury. The "pobre niña rica" as his friends sometimes called her. She *was* rich, from one of the wealthiest Latinx families in the country. And she'd always seemed so sad, so quiet. But to him she'd been intriguing, and beautiful. *So damn beautiful.* She brought out his protective instincts like no one outside his mother and sister ever had. He'd been drawn to her from the first moment, and once he'd actually gotten to know her and realized how brilliant and funny she was—he'd fallen hard.

People underestimated Perla, never seeing the fire hiding under those bland clothes and nerdy glasses. She was always so fastidiously put together. She was fine-boned and small, almost waifish, with big gray eyes he'd felt like he could drown in. And she'd dressed to go unnoticed. Pencil skirts and cardigan sets with ballet flats, in every shade of pastel you could imagine. *Cashmere* cardigans, and *designer* skirts and flats, but forgettable, almost old-fashioned. But still, she'd been like a beacon to Gael.

Back then he'd been the big man on campus, at least the part of campus that cared about drama majors and theater. He was poised to be the one star from their graduating class. And once all that potential his teachers kept telling him he had actually turned into acting opportunities, he'd had no idea how to handle it. He'd come from humble beginnings, after all. And almost without warning he'd been thrown into a world of wealth and fame he'd felt lost in.

He was tough, a hard worker, and he was no dummy. But he'd needed some insight in how to carry himself in that environment, and Perla had given him all the help he'd needed. She'd taught him where to get his suits and who to go to for a haircut. The right place to rent an apartment in New York City and even what car to drive. She'd been his guide in navigating the world of the one percent, and just when he was poised to soar, he'd left her behind.

He still remembered that night. Could even recall the old Yale sweatshirt he'd been wearing. He could smell the microwave popcorn Perla had made for him that was sitting on her coffee table when he walked into her apartment. After days, weeks of him ignoring his uncle's warnings that his relationship with Perla was hurting his image, it all came to a head when a tabloid plastered a photo of Gael and Perla walking in Manhattan. The headline with the words *Plain Perla* plastered in red had been Manolo's smoking gun. Manolo laid into him about how it was better for everyone to end things. That staying together would be bad for his career and would almost certainly be bad for her mental health. That the media was ruthless, and no matter how hard he tried to protect Perla, her connection to him would end up hurting her. So he'd done it. He cut her out of his life.

Six months after their breakup she'd started popping up in gossip websites and on Page Six, jet-setting around the world. The pastel cardigans all gone and replaced with a bolder, more Instagram-ready version of his shy ex-girlfriend. But once her father died, she seemed to have dropped off the face of the earth. Except now she was on her way to his house. And he wasn't sure how he felt about any of it.

The sound of gravel on his enormous circular driveway jolted his attention back to the present and the car coming

toward him. He frowned as a sleek, black Maserati SUV
rolled to a stop just a few yards from where he stood. He
could feel his forehead scrunching with a frown as he tried
to get a closer look at the driver. He'd been expecting a
variation on the BMW sedans Perla always drove. Her car
choices had always been in line with her modest—for rich
people—tastes in fashion. But this was the kind of car you
drove to make a statement. He moved closer to it, heart
hammering in his chest as he saw the door open.

His plan was to stave Perla off, meet her in the driveway
before his mother had a chance to see her, and tell her this
was not going to work out. That there was too much baggage for them to be around each other. He moved his feet
to reach her car, and even opened his mouth to say it, but
once he got a glimpse of her, the words never came. He
just stood there, mouth gaping as she slowly opened the
door and gave him a full view of the new Perla. This was
not the same girl from college or even from those early
Instagram posts.

Gone was her usual high ponytail and scrupulously
highlighted blond hair. In its place was a raven-black pixie
cut that made her big gray eyes sparkle. The winged eyeliner was a surprise, too, and when his eyes drifted down
to her mouth, her lips were a cherry red. Perla had never
been one to be flashy about her wealth, but if you knew
what to look for, you could find it all over her. The vintage
Piaget watch on her wrist. The big green Bottega Veneta
he recognized from a runway show he'd been dragged to
during fashion week.

Everything about Perla Sambrano had always given off
old money vibes, but she wore it differently now. There
was a boldness to her that hadn't been there before. And
she was certainly dressing differently. She had big gold
hoops in her ears and the subdued clothing choices of the

past were replaced by a black sweater dress and black faux leather leggings. He raised an eyebrow when he noticed the sneakers on her feet. Perla Sambrano in red sneakers. Balenciaga sneakers, but still.

But as she made her way to him, he saw that her outfit and car were not the only things that were different. She threw her head back to put on a pair of oversize sunglasses and when she saw him, the smile on her lips was not the shy expression from the old days. This was the smile of a woman who meant business.

"Gael," she called as she reached him. They were both Latinx, after all, so when she lifted her face to his, he pressed his cheek to hers in hello. His skin tightened as it touched hers and an electric current ran through his limbs. He told himself it must be the chill in the air. That his surprise was the natural reaction to seeing someone after so long. She looked *so different*, he was surprised, that was all. He opened his mouth to say something, anything, then blurted out the one thing that would almost certainly piss her off. "When did you start wearing red lipstick?"

She leaned back like she didn't know what to make of his outburst, then she grinned. The old Perla would've recoiled at his question. In the past, feeling judged had been the fastest way for Perla to clam up. But today she just lifted a shoulder and grinned, cheeky and unfazed by his grumpiness.

"I thought I'd try something new. I got a little tired of neutral." He knew he was glaring, but he didn't seem to be able to come up with words just then. Perla didn't seem to notice his silence. "Thanks for agreeing to do this." She smiled sweetly and something primal pulsed in his chest. Whatever it was, he shut it down immediately.

"Don't thank me. Thank Gabi's pushiness," he groused,

sounding harsher than he intended. But Perla's smile deepened at the mention of his sister, unaffected by his surliness.

"Knowing Gabi, I imagine she delivered the news with the subtlety of a freight train," she joked, surprising a laugh out of him. But after a moment a taut silence descended, and they both seemed to run out of pleasantries at the same time. There was no pretending this wasn't awkward. How does anyone handle meeting the person that at one time had meant everything to them? It felt like coming out of a bunker after six years underground and realizing the world had moved on without him. He'd been stagnant, and she'd blossomed.

He'd refused to dwell on his decision to end things after it happened. His whole approach had been to ignore what the breakup did to him. He'd told himself he didn't deserve to mope around when he wasn't the one who got dumped, and he'd put her and everything he lost out of his mind for six years. And that was not something he had any interest in revisiting. Maybe Manolo was right and considering this project was a mistake. He'd only been around Perla for a couple of minutes, and he was already unearthing ancient history.

"Here." He gestured to the steps that led to their house. "Let's go inside and we can talk there."

She nodded, following him. Gael didn't miss that she kept herself a few feet away from him. When it was time to climb the steps to the door, she let him go first and then stood away from him as he pushed it open.

One thing was clear: Perla was here for one thing and one thing only, and that was business.

Three

Perla had been prepared for the cold shoulder. For Gael acting like he'd forgotten who she was, but what she had not been prepared for was the effect Gael Montez's appreciative gaze would have on her. Well, that was a lie—she remembered only too well how being close to him affected her; she'd just hoped time and distance had diluted that vulnerability.

It hadn't.

And if possible, he was even more beautiful now. Larger than life in a way that was…distracting. Gael had always been movie-star handsome. Charisma to spare and the looks to turn heads whenever he walked into the room. People were drawn to him, and he knew how to keep their attention. He'd always been able to command Perla's.

But in six years he'd gone from boyishly handsome to a rugged, almost dangerous masculinity. He'd always stood nearly a foot taller than she did, but since she'd seen him last he'd gotten bigger, more muscular. All the soft edges gone. He was sporting a beard and had his chin-length hair framing his face. She was not usually into the Winter Soldier look, but Gael pulled it off. He more than pulled it off. God, he could be a Carib warrior with that golden-brown skin, green eyes and chiseled jaw. Yeah, it was for the best that she'd only be here for a couple of hours.

As they made their way up the steps to his impressive home, she caught him sending looks in her direction. Despite her best efforts to remain unbothered, her belly fluttered and a smile tugged up her lips, because she knew what those looks were about. He was intrigued.

In the past year she'd gone for a completely different style. Something that reflected a bit more of her personality. Her whole life she'd taken direction from her mother about everything. From her hair color to the shoes she wore, but she'd freed herself of all that. Perla liked this new version of herself, and from the way Gael kept glomming her up with his eyes, she was thinking he appreciated it, too.

"Here we are," he announced, opening the red door that led to the foyer of the home. It was a stunning place. Built in the Cape Cod style, the exterior was painted in a traditional light blue with white shutters. The interior was modern and with an open floor plan and lots of glass. The better for taking in the gorgeous views of the Long Island Sound.

"This is beautiful," she complimented sincerely as he took her coat. She looked around, admiring the gleaming teak flooring and light gray walls of the foyer. From there she could see the floor-to-ceiling stone fireplace in the living room, which was decorated with garland and tiny white twinkling lights. There was garland everywhere actually, and she expected there would be a huge tree somewhere. Gael's mother had always loved Christmas. Even when they'd lived in their little house in Bridgeport she'd made the space beautiful and festive. Perla was about to ask about his mother when she heard a familiar warm voice call her name.

"Perlita, querida!" Gael shook his head at his mother's exclamation, and Perla couldn't help smiling as she saw the woman come over to her with her arms open wide. Veronica was wearing an old Yale Mom sweatshirt and jeans, her shoulder-length hair now fully white. She looked warm and approachable. The polar opposite of Perla's own mother, who was always groomed to within an inch of her life.

"Doña Veronica," Perla said as she was engulfed into a warm hug. Veronica always smelled like vanilla and warm bread. Perla closed her eyes as the woman cooed over her.

"It's been too long, sweetheart. More than a year now. And what is this Doña business. You call me Veronica, okay?"

Perla smiled at the feigned reproach, but before she could respond there was a sound from behind her, which she assumed came from Gael. "A year?"

Veronica nodded at her son's comment without taking her eyes off Perla. "Yes, Perlita came to see me after that first surgery. You were in Italy shooting the second Space Squadron."

"Oh."

Perla's face heated at the affronted surprise in Gael's voice, but she wasn't looking up at him. Letting him see her blushing was not advisable. Thankfully, Veronica was not done with her greeting.

"I'm so happy to have you here with us. I love your new style. It suits you." Veronica pulled back to get a better look and smiled down at Perla. It was so good to see her again, but when Perla looked closely, she could see the deep lines around the older woman's eyes. Veronica still had her en-

ergy and spark, but Gael's mother had the look of someone who'd just fought a hard battle and won it by the skin
of her teeth. "You have to have lunch with us. I want to
hear what you've been up to. Gabi said you're working at
Sambrano." The older woman paused then and squeezed
Perla's hand. "I heard in the news about the changes going
on at the studio." Veronica had too many manners to say
that she'd seen Perla's family drama plastered all over the
news, including how her mother had tried her best to destroy her father's legacy.

"Thank you," Perla said dutifully, not wanting to delve
into her still-complicated feelings about her family, her father's death and the mess he'd left for all of them to pick
up. He'd been a proud man, hardworking and brilliant, but
he'd never been affectionate. He'd given all his children
names of gems, but never treated them like they were precious to him. Perla, being the youngest, felt completely in-
visible to her father. And now that he was gone, realizing
she hadn't known her father enough to truly miss him, was
almost too painful to dwell on.

"Gael, you need to make sure you're done by lunchtime, so I can visit with Perla!" Veronica's voice brought
Perla back to the moment, and she had to smile at the older
woman's loving chastisement of her son.

"Sure, Mami."

Perla turned to look at Gael and she saw in the set of
his shoulders and the tightness around his mouth that he
was looking for any indication that his mother was in pain.
He'd always been protective of her. Well, he was protective of everyone; that was one of the many reasons Perla
had fallen fast and hard for Gael. But his mother had always been his main priority. Perla never had the unconditional love Gael had always received from his mother, but
she knew the responsibility he felt for taking care of the

woman who raised him. Gael was a man who never shied
from his duty. He always did what it took to take care of
his people. She'd loved that about him...and that was *not*
where her head needed to be at all.

"We should get going. I have a flight later today and
need to be on the road in a couple of hours," she said tersely.

"Sure." Gael nodded, giving her a questioning look. But
whatever he was wondering about, he didn't ask it. After
letting her say a quick goodbye to his mother he briskly
led her through the living room, which indeed had an enormous tree in the corner. They walked by framed windows
showcasing an awe-inspiring view of the ocean, and walls
lined with family photographs and quite a few pieces of art.

Unlike her own mother's house, which looked like a
Versace home showroom, Veronica's house was furnished
for comfort. Dozens of photos of Gael, Gabi and Veronica and other family members hanging on the walls or in
frames on practically every surface. The brown leather
sectional looked inviting, like it could easily sit half a
dozen people. There were also armchairs and ottomans
scattered around the room. All of them looked well used.
The Montez home was a place for family. In the past she'd
yearned to be one of them. To belong to these people who
loved each other so deeply, but Gael had not seen her as
his forever.

"This is very nice, Gael." She knew buying a home
in the Hamptons for his mother was one of his dreams.
When they'd been together, he told her that when he was
in middle school his mom worked as a housekeeper for a
wealthy family in Southampton during the summer. The
estate had a small apartment over the stable and she would
bring Gael and Gabi with her. He told Perla he'd loved
and hated those summers. Loved the beautiful coast and
playing on the beach with his sister but hated how the

family treated his mother. He'd confessed to Perla that one night after he'd seen his mom almost pass out from exhaustion, he'd promised himself that one day he would be rich and buy her one of those big houses…and he had. She wanted to ask him if he remembered telling her that. Instead, she turned around, admiring the room in silence, until she trusted herself to speak. "Your mother must be very pleased."

He made a noise that was more of a groan than a yes and stopped right as they reached the fireplace, which was blazing happily. "You know how she is." He smiled wryly and looked around the big room with the ten-million-dollar view he'd bought for his mother. "It took six months to convince her we needed a decorator to help her."

"I can imagine." Perla smiled knowingly as she admired the room. Gael's mother would probably not be one to think spending money on something as frivolous as a decorator was necessary.

"Come," he said, breaking the tense silence between them. "We can do the reading in the study." He laughed awkwardly as he opened the door to the massive room. "I'm not sure what else to call it."

"Wow, this is amazing," Perla said in a reverent whisper as she followed him to the doorway and took in the rows and rows of books along the walls. Like in the living room, there was a blazing fire here, and there was an ocean view, too. But what captured her attention were the bookshelves and the enormous screen in the far end. There were four brown leather armchairs in a semicircle in front of a screen that wouldn't have been out of place in a movie house. She turned to look at the other end of the room where there was a love seat and a Herman Miller chair, presumably for reading. This place was for two things: books and movies.

Gael's—*and Perla's*—two favorite things.

Dissecting books and movies they both loved had been one of the ways they'd bonded when they first became friends. Later, when they'd been much more than that, their shared passion had been one of the things that convinced Perla they were perfect for each other. That despite their outward differences in background and even personality, at the core they were kindred spirits. And she absolutely had to stop reminiscing; she was already on a slippery slope as it was.

Forcing herself to shake off the maudlin thoughts flooding her, she stepped into the large room. The walls were covered in a midnight blue wallpaper with little flecks of gold. The effect almost gave the sensation of being surrounded by a starry night sky. The dark wood of the built-in bookshelves and warm lighting made it cozy and inviting. It was a room for slowing down and doing the things you enjoyed. She had her own version of it in her apartment on the Upper West Side of Manhattan.

"Come over here," Gael called, piercing through her thoughts. She turned her head to find him standing by the bookshelves. He was pointing at one of them, presumably for her to look at, but her eyes kept wanting to drift over him. He was dressed simply, in black joggers and hoodie, and he still looked imposing. Those wide shoulders tapering down to a trim waist. His powerful thighs stretching the fabric of his pants so that she could almost see the outline of his muscles. He was so intensely male. It was hard not to stare at that powerful, virile body.

"I think you'll get a kick out of these." Again, his voice startled her.

"Sorry," she told him as she came closer. "I got distracted." He gave her a long look, but didn't comment on her obvious flustered state.

Once she was close enough, she leaned in to scan the

shelf and gasped as she saw the titles of all of Gabriel García Márquez's books. The Nobel Laureate was Perla's favorite author, and it seemed like Gael had collected *all* of his books. "Are these first editions?" she asked, feeling a little dazed. She owned a few herself, but some of the titles he had were practically impossible to find.

"They are." He sounded more than a little pleased with himself. And she would not be foolish enough to think this man was attempting to impress her. "You might also like what I have in the next shelf." She turned and squealed with delight to find rows and rows of romance novels. Also her favorite, and something she'd gotten Gael into in college. She'd talked him into trying them by saying he could learn about capturing the inner life of the characters, especially the heroes in the stories. She'd told him romance authors wrote big emotions like no one else, and it would help him when he needed to get into a character's head. Gael hadn't been too convinced, but he'd read them—he was always willing to try anything that would help him be better at his job. It didn't take long for him to get hooked on them and soon they were swapping books.

Suddenly feeling a bit overwhelmed, Perla forced herself to straighten and step back from the old editions of Johanna Lindsey books, and turned to Gael.

"This is a lovely collection," she said coolly, needing to keep herself at a distance. "But let's talk business." She forced herself to offer him a smile as she tried to shake her nerves off. "I know you probably want me out of your hair." She didn't wait for an answer and launched into her pitch for the show. She talked rapidly as she pulled out the full script from her bag. "I know you're interested in this role," she told him in a tone that brooked no argument. He just leaned into the bookshelf, a neutral look on his face.

"This is a special project," she said, confidently. "Caballero-Mendez came to us asking to write the screenplay."

He arched an eyebrow at that, interest edging out his feigned indifference. Good call, Gabi. "Everyone involved in this project is an all-star. This project could cement your versatility as an actor." Perla mentally patted herself on the back for managing to deliver that with a lot more confidence than she felt.

He eyed her from his stance a few feet away as if he was trying to read something on her face. Her skin heated from the intensity of his stare, and just when she was about to break, he finally spoke.

"I'm surprised you're working for Sambrano." That was not where she expected the conversation to go. Even if the comment was fair enough. Back when they'd been together, Perla never wasted an opportunity to affirm she had no interest in working for her father's company.

"My family owns the studio," she hedged and in response he arched an eyebrow that said *That's always been the case.* She raised a shoulder, as if she was bored with the conversation, buying herself time to come up with an answer. "My sister's the president now, and…" She trailed off, not wanting to get into this with Gael. She'd always had a tendency to spill her feelings whenever he was around.

"You never had an interest in working for your father *or* the company."

"That was a long time ago, Gael." She was going to say, *You have no idea about what I'm interested in,* but she decided that antagonizing him was not the way to go, and before she knew it, she was telling him the truth. "My sister's a very different leader than my father was, and she wants me there, views me as an asset. And you know what else?" She crossed her arms in an identical gesture to his. "I believe in the vision she has for the studio."

"You've really changed," he said, and she almost bristled. But his tone wasn't judgmental or sharp. It was almost like he was thinking aloud. Putting things together.

"I have," she confirmed, unable to keep the challenge out of her voice.

He stared at her again in that unnerving way he'd been doing since they'd come into the room. After a moment he shook himself and grabbed the script from where she'd put it on the love seat.

"All right, then. Let's see what magic Caballero-Mendez did with this script." With that he came to stand barely a foot away from her and opened the binder to a scene in the middle of the screenplay. "Read with me."

Four

This was what he got from trying to be all cavalier. A fucking disaster.

"I don't think this scene is a good idea," Gael said through gritted teeth, while Perla looked at him with angelic eyes. He'd been surprised by the calm and steady way in which she talked about her work and her family. This version of Perla was so different than the girl he'd fallen in love with. He felt thrown by her presence and whenever Gael felt unsteady, he was impulsive. And now he'd impulsed himself into doing a kissing scene with Perla Sambrano. Who seemed not only unbothered, but kind of amused about his little freak-out.

"Lighten up, Gael. It's just a kiss. You're a professional, and I didn't think you'd forget that I was an arts major, too. I can handle a fake kiss. Believe me, I know it's not going to be the real thing."

She was goading him. He looked down at her as she

stood there, her face fixed in an expression of absolute calm. The only thing that betrayed the little game she was playing was the barely visible tremor on her top lip. She was nervous, too.

"So you're cool about us kissing, then? No big deal?" The skin on his face tightening as adrenaline roared through his veins. She wanted to pretend, to play like this wasn't getting to her. He was going to call her bluff.

"Yep." She nodded and again he almost missed that her smile was just on this side of panicked.

"All right, then," he said, voice like gravel from the sudden pulsing in his groin. And that was so unprofessional. What was going on with him? He was better than this. He was an experienced actor; he knew how to keep himself in check in intimate scenes, had done them hundreds of times. But the prospect of a kiss with Perla had beads of sweat dripping down his back. This was a stupid, reckless idea. He should just end this. Tell Perla he knew she was bluffing. That this little game she was playing to get back at him for the way things ended between them was not going anywhere.

The Perla he'd known would've never pulled something petty like this. If he had any sense at all he'd back off from this whole thing, tell her he wasn't going to take the part. That Gabi misjudged his level of interest. That was the *sane* thing to do, but he didn't do any of it. Instead, he took a step closer, his hand crushing the script, and his gaze fixed on Perla's cherry-red lips.

"Ready?" She gave one terse nod and moved within kissing range.

The scene was the moment when Francisco Rios and Claudia Mieses kissed for the first time. They were supposed to be walking in Cambridge late at night. It was fall and a little chilly. Claudia was shivering, and Francisco stopped and embraced her, then he kissed her.

"Tienes frío," he said, following the lines as he gathered her in his arms. Perla looked surprised that he'd started without warning, but soon she went with it. She glanced up at him, and there was something in her eyes he could not quite read. Something he'd never seen before. A fiery, challenging gaze that came with this more brazen version of Perla.

"Francisco, kiss me," she pleaded. And there was a tremor in her voice, like she could barely control the urgency, the need for his touch. The words ignited something hot and wild in him, even as he reminded himself she was only reading her lines. That the trembling in her voice was just acting.

That it was all fake.

He strived to clear his head as he pressed closer. Tried desperately to find his focus, to channel what he needed to convey. His heart was punching into the walls of his chest as he bent his head to reach her mouth. Those full red lips were beckoning to him, and it was useless telling himself this was like any other kiss on a set. Perla was a full assault on his senses. The curves of her, her pert breasts pressed to his chest, her warm softness brushing against him, set him on fire.

Focus, Gael. Focus. You are Francisco and this is Claudia. There's no history and no baggage here. Just two actors infusing themselves into their roles.

He ran his finger across Perla's hairline. Francisco was supposed to tug on an errant curl on Claudia's forehead, but Perla's short hair didn't allow for that. She sighed when he touched her and he bent down, his eyes wide open, taking her in. She was so beautiful, he'd always known that, but now it wasn't just some piece of information he stored to never examine again. It was a palpable, undeniable fact. From the notes, he knew this scene took place after Francisco and Claudia had been dancing around each other for months. That they'd been resisting the growing, undeniable attraction between them until this moment. The prelude to this kiss was the final instant before they tore down the last wall and took their friendship to a new place. A place that would lead to an epic love story, to marriage, children. It was a kiss that would change the course of their lives. And when his lips finally crashed onto Perla's and she melted against him, tightening her slender arms around his neck, Gael tossed out any attempt at pretending this was an act.

Perla had forced herself to not think about Gael's kisses for the past six years. Had told herself again and again that the breakup had been for the best. That she was not cut out for life in the spotlight. That she was too much of an introvert, and he was too gregarious for them to ever work long-term. That even if it had hurt like hell, Gael had been right, that *they* weren't right. She'd drilled into her head that his kisses weren't perfect. That his arms hadn't been the one place in the world where she felt safe.

She'd been deluding herself.

Just a moment in the man's arms and she knew if she didn't pull away, she'd be ruined. Gael's grunt of pleasure as their lips met was a deep, possessive sound, and in an instant she was lost to him. She bit on his bottom lip and her tongue went exploring. That elicited another satisfied groan, and soon they were devouring each other. The thought occurred to her that for all that they were different, one thing remained very much the same: he was still the only man she'd completely given herself to.

She'd made up endless excuses for why that was still the case. That she needed more time, that she had trust issues...but it was all nonsense, because the real reason was that she'd fallen for the wrong man and she'd never gotten over him. And that man was currently ravishing her mouth like he wanted to consume her.

He was acting, she told herself as lust threatened to edge out every sensible thought in her head. This wasn't Gael, who had finally realized that Perla had been the one all along. That they were perfect for each other. No, this was an actor doing his job. Performing, pretending that he was burning up for the woman in his arms. This was Francisco Rios kissing Claudia Mieses. In a minute, less than that, they would pull back. Their bodies would unlock from this searing embrace, she'd politely thank Gael for considering the role and she would get in her car and drive away.

That was what had to happen. Perla wasn't foolish enough to think this was anything other than a job for Gael. But it was hard to be sensible when her tongue was sensuously sliding against his, and his big, rough hands gripped her like he would never let her go. The scruff of his beard grazing against her cheek electrified her, and his rosemary-and-mint shampoo was all she could smell. She was wrapped up in Gael again, just like she'd dreamed a thousand times.

Somewhere in the recesses of her mind, Perla thought she heard a door open, that she sensed footsteps on one of the Serapi rugs in the room. She wondered if she should tell Gael, but his lips were on her neck and his hands were on her backside, and she would do almost anything to stay just like this for a second longer. No matter what she'd told herself on the drive here and no matter what she would most likely lecture herself with for the rest of her life, this moment was too good to cut short.

"Yo lo sabía!" Veronica's delighted voice broke the spell, causing Perla to practically fly out of Gael's arms.

"I told Gabi you two had finally seen the light. I've been praying for this for years." Perla didn't even know where to look. She'd never had much luck when it came to public humiliation, and it seemed her streak of doom was not done yet. Gael's mother approached Perla with what, to her utter horror, looked very much like tears in her eyes, and gave her a strong hug, which she helplessly reciprocated. She had no idea what to do or say, and hoped that Gael would react at some point and tell his mother what was actually going on. But Veronica was in the throes of euphoria.

"You two are just so perfect for each other," Veronica exclaimed. "I've been telling him for six years he made the biggest mistake of his life when he let you go. I've never seen my baby happier than when you two—"

"Ma! Por favor," Gael called from whichever corner of the room he'd run off to when he'd been caught with both hands on Perla's ass and his mouth on her neck.

"I'm just happy for you, mijo." Veronica raised her gaze in her son's direction, her radiant smile still firmly in place.

This was brutal.

Perla had always known Gael's mother cared for her. The woman had welcomed her into their home from that first time she came to visit with Gabi after they'd ended up in the same dorm. With the Montez family Perla had finally understood what it meant to feel like you belonged. They always acted like she was not just welcome, but that she was also expected. And now seeing the real joy in Veronica's face at the idea that she and Gael were an item again…it was like getting punched in the stomach.

Because the one thing she would not let herself dwell on were the "what-ifs" when it came to Gael. Seeing Veronica's reaction, her words, it was too painful, and dammit, she was not going to fix this. Gael was the one who pushed that kiss, who touched her like he wanted her, who made her forget herself. He had to fix this now.

"It's just been so long since I saw you happy, Gael. You two together, it's my Christmas miracle." Veronica let her out of the embrace but kept her hand firmly in Perla's, like she couldn't stand to let this moment slip away.

"Mami," Gael groaned, his gaze fixed in the far distance like there was something there he desperately wanted to reach—probably his patience. "This is not what you think. Perla and I—"

He paused, his mouth in a hard line. And things between them hadn't been over so long Perla couldn't see that Gael was trying to get himself under control. His mother would see it, too, but Veronica waited him out. Like if she gave him enough time he'd realize she was right about what she'd seen.

Finally, after what seemed like hours, Gael looked at Perla and then at his mother, his eyes boring in on whatever he saw on the older woman's face. His expression was unreadable. He walked over to them, focused on his mother, and Perla braced herself for when he would finally put all this to rest. When he let his mother know she'd misread the situation.

But instead, he reached for Perla, and with a fake smile tugging up his lips, he opened his gorgeous mouth and lied his face off.

Five

Perla was stiff as a board in his arms, and he couldn't blame her. He'd just told his mother that they were back together. He didn't dare look down at his fake significant other, because she was probably ready to murder him. And he *had been* intending to come clean, but when he saw the tears of joy in his mother's eyes, he hadn't been able to do it. This was the happiest he'd seen her since she got really sick last year. She'd been giddy to find them necking in the study, and he would be damned if he took that from this woman after the hell she'd been through.

"We just didn't want to tell you until I was back home. You know how it is, better to give the news in person." He lied to the woman who brought him into the world as he put an arm around the woman who was most likely plotting how to take him out of it, if the murder noises Perla was making were any indication.

"Of course I understand! This kind of news is best given

in person!" his mother exclaimed with a knowing wink as she leaned in to kiss him on the cheek, and then moved in to give another hug to Perla, who was looking a little pale. "You wanted to have Perlita here when you told us. Querida," his mother said, turning to his supposed girlfriend, who so far had not uttered a single word. "I'm so glad we get you for a little visit, but can you stay a little longer?"

That request seemed to finally snap Perla out of her shock. "I have to catch my flight, Veronica. I can't stay very long."

The frown on Gael's mother's face was the one that usually came before emotional extortion a la Latin mom ensued. "Ay pero, just for a little bit. We want to see you, too, and this muchacho has kept you all to himself since you got here. I knew you couldn't really be here for work. It's Christmas! And since you can't be with us for Nochebuena we have to get some quality time with you." Her eyes widened as if she'd just had a great idea. "We just made alcapurrias this morning. I can fry some up for you! You used to love them."

Gael could tell that she was about to throw in the towel, and who could blame her? Veronica Montez could always wield a hard bargain with her culinary offerings.

"I still do," Perla said, admitting defeat.

"Great!" His mother was giddy. "Just give me ten minutes, okay?" Without waiting for an answer, his mother flew out of the room completely unaware of the fiasco currently unfolding.

"You are *unbelievable*," Perla accused as she stepped out from under his arm.

"What's so unbelievable about me not wanting to break my mother's heart during the holidays?" Gael knew he was being an unreasonable bastard, but in the past few minutes, keeping this lie going had turned into his one mission in life. "Not that this is your problem, but she almost died, Perla. I managed to keep it out of the tabloids but that one surgery she had ended up being like five surgeries, and after the last one we didn't think she'd walk again. This is the first time I've seen her really smile in almost six months." Perla's face crumpled at that, and he saw when his words began to edge out her annoyance at him. "I know I don't have any right to ask you for this, but it's going to be an hour maybe two of pretending we're seeing each other."

"I don't like lies," she protested weakly, her gaze on the door his mother had practically skipped out of earlier.

"I know." He rubbed his face hard with the palm of his hand. "This is a lot to ask. But you'll be out of here and on the way to the airport after lunch," he reminded her. "After the holidays and once things have calmed down a bit, I'll tell her that we couldn't make the long-distance thing work."

"I don't know, Gael," she said nervously. He was aware this was not a small concession. He also knew Perla had made the trip over here for a reason. He had something she wanted, something she'd been willing to do despite their history and the baggage she'd be dragging back to the surface, and he was enough of a bastard to use it.

"I'll take the role," he offered, before he could talk himself out of it. He had to suppress a smile at the way she perked up. If she had antennae they'd be twitching on top of her head. Yeah, people saw Perla Sambrano, the pampered rich girl, and they had no idea there was a driven, fierce perfectionist under all that. Perla liked to be good at things, and she liked to make the people she loved proud of her; she liked to make them happy. If her sister wanted this, Perla would do whatever it took to deliver it.

"You'll commit knowing virtually nothing about the

terms of the project in exchange for me pretending that we're dating for the duration of a meal?" She sounded irritated, which made his dick pulse in his sweats. She was so sexy like this, with that hint of bloodthirst in her eyes.

"You informed me earlier that all I needed to know was that I'd be a fool not to be a part of this project."

"True." She flashed a little smart-ass grin at that, and he almost scooped her clear off the floor and kissed her senseless, but the priority was his mother. He had to stay on task.

"You know I'd do anything for my mother, Perla. I realize you don't think much of me." He put both his hands up in a conciliatory gesture when her gray eyes narrowed to slits. "You have good reason to hate me, but I at least hope you could remember that."

"I don't hate—" She started to protest, but whatever she saw in his expression made her close her mouth.

She turned her face up to him. He towered over her by almost a foot, which meant that she had to turn her head almost ninety degrees to face him and something primitive in him reveled in that.

"I go out there and pretend we're dating, have lunch with your family, then leave and you will play Francisco Rios in our series?" she asked.

Gael nodded, his arms crossed on his chest to curb the insane urge to pull her to him.

"And you break the news to her afterward. I won't be expected to pretend later, and you won't make me the bad guy in any of this."

"Correct," he confirmed through gritted teeth, and he wanted to rip out the swarm of bees that had taken residence in his chest. Blood rushed to his ears as he waited for her answer.

Her eyebrows almost came together as she considered

his words, clearly trying to figure out where the catch was, but after a moment her arms dropped to her sides and she exhaled, gaze still locked on his. "Fine, two alcapurrias and I'm out of here."

She stormed out of the room in a cloud of black and cherry red and he stayed rooted in place watching her pert little ass as she made her way to his mother's kitchen.

"Perla!" The welcoming choir from the kitchen put a smile on Perla's face despite how out of sorts she was feeling.

"Come give me a hug, niña," Gael's grandmother demanded as she turned golden-brown empanadas in a pot of bubbling hot oil.

"Doña Juana," Perla said as she put an arm around the small woman.

"Call me Abuela, querida, and especially now that my grandson has finally wised up and gotten you back." The older woman carefully plucked the last of the empanadas out of the oil as she talked and turned off the gas, then turned around to wrap Perla into a fierce hug. The roughened palm patting her cheek with such tender affection had tears prickling her eyes.

"I'm so happy you're here. Now get those empanadas and put them on the table. Then we can talk about your new look. Gaelito can't keep his eyes off you," Juana teased and Perla looked up to find the Hollywood actor in question leaning against the arch that led from the kitchen to the dining room. The house had enough square footage to easily accommodate a dozen people, just in the kitchen, so Perla hadn't noticed Gael walking in. And he *was* looking at her, very intensely looking at her. He was too damn fine for words, and she really, really wished he'd stop being this damn sexy all the time.

"Here, let me help you," he said, pushing off the wall. He picked up the plate of empanadas and she followed him into the next room. She imagined all that sinew and muscle she'd gripped and felt against her when they kissed, shifting and flexing as he moved. Her lips were still bruised from the kiss, and Perla couldn't help sliding her tongue over the spot on her bottom lip where he'd sucked on it. He must've noticed the gesture because he froze for a second and a flush of heat spread through her just from that. She had to turn around and occupy herself with the task of arranging the food on a dish to keep from doing something supremely stupid.

Even looking at the man was dangerous.

With every word exchanged, every touch, feelings and yearnings she'd hoped had been buried and dead long ago cropped up like crocuses announcing the end of a long, dark winter. But she could do this; it was only two hours. Veronica would have her Christmas without drama, and Perla would deliver Gael Montez for *The Liberator and His Love.* All she had to do was keep her head in the game. If there was something Perla knew how to do it was repress every emotion. To pretend nothing was wrong, even when she could barely hold it together. Her mother had made sure her children could always present a happy face, no matter how miserable they felt. She was a pro at "fake it till you make it" and she would not falter in this. One meal with Gael and his family. Then she'd drive away and call her sister with the good news.

She needed this win. Not because Esmeralda was putting pressure on her, but because she wanted to prove to herself she could see this through.

All she had to do to fulfill her end of the bargain was pretend for a little bit. She didn't like lying to Veronica — she was sure Gael wasn't thrilled about it either, but he'd do what he needed to, in order to make his mother happy. In college she'd found it utterly disarming that the rough, brilliant, beautiful boy who seemed to have every girl on campus dying to be on his arm, would leave New Haven every Saturday afternoon and make his way down to Bridgeport so he could see his mother. One of the many things about Gael that had made her fall hard.

"Mami, I'm back!"

Gabi's voice pierced through Perla's musings. She should've assumed Gael's sister would make an appearance, but the past twenty minutes had been so chaotic she hadn't had time to think about who else they'd have to involve in this farce. Gabi would not buy that they were dating. First, Gael told his sister everything, and second, Gabi knew exactly why she was here. And as good an actor as her brother was, Gabi did not have a poker face. Perla turned from the platter of empanadas she was pretending to arrange and put her arms around Gael's neck. Her mouth barely reached his throat, so she had to rise on her tiptoes to speak close to his ear.

She wished that he didn't feel this good. That the reality of him didn't make every one of her many fantasies pale in comparison. A wicked and not a little bit reckless thought occurred to her as they stood there pressed together in his family's dining room: she had the next couple of hours to touch Gael Montez as much as she wanted.

It would be a problem later; she knew that. She was already halfway back to that emotional chaos that only Gael could cause in her, but she found that she didn't much care. How could she deny herself this feast of a man when he was literally offering himself up on a silver platter? Was it reckless? Yes. But he'd asked her to pretend. No, not asked, demanded. He'd demanded she play this role for the next two hours. The role of besotted girlfriend, that they convince his mother they were an item once again. And that was how they'd been back then. Constantly touching, Veronica, Gabi and Abuela had mercilessly teased them about "all the PDA."

"What are you doing?" he asked tersely, without pulling back.

"Did you tell Gabi?" Immediately he tightened his arms around her. His massive chest like a living, breathing wall against her.

He nodded before he opened his mouth and the way his scruff grazed against her skin made shivers course all through her body. "Gabi knows. I caught her before she went to take the dogs out."

"Okay," Perla answered in a breathy tone, her lips brushing the side of his neck. She smiled at the strangled noise that came out of him in response. Something between a growl and a groan, and almost instantly he moved them until she had her back against the wall.

"If you're trying to play games with me, don't," he gritted out, his big body pressed to her. "I will call your bluff, every time, Perla. I thought you'd know that by now. Or was that kiss in the study not enough of a warning for you?"

She didn't know why she was provoking him. But her better judgment seemed to be on permanent hiatus when it came to Gael Montez. And there was something else she was testing. Another motive behind her urge to push him. She was trying to answer the question she'd been asking herself for six years. How had Gael gone from being devoted to her to heartlessly indifferent practically overnight?

She'd never quite figured out where things had gone so wrong with them. Because Gael had never given her reason to doubt his devotion to her. Then without explanation he'd let her go. Now that she was with him, that she could touch him and feel his reaction to her, it was beyond her to not find out if she still had that effect on him.

She tipped her face up so that her lips were just inches from his. "And here I was thinking that was just how you kissed on all your auditions."

He scowled at that, biting his bottom lip, like he had no idea what to do with her. "What's going on with you, Perla? You're not like this." He sounded confused, and something else that she could not quite pinpoint. Annoyed or not, his arms enveloped her and she felt a shiver course through his body as he held her. Still, that he saw her as some frail waif nettled.

"You haven't known what I'm like for a very long time, Gael," she retorted, sliding from under the cage he'd made with his body. "And what could possibly be going on with me? Other than having to lie to your whole family."

The meal was wonderful. The food delicious and full of all her favorite Puerto Rican treats. The kind of stuff her mother had never served when they were kids, but that her grandmother would make whenever she'd come for a visit from the DR. But it wasn't just the food, it was the company. She'd grown up in a home where there wasn't much warmth. Perla's parents had a toxic, tempestuous relationship that sucked the joy out of every moment. Which was why her time with the Montez family had been such a balm. People who sat around the table and talked. Laughed with each other, *liked* each other.

She'd told herself the whole ordeal would be agonizing, that Gael would be awkward and that she'd be flustered counting the minutes until it was over. But she could not have been more wrong. The moment they'd all sat down, it felt like the old days. Like one of the many weekends when Perla had driven down with Gael for a meal. Forgone a fancy weekend somewhere with her own family to be with the Montez crew. No matter what she might have told herself, she'd missed these people; she'd missed him.

"It's been so nice to have you with us, Perlita," Veronica said for what had to be the tenth time since they'd sat down to eat. All through the meal she'd been getting sly smiles from Abuela and Veronica as if they'd approved of her and Gael getting all handsy in the dining room. "You have to come and spend some time with us after you get back from Punta Cana. You know you can come here even if this boy is off on location, doing all that fancy stuff he does."

"I will," she lied, reaching for her glass of water. Her gaze fixed on one of the wreaths stamped all over the tablecloth.

"I'm so sad you have to rush off," Gabi said and Perla almost believed she was being sincere.

"Perla has to go to the airport," Gael protested, and even though it really shouldn't, it still hurt that he seemed in such a rush to get her out of his hair. And she *should* be heading out. She had been looking forward to spending time with Esmeralda and Rodrigo. Esme's mother and tias had been warm and welcoming on the few occasions Perla had met them. But it wouldn't be like it was with these people, who had always let her be herself. She repressed the sigh in her chest and looked around the table one more time. Steeling herself for the "see you soons" that were coming when she knew there would be no visits or times with Gael and his family ever again.

"But her flight isn't until late tonight and it's not even 3:00 p.m.," Abuela argued. "You still have a little time," the adorable, wily older woman said in that way that made it impossible to deny her anything. "Come down to the basement kitchen with us to help make the pasteles de yuca for a little bit and *then* go," Abuela suggested, knowing Perla had a weakness for pasteles. "I need to get some information about *La Venganza*. These cliffhangers are killing me and I know you have the scoop!" Perla laughed at the reference of the very popular telenovela being aired on one of Sambrano's networks.

"That's confidential information, Abuela," she said with a smile as she stood up, helping clear the plates.

"Mama's right, Gael. She can come down and help us for a bit. That way we can send you with some for your sister," Veronica cajoled, making Perla thaw a little more to the idea of sticking around. She *could* stay a little longer.

Without looking at Gael—and encountering his most likely disapproving expression—Perla conceded. "Abuela's pasteles are very hard to resist. Are you going to help us, babe?" she asked Gael sweetly. She knew at this point she was poking the angry bear, but hey, he had started this fiasco so he was going to suffer with her.

He pasted on a smile so fake she was tempted to ask if that was the best he could do for the millions he got per film. But when he reached for his mom, and kissed the top of her head then whispered an earnest, "Whatever makes you happy, Mami," Perla melted into a puddle before following their lead downstairs, ready to take part in the Montez family Christmas tradition.

Six

"Pass me the filling, querida," Gael's mother asked Perla, and his pretend girlfriend promptly picked up the bowl of shredded pork and handed it over without missing a beat. It was like time hadn't passed at all. Perla had been folded into his family like she'd never left.

The most irritating part of all was that he kept forgetting none of this was real.

For the past hour they'd all been making the pasteles. Every year his family made a few dozen of the Caribbean version of tamales to give to relatives and enjoy as part of their Nochebuena dinner. Even when his mom had been struggling to keep a roof over their heads, working three jobs to make ends meet, she'd somehow managed to get the stuff to make a few pasteles. In those lean years they'd eaten a rotisserie chicken instead of a pernil, and the arroz con gandules had only been enough for one serving each. But their mom would set the table like they were having a lavish meal. She made sure there were a few small gifts to open on Christmas Day.

Gael sometimes was a little numb to his career success. Once the opportunities finally started coming in, it seemed like he could barely keep up with the demands, much less enjoy what he already had. Then there were these moments. Getting to watch his mother and grandmother make pasteles in one of the two big kitchens of the mansion he'd bought. He was proud of this.

And almost as if she'd been reading his mind, Perla opened her mouth. "I'm so glad I got to see the house with all the Christmas decor up."

His mother smiled, looking up from wrapping a pastel in banana leaves. "Gael likes to spoil the people he loves. Don't you, mijo?"

"You deserve it," he muttered huskily, and felt Perla's eyes boring into his side. She'd always done that, been able to see more than anyone else. But this was not the time to dwell on the past. All of that was water under the bridge. One of the many sacrifices he'd made along the way in order to make sure his career thrived. In order to make sure his mother never went without ever again.

He just needed to keep it together a little longer and things would be back to normal. Continuing to be in the same room with Perla when everyone expected them to touch was flirting with disaster; that was a fact. But they were on the home stretch. His mother got her QT with Perla and now it was time for her to go, and if something hot and angry pulsed in his chest at the idea of her leaving, then that was to be dealt with later.

"Tell me about your new job, Perlita?" Veronica asked, and even though Gael kept his eyes on the batter he was spooning, his attention was on what Perla would say.

"I'm doing all the talent acquisitions for the studio's big-

ger projects and overseeing all our casting departments."
He could hear the excitement in her voice, and despite this
shit show the two of them had started, he was glad for her.
"My sister, Esmeralda, and her fiancé, Rodrigo, have been
at the helm for a year now and they're both very invested
in bringing back the kind of programming the studio had
at the start. More shows that reflect all the faces of Latin
America. Our mission is to show as much as we possibly
can of the seven hundred million people who are part of
the Latinx world."

Gael's abuela made a sound of approval at Perla's words.
"That's good, mija. I noticed that the shows weren't the
same. I remember that Sambrano was the first network
to have a Black Puerto Rican couple as protagonists in a
telenovela. That made me a fan for life, but in the past few
years it's been different."

Gael looked at Perla then, wondering what her reaction would be to his grandmother's comment. He found
her giving the older woman an apologetic smile. "You're
right, Abuela. We lost our way for a while there, but we're
determined to bring the network back to that mission. I'm
proud to be part of the effort."

Before Gael could stop himself he opened his mouth,
"You're really enjoying the work, then."

Perla gave him a baleful look. "I do enjoy it, and I'm
even good at it." The look she gave him, like she expected
him to say something dismissive, cut a bit, but he guessed
he deserved it.

"I don't doubt it. You're brilliant," he told her. It wasn't
like it was a lie. God, his head was a mess; too many feelings that he did not want to be cropping up were practically flooding him. The longer he was with her the worse
it would get. And he knew where it would all end, badly,
just like it had before. It was time to end this.

"It's almost 4:00. You said you wanted to be on the road before it got totally dark." He sounded like an ogre, but there was no helping it.

"Sure." Perla nodded, looking hurt. And dammit, it was not his job to keep Perla Sambrano happy no matter how much he ached to see that frown on her face disappear. "Darn, I must've left my phone in my bag upstairs," she said as she rinsed her hands. "I'm supposed to check in with the crew at the airport in case there are any issues. It was so good to visit with you all." She moved around the basement kitchen island and put her arm around Veronica, but his mother shook her head.

"No, we'll go up with you. We have to see you off properly. Mami's getting some pasteles packed up for you." Within seconds they were all walking up to the main floor of the house and that was when Gael noticed the sound of the wind. A glance out the window confirmed that the gusts were intense and snow was coming down hard. He could barely see anything, the usual view of sky and sea completely blurred out by the heavy snow.

"Oh, no," Gabi said ominously. "Perla, you can't drive out in that."

"But I have my flight," she declared as she warily looked out the window.

"You cannot go out in this, Perla." It wasn't a command, but just barely.

He had to shove his fists in his pockets to keep from grabbing her when she made a move for the door like she was actually planning to drive in that blizzard. Gael could see his mother furrowing her brow, too. And he knew it was only a matter of seconds before she suggested Perla stay with them until the weather improved. And yeah, that would be a major disaster, but he wasn't going to risk her getting into an accident.

"Sure I can," she told him, like he was overreacting. "The SUV has all-wheel drive." With every word out of her mouth Gael had a harder time not forbidding her to leave the house, especially when she kept putting on layers like she was going somewhere. "I bet it's just a squall. I'll probably drive right out of it once I'm farther from the coast," she assured them as she plucked her purse from the couch and set it on the floor by the door. "Here, let me check my messages." She was only in her socks, but had pulled out her sneakers from the rack by the door. The urge to grab her and keep her safely in his house until the snow stopped was so intense he was practically levitating.

If she stayed, she would stay there as his girlfriend, and these past two hours had already frayed his nerves raw. He didn't give a damn. All he cared about was keeping her safe.

"Shoot."

The tension in his neck and shoulders barely allowed him to snap his head back in her direction. He could hear the edge of panic in her voice as she read through whatever was on her phone. She squeezed her eyes shut for a moment and before she opened her mouth, he knew what she'd say. "The flight's canceled until noon tomorrow at least. The crew from the jet said they can't be cleared for take-off because there's a weather system coming through over the next eighteen hours."

He was still considering why his chest was tight enough to suffocate him, when his mother's scream of delight broke through the tension in the room.

"Well, you can just stay here! And if the flight can't go out tomorrow, you'll celebrate Nochebuena with us. I'm sure your sister will want you to stay put until it's safe to fly again." Gael's lips tugged up a little at how pleased his mother looked. Even if this was definitely a terrible turn of events.

Perla kept sending him looks that practically screamed "This is all your fault," and maybe it was, but he certainly was not sending her out in these conditions. They would just have to extend their fake relationship for a little longer, and that was that.

"Mami, take it easy on poor Perla," he said, trying very hard to sound at ease as he made his way to her. "You're going to scare her off. Give me your keys," he said, extending out his hand to her. "I'll get your bag for you."

"My bag?" she asked, like she had no idea what the word meant.

"*Your bag*, so you can have your stuff for tonight." He kept his hand out while she glared at him and the rest of his family looked on. He knew his mother was poised to go into full-on mama bear mode as soon as Perla relented.

Perla looked up at him, her face defiant, and moved in until she could bring his head down low enough for her to talk into his ear. She wrapped her arms around his neck and he thought he heard an *aww* or two coming from the direction of his female relatives. She pulled until he moved closer and their heads were brushing together. Her teeth grazed his earlobe and he had to bite the inside of his cheek to keep from moaning. He was sure from a safe distance this looked like a couple's embrace, but he could feel the menace coming off in waves from the woman in his arms, and still his cock throbbed from the closeness.

"This is all your fault, Gael Montez," she hissed. "We have to come clean. We can't keep pretending until I leave tomorrow." There was a little panic in her voice, but there was also a breathlessness there that he thought had more to do with how close they were standing than their conundrum.

He cursed the frisson of pure lust—yes, lust; he was

done fooling himself that it was anything else—and gripped her hips, eliciting an extremely satisfying surprised gasp out of her. "I'm not the one who drove out here when there was a storm warning for the afternoon, Perla. And you can't take it back. A deal's a deal. You know we can't tell my mother we were lying."

"Get a room, you two!" Gabi, that instigator, yelled from the couch where she was playing with the dogs.

"Keys, sweetheart," he teased and this time her teeth did a lot more than graze his ear.

"So testy," he said, pulling away from her before she pulled a Mike Tyson.

"I'll go get your stuff." He winked at her as she sent him a dirty look, which made his dick impossibly harder. If he could, he'd put her over his shoulder and carry her to the nearest bedroom until he had her screaming his name.

"Did Brigida clean the cottage this morning, Gaelito? I don't want Perla staying over there if it's not clean." And he needed to get himself together; his mother and grandmother were in the room.

"Cottage?" Perla asked cautiously, and Gael almost grinned as he heard his sister's explanation.

"Yeah, you two will have your own little love nest."

Nightmare. She was in a nightmare. And the kicker was that if this wasn't a hellscape of her own making, this would've been the stuff of her wildest fantasies. Snowed in with the man she'd been in love with for as long as she could remember, in a picturesque little beach cottage while his family—whom she adored—made cooing noises at what a cute couple they made.

Yeah, it would've been her literal dream if it wasn't a real-life horror show. And the snow was still falling in heavy sheets, covering the entire property in fluffy white powder. She was looking out the window at the "cottage" she'd be staying in, which was just a few yards away from the main house. After Perla recovered from the initial shock of being stranded with Gael and his family, Gabi explained the cottage was Gael's private space. Speaking of Gael—that coward—he'd run off somewhere as soon as she'd caved and agreed to stay until the snow passed. Probably to figure out how to torture her some more.

And damn it all, the cottage was darling. From where she stood, she could see the two picture windows on either side of the door and the small stone fireplace.

"It's pretty cozy in there. Are you sure you're up for it?" Perla jumped when she heard Gabi's friendly voice behind her, and even though she was strung as tightly as she'd ever been, hearing her old friend did help her frazzled nerves.

"This is a really bad idea, Gabi," Perla whispered, looking around the kitchen like a caged animal, expecting Abuela or Veronica to find them and uncover the lie.

"Well, no. It's not a good idea at all." Perla's stomach flipped at Gabi's typically unfiltered honesty. "But it's too late to take it back now. Mami had a really rough couple of years, Perla. Like really bad." Gabi's voice broke on the last few words, and now that Perla was looking closely, she could see the drawn expression on her face. Veronica's health crisis had taken its toll on the whole family. "She's so happy to have you here. Last year we spent the holidays with her in the ICU."

Perla's heart lurched as she saw the pain on her old friend's face. Veronica's health was not Perla's responsibility, that was true, but she couldn't bring herself to resent Gabi or Gael for trying to keep their mom happy. She didn't have a mother who meant the world to her, who had protected her or whom she felt protective toward. But she knew that was what Veronica was to her children, and no matter how annoyed she was at Gael, she would not mess up the Montez's Nochebuena.

"All right," she said without anger. "But you need to talk to your brother. There will be no funny business. I get my own bed."

Gabi's face paled slightly at the mention of the bed. "Please tell me there's more than one bed, Gabriela."

"There's a pull-out couch," Gael's sister hedged. "The cottage's more like a suite than an apartment," Gabi explained, and Perla wanted to scream. But before she could list her many concerns with the plan, Veronica and Gael walked in. At least he had the decency of looking somewhat worried.

"Okay, querida. I took a quick look at the cottage—"

"You didn't have to do that. It must be freezing out there and slippery," Perla said with concern, but Veronica waved her off with a smile.

"Gaelito built a covered walkway from the main house to it. Always so smart," she told her son, pushing up to kiss him on the cheek. "You've got fresh blankets and towels in there and I brought some almond creamer. I know you can't do regular milk in coffee." If she'd had any doubts about staying they were laid to rest in that instant. Veronica was positively beaming at the prospect of having Perla stay with them. She couldn't be selfish, not on this. "If I would've been informed about my son's new relationship status..." She offered a wink to soften the admonishment. "I would've made sure I had all the things you like, Perlita, but someone was keeping his secrets extremely under wraps as usual."

Despite Veronica's attempt to chastise them, Perla felt her throat tighten with emotion at her words. How did she remember? Perla had not had a cup of coffee with these people in at least six years, and still they knew how she liked it. Her own mother would probably be hard-pressed to list even two of her favorite foods, let alone details like what kind of creamer she liked.

"That's so kind of you. Thank you. And this relationship status change is very recent."

"Like super *super* recent, veritable breaking news," drolled Gabi, making Perla's face heat.

"Of course, mija. And don't be embarrassed about staying with Gael. We're a modern family," Veronica assured Perla, with a peck on the cheek. "Gabi's girlfriend stayed with us for Thanksgiving and we were so happy to have her here. I just want my kids and their partners at home with us."

The word *partner* landed like a punch to the gut. She looked up at Gael and saw that he wasn't faring much better. This white lie was turning into something perilous, and Perla was very aware that the biggest casualty would be her heart.

"Vamos, let me get you settled in," Gael said as he tugged on her hand. She should pull away. She should be furious with him, but he was looking at her with concern and with a tenderness she craved more than she would like to admit. She let him lead her to the mudroom, where she donned her coat and slipped her feet into too-big rain boots. They stepped out to find the wind howling all around them. The covered path protected them, but not completely, and it was freezing. The drive to the airport would've been terrifying in this. Even a thirty-second walk felt like a battle against the elements. But Gael's big body was right behind her as they made their way up the path, and no matter how things had been with them recently, she knew in her heart that if she stumbled he would catch her.

"Welcome to my casita," he announced without a hint of irony in his voice as they reached the red door with a circular window that let her see into the place she'd be spending the night.

They left their boots outside and stepped into the small cottage. The fire was roaring, making the space warm and toasty. The furniture was all designer. Lots of dark wood and soft, supple leather. Still, it looked inviting, like everything in Gael's home did. Except here there were not colorful cushions or knickknacks on the mantel. This place was more subdued, more masculine.

This was Gael's private space.

It was an open floor plan, just like the house. A small kitchen to the side, with stainless steel appliances and glass-front cabinets. A small table for two was set, there was an armchair with a reading lamp by the fireplace, and right beyond it he'd installed a floor-to-ceiling bookshelf. That was when she noticed the two paintings above his fireplace, and butterflies started flying in circles in her belly.

"You got the Jorge Meriño pieces," she said in surprise.

"I did." He was so nonchalant about it, as if it was no big deal for him to have two paintings by her favorite artist prominently displayed here. To be fair, Gael liked Meriño, too. He also knew the artist was her absolute favorite. This had been another thing they'd had in common, after all.

Perla always loved art; one of the few good things she'd gotten from her mother was her eye for it. When she and Gael started seeing each other, she'd discovered that he was also an art lover. They'd loved to go down to the city for shows and art gallery openings, especially ones displaying up-and-coming Latinx artists.

Their shared passion for art was something she hadn't thought about in years. Unlike the books and movies there was a difference in access to art for them that made it less real somehow. Back then Perla arrived to the shows like a collector, ready to buy a piece if she liked something. Meanwhile, Gael had only been an admirer, and on the occasions she offered to buy him something as a gift, he'd turned her down. But now he was a movie star, a man who could have anything and anyone he wanted.

Seeing one more thing they'd shared just made the fact that he wasn't truly hers, that he'd never be hers, again more painful. She held her breath and let it out slowly as she took in the pieces. She loved Meriño's aesthetic. He painted beautiful women with skin the color of graphite dressed in flowing gowns. They always wore white and had bright red hibiscus flowers in their hair. One of Perla's most prized possessions was one of his paintings. "When did you get these?" she asked, a little breathless, trying and failing not to read too much into this.

"The Luna Gallery in Tribeca. They just had a show of contemporary Ethiopian artists—I got a painting for my place in LA. I've bought a few pieces from them over the years."

That Ethiopian artist exhibit had been for VIPs only. She hadn't been able to go, but heard that the pieces all sold within a few hours. That meant Gael had been there on opening night. She'd taken him to Luna years ago when they were dating. But she had no idea he'd continued to go there on his own. This was…she didn't know what it was.

He was looking at her with that coy expression she remembered. It usually meant he knew he was about to get called out on something and was thoroughly prepared with a smart-ass comment. And Perla *had* questions. Why did he have these paintings in particular? Why did he keep going to the gallery she'd taken him to so long ago? What did this all mean? But as much as she wanted to ask, the truth was, none of it was any of her business anymore.

Gael Montez was not her business.

She returned her gaze to the two paintings and admired them for a moment, before offering him the sincerest smile she could muster. She needed some distance from Gael before she said something that would make the next twenty-four hours a lot more awkward than necessary. "They look really nice. I think I'm going to go back to the house," she said with a casual shrug she was not feeling. "I told your mom I'd come back to play dominoes with her, Gabi and Abuela. I also have to call Esmeralda."

She expected him to feign indifference, to let her walk out like he didn't care what she did. Instead, he answered the questions she hadn't asked out loud. "I got them because they reminded me of you." There was a tightness to his voice that she wanted very much not to read into. She had to get away from him before she said something she could not take back.

She stopped right by the door, reeling from the emotions she'd felt in the past couple of hours. She should probably confront him. Remind him it had been because of his choices that he'd lost her. Tell him how much it hurt her when he cast her aside. But she wouldn't give him any more of herself. Gael would never get any more of her tears. She just walked to the door instead. Before she walked out, she looked at him over her shoulder and said, "I never took you for the sentimental type."

She didn't feel an ounce of satisfaction in finally getting the last word.

Seven

"I can't believe the planes are grounded for the next day and a half," Perla lamented, tossing her cell phone aside after her call with the crew. She picked up the domino she'd been about to use for a play and tapped it on the table. She looked worried, upset. And he wished it didn't hurt to know that it was because she didn't want to be around him.

"You can stay with us as long as necessary, mi amor," his mother said sincerely. "It's been a delight to have you here." Veronica's comforting words only seemed to sink Perla into a deeper misery.

"I can't impose on all of you like that," Perla protested as his mother, sister and grandmother plied her with words of encouragement.

They'd made a mess of this.

Scratch that. *He'd* made a mess of this.

Against his best judgment, he walked over and put an arm around her, and it was a testament to how upset she was that she didn't fight him. She just sighed and burrowed into him. She let the whole weight of her body rest against him and he held her up. She looked up at him for a second, the winged eyeliner a little smudged now at the end of an emotional and chaotic day. "It was going to be my first Christmas with Esme's family," she explained, and she didn't have to say why that meant a lot to her. He knew how things had been with her mother. She was going to finally spend the holidays with family who treated her like they wanted her there. And now she would miss it. Right then Gael decided he would do whatever it took to give her a good Christmas. In a couple of days she would drive out of his life for good, but he'd give her two perfect days.

He lifted her chin so that she looked at him. "You're with family here, Perla. We'll take care of you." She didn't look convinced in the slightest, but she had too much home training to scoff in front of his mother and grandmother.

The girl he'd known and loved—yes, loved—had turned into a woman who was still searching for home. Perla may have found her confidence, but in some ways she was still lost, still looking for the unconditional love she'd never had, and he would make it his mission to ensure she got as much warmth and family as she could take in the next forty-eight hours. And because his family was the most extra in the world, soon they had Abuela, Gabi, Veronica and even the dogs coming in for a group hug.

"Mija, I know you're disappointed that you won't be with your sister in Punta Cana, but we will make sure you have a great Nochebuena with us," Veronica assured Perla as she pressed a kiss to her head.

"That's right, and I already have a few jobs for you, especially setting the table and getting everything pretty for our dinner. I was going to have Gaelito do them, but we know that boy has no finesse." Everyone laughed at Abuela's teasing, and Perla gave them all a watery smile.

"Thank you. I feel terrible about crashing your holiday plans like this—"

"Crashing?" his mother cried in horror at the suggestion Perla was not implicitly a part of every Montez family holiday. "You're family, baby. Gaelito's girlfriend." Gael felt her stiffen in his arms at the mention of their "relationship," but Perla was back on full fake-it-till-you-make-it mode, and just nodded.

"Thank you," she said, again, and when she looked up at Gael with those big stormy eyes, watery from unshed tears, something inside him cracked wide open.

"You're exactly where you belong," he told her, and to his surprise he felt the truth of those words in his very soul. He'd make sure he delivered on his promise to her.

"What are you doing?" Perla jumped at least a foot in the air when she heard Gael's voice, and then almost passed out when she turned to answer him and ended up face-to-face with a naked and very muscular tanned torso.

"Aren't you cold?" she asked irritably, instead of answering his question. Not that she could even put thoughts together when her brain kept trying to make her count the abs on his stomach.

Was that an eight-pack?

In college he'd had a swimmer's body, tight and lean, but not much bulk. He was so tall, it wasn't as if he needed the muscles to garner attention, but she guessed in Hollywood the more the better, at least when it came to brawn.

"I'm not," he said, running a hand over his chest as a self-satisfied smile tugged up his stupid, gorgeous mouth. "I asked you a question, Perla."

She furrowed her brow, trying extremely hard to recall what she could've possibly been doing before Gael short-circuited her brain with his abdominal muscles and extremely smooth, deeply bronzed skin.

"Um, what was I doing?" She looked down at her hands and finally her brain came back online. "I was decorating your tree." She'd found the little fake fir hidden in a corner next to a box full of ornaments and lights. "I wanted to make the place a bit more festive since all the Christmas spirit seems to be relegated to the main house." Apparently she said the wrong thing because now he was the one looking all flustered.

"Aren't *you* cold?" he asked—or growled if one was to get specific—pointing at her legs. She'd changed into something more comfortable while he was in the shower, and it seemed he'd noticed. He ran his gaze over her pajamas a few times, and she did not miss that he kept stalling on the spot where her shorts ended and her butt began. His eyes left a trail of heat all over her skin, enough to make her shiver. And yeah, they were *pretty short* shorts. In her defense, she had packed for a trip to the tropics.

"I am, a little, but this is the only kind of pj's I have, and as much as I love those faux leather leggings, they're not very comfortable to sleep in."

Okay, the hard staring was getting a little awkward.

And now he was walking away and going to the bedroom. God, had he always been this rude? With his family he'd been more or less normal, but since they'd come back to the cottage he'd been broody and short with her. And okay, she hadn't exactly been warm either, but this situation was nerve-racking.

"Here." His sharp voice resounded in the small space, and Perla looked up to find Gael holding up what looked like a pair of joggers.

She narrowed her eyes at him without making a move to take the pants. "Gael, you're almost a full foot taller than me. Those won't fit me. Also, I'm a bit curvier in certain areas." He directed his gaze at the area she was referring to, lips wrapped around his teeth, before facing her again.

"You can cuff them."

Was he giving her orders?

She crossed her arms over her chest, suddenly feeling contrary. "*No.* If you have a problem with what I'm wearing, I suggest you stop looking." With that she turned around and made sure her bottom was on full display as she bent down to pick up the box of ornaments she'd found. He could sound as mad as he wanted, but she'd seen him checking her out. She'd gained a bit of weight in the past few years, but for the first time in her life she felt comfortable in her own skin. Her mother had always drilled into her that she didn't have "the height for curves" and she'd always obsessed about dieting and her weight, but like most of the things her mother advised her on, Perla realized it hadn't been good for her.

So yeah, her butt was a bit bigger and her curves more generous, and she loved her body this way. And from the groaning and teeth-sucking behind her she assumed Gael didn't hate it, either. But for the sake of her own sanity, she ignored him and focused on wrapping fairy lights around the tiny tree.

"I don't want a tree in here," he finally said, his voice tight. He was such a grump about everything. He'd never been much for holiday cheer, but this year he was a full-on grinch. She turned around and found him looking at her with that terse expression, like having her in his space made his skin crawl.

"What's your problem, Gael? There are trees next door and you don't glare at them like you want to murder them. You used to be fine with decorating." She remembered driving over from her family's sumptuously decorated

mansion in Greenwich to his house one year and going to
Target with Gael to buy a new tree and outdoor decora-
tions. It had been after he'd gotten paid for one of his first
commercials. He picked out every ornament with such
care. Perla had noticed some of them had been hanging
on the new tree in his mother's living room. But as cheerful as things were in the main house, Gael's little space
was...stark.

"I've had a hard time getting into the Christmas spirit
in the past few years," he muttered and wouldn't even look
at her as he talked. When they'd been together he'd confessed to her that his father had left their family during
the holidays, and she wondered if that was what all this
was about. Or if it had to do with...nope, not going there.

"Why are you being like this, Gael?" she asked, and his
nostrils flared, his big hands twitching at his sides. She
felt diminutive in front of him. His massive body towering
over her. Gael had always been beautiful, but now he was
Hollywood handsome. Almost too perfect. Skin polished,
bright white veneers in his mouth, everything about him
groomed to the maximum. Even in joggers and a sweatshirt
there was something about him that made her want to stare.
And that should intimidate her, because aware as she was
of his perfection, she knew she was far from it. She was
pretty; she knew that. And she appreciated her looks and
knew what complemented her attributes. But she wasn't
movie-star beautiful and that was what Gael was around
every day. People whose job description included achieving almost unnatural levels of physical exquisiteness.

And yet, there was no denying the heat in his eyes as
he looked at her. It was almost menacing in its intensity,
but she knew now, like she always had, that she would always be safe with Gael Montez. Well, at least her body
would be—her heart was another story.

"I don't want to talk about any of that, and I'm sure you don't want to hear it," he said, reminding her that she'd posed a question.

"Sure, why don't you tell me how to feel, Gael? That's always been a special skill of yours." She knew that was not the way they would arrive at civility, but she was tired of his sulking.

She could see his jaw working, and a flush of pink working up his throat. She should leave this alone. This could not lead anywhere good. She'd already felt what his touch did to her. Already confirmed that the years and the distance had done nothing to temper her feelings for him, and here she was provoking him. Goading an answer out of him that would wreck her no matter what it was. And he *would* tell her, because Gael had never been a coward. And he'd already called her bluff once today.

He moved fast and soon she was pressed to a wall or a door, she didn't really care, because all of her concentration was going toward Gael's hands on her. His massive, rock-hard body pressed to her, and she wished, really wished, she had the strength to resist him. But all she did was hold on tighter when he pressed his hot mouth to her ear.

"I've told myself a thousand times today that I'm not supposed to want you as much as I do." He sounded furious and if she hadn't known him as well as she did she would've missed the regret lacing his words. He gripped her to him, and desire shot up inside her like Fourth of July fireworks, from her toes and exploding inside her chest.

"Wouldn't it be something if we could make ourselves want the things that we can actually have?" she said bitterly. He scoffed at that, and she didn't know if it was in agreement or denial of what she'd said. It was impossible to focus with his hands sliding over her like they were. She had never been able to put up much resistance when Gael had his focus on her. After a moment he pulled back. His eyes were bleak as he looked at her, and she dearly wished knowing he hadn't walked away unscathed didn't matter as much as it did.

"I don't want to talk about it." It. I-T. She had no idea what the *it* even was. It could've been so many things. His father's abandonment, their relationship and how it had been laid to waste. The years they'd had and lost, everything they could never get back. Two letters to encompass so much loss and heartbreak. There were things to say, so many. But she could not make herself say a word. The pain in his eyes wouldn't let her.

He ran a hand over his head, like he didn't know where to start. Like this was all too much for him, and for a moment she thought he would actually walk away, leave her standing there.

He kissed her instead.

Eight

He'd almost told her everything. About what his father had said the night he walked out on Gael, his mom and sister. Almost confessed the real reason why he broke it off with her six years ago. Truth was like an avalanche roiling in him. But that was his baggage to carry, not hers. He could not change what was, the way he'd hurt her or the fate of the men in his family. But he could make these days good for her. He could get all the way out of his feelings and focus on Perla. He *could* take charge and give them both a much-needed release. The feel of her lips on him had dogged him all day. And now here she was, perfect and soft in his arms. Kissing him with a hunger that set his blood on fire. He tried to think of something in the past six years that had felt this real, and he could not come up with a single one.

"I can't stop thinking about your mouth," he said, almost grudgingly, as she grazed his neck with her teeth.

"Well, if it makes you feel any better it's definitely mutual," she answered with a sexy little growl as she hooked her legs around him.

He'd told himself so many times after the breakup that she deserved better. Someone who could love her like she needed. Someone who could protect her heart. Told himself again and again that person couldn't be him. That no matter how much he tried, he was destined to break her heart. That his feelings for her had just been fleeting, a passing infatuation. But his reaction to her now, the frantic hunger he felt for her, told a very different story.

"Can I?" he asked as he rubbed his thumb over a hard nipple. He was eager to see her reactions; he'd always loved how expressive she was. How she didn't know how to hide her desire. She always showed him everything he made her feel. It had been like an addiction when they'd been together. He would spend hours exploring her. His hands on her skin, and his eyes pinned to her face, marveling at the way she'd squeeze her eyes shut, or let her mouth fall open from pleasure.

"Mmm," she moaned as he circled one taut tip with his thumb. And his mouth watered with the need to taste all the places he hadn't touched in so long. Perla had been...inexperienced in college. Gael had been her first everything. And even if he'd never admitted it, he'd fucking loved being the first man to ever see her fall apart in his arms.

"You like it when I touch you like this?" he asked, before dipping his head to mouth a nipple over her shirt.

"You know I do." He smiled at how put off she sounded, but her gray eyes, which had been so cold only a minute ago, were glowing. Gael wanted to see her burning for him.

He liked his sex dirty. And this woman right here, she had his head full of all kinds of filthy things. And right below that urge, there was a much more dangerous impulse, but he smothered that thought before it could get any oxygen. He brought his focus back to Perla. To the way she felt under his hands, perfect.

Still, she looked a bit shy as she took his hand, guiding it under her T-shirt. It was a black, long-sleeved tee that had the words Gracefully Furious in pink font. He had to bite back a smile, because that was exactly how he would describe her. He'd always been drawn to her wit and that palpable fragility in her, but now there was a boldness there, too, and that made her irresistible.

Every thought other than touching her flew out of his head when he palmed the warm, soft skin under her shirt. She didn't say a word as he ran the heel of his hand up her ribs and then to the slope of her breast. They were small and pert, and they were...bare.

"No bra? That's different," he said, voice dripping with want as he worried a nipple between his thumb and index finger, making her mouth open in a silent moan.

"I don't like them. I never did. And now I only wear them if I have to," she told him, her back arching as she pushed herself into his hand.

"That is a dangerous piece of information to have. How will I get through the next day knowing the only thing between my hand and these beauties is one layer of clothes?" He leaned in to kiss her, a quick glide of his tongue with hers, and she opened up for him hungrily. Her mouth hot on his as he took small nips of her bottom lip. God, he could devour her. "I'm going to put my mouth on them now."

"Please." The little sounds she made were driving him absolutely crazy. This woman begging for him was almost overwhelming. He applied himself to touching her, ran the pads of his thumbs over each of her nipples, tracing with his fingers the places he'd taste.

"There's a rosy pink right under the brown of your skin, and when you're like this it flushes. I want to see the other places where you're a little pink, baby." And there was no stopping his mouth.

"Oh, my God," Perla moaned as she writhed in his hands. He bent his head and circled the hard tip of his tongue around the peaks of her breasts and when he flicked them with his finger...that got him another delicious sound of pleasure. With every touch, she pressed herself closer to him and now her legs were wrapped around him, so tightly that he could feel her heat through those sinful little shorts, and he was sure she could feel the base of his painfully hard cock.

"You feel that, sweetheart?" he asked as he nipped on one of her earlobes. "You feel how hard I am for you?" He thrust against her, and she rocked to meet him. He was careening into a series of extremely bad decisions, he knew that, and still his hands roamed down to the soft skin of her belly.

"Are you ready for me?" he asked as his hand snaked down to her core.

"So ready," she gasped when his fingers grazed against the curls covering her folds.

"You're aching for this, aren't you? When was the last time someone touched you like this?" He had no idea why he was going there. If he was smart he'd leave that door firmly shut, but something in him needed to hear that no one made her feel like he did.

"Six years to be exact," she said in a breathy whisper as she reached for his hard cock. Her grip was like a vise and he could not think. He plunged into her hand viciously, even as he tried to process what he'd just said.

"Mmm," he grunted, dizzy from pleasure. "Six years?" he asked, fuzzy thoughts starting to become clearer. Six years; she hadn't been with anyone in six years? He'd broken her heart so badly that she hadn't been with anyone else?

And now he was doing this with her when he knew there was no possible future for them.

Fuck. He needed to stop this. *Now.*

"What?" she asked breathlessly as he unwound her legs from around his waist, jumping back like her skin was scalding him. She looked drunk from his kisses, so utterly edible. But he knew what the right thing to do was. He wouldn't go any further without being certain she would not regret this later. And today had been too much of a roller coaster for sex to be anything other than a terrible idea. But it seemed Perla was going to be pissed at him anyway.

"You're going to regret this later," he told her, rubbing his mouth with the back of a shaky hand.

She flinched like he'd slapped her. Her expression went from dreamy and warm, to shuttered and embarrassed. "You don't have the slightest clue about my regrets, Gael," she said stonily, "but you're right about one thing. This is a mistake." She was already pushing him back so she could get away.

"It's not a mistake. I just don't want to complicate things more than they already are." *Because I'm almost certain that I still have feelings for you, and doing this will probably end with you hating me even more than before.*

"It's not that I don't want you, Perla—"

"Oh, my God," she screamed, her face a mask of horrified embarrassment. "Please, Gael, spare me the 'it's not you, it's me' rerun from college." Perla was not even looking at him. Her hands crossed over her chest and her face miserable. She seemed seconds from starting to cry. "I haven't forgotten what you said." She held up a hand at him, her expression forbidding. "No need to tell me again. Let's just pretend none of this happened and try to get through tonight and tomorrow," she said miserably and stormed off to the bedroom. He could hear her moving around the room quietly as he stood there like a statue looking at the bare little tree with its twinkling lights. She never even got to put on the ornaments.

He was *such* an asshole. He knew that adding a fake relationship with Perla to the already shitty mix of feelings that usually cropped up for him around the holidays was a terrible idea, and less than twelve hours in, he already had her on the verge of tears. His father had been right; the Montez men really could not stop themselves from hurting the women they cared about.

All those years ago, on another Christmas Eve when his life had fallen apart, his father had warned him of that fact. After disappearing for over a week, Gabriel Montez had shown up at dinnertime on Nochebuena smelling like booze and another woman's perfume. His mother, finally done with years of putting up with her husband's philandering, had kicked him out.

Gael wasn't sure what it was about that particular time, after so many others, that seemed to take. But she'd stood firm in her best red dress with Gabi crying against her legs and demanded he leave them alone. Gael remembered that he expected his dad to do his usual round of begging. To fling excuses and endearments at his mother until she relented. To his surprise, without a word, his father had gone to the bedroom he'd shared with his wife for over fifteen years, packed a suitcase and after kissing him and his sister goodbye, walked out of their house for the last time.

Gabi and Veronica watched the man go with tears streaming down their faces, but Gael ran after him. Angry and confused, he demanded that his father explain why he was abandoning his family. Why he kept hurting his mother. Why he didn't love them. His father had lifted a shoulder and said, "The Montez men are no good to their

women, mijo. No matter what we do, we end up destroy-
ing the women we love." He shook his head sadly, like he
could not understand it himself. "It's a curse." With that,
he bent down to kiss ten-year-old Gael on the forehead,
got in his car and drove away.

Over the years Gael told himself a lot of things regarding what his father had said that night. That his dad had
been weak and selfish, and trying to make excuses for his
bad behavior. That he'd chosen to fail his family, that he
cheated because he wanted to. That he would never be that
kind of man. He'd spent eighteen years telling himself that
he'd be different from his father, and here he was hurting
this woman, again. And what was any of this for? To pretend for a few days and then leave them both done in again?

Manolo had been right about one thing; with Perla and
him it had to be all or nothing. He could not pretend with
her; he couldn't only have her halfway. And that was why
staying away from her had been the right thing, the safe
thing. No matter how much he wanted her, how deep his
need ran for her, he would *hurt her*.

It didn't matter what he wanted or, in this case, who. He
was a Montez and Montez men ended up alone.

Perla: SOS… SOS!

Perla was well aware that her texting was a bit on the
dramatic side today, but desperate times, and all that. She'd
kissed Gael *again*. She almost did more than that, and then
he'd pushed her away. God, how many times would she
set herself up to be humiliated like that?

She'd just hide in the bedroom and pretend she was
asleep when he came in to bed. Or maybe he'd sleep on
the couch. She wished the idea made her feel better, but

the thought of him sleeping in discomfort because he was trying to avoid her only sank her mood further.

He must think she was desperate. And the worst part was that she would've let him have her right there. She'd been aching for it. It was like she was a completely different person when she was with Gael. Reckless and impulsive, ruled by her desires.

She needed someone to talk her off this cliff, which seemed to be crumbling under her feet almost by the minute. Perla fired another message off to Marquito, Rodrigo's brother—and her closest friend. He was supposed to fly to the DR for Christmas, too, but had pulled out at the last minute, saying he had too much work with the awards season starting in January. Marquito was a stylist to some of Hollywood's A+ list, so he was spending the holidays in LA on his own. And Perla had been so caught up in drama today that she hadn't even checked up on him.

Marcos: Girl, you're not still trying to get on a plane, are you? I thought you were grounded until the storm passes.

The details of her breakup with Gael Montez weren't exactly public knowledge. She wasn't sure how he'd done it, but he'd managed to keep any mention of how their relationship ended out of the news. But she and Marquito went way back. Since his relationship with her asshole brother, Onyx, had crashed and burned years ago. And in the past year since their siblings rekindled their own romance they'd grown closer than ever. Which meant he knew all the sordid details about her and the Hollywood heartthrob.

Perla: No, I'm still in New York. No one's flying out of here for a while. I'm snowed in at Gael Montez's house in the Hamptons.

The three dots indicating that Marquito was typing up a message appeared immediately.

Marcos: You're what?! OMG PERLA SAMBRANO! Can I call you?

Perla cringed at the idea of Gael hearing her gab about her thirst for him while he was in the other room.

Perla: I can't. I'm in Gael's private cottage…because we sort of told his mom we're dating again.

A string of gifs appeared, which Perla supposed were trying to convey Marquito was not computing.

Marquito: For the love of all that is holy please let me call you.

As she considered what to do she heard a door open and close in the cottage. And a moment later through the bedroom window she saw Gael's tall figure walking out on to the boardwalk leading to the ocean. He looked so sad and alone, and Perla once again wondered what the hell she thought she was doing with this man. Sullenly, she tapped her screen and called Marquito. It didn't fully ring once before he picked up.

"I want the tea. All of it!"

Despite herself, Perla smiled at her friend's nosiness. "You're a chismoso," she told him, unable to mask the genuine affection in her voice.

"I do love my gossip, but come on, friend. *This is major.* What's going on? How did you end up in the Hamptons?"

She sighed before launching into a detailed explanation of the day's occurrences and almost couldn't believe herself that all that had happened in less than twelve hours.

"So you're spending Nochebuena with him and his family, pretending to be his girlfriend?" Marquito recapped.

"Correct."

"And you've already made out twice and are sleeping in the same bed tonight?"

Perla growled at Marquito's giddiness. "This is such a fun game. I'm so glad I called you."

"Perlita, babe, are you having just pants feelings for this boy or is your heart in the mix, too?"

And that was the question, wasn't it? One that she would be smart to answer sooner rather than later.

Still looking where she'd seen Gael's tall figure long after he disappeared from view, Perla sighed. "Maybe..." Lies. "Okay, not maybe, I do." She slumped on the bed feeling wrung out from the admission. It was one thing to barely acknowledge it to herself, but a whole other to say it out loud.

"Oh, friend." Marquito's gentleness as he spoke to her stung. She hated feeling pitiful and foolish.

"You know what's even more absurd?" Perla asked into the silence of the room as she shifted to get under the covers.

"What?" Marquito asked cautiously.

"I'd convinced myself that I was over him. It's barely been twelve hours, Marcos, and I can't breathe right if he's around. I can't *think* when I'm close to him." Perla squeezed her eyes shut as she thought of the way he'd touched her just minutes ago. The way his big hands had felt on her skin. "I've let him kiss me twice, and I know I'll do it again if he asks me."

"Oh, boy… Perla Marina Sambrano, you in danger, girl."

"I know," she said, resigned, and considered her options. This thing with Gael would end poorly. He was not interested in a relationship. As far as she could tell he hadn't had a serious girlfriend since they split up. It was probably unhealthy of her, but over the years she'd kept up with him, or at least with what the tabloids had to say, and he had not had a long-term relationship. He'd casually dated a model or a costar, but they never lasted.

Not that she was one to talk. She couldn't remember the last time she'd gone past a first date. But she had a lot going on; she didn't have the bandwidth for a relationship. She was just starting this new chapter in the family business. She was finally on her own and free from her mother's clutches for the first time in her life. She'd told herself she would focus on her career, that she'd take this time to figure out what she wanted. In conclusion, she should not want Gael Montez, but she still did.

"Perlita, are you still there?" Marquito's raspy voice yanked her out of her thoughts.

"I'm going to see where things go."

Perla thought Marquito's long exhale would be a preface to him trying to talk her out of it, but when he spoke, he surprised her. "Who am I to lecture you, babe? I keep falling headfirst into someone that I know isn't good for me. But I love him." Perla's heart ached for her friend, and she wished her brother wasn't such a selfish jerk.

"I'm sorry," she said sincerely. "I wish Onyx would get his head out of his ass."

"Nope, we're not touching my drama tonight. Perla. If you want that man, let yourself have him."

"I think I might," she assured her friend before ending the call. Anticipation roared under Perla's skin like the flames of a fire as she lay in Gael's bed. This was not a smart plan, but maybe that was why it needed to happen, because from how they'd both been thirsting after each other all day she knew all of this tension would need to be popped somehow. And wasn't it better to do it now? To stop fighting the inevitable and slake this lust that was clouding her judgment? No one had ever done to her what Gael could. He made her feel like a goddess when he looked at her with lust burning in his eyes. It was impossible not to want to snatch some of that when it was within her grasp.

She'd known that was the reason why she'd barely even kissed another man in all these years. It was like having to live on fast food when you'd gotten used to filet mignon. And she wanted another taste of him, even if was just one last goodbye. She'd wait for him to get back, and she'd fill Gael Montez in on why the only way for them to fake this relationship convincingly was to burn off some of this sexual tension. She had a few suggestions on how exactly they could do that.

Nine

"Damn, bro. I can feel the waves of tension coming off you all the way from here."

"Can't I have ten seconds to myself in this place?" Gael made a frustrated noise with his back to his sister. He'd come here after Manolo had called him for the fourth time in an hour to talk about the project he was insisting Gael take, even after he'd told him on the plane he wasn't interested. Manolo, as always, had not been happy that Gael didn't take his advice, but his uncle had gone into a full rage when Gael told him he'd accepted the role for the Rios series. The man had launched into a tirade about how he was throwing away the work they'd done to build his brand. Gael hadn't been in a mood to be handled and had ended the call. Hell, he wasn't in the mood for anything. Not after how things had gone with Perla.

He was leaning on the rails on the small pier he'd built on the property. There were lamps overhead lighting the path, but Gael had chosen a dark corner to come and think.

He was still at a loss of what to do about the woman he'd left in his house looking miserable.

"So testy," Gabi responded without heat, and walked over to him until they were standing side by side. She didn't say anything, just kept watch with him in silence until he was ready to talk.

"We should've gone to the condo in Ponce," he told her.

Gabi scoffed and wrapped an arm around his waist. "You know Mami can't handle Christmas in Puerto Rico yet. She'll want to go visit everybody, and there'll be people coming through the house all day. She's not well enough for all that. Besides, she loves it here. This is her favorite place." His sister tightened her hold on him and he was grateful for her anchoring presence in this moment when he felt so close to drifting away.

His mother did love the ocean. When he was a kid, she'd talk about her own childhood in Puerto Rico. Of growing up in Ponce and walking to the beach for a swim every morning, and he'd dreamed of giving her that. Of buying a little corner of ocean for her. And now he'd done more than that. His mother had an oceanfront condo in her beloved Ponce, a house in the Los Angeles hills with stunning views of the Pacific Ocean, and a mansion in the Hamptons with a private beach. He dearly wished he could feel something other than exhaustion when he thought about all of it.

"I've made a mess of things with Perla," he blurted out. "Again."

His sister let out a long, sympathetic sigh, and he could feel her head shaking against his shoulder. "You two are hopeless. I thought Perla would be smarter than you, but it seems like you have very adverse effects on each other's intelligence. Dummies." Gabi's sad laugh blended with the crashing waves of the ocean. It was too dark to see her, but he could picture the sardonic smile on her lips. "You kissed her again, didn't you?"

"Yes." Gael put his head in his gloved hands as he waited for his sister to ream him out. Whatever she was about to tell him, he deserved it. Because he knew better. The kindest thing a Montez man could do for a woman he cared about was to leave her alone. What he ought to do right now was walk into the house and come clean to his mother, then stay as far from his ex as he could.

But the need to be around her was like a sickness. "I thought I was past this."

"Past lusting after the woman you've been in love with since sophomore year of college?"

"I'm not in love with Perla," he argued weakly. "I *can't* be in love with her. I can't be in love with anyone—*you know why.*"

This time his sister's sigh was the opposite of sympathetic. "Gael, please, you have to stop with this 'I'm cursed' nonsense. Our father was a no-good bum, and he should've never—"

"It's true, though." Gael turned to his sister, grateful for the semidarkness, hoping it hid some of the agony on his face.

The blue tint of the moonlight cast his sister in a gloomy light, and he wondered how much her somber expression mirrored his. "I wish I'd told Mami about that bullshit you've had in your head all this time."

"You can't," Gael warned.

"I won't," she sighed, tiredly. "If I haven't done it in all this time, I'm not going to do it when she's so frail. It would kill her to know you've been doing this to yourself."

"I'm not doing anything to myself," he answered stubbornly. "I should've been more careful, but as soon as I saw her it was like all the lectures I'd been giving myself burned to ashes. I've fronted like this was all for Mami. But that's bullshit. I wanted her. It's like my self-control evaporates whenever Perla's near. And all I do is hurt her."

"God, you're such an idiot." As far as confidantes went, his sister was not a coddler, but at least she was honest.

"You hurt her because you keep hanging on to that stupid curse idea and listening to Manolo. There's no curse, Gael. You broke up with her in college because you let Manolo convince you that your career was going to suffer if you had a girlfriend. And you're hurting her now because you're choosing to believe our father's ridiculous excuse to justify his cheating. The man could not take responsibility for anything."

"If none of it is true, how come I left Perla crying in the cottage? I've barely been around her for a day and I've already made her miserable."

"Why is she crying?" His sister's tone told him she already knew the answer.

"Because I told her she'd regret it if things went further."

Gabi made a sound that was a cross between sympathy and frustration. "You know, it's a good thing you figured out a way to channel this melodramatic streak of yours into an exorbitantly lucrative career, because you are too much sometimes."

"Way to kick a guy when he's down, sis."

"I'm not kicking you while you're down. I'm telling you to get over yourself. I don't know what you two were up to in that cottage, but by the way you were eyeing each other all day, I assume it had something to do with you and your very poorly concealed thirst." She held her hand up, as if she could sense he was about to protest. "Nope, I'm talking. You keep hurting Perla because you refuse to accept your feelings for her, and you're stubborn as hell.

If it wasn't because this role came up, you would've spent the rest of your life wondering where you went wrong. What is so bad about you wanting Perla and her wanting you back?"

"Because it can't work." Gael wondered who exactly he was trying to convince.

"It certainly won't with that attitude," Gabi retorted, and she sounded like she was about to completely lose her patience. "Have you ever considered that if you just go with it, things may not seem so monumental? You're both young, hot and with money to burn. If you want something or someone, all you have to do is reach for it…or her."

"I don't know, sis." Gael considered his sister's words. Being around Perla today he felt like he had ants under his skin. Unsettled and frantic from wanting her. But maybe that was what he had to do. Just let this thing between them happen. Just let them run their course and then she would leave and his life would go back to normal. They were both adults, after all. If they went in with their eyes open, then they could walk away once it was over.

"You know what, Gabi?" he asked, a plan hatching in his head already. "I think you're right. I think I just need to go with it."

"What are you up to, Gael Alberto Montez?" Gabi asked suspiciously as they turned and headed back up the pier.

"You should be happy. I'm finally taking your advice," he said distractedly, his mind already picturing how he'd find Perla. Maybe she was already in bed.

"That's what I'm worried about."

"Don't worry about me, little sister," he told her as he bent down to kiss her forehead. "I have it all under control."

The last thing he heard as he walked up the stone path to the cottage was his sister's laughter. "Famous last words."

* * *

Perla woke up on a slab of granite. Of very warm, very bronzed granite.

"Oh, Lord," she whispered as the events of the previous night, and day, came roaring back to her. She was in bed with Gael Montez, and despite it being a California King, she'd somehow ended up sprawled on top of him. He was significantly larger than she was, which meant that with her fully on top of him, she could still see a lot of golden brown skin. She opened one eye, and yes, there was a good amount of sculpted muscle and delicious collarbone to admire. Her lips, which at the moment were exactly in the valley between his pecs, itched to pucker up and press a kiss on that smooth skin.

God, she couldn't even count the number of times she'd yearned to wake up like this again. Of getting to look her fill, to touch as much as she wanted. And she wanted. She wanted *so much*. She'd fallen asleep waiting for him to return, so she didn't get a chance to propose her plan to him. But she would as soon as he woke up. She'd be a fool to waste this chance. Because if one thing was certain, it was that this lust was not going anywhere.

She sensed something stirring at the foot of the bed and stiffened, wondering if she'd been thinking so loud she'd woken up Gael, then she felt it, a very warm vibration by her feet.

She sat up startled, and Gael, with his eyes still closed, shifted, until something started moving up his body under the blankets.

"What the hell?"

"It's just Chavi," he explained and lifted a hairless sphynx cat from under the covers.

"Oh, my," Perla said as the cat rubbed its tiny bald head

against Gael's wrists. She purred like a little motorboat. "I thought you didn't like cats."

"I don't," he assured her as he ran a hand over the animal's back. "But she likes me, and my mother insists I need 'some kind of company.' Which means I got Chavienda for my birthday this year."

She couldn't help the laugh that exploded out of her. "You named your cat nuisance?"

He grinned at her and then winked, and goodness, the man really was beautiful. He was sitting up now and she could see the notches of his hips and that trail of brown hair leading to his...

"My eyes are up here, Perla." Oh, that was his sex voice, and wow, it still had a very strong effect on her. "And her name's nuisance in *Puerto Rican slang*." Gael's voice snapped her out of lusting for him, and she kind of melted when she saw how gentle he was with the cat. "It's very fitting given her family situation."

Perla could not help the grin that tugged at her mouth. "So far she's been extremely well behaved, so she's not much of a nuisance. This is kitty slander."

"That's because you haven't looked closely at my coffee table. She loves to file her claws on it," Gael harrumphed as he swiftly grabbed the cat, put her out of the room and closed the door. He flopped back into the bed and smiled up at her.

"How did you sleep?" He sounded tentative, but there was something in his voice this morning that had not been there last night. Like some of that distance he'd been putting between them had been bridged.

"Good," she quipped as she warmed under his attentive gaze.

"I'm glad." He shifted so that the sheets revealed more of his skin.

It was exceedingly difficult to focus on what he was saying when she had over six feet of Puerto Rican male in his prime two feet away.

His mouth had always been a particular fixation of hers. The bottom lip was fleshier, but both were perfectly shaped, the top one a shade darker than the rest of him, but the bottom one was this enticing pink, and God, she loved tugging on it with her teeth. Sucking on it until she made his breath hitch. Her gaze locked on that mobile mouth. The way it stretched when he smiled, and parted just a little when he was deep in thought.

She'd never stopped wanting him. She might never stop. She wished she could be bold and ask for what she desired, but she didn't want him to push her away. Gael sucked in a breath as she worried her thumb over his lip, and then moved to clamp a hand on her wrist.

"Te agarre," he said, and that was exactly how she felt. Caught. Caught looking, caught wanting something she shouldn't and craved anyway.

Her body flushed hot and cold and her stomach fluttered frantically at his touch. His gaze moved up until they were looking at each other. And she could see it there, that fire in his eyes, *that want*. Gael may not be able to love her. He might not want a future with her, but he desired her. That heat in his eyes could be nothing else. And if this was all he could give her...she would take it. He pulled on her arm until their mouths were inches away, and her heart felt like it would burst through her chest.

"Quiero besarte," Gael whispered against her lips.

"But morning breath," she hedged breathlessly.

He smiled against her mouth and moved in closer until their foreheads were pressed together. "It doesn't bother me, sweetheart." She was melting, her bones and muscles softening with every word and every touch.

"Okay." She could hear the tremor in her voice as he moved in closer and shifted them until she was on her back and he was covering her. He was so big. This lusty god was everything she could see and feel, a complete assault on her senses. He brought their mouths together and gave her an achingly sweet kiss. While the others had been rushed and ravenous, this one was sultry and sensuous. He licked at the seam of her mouth, his tongue warm as he explored her, gliding against her own. All the while his hands roamed her body; he caressed her thighs, her calves, palmed her belly. Like he wanted to map every part of her. She ached for him with bewildering urgency. It was like she'd forgotten how to feel in these past six years and Gael's hands and mouth had woken up all those dormant sensations.

She ached for him. A dull, throbbing need pulsing at the apex of her thighs.

"Please, Gael," she whispered against his mouth, arching her back to press even closer to him.

"Mmm," he moaned and moved them again until she was astride his hips. She could feel his erection prodding against her backside, and a shiver of lust coursed through her body. She wanted that, too, him deep inside her. She rubbed herself against Gael, eliciting a tortured sound from him.

"Come here," he told her, already reaching for her, and the demand in his voice with just a hint of possessiveness ignited her blood. She had no idea what happened between last night and the morning to change Gael's mind, but she would not question it. He kissed her hungrily, one hand at the nape of her neck, while the other skated up her belly. "Can I touch you here?" he asked as the tips of his fingers brushed the underside of her breast.

"Please," she begged as she went in for another kiss.

Their tongues languidly tangled together as he played with her breasts. He plucked on a nipple and then the other, making liquid heat pool in her core.

"Oh, God," she gasped as he brought his other hand under her shirt.

"You like this?" he asked, and she only nodded, too turned on to make words. The way he touched her, like he owned her—it made her dizzy with lust. She wanted to ask for more, to take his hand and press it to where she pulsed for him, and just as she was about to do it, the door of the cottage crashed open, sending them both scrambling.

Ten

"Are you okay?" Gael asked Perla as she rushed to put on the jogger pants he'd gotten her, which *were* way too long, but still distractingly hugged the curves of her ass and hips.

It was going to be very hard to keep his hands off her today. And he still had no idea what he was doing. He had to talk to her, tell her that he still could not give her what she wanted. That he would not take more chances with her heart when he knew he'd never be able to be the man she deserved. That they could do this until she left. But right now he had to deal with his sister, who was hollering like a lunatic outside the bedroom.

"Jesus," Gael exhaled as he slid on a Henley and hurried to open the door of the bedroom. "I'll go deal with her. Take your time," he said to Perla, who was now looking through her bag.

"All right, thanks," she said, looking up at him. Her cheeks were still flushed, and her lips looked a little swollen from his kisses. He wished to every deity he could just kick his sister out and go back to what he was doing. But there was no way that was happening. Not on Christmas Eve.

"Chill out, Gabriela! What the hell?" he grumbled, reluctantly closing the door behind Perla.

The moment he set foot in the living room his pest of a sister wolf-whistled as she gave him a very thorough once-over and a goofy grin appeared on her face. "Oh, I see how it is."

"You see nothing," he muttered and pointed at the three insulated tumblers on the table. "Is one of those for me?"

Gabi nodded as she stared at the closed bedroom door. "Yes, the blue one's yours. So what exactly was occurring before I arrived?"

Gael ignored his sister's nosiness and picked up the piece of paper next to the coffee. It was a to-do list in his mother's handwriting. He smiled as he got himself caffeinated. First on the list was "come over and have breakfast with your elders." "Mami's in a mood today."

Gabi smiled and grabbed her own cup. "She is. She wants you to make the chocoflan and tres leches. I'm in charge of the pernil and the playlist." She glanced at the door again and smiled wide. "Abuela's requested that your girlfriend be in charge of setting the table."

Gael raised an eyebrow at that. "I'll tell her when she gets out of the shower."

"I take it things are marching smoothly, then?" Gabi thought she was cute.

Gael only nodded and kept gulping down coffee.

"You're no fun," his sister groused.

"And you're a busybody. We'll be at the house in twenty and then I'll bring all the stuff for the dessert here. That way Mami and Abuela have the big kitchen to themselves."

They talked about the plans for the evening as they sipped coffee, and after a while Perla stepped out of the bedroom. She looked adorable in another oversize sweater, this one a forest green, with very skinny jeans. Her face was free of makeup and her short black hair was sticking up in every direction. He wanted to ravage her. His heart pounded and his skin prickled whenever he saw her. He could tell himself, his sister and even Perla whatever he wanted, but in that moment he gave up on telling himself lies about what he was feeling for this woman.

"Morning," Perla said shyly as Gabi handed her the third coffee tumbler.

"Good morning," Gabi said cheerfully, while Gael put his arm around Perla and brought his mouth down to hers for a kiss.

"You used my toothpaste," he muttered against her mouth, tasting cinnamon and clove.

"Yes, I forgot mine," she told him a little breathlessly as they pulled apart.

He was a little deprived of oxygen himself, and still this felt right. Even if it was only for today.

"Mami sent Gabi with a list of what she needs us to help with and she wants us at the house for breakfast. Are you okay with that?" he asked quietly as Gabi sat on the couch playing with the cat.

Perla didn't respond immediately, her gaze fixed on something behind them. "You finished it," she said, pointing at the other side of the room. When he turned, he saw the little Christmas tree that he'd decorated after he'd come back and found her asleep.

"Yeah," he confirmed as Perla walked over to it, getting his sister's attention.

"Acho, Gael. Did you actually put up the tree?"

Perla turned to look at him, obviously curious for what he'd tell his sister. "Perla wanted it up."

"I did. Thank you." His pretend girlfriend offered him a happy little smile, and the warmth of it blazed all the way to his bones.

"Oh." There was a whole lot more to that one syllable that his sister kept to herself, but he wasn't trying to encourage Gabi and her opinions. His head was enough of a mess as it was. He took the few steps to reach Perla and put his arms around her. He'd always been like this with her. Couldn't keep his hands to himself.

"All right, lovebirds, Mami texted. Food will be ready in fifteen minutes. Gael, go brush your teeth," Gabi said with a flutter of her hand. "Go now while I'm still here. I'll keep Perla company."

He didn't call his sister a cockblock as he walked into the bedroom, but he thought it. He still couldn't muster up a negative feeling as he stepped into the shower. All he could think was that for the first time in a long time, he was looking forward to Nochebuena.

Things were decidedly different this morning. Gael not only had been extra handsy, but he'd also been like that in front of his *sister*. Now they were stepping out to go have breakfast with his mother and he was holding Perla's hand as they walked, like it was the most natural thing in the world.

"Are you still doing your famous desserts?" Perla asked as they carefully walked the path to the house. Gabi had filled her in on the duties that had been assigned to Gael.

"You remember that?" Gael sounded surprised. If he only knew that she had every detail about him permanently on tap. That there was nothing he'd ever told her that she didn't remember.

"Of course I do. Chocoflan and tres leches are your specialties. Do you still make extras?" She smiled at a memory of them making desserts the year before everything fell apart. As they worked, Veronica had informed her that Gael was a neighborhood legend due to his skills making the two desserts. After getting a job at one of the Latin markets in town when he was in high school, Gael started making them for his family and made extras for the neighbors. Every year after that the list of people he gave them to grew, and by the time he was in college he made a couple of dozen desserts every year, which he distributed to people in the neighborhood and a local senior center.

"Kind of. Not like I used to," he answered, pulling her out of her own head. Gael must've noticed something in her expression because he put a finger under her chin and tipped her face up to him. "Is something wrong?"

"What are we doing, Gael?" The words were out of her mouth before she could stop herself. It wasn't like the question wasn't warranted. He pursed his mouth as he considered what to say and she wished he wasn't wearing his sunglasses so she could look into his eyes.

"Right now the only thing I know for sure is that while you're here, I want more of you." He shook his head and his long hair grazed against his chin. She almost smiled thinking that now she was the one with the shorn hair and his was long enough to braid. "Having you in my bed this morning felt good. And holding you when my sister was with us felt even better. I don't have any answers other than that. I can't offer anything beyond this day and tonight."

She should've prodded then and told him he was acting like she was only a warm body, a convenient distraction. But she realized that even if he was, she wanted him anyway. If he felt the same, then today she'd pretend that he really was hers. Tonight she'd ask him to make love to her just as she'd intended, and in the morning she'd get in her car and finally move on with her life. Finally say goodbye to Gael Montez.

"We have today, then," she said, and pushed up to kiss him.

Eleven

"Gael!" Gabi called from behind him and as soon as he turned, a wet, cold clump of snow hit him right in the face.

"Eat it, sucker!"

He didn't have the chance to ask if it was on purpose, because his pain in the ass of a sister was already running toward him with another snowball.

"Oh, no, you don't," he called, bending down to pile some snow in his hands. "Perla, get behind me. She's ruthless."

He heard a snicker and turned around to see Perla packing a ball of her own.

"Good. I'll need reinforcements," he said, affecting the voice of his character in the Space Squadron, a military general who could blast fireballs from his hands. "Heads up," he bellowed as he avoided another face full of snow and pelted his sister on the elbow.

Perla was small but fast, and soon she was also chucking snowballs in Gabi's direction. "Perla Sambrano, *do not* throw snow at my head!" his twin sister shrieked. "You know I don't like getting my hair wet." Gael grinned like a loon when he heard Perla's apology and then saw a snowball hit Gabi right in the solar plexus.

"Yes!" he crowed, throwing a fist in the air as he ran for cover. "Get her, babe!" The word was out of his mouth before he could stop himself. Perla's hand froze and the snowball she was packing crumbled on her palm as she looked at him. What the hell was going on with him? Why did he have to keep testing the boundaries? He had just come to a place that worked for both of them, and already he was trying to push past it into something else. But his annoying sister wasn't done throwing snow at him.

"You're really gonna get it now, Gabriela Montez!" he yelled as he brushed snow off the back of his head, grateful the fight distracted Perla from what he'd just said. As soon as he stood up, snow hit him from all directions; he gave up trying to throw his own and covered his face with his hands. "Et tu, Perla?" he joked and heard both women cackle with laughter.

"You've been defeated," Perla boasted as she made her way to him. She looked so happy, her face open. Beaming. It was a wonder how he'd fooled himself as long as he had when it came to his feelings for her. She filled him up. Seeing her smile always nourished something in him no one else ever could. There was this constant yawning void in him that even his loving family couldn't fill. It gnawed at him constantly, but her presence had always eased it. He'd felt the difference when he'd met her in college. And since he'd given her up it had just grown bigger. Fame, fortune…none of it could make it better. But today, seeing this Perla, whom he thought was lost to him forever, laughing with glee as she tossed snow up in the air, made his cup run over. Fulfilled and overflowing.

"I've been betrayed by my comrade," he said dramatically as he pulled on her snow-crusted glove and brought her in for an embrace. "I'm wounded," he whispered as he pressed his lips to her cold cheek.

"I can kiss it better," she told him, turning her face to him. Gael's whole body pulsed with something very close to happiness.

"Ew, get a room, you two. Come on, Mami's waiting!" Gabi yelled at them as she headed up the path to the house, but they ignored her, completely caught up in each other.

"Poor baby." Perla's voice was raspy as she brushed kisses on the spot on his neck where the snowball had landed. The skin there tingled from the icy flakes, and probably from feeling her hands on him. He wanted to say she had already made it better. He almost told her that he could see in color for the first time in years. That he could feel the chill on his face and the snow beneath his feet more vividly than he had almost anything else in these past six years. But he didn't say any of it. He wouldn't make declarations to this woman whom he would later betray. He would not make promises that he knew he'd never be able to keep.

"Are you sure you don't want to come make the desserts with us?" Perla asked as she put the lid on the bin of ingredients Veronica had lined up for them.

"Nah, my brother is the pro at the sweet stuff. I'm going to work on the playlist and get the living room set up for dancing while the pernil's in the oven. It'll just be us, but some of our neighbors may come by after dinner."

Gabi gave Perla one of those assessing looks she remembered from when they lived together in a college dorm. "Seems like you guys have figured out a way to make things work," she said, and if Perla didn't know her as well as she did, she wouldn't have heard the underlying question there. *Are you two really going to be able to keep it casual?*

Perla had no clue, and it seemed Gael wasn't faring any better. She'd practically swooned when he'd called her *babe*.

"Gael said he still makes the flans for the neighbors," she told Gabi in an attempt to deviate the conversation from feelings. "I can't believe he still does that."

Gabi furrowed her brow as if she wasn't certain what Perla was talking about, then realization washed over her face.

"He told you he only gives them to the neighbors?" Gabi asked, obviously surprised.

"I asked him if he still did a bunch to give away and he said 'kind of,' but not like he used to." It was hard to read what exactly was going on in Gabi's face, but it was somewhere between disbelief and affection.

"My brother's a piece of work." Gabi shook her head as she chomped on a grape. "Mami, come hear this," she yelled and a moment later Veronica walked into the kitchen.

"Que fue, mija?" the older woman asked. She had a duster in her hands, which almost made Perla laugh since the entire house was spotless. Never mind Gael also had a whole staff taking care of the cleaning. But Perla knew from experience that there was clean and then there was Caribbean people clean.

"Gael told Perla that he still 'kind of' gave desserts to the people in the neighborhood." Okay, Gael had obviously been lying.

Veronica clicked her tongue and looked at Perla with a sad smile. "My son works so hard on hiding the kind of man he really is."

"He doesn't do the flans for neighbors?"

Abuela, who had also drifted into the room, didn't give

Veronica a chance to respond. "He stopped making them when his schedule got too busy, but he started a charity that provides Thanksgiving and Nochebuena meals for thousands of families. He started it just in Connecticut, but last year he expanded it and they do it in Puerto Rico, too. That boy is too humble. He won't let us tell anyone it's him."

"But why wouldn't he tell me that?" Perla asked, hurt that he didn't trust her enough to share what he'd done.

Veronica shook her head as she walked over to Perla, her brows furrowed. "Gael's been closed off for a long time."

"Mami," Gabi warned as if trying to stave off whatever her mother would do next, but Veronica waved her off.

"Dejame, Gabriela. I'm just letting Perlita know the truth. He was never the same after your relationship ended, mija." Veronica held Perla's hand in hers. "I'm glad you're back in each other's lives. Gaelito looks happier already."

"I don't know if it's just me causing that. He's so happy that you're recovered."

Veronica shook her head, a small, knowing smile on her lips. "He's very happy about that, but it's not what put a smile on his face at breakfast this morning."

Perla wanted to hide away from the hope she saw in Veronica's eyes. Not only because they were lying to everyone, but also because Perla wished more than anything that what was happening between them was real. She would pay dearly for what she started with Gael, just like she had the first time. But she would be damned if she was going to stop. She was willing to live with the fallout, whatever that was.

Twelve

"Perla, did you hear me?"

"Oh, sorry. What did you need?" She'd been distracted since she came back from the house. Some of the warmth and playfulness from the morning was replaced by aloofness.

"The Chantilly cream for the tres leches," he reminded her, pointing at the mixing bowl of snowy-white whipped cream. She handed it over distractedly as she looked out the window.

"Is something wrong? Did you hear from Carmelina?" He wasn't sure how things stood with Perla and her mother, but their relationship had always been strained. Especially around the holidays. She shook her head in response and looked up at him with those sad gray eyes.

"My mom's barely talking to me these days. She didn't take it well when I sold my shares to help Esmeralda."

"I can imagine."

He'd heard about that. It had been all over the news

when Perla's half sister took over as president of the studio, and Rodrigo Almanzar, the former chief content officer, was officially appointed by the board as CEO of Sambrano. Rodrigo had a long history with the Sambranos, but it had surprised everyone when it leaked that Perla had sold her stake in the family business to him. Carmelina Sambrano, Perla's mother, was as blue blood as they came. Her very conservative Latin family owned a chain of high-end restaurants, which was now apparently in financial trouble. And it certainly would not have made her happy to lose access to her daughter's fortune in company shares.

"Do you want to talk about it?" he asked, finding it increasingly harder to see her upset and not be able to do anything about it.

"Why didn't you tell me about your charity? That you give dinners to families for the holidays?" she asked almost in an accusatory tone, her eyes flashing with something that looked like genuine hurt.

This was what had her upset? He sighed, silently cursing his sister and her big mouth. "I don't know. I didn't want you to think I was trying to impress you with my 'good deeds.'"

"Impress me? Gael, *you're* the movie star."

"That's not who I am to you, though. I'm just Gael from Bridgeport to you."

"You've never been *just* anything to me, Gael." The way she said it, like it was the last thing she wanted to come out of her mouth but she couldn't keep it inside anymore, rocked him.

"Why are you really here, Perla?" he asked, even if he knew the answer would only make things worse.

She eyed him as she worked on making caramel for the flan. "I'm here because I wanted you to take the part. I came because I remember this being the kind of role you dreamed about in college." She stopped fussing with the melted sugar and braced her hands on the counter like she was trying to find her strength for the conversation, then she hung her head for a moment. He watched as her back lifted and then slumped. Noticed how there was a tiny red bruise on her neck, which looked very much like teeth marks, and he wished he could be the man this woman deserved.

"You're the best person for the job," she said matter-of-factly, "and I could put my feelings aside and get the actor who could make the project a success or I could sulk. You're not the only one who can put business first," she added with finality as she looked him dead in the eyes.

Something bruised and feral howled inside his chest at her answer. Deep down he'd wanted her to tell him she'd come to see him, that she'd wanted to know if things between them could still work. But he couldn't blame her for protecting herself. It was the only smart thing either of them had done since she'd arrived.

"So this was purely professional. It had nothing to do with our history?" he asked, and she turned her eyes down. He wondered what the hell he was trying to accomplish rehashing all this.

"I'm not sure what you're fishing for, Gael." She sounded exasperated as she cleaned her hands on a tea towel and moved toward him. "But I can tell you this. No matter what my plan was when I got here yesterday, sleeping with you was not part of it." He swallowed hard as she came to stand right in front of him, her slight body pressed to his front. The urge to touch her made his heart punch against his chest. "And you know what?"

"What?" Speech was becoming more and more elusive with every passing second.

Her smile deepened at his one-word question, and the

expression made her look thoroughly wicked. He gasped as her nails scraped the back of his neck; the jolt of sensation went straight to his groin.

"I'm not going to spend any more time hesitating. I want you." She let the words linger as she snaked a hand down to the front of his joggers and palmed his hard cock. He stiffened at the lazy stroking motion, gritting his teeth to keep from taking her right on this counter. "Mmm." Those sounds she made were going to end him. "And I think you want me." He let out a pained sound, too turned on to make words. "We have this…just for the holidays. What do you say?"

Just for the holidays.

Sure, he could say no, but he wasn't going to. Not when she was offering and he was desperate to take everything she could give him. He let his hands slide down to her backside and dug in, the denim of her jeans rough against his palms, and thrust into her hand. "I say you better stop stroking my dick, unless you want me to bend you over this kitchen island," he said through a clenched jaw.

"Mmm, that sounds hot," she answered before she licked into his mouth. After a moment she pulled back with a very wicked grin. "But later," she declared. "After dinner tonight, when we have time."

He was going to come just from that throaty laugh of hers. "You're playing with fire, Perla Sambrano," he warned as he went in for a hungry kiss. They ate at each other's mouths for a few breathless moments until they both pulled back, panting. He had to bite back a grin at the dazed expression on her face.

"I'm looking forward to being burned, Gael Montez," she said a little wobblier than just a second ago, but no less sexy. He could not wait to get this woman in his bed and wreck her completely.

"Now, let's finish this flan before another one of your family members walks in on us half-naked," she teased, and despite the extreme case of blue balls he was experiencing, he laughed.

"Family's overrated," he groused as he worked on getting his erection and his breathing under control.

She clicked her tongue, shaking her head in feigned disapproval. "You're crazy about your family," she told him with a smile that beckoned him to go back in for another kiss.

I'm crazy about you, but that's just going to leave us both in pieces like it did the last time.

"I'm almost done," Perla called from the bedroom as she finished putting on her diamond studs. She stood straight as she took in her reflection in the mirror. She was wearing a replica of a black Balenciaga gown from the 1965 winter collection. She'd bought the original dress at auction to donate to the Fashion Institute in New York, and the House of Balenciaga had offered to make her this one when they'd heard. It was a sleek and simple design in the front, with long sleeves and a knot at the waist that brought attention to the A-line skirt. But the back was what drew her to the dress. It had a deep scoop that showed a lot of skin. It made the dress sexy and elegant at the same time.

She loved vintage couture and had amassed quite a valuable collection over the years, though this one was one of her favorites. She'd intended to wear it for Nochebuena in Punta Cana but if she was honest, it was more fitting for an evening dining by a fireplace. She'd done little with her makeup—just a bit of mascara, her new trademark winged eyeliner and red lipstick.

She looked good. Healthy and elegant, but more than

anything she loved how she felt in this dress. In her own skin. She ran her hands over the skirt, looking at her reflection. Her skin buzzed with anticipation. In part it was that she was looking forward to spending time with Gael's family, but mostly she couldn't stop thinking about what would happen after. All day they'd been circling each other, only to clash into frantic, breath-stealing kisses. It had always been like this for her when it came to Gael, like her body was dormant for anyone else, but with him the fire inside her roared to life in an instant. It was more than desire; it was a bone-deep wild need.

The truth was that she'd probably never stop wanting Gael. That no matter how much of him she got she'd always want more. They'd agreed that this thing they were doing could only go on until she left. And she should be glad. She'd gotten what she came to do; he'd agreed to take the role. And this time she knew what was coming. She would have time to prepare for the goodbye.

"That really doesn't make any of it better," she sighed as she stepped into her Louboutin heels. She'd have to take them off in a minute and switch into snow boots for the walk to the main house, but she wanted to see the whole outfit together. "I look kind of hot," she told herself, even if the smile from before had waned a little.

She heard a light knock on the door before it opened just a couple of inches.

"Can I come in?"

Her heart kicked up in her chest to a gallop, as butterflies fluttered in her belly from hearing Gael's voice. "Sure, come on in." He'd let her have the bedroom while he changed in the other room, so she hadn't seen him in his own Nochebuena best yet. She closed her eyes for a second, bracing herself for the sight of Gael Montez in a suit.

"Perla," he breathed out as she turned around to face

him. His eyes roamed over her hungrily, and she would've flushed at the attention, but she was too busy staring at him. He was wearing a burgundy velvet jacket—which she recognized from Tom Ford's latest collection—and black slacks. His chin-length hair was parted at the center and framed his gorgeous face perfectly. The man really was movie-star handsome. Those shoulders filled out the jacket perfectly and her hands itched to touch him. And lucky for her there was nothing and no one stopping her from doing it all night.

"You look amazing," he told her as he came closer. Without hesitation he took her in his arms and kissed her cheek. "Tan bella." No one had ever called her beautiful before Gael. Or maybe they had, but with him it was the first time she'd believed it. Because there was no way to mistake what she saw in his eyes when he looked at her. The mix of tenderness and barely contained hunger with which he touched her. It was why it had been such a shock when he'd ended things. But that was not relevant now, not when Gael was holding her like she was everything he needed.

"I have something for you," he whispered in her ear, bringing her focus back to him.

"You do?" She could hear the smile in her voice and goodness, how was that possible after knowing everything she knew? After the heartache. After so much time. How could this man still turn her inside out? She felt him reach into his pocket and then he brought a hand up to show her. In his palm was a pair of pearl drop earrings.

"Where did you get this?" she asked as she plucked one out of his hand. It was clearly vintage, done in an Art-Deco style. The perfect tear-shaped pearl dangled from a row of baguette-cut diamonds, and at the top was a perfect round-cut ruby encircled by tiny diamonds. When she turned it around, she saw the Cartier stamp along the clasp.

"Do you like them?" She just looked up at him, too stunned to do anything but shake her head. *Like them?* If he would've given her hundreds of earrings to choose from, these would've been the ones she'd pick.

"I love them," she told him as she moved to take off the ones she was wearing, so she could put the new ones on. "Seriously, though, where did you get them?"

He grinned at her, having a little too much fun with his vintage jewelry prowess. "Remember when I slipped out while you were helping set the table?"

"Yes…" The rest of what she was going to say died in her throat as he moved to help her put on the earrings.

"Our next-door neighbor owns an antique jewelry store in town. She usually has some pieces at home," he informed her as he nimbly hooked an earring on one side and then the other. "There," he told her before pressing a kiss on her cheek and stepping back to look at her. Good grief. It was like he could tell whenever she'd managed to convince herself she could walk away from this unscathed, and then intentionally said or did something to remind her she was fooling herself.

"Perfect." The way he said it sounded like he wasn't just referring to the earrings, but she was not reckless enough to assume he was talking about them. Without saying a word she let him put his hands on her shoulders and move her until she was facing the mirror again.

"Gael," she said, too afraid of what would come out of her mouth to risk another word. He was right; they were perfect. The ideal complement to her gown. He was standing right behind her, and even in her heels he towered over her. He ran his hands possessively over her flanks, waist and hips.

"I can't stop thinking about tonight," he whispered hotly against her ear, and she had to bite down not to moan. "As soon as we come back tonight, I'm going to take off this dress and put my mouth right here." He placed the heel of his hand right at the apex of her thighs, and pressed hard.

"Ah," Perla gasped, and her head lolled on his shoulder. The lids of her eyes felt heavy and she lowered them until she could barely see through. It was thrilling to look at them both in the mirror while he touched her like this. "We need to go to dinner soon," she said in a reedy voice she could hardly recognize.

"We will, but as soon as we're back here I'm going to have you screaming for me, Perla. I'm going to lick and taste you until you come on my tongue, and then I'm going to take my sweet time with you." He punctuated each word with a roll of his hips, letting her feel exactly what it was that he was going to give her. This was them, always. Sweet and sinful all at once, a perfect match. They *looked* perfect, too. Elegant, young and perfect. Like they belonged together. That thought went a long way to suffuse the fire roiling in her blood, and she smiled sadly at the picture they made. She turned to look up at him and for a second she thought she saw a flash of her own regret in his eyes.

She turned her back on the reflection of everything she wanted and could not have. "I'm ready," she told him without daring to look in his eyes again.

He looked at her for a second, as if there was something he wanted to tell her. But after a moment he shook his head and smiled. "Are you sure you're ready for the madness of Nochebuena with the Montezes?"

"More than ready," she assured him, ignoring the stab of longing she felt. And the truth was she did look forward to this evening, and all that it would entail. Fake or not, this was the closest thing to real happiness she'd felt in a while. She wouldn't waste a moment of it. Life would come calling soon enough.

Thirteen

"Let me help with that, Veronica."

Gael grinned as he found Perla gently coaxing his mother to stop taking dishes to the kitchen. They'd finished dinner moments ago and despite there being staff to help with the cleaning, his mother and grandmother could not quite relax.

"Mami, listen to Perla," he said as he wrapped his arms around his mother's thin shoulders while winking at his fake girlfriend. Although nothing about the way he'd been feeling about Perla felt anywhere near fake.

"Ay, Gael, I'm fine," his mother groused as he nudged her out of the kitchen.

"I know you're fine, but you've also been cooking all day since you refused to let the chef help you."

"I like to make my family's Nochebuena dinner myself." He grinned at his mother's stubbornness.

"And we appreciate your efforts. That arroz con gandules was really the best I've ever had," Perla interjected as she joined them.

"See, this is why I like you better than my kids. You always know what to say," Veronica teased as she leaned to place a hand on Perla's cheek. "We're so happy to have you here with us this year, Perlita. I hope we get you for many more Nochebuenas." Guilt pierced Gael's chest, and right underneath that he felt the undeniable yearning that his mother's words evoked. No matter how much he knew things with Perla could never work, he still wanted her forever. Especially now when she was moving around their house like she belonged here. When he could barely keep it together, knowing what awaited them once they were alone. But he was still a Montez, and no matter how hard he tried he would end up breaking her heart.

"Ay, mi canción," his mother squealed, bringing both Perla and his attention to the older woman. "Ven, Gaelito, take your mother out on the dance floor for a song or two. You know I can't sit still when El Gran Combo is playing."

"You heard your mother, Gael. A bailar." Perla fluttered her hands in the direction of the clearing in the living room.

He resisted the urge to pull her hand and bring her in for a kiss and did as he was told. When he and his mother were moving around the living room, dancing to the old salsa classic, he couldn't help looking back in Perla's direction.

"Your uncle has been trying to call you. He said that you hadn't picked up the phone." The mention of Manolo was a bucket of cold water on his fevered thoughts about Perla.

"We've talked twice already, and I have nothing more to say to him right now." Gael sighed, causing his mother to raise an eyebrow in question.

"What's going on, mijo?"

Manolo was supposed to come back for Nochebuena,

but the same snowstorm that stranded Perla with them ended up keeping his uncle in the city. And even if he'd never tell his mother, he was glad his uncle hadn't been here to interfere with this decision about the Rios project. He suppressed another sigh as his mother scrutinized whatever she was seeing in his face. "Is something going on with you two?"

"Tio doesn't want me to take the project Perla's studio is producing." His mother pursed her lips at that but didn't interrupt. "He thinks it will hurt my career to pigeonhole me by playing such a 'Latinx' role."

She scoffed at that, making Gael grin. "And since when does Manolo know better than you do where you can take your career?" His mother was a beautiful dancer and could move to the music instinctually, so she had no problem having a serious conversation and keeping to the beat.

"Manolo has been a good manager. I take his advice seriously. And for the most part it hasn't led me astray." He admitted this because it was the truth, mostly. No one knew about the advice Manolo had given Gael about Perla six years ago. He never told his mother, not even when she rebuked Gael for "breaking that sweet girl's heart," that it had been Manolo pressuring him that pushed him to end things.

His mother was sentimental and would've seen the decision as mercenary. But Gael had understood Manolo's reasoning. He'd been on the rise, and the media loved an eligible bachelor. His career had skyrocketed after the news got out that he was single. It had made sense at the time, but it was undeniable that the cost turned out to be much higher than he'd imagined.

"Manolo has been good to us, that's true," his mother said, bringing him out of his thoughts. "But you have made him a very rich man, son." His mother raised her hand to caress his cheek and gave a regretful little shake of the head. "He stepped in to be a father figure to you when Gabriel left, but he did that *by choice*. Besides, that's my debt to Manolo, not yours."

People saw his mother and her gentle demeanor and didn't realize there was a lioness hidden inside her. He owed everything he was to this woman. But even if she was right about not being beholden to Manolo, things were still complicated when it came to him and Perla.

"Mami, even if I take the role—"

"If?" his mother asked, making him laugh.

"Okay, mujer. Fine. I have decided to take the role, but that still doesn't mean things between Perla and me are fine. I don't—"

"You don't what?" Telling his mother he was certain he'd hurt Perla would not go over well, since the woman was convinced both her children were angels. But not even she couldn't deny that his lifestyle didn't exactly allow for relationships. And it was probably smart to start planting the seed that Perla would not be a permanent addition to family gatherings, even if the very thought of that hit him like a punch to the gut.

"I don't know if I can be the type of person Perla needs for the long run," he said, and his eyes instinctually scanned the room, searching for the woman in question, until he found her. As if she could sense him looking at her, she turned around and smiled at him. The effect of those gray eyes on him was forceful and absolute. He would never want anything like he wanted Perla Sambrano.

"I like how you look at her. And I *love* the way she looks at you. I can tell she sees in you the same thing I do."

"And what's that, Mami?" he asked, unable to help himself.

"A good man. A good son. A good brother. A keeper,"

his mother told him happily. And his gut clenched at the reckoning he knew was coming.

"How do *I* look at her?" he asked, eager to keep hearing what his mother saw between them, as if that wouldn't just make all this worse later.

"With fire in your eyes, querido. You always did, and that passion has been gone since you two split up." His mother clicked her tongue, head shaking as if the situation had been a very sorry one indeed. "I know you love your job, and what a blessing it is that the world sees and values your gift. You're a wonder, my son, so remarkable." Sadness moved through her face from whatever she was recalling. "But I know you're not happy. I know you said you'd both decided to end it, but I knew you still had feelings for her and now I see it. The light is back in your eyes."

"I'm happy because you're healthy again, Mami," he assured her.

"I know you are," she told him, squeezing the hand he was holding as he led her across the dance floor. "But maybe now that I'm doing better you'll be a little selfish and focus on your woman. And I don't care what Manolo says. You do whatever you want to do. If he doesn't like it, too bad."

"Mami...you're being pushy," he warned as a surge of possessiveness coursed through him at the words *your woman*.

"Looks like someone wants to give you some competition," his mother quipped and he turned his head to watch Perla getting pulled onto the dance floor by the son of one of their neighbors. Since they lived in one of the most exclusive zip codes in the country everyone at their little Nochebuena dinner after-party was loaded, and it seemed like Perla had garnered the attention of the heir to a Latinx fashion empire. Miguel Correa was a little older

than Gael, but undisputedly handsome, and he was looking at Gael's fake girlfriend like he wanted to swallow her
whole. Gael's eyes zeroed in on the spot on Perla's wrist
where Miguel had placed his hand and made a menacing
sound. He wanted to go and physically remove him from
her vicinity.

His mother's knowing laugh pulled him out of his
bloodthirsty thoughts. "You're absolutely not allowed to
rip our guests arms out, mijo."

If Miguel didn't stop with the touching and close-talk-
ing, he would be lucky if his arm was all he lost.

"Why don't you go rescue her and I'll go talk to Gabi
and Abuela? We should be wrapping up soon. Your vieja
can't party like she used to." His mother's joke went a long
way to cool off his fury, but after giving her a kiss and
walking her over to the couch where Gabi and Abuela were
observing the proceedings, he went right back to glaring
at Perla and her suitor.

"Bendito, bro, are you going to let Miguel outdo you
like that?" Gabi teased like the smart-ass she was, and Gael
had to make an effort not to grind his molars to dust as
he watched the man glide through their living room with
Perla. Blood rushed to his head as a choir of "mine, mine,
mine" rang through his head.

"I'll be back in a minute."

"Go get her, tiger." His sister was such a pain in the ass.

Gael moved purposefully the few yards to the middle
of the room. Perla danced gracefully, her hips swaying
to an old-school merengue. Miguel was giving it his all,
moving his feet with perfect form, but Perla seemed distracted, her eyes roaming the room until they landed on
him, and her whole face lit up.

And damn, Gael was in so much trouble. He had no idea
how he was supposed to walk away from this. The way her

eyes roamed over him made his heart claw at the inside of his chest. As he reached her he took one long breath in through his nose and let it out slowly before he opened his mouth, trying to calm the storm brewing inside him. How could he still want her this much? How could he let her go?

"May I interrupt?" he asked after unclenching his teeth, his heavy hand on one of Miguel's shoulders. Miguel did a double take at whatever he saw in Gael's face, and immediately let go of Perla.

"Your girl can dance, man. If you don't watch out I might try to steal her from you."

I'd love to see you try, asshole.

Gael bared his teeth in answer and slid his arm around's Perla's waist. Within seconds he'd taken his woman as far away from Miguel Correa's greasy hands as he could.

Perla shook her head and laughed as he started moving them around the room. "Well, this is not a very flattering side of you," she told him, but her eyes were twinkling.

"You love it." He was practically growling, and she threw her head back and laughed in earnest.

"I wouldn't say *love*," she told him with a wink. "But it's kind of flattering to see you drop your stoic mask for a bit. I've always liked it when you let your passions run wild, Gael."

And that was where this woman would end him. The way she let him see everything. Unafraid to show him that he'd pleased her. He'd been in Hollywood for so long he'd forgotten what it was like to have someone who didn't pretend. Who said what she meant and meant what she said. Someone who despite the ways she'd been hurt—*hurt by him*—could still be this open.

The song changed from a faster tempo merengue to "Veinte Años," a slow, moody bolero about a story of a twenty-year-old love affair that cannot be forgotten. Because his sister was in charge of the music and she loved messing with his head. But as Perla melted into his arms, he pressed her to him and let himself have this moment. For so long he'd refused to dwell in his feelings and when a light had gone out inside him, he'd told himself it was for the best. That he didn't have time for love; he had responsibilities. His entire family was depending on him. And until this moment, he hadn't permitted himself to admit that breaking up with Perla had carved out a piece of his soul and it had never grown back.

"Are my moves not to your liking or do you just enjoy scowling?" Perla asked jokingly, looking up at him. Her cheeks were flushed from dancing. She looked so beautiful. And her moves were more than to his liking. He had a hand on her hip and could feel them sway seductively to the music. Unbidden a memory of her astride him, rocking with him in that same sensual rhythm, robbed him of breath. Suddenly, he couldn't wait any longer; all he wanted was to drag her out of that room and finish what they'd started that morning.

"You know your dancing is fire," he told her and laughed when she made a show of fanning herself at his compliment. God, this woman—he didn't just find her irresistible, he also liked her. He liked her so damn much. Impulsively, he bent down to press a kiss to her mouth. As expected, there was a flurry of cheers and whistles coming from where his family was sitting, but he couldn't even be bothered to care. He wanted every person in this room to see how much he wanted Perla Sambrano.

He pressed his fingers into her skin until she was flush against him, and every nerve in his body buzzed with electricity. They were still clutching hands, and he squeezed her tighter. Needing to ground them both in this kiss. He tasted her gently, a sharing of breath that seemed to fill his lungs with oxygen. He imagined their hearts speeding up in unison as he deepened the caress. He was wondering how much longer they'd have to stay at the party before he took her back to the cottage, when something buzzed against his leg and almost instantly Perla stiffened.

She pulled back, the haziness in her eyes gone, replaced by uncomfortable alertness. That was when he heard the faint ringtone. It sounded like a horn of some sort.

"Is that your phone?" he asked curiously as she unclenched her hand from his and slid it in the pocket of her dress.

"It's my mom," she whispered with a grimace and she signaled to the hallway at the other end of the room that led to the den. "I've been avoiding her all day." He nodded and made a move to follow her, feeling protective. He suspected her mother was probably calling just to ruin her evening, and he didn't want to leave her to face it all alone. Then he reminded herself that no matter what his dick or his family thought about the situation, he was not actually her man. Not in any way that gave him the right to walk out of this room with her or intrude in a private conversation.

And thankfully, she had her head on straight better than he did, because she slipped out of his hands with the phone pressed to her ear and walked out of the room without a single glance in his direction.

Fourteen

"Are you okay?" he asked again as they walked into the cottage.

"You know how my mother is," she told him in a brittle, subdued voice as she worked to take off her coat and boots. Her mother could always do that to Perla, suck the joy right out of her. He'd seen it so many times when they were together. Perla would take her mother's call glowing and happy and after a two-minute conversation, she'd walk back into the room ashen and looking a little lost. Carmelina's poisonous words always struck true; a few well-aimed barbs and she could incinerate Perla's happiness down to ashes.

"I'm sorry," he said, biting back angry words. She didn't need to hear what he thought about her mother. That would only hurt Perla, and Carmelina had taken enough from her already. If she was his, he'd make sure she never…no, there was no point going there. She had already been his and he'd squandered her love, just like her family had, and she deserved so much better than that, from everyone in her life.

"I don't want to think about her anymore," Perla said as if she could read his mind.

He knew all too well what it was like to have a parent who made you feel like shit. But his father at least had the decency to stay out of his life. Perla's mother on the other hand—despite acting like she couldn't stand her children—seemed unable to stay out of their lives.

He hated how resigned she seemed to always fall short in her mother's eyes, how it still hurt her. He knew he couldn't spare her that. But he could make her feel good. Tonight, if she let him, he would worship her. Show her with his body and his hands that every inch of her was precious to him.

"Here, let me help you." He quickly took his own coat off and reached for Perla as she attempted to slide out of hers. He carefully pulled it off her arms, and she shivered as the air hit her bare shoulders and back. He couldn't help staring at the lines of her. He could write poetry about the way her soft curves felt under the palm of his hand. About the feel of her skin on his lips. The hunger she awakened in him.

He hung her coat on a hook and moved to stand behind her. He rubbed his hands together before placing them on her shoulders and bent down to kiss the nape of her neck. "You looked beautiful tonight," he whispered against her warm skin, making her tremble in his arms. He loved this new style of hers. Vampy and a little mysterious. Made him want to discover all the things about her that he'd been too afraid to explore before. He'd suspected it six years ago and he was certain of it now. He could spend his life discovering this woman, finding a million different ways to make her feel loved. To make her believe that she was every inch as valuable as her name.

A pearl. A treasure.

He kept kissing her as she swayed in his arms. Pressing his lips down her neck and over to her shoulders. Pausing to take in her smell, greedily tasting her velvety skin. He wanted to consume her. He'd been getting nibbles when what he wanted was to feast on her. Take his time with every delectable part of her body he hadn't yet tended to.

"Your hands feel like heaven," she said in a breathy, low voice, like warm honey.

"I want you," he confessed against her ear as his fingers worked on undoing the small buttons at the back of her gown.

"I want you, too. So much," Perla gasped, brushing her ass against his hard cock. His hands shook with the need to possess her. He fought for control as he slowly revealed more of her skin. She'd gone without a bra since the back of the dress was so low. The thought of those brown peaks brushing against the soft material of her gown made him go impossibly harder.

"Perfect," he said as he helped her step out of it. A primal noise rumbled in his chest as his hands slid down her back to the lacy edge of her panties. The black lace covered very little and it framed her delicious backside in a way that made his mouth water.

"What do you want?" he asked, holding himself back. He needed to ask if he was allowed to touch, because once he started he wasn't stopping until there wasn't a single inch of her left for him to savor.

"You," she told him, and he wished he could give her all of him, forever. But they had tonight. Every ounce of his focus, every second of his attention, would be for her. Without hesitation he scooped her up, eliciting a surprised little squeal out of her. But she didn't fight him; she just wrapped her arms around his neck and let him take her to the bedroom.

He was fully dressed, but for his shoes, and there was something carnal and raw about having her almost naked in his arms. He bent his head, seeking her mouth, and licked into her as he placed her down on the edge of the bed. He knelt between her spread thighs and took her in. With this woman in front of him like this, open and ready for him, Gael imagined himself on the edge of a crossroad that could take his life on a completely different path. One he could not come back from. Like every step forward would burn what he left behind.

He looked up at pert breasts lifting and descending with her quick breaths. Her mouth was swollen from his kisses, the embodiment of everything he'd ever wanted.

"Perla." Her name was a commandment, a calling. A vow he would surely break. "Show me where you want me to touch you," he demanded, and smiled when a flush of pink appeared on the apples of her cheeks.

His sweet Perla. She looked so different now than the girl he'd known. Her hair, her clothes, her body. She was more luscious now, grown. And yet, that shyness, that untainted pureness, was still there.

"Here," she said and followed the command by palming her breast with one hand, and with the other she slid her panties down and off. Gael felt like all the air left his lungs at once. "Make love to me."

"Are you sure?" he asked as his cock turned to granite in his briefs.

"I've missed you," she said, simply. No games. Just the truth. Then she turned those gray eyes on him. Like rolling clouds before a storm. "And don't act like I'm a delicate flower. I may not have done this in a while, but I do know how bad I want this."

"You're going to kill me," he said in a hoarse, taut voice as he ran the pads of his thumbs over her pussy. Her confession of not having sex with anyone else after they broke up should have made him feel like the worst kind of bastard, but his chest pulsed with the knowledge that he was still the only man to have ever been inside her. That when he entered her, he'd be the only one to ever fill her up. The only one to move inside her while she shattered in his arms. That no other man had felt the hot, delicious grip of her body. He let his hands roam over the silky skin of her legs, pressed his palms to the inside of her thighs so he could spread her for his view. He sucked in a breath when he saw the brown-and-pink dewy petals at her core.

"Gorgeous." He looked up, already licking his lips in anticipation for her taste. "I'm starving for you."

"Then consume me, Gael," she demanded like an empress as she leaned back on her hands, her half-closed eyes focused on him. Without taking his gaze off her he brought one hand up to her breasts and pulled on the hard, brown tips.

"Ah," she moaned, and arched her back to give him more access. And because he couldn't help himself he lifted his mouth until he could suck on her nipples. He lazily circled one areola and the other, then ran the flat of his tongue between her breasts before returning to the place he craved.

He nudged her legs open and pressed his nose to the furrow of her labia. "I'm going to lick you. Circle this sweet little *pearl* with my tongue until you come."

She laughed, a husky sensual laugh that made his dick pulse painfully in his slacks. He started with one long and slow lick with the flat of his tongue, which rewarded him with breathy little moans. "Suck on your fingers, babe," he instructed her. "Play with your clit while I taste your honey. Show me how you make yourself come when you're on your own."

His head felt hot as she watched her do exactly as he asked her. She lifted one hand and inserted three fingers into her mouth. Sucked on them for a few seconds and swirled her tongue around them.

"Fuck, that's hot," he muttered, lips right against her heat before he speared her with his tongue. Her sweetness flooded his senses and he almost came on the spot. He lapped at her a few more times before he made himself stop. He grabbed her wrist and brought her wet fingers to her pussy. "Show me."

"Bossy," she panted as a wicked grin pulled up her lips. This woman didn't stop surprising him. There was this untarnished purity to her, but she had a fire inside that could burn him to ashes. Gael had forced himself to forget how it had been with her. The way she ignited his blood every time they were together. The way that for him she was an incandescent flame no one else got to see. She always gave him everything. That was why no one since had ever come close. No one could undo him like Perla could.

"Keep going, amor," he urged her, and she brought the pads of her fingers to her heat and touched herself. First, two fingers rubbing on her clitoris, then three. She circled them fast, spreading her legs wider.

"You're so close," he groaned as his dick pulsed in his pants.

"Yes," she panted as she pumped two fingers inside herself, and he had to taste her. He spread her labia and put his mouth on her. She moaned low, rolling her hips into his mouth, and soon her legs were trembling as an orgasm washed over her.

He was going to die if he didn't get inside her soon. He lapped and sucked at her a few more times while she lay on her back, sated and so beautiful it almost hurt to look at her. He made quick work of his clothes and soon he was kneeling between her thighs. He took a moment to admire the wild beauty on his bed. The woman whom he'd been telling himself for so long he couldn't love. And what empty, cowardly lies those had been. He was *full* of love for her, and even if that meant having to let her go, he would not waste what she was offering him.

"Mmm." She pushed into his touch as he slid the palms of his hands over her. First, her calves, then up her legs, the inside of her thighs. He pressed the heel of his hand to her core, making her suck in a breath. He gripped her hips and caressed the softness of her belly, pressing his lips at her navel. He cupped her breasts and pinched her nipples, making her arch for him.

"You're so beautiful," he told her as he touched her. He bent down and kissed her, her taste still on his tongue. He felt her hands on his shoulders, on his back, and it was like his skin was coming back to life. Each caress woke up a part of him that had been asleep for far too long.

He pulled back for a second and hovered over her. "Hi," she told him through a smile, and he felt his heart crack a little from how sweet she was. How would he ever walk away from this?

"When do I get to see if you still have the magic touch?" Perla asked as she stroked Gael. She felt him shiver as she squeezed on the head of his penis.

"Very, very soon," he promised her, and made his way down her body. Her first orgasm had already been so intense that she feared she'd be too sensitive, but as soon as he touched, she instinctively spread her legs wide to give him more access. Gael's hands were a marvel. Gentle and rough at once. His fingertips could flutter over her skin like butterfly wings one moment and the next roughly bring her to her climax. If this wasn't so good, she'd almost regret doing it. Because she *knew* the descent would be grim. Losing him the last time had been almost unbearable, and she knew this time it would be worse. He hadn't made her any promises beyond this day, but how she wished this man could be hers forever.

"Oh," she gasped as she felt slick fingers at her vulva. She'd seen him grab the lube and now she felt the slippery gel as he applied it on her. He smoothly slid two fingers in, then flipped his hand so that he could massage that spot inside that made her tremble. "Mmm...right there, Gael."

"You love that," he purred as his hands expertly caressed her. "You're so wet and hot, clenching my fingers. So tight. I can't wait to be inside you."

"Can we test that theory soon?" she panted as he did something delicious to her with his thumbs. "Please."

"Since you asked so nicely." She opened her eyes and found that his face was a lot more serious than his words had been. She looked down her body and saw that he was rolling on a condom. Perla raised her knees so he could see that she welcomed this. More than welcomed—she burned for him. Had dreamt about this moment so many times, it almost felt surreal. And even if Gael would never be hers again, right now the only thing that mattered was having him inside her. After coating himself with lube he put a pillow under her hips, and soon the tip of his cock was nudging at her entrance.

"Are you ready for me, sweetheart?" His eyes were wide open and the way his lips tugged up into a sexy smile made all the air rush out of her lungs. The way he touched her would be what she'd always remember from this night *and she would remember.* The intensity of his gaze, the raw need, was electrifying. To know she made this strong, beautiful man—whom millions of women thought of as the perfect male specimen—tremble with desire was overwhelming.

"Wrap your legs around me," he demanded as he pushed in. He gritted his teeth as he entered her with excruciating patience until he was in to the hilt. She felt so full, like he was inside her and around her.

"How does it feel?" he asked tautly.

"Like it's almost too much. Like you're stretching me all the way to the edge before pain but, instead of less of you, I want more," she confessed.

"God, the things you say, baby," he said and shuddered out a breath, and his face twisted in what looked like a mix of agony and ecstasy. "This is so sweet." He was moving in her now and when he thrust in she felt a tightness and then a moment of real pain; it had been a very long time since she'd done this.

He looked down at her, face full of concern. "Do you need me to stop? I can pull out—"

She tightened her legs around him and shook her head. "Don't you dare, Gael Montez. I've waited too long for this. I just need a moment."

"Okay," he said before pressing his lips to hers. He tipped her in a way that made her feel full to the brim. He rolled his hips into her and she met him stroke for stroke until the burning stretch turned into something languid and delicious.

She gasped when he pulled out and flipped her onto her stomach and then entered her again from behind. His hands pinched her breasts as he surged into her, making her cry out with mindless pleasure. Then, like he could read her thoughts, he brought his hand down and stroked her clit as he took her hard. Within moments she was crying out her orgasm and he followed her a moment later. His gasp of tortured pleasure, hot against her ear.

He held her to him for a few moments, their bodies still joined. He kissed her gently, her sweaty brow, her cheeks, and as he left her body he trailed kissed down her spine. "Thank you," he whispered so low she thought she imagined it.

She almost thanked him, too, but she didn't want to shatter the moment with words. Morning and reality were coming and she wanted to keep this perfect cocoon they'd built around them for as long as she could.

"Regrets?" he asked her as he ran a warm washcloth between her legs. Caring for her in a way that made her almost want to weep. He'd tried to sound neutral but she could see a wariness in his gorgeous eyes.

She shook her head and told him the truth. "Not a single one. It was worth the wait." *You were worth the wait.*

Fifteen

"Feliz Navidad, cariño," Gael whispered in Perla's ear and yeah, this was a far superior Christmas morning wake-up than any she'd had in recent memory.

"Mmm…good morning," she said as she stretched languidly in his arms. She was deliciously naked under layers of fluffy warm blankets and quite literally wrapped up in the man who had owned her heart since she was nineteen. She wanted to hold on to this feeling forever.

Gael rolled his hips into her, his hardness pressing into her backside, and just like that she was burning for him again.

"Someone has a special gift for me," she teased as his hands roamed over her.

"I do," he whispered hotly in her ear, while his hands plucked the tips of her breasts.

"Ah," she gasped as he touched her while he slid a muscular thigh between her legs until she was open to him. "Gael, please." She had no idea what she was begging for;

she just knew she ached for more of him. She needed him to make every thought evaporate from her mind.

"Mmm... I love it when you get like this." His voice in her ear was as languorous as his hands on her body. He slowly slid one down her torso until he was at the hot center of her. He palmed her there, and she pressed into his touch. One of his fingers slid into her, and she instinctively tightened around him. "I love how you feel, so wet." He sounded drunk with lust, and that only ignited her own desire further, until it was bubbling like boiling water under her skin. She made a desperate sound as he pushed a second finger in while circling her clitoris with his thumb. She was so open to him, completely at his mercy. His big body enveloping her as his hands pleasured her. Her orgasm was a frenzied, frantic force that rocked through her.

"Gael!" She screamed his name until she was hoarse and still he kept touching her, coaxing more and more sensation out of her until she was limp in his arms.

"You're an excellent Christmas present," Gael told her as he peppered kisses on her neck. He'd moved them so she was sitting against him, and it was pretty perfect.

"You're not too bad yourself, Mr. Montez." She pressed into the erection that was still hot and hard and looked up at him. "Are we going to take care of this?"

"Later," he said, putting his arms around her. "That was just for you."

"Are you trying to ruin me?" Perla asked, not entirely joking, eliciting a wounded grunt from Gael. She wished she could tell him that these past two days had made it perfectly clear why she never seemed to get past the first date with anyone else. Because he was *it* for her. A man with a hard body and clever hands was not all that hard to find. But someone who could own her body and her heart, *that* she'd only ever had with this man. Perla looked out the window and saw the bright blue sky that promised a clear, sunny day, and her heart fell. She'd have to leave him soon. She had so much more than she used to when it came to family and a support system, and yet she knew she'd feel his absence like a dark, gaping void.

"Looks like it should be safe for me to drive back today," she told him, even as she tightened her arms over his. Forcing him to hold her closer.

"Hmm." She felt the rumbling in his chest as he worked on what to say to her. "You could stay here with us." Everything in her wanted to jump on that offer. The temptation to ignore the outside world and lose herself in this man and in his family was hard to resist. But this didn't belong to her. It was a mirage. She couldn't have any of it. He'd made that clear, and the longer she stayed the harder it would be to walk away.

"My sister's waiting for me and I've imposed on your family time long enough."

"Perla." He sounded reproachful, as if she'd said something egregious. "My mother has spent the last day and a half telling you that you're her Christmas miracle."

She laughed at his grumpiness, but she couldn't let him talk her into staying. This was about self-preservation. And as if the universe was in total agreement that she needed an exit plan, her phone started ringing.

"Leave it," Gael said as he did delicious things to her neck, but as tempting as he was, she needed to start drifting back to her life.

"I can't. It could be about the flight." She leaned to grab the phone and confirmed she'd been right. It was from the crew. A thirty-second exchange informed her they'd been cleared to fly, and her private flight to Punta Cana would be departing the next morning. Needing a second to push down the disappointment and despair threatening to flood

her at the thought of leaving Gael, she distracted herself
with texting her sister.

Perla: All set for tomorrow. I'll be there in the early afternoon. Will send details when I'm on the plane.

"Sounds like I'll be trading chilly snow for sandy
beaches." For the life of her she could not make herself
sound enthused about it and that only made Perla even
more annoyed at herself. Because this had never been the
plan. She should've already been in the DR with her family. Jumping in bed with Gael was just the cherry on top of
the cake of bad choices of the last forty-eight hours. And
yet, she didn't regret any of it, not when he felt so solid and
warm, not when he wrapped his strong arms around her
and, without a word, soothed her frayed nerves.

"What are we going to do?" she asked. He grunted, then
pressed a kiss to her temple. "I think you already know
the answer to that question."

It was on the tip of her tongue to say she had no clue
what he was talking about, but her heart seemed to catch
on before she did, racing in response to his words. Not just
what he said, but *how* he said it. There was determination
there. A conviction. Like he was ready to make promises.

"I'm not sure—"

"Yes, you are. You're sure, like I'm sure."

She stopped talking when he started moving, sliding out
from behind her until he was standing in front of her next
to the bed. And yeah, there was no way she could focus
with Gael Montez in his full naked glory.

"*I'm* sure?" she asked, the question more for herself
than for him.

"I think you are," he told her as he wrapped a gentle
hand around her throat and tipped her face up to look

at him. He was smiling pleasantly enough, but his eyes looked like they were working at boring right through her skull. "I'm not ready to close the door on what's happening here," he said as he waved a hand in the space between them. "I'm not sure what it'll look like, but I can't just let you drive out of my life."

He was deadly serious now. But she could see the hesitation in his eyes. He didn't know how any of this could work, not any more than she did. The difference was that right under his uncertainty she saw determination. He was willing to make this work.

"What does that mean?" she asked as anticipation, hope, lust and...love swirled inside her like the most intoxicating of cocktails.

"It means I finally understand that I was walking around with a giant piece of my heart missing." Oh, God, what was he doing? "The way that you walked in here yesterday, with your head high, you're so strong, baby. I don't deserve this second chance, but I want to try and earn it." She could see his throat working, and his eyes were shining with something that looked a lot like...no, she wasn't even going to think it.

"Perla, you were the first amazing thing that ever happened to me, and you are still the best. I can't give you up." She had no words, but she didn't need them because he pulled her to him, and for a moment, bent down to press their foreheads together. They took a few breaths in unison, letting the things he'd said sit between them. "I want to drive into the city with you. I..." He heaved a sigh, and she could feel the urgency rolling off him. "I want to spend tonight with you, just us. And I want to talk about how to keep seeing each other. And then you'll go to the DR and I'll go do my press tour in Asia and we'll have a lot of phone sex for those two weeks. Then I'm going to kidnap you and take you to Hawaii for a week and we'll do nothing but stay in bed and eat seafood on the beach."

He was saying everything she wanted to hear, and she wished she could just snatch what he was offering. No questions, no doubt, but she was not the girl who'd trusted blindly in the love he had for her. She knew all too well how life could get between two people, no matter how much they loved each other.

"You don't know how many times I dreamed of hearing you say this," she told him honestly as he distractingly ran his thumb over her bottom lip. "But nothing's changed in the last two days, Gael. You're the same. I'm the same, and we'd agreed that it was too complicated."

He didn't shake his head, or even contradict her for a long moment. "That's the thing, though. Everything seems to be the same, but I *feel* different, and I see you now, here in my bed, with my marks on you." He brushed two fingers over a little sore spot on her collarbone where he'd left a love bite. "And you look different to me, too. I know you feel it," he said with certainty, and bent down to kiss her. It was bruising and thorough, like he was trying to make his final argument with the kiss itself. Like them together was all the evidence he needed to show her just how different everything was. He pulled back, leaving her panting, and she knew before she said it that she'd let herself believe in everything he was offering her, even if she was certain life would undo it all in the end.

"Okay," she whispered as she gripped the hand on her neck and pulled it so he was standing between her legs. His groin was just inches away and her mouth was practically watering from the need to taste him. She fisted the base of his erection as she looked up at him. She searched his face for something, a sign that told her that trusting him was a stupid idea, but all she saw was the same lust burning through every ounce of her resistance.

"You have plans for that?" Gael asked roughly, through clenched teeth as she flicked the head with the tip of her tongue.

"Maybe. You have any ideas?"

He grunted and pushed in. "Let me in, baby," he coaxed her and she did, hungry for him again…before long all her doubts were floating away in the deep, tumultuous waters of her love for Gael Montez.

"Manolo, I can't do this right now," Gael told his uncle as he struggled to keep his voice down.

"You don't have five minutes to discuss the terms of a project you accepted without consulting me?"

Gael gritted his teeth at Manolo's reproaching tone. His uncle insisted on treating him like he was still a kid, and he was done with this shit. His mother was right. Manolo made a very good living off Gael's work and he was done acting like the old man did this as a favor to him.

Gael walked over to the window in the study and watched as two workers plowed the driveway and the path to the main road. Some days he could hardly believe he owned all this. But he'd have to start reminding himself— and his uncle—who was really running the show here.

"Manolo, let's get something straight. You're my uncle and I love you. But *you* work for *me*." He heard the older man suck in a breath, but Gael wasn't tiptoeing around Manolo's fragile ego today. "I'm taking the Francisco Rios part because it's what I want to do. End of discussion."

"And what am I supposed to tell the other studio about the lead role for that superhero franchise, Gael? I gave them my word." Manolo's voice rose on that last part, and that only worked to infuriate Gael even more.

"If you made promises on my behalf, then it's your problem how you rectify it."

"It's that girl, isn't it? You were never able to think straight when she was in the picture. Getting dicked around just like your father—"

"Manolo," Gael roared into the phone. "I suggest you rethink whatever it is you were about to say. And you better get used to seeing Perla around again."

"What does that mean?" his uncle scoffed.

"I need to go. We're about to head into Manhattan," Gael said when he heard a light knock on the door, and saw a raven-haired head pop inside. His body instantly reacted to her presence. Good God, he needed to get a grip.

"What do you mean, Manhattan? And who's *we*? I'm on my way to Sagaponack to talk to you and you're taking off?"

"I won't be here when you get in," he told his uncle as he gestured for Perla to come in. "Drive safely, Manolo."

Perla's eyes widened as she heard the name, but Gael waved off her concern.

"Is everything okay?" she asked, worry clear in her voice. He hated that he'd never stood up for her back when Manolo acted like her presence was an imposition. Once things between them were settled and he came back from his press tour, he'd really have to reconsider if it was in his career's best interest to keep him as his manager. But right now it was all about Perla and him. Everything else could wait.

"Nothing," he told her as he brought her closer. "Just checking in. Looks like the contract for the Rios project came in yesterday."

She smiled up at him when she heard that. "I told you the producers were desperate to get you."

"Well, they have me."

"I thought *I* had you."

This woman was going to end him. They'd just made love for over an hour in the cottage and he already needed her again.

"They have my acting skills. You get everything else."

"Mmm, is that a promise?" What he told her earlier wasn't a lie; he knew he didn't deserve a second chance with this woman, but he did not plan to waste it.

"That's absolutely a promise. What do you think about staying at my place tonight?" he asked as he ran his hands over her pert backside. "I can drive you to the airport tomorrow, before I head back here."

"If you make it worth my while, Mr. Montez." Damn but her hands were like fire on his skin.

"If anyone saw you looking at me with those big gray eyes, they'd have no idea what those hands were getting up to this morning."

She laughed wickedly in response as she stroked him.

"Maybe I'll give you a preview of my plans for the evening now," he suggested, already moving them toward the couch. "I'd love a replay of your lips wrapped around my co—"

"Here you are!" his mother called, then screamed, covering her eyes. "Oh, my God, Gaelito, take your hands off that poor girl. She hasn't even had breakfast yet." That caused Perla to dissolve into fits of laughter, while Gael tried to use her as a shield for his raging erection.

"Mami! Can you give me a minute?"

"Take five, mijo," his mother said reproachingly as she gestured toward Perla. "Ven, Perlita. I want to spend a little more time with you before you leave us. And you better get yourself together, little boy. I don't want to hear about you getting all handsy in that car. That black ice is dangerous out here."

"Fine," he called after his mother, who was already walking out of the room with Perla. He'd come into the house while Perla was packing up and let his mother know he was going into the city with her. To his surprise, she'd been all for it. She told him she was in support of anything that kept him smiling like that. He couldn't disagree. Gael could not wait to finally get Perla alone for a few hours somewhere where there were not nosy relatives underfoot. And once he did, he was going to make sure she understood that he was willing to do whatever it took to make things between them work. And then he'd make it clear to Manolo that his priorities had changed. His sister and mother were right. It was about time he was a little selfish.

Sixteen

Perla looked at Gael's phone, which flashed with yet another incoming call from his uncle. But if he noticed the phone vibrating in the console between their bucket seats, he did not show it. He kept his eyes on the road as he drove her SUV into Manhattan.

"Seems like Manolo really needs to talk to you," she told him as casually as possible. She didn't want to pry, but from what she'd overheard earlier, things sounded tense. Not that he gave any indication that he was having second thoughts about *The Liberator and His Love*. On the contrary, they'd talked about his ideas regarding the role for a decent part of the two-hour drive into the city.

"Do you remember when you did that monologue junior year?" she asked out of nowhere, and instantly saw a change come over his face. The tightness around his mouth that had been there since he'd spoken with Manolo smoothed, and his beautiful lips turned up into a wide smile.

"*You* remember that?" he countered, clearly surprised, and soon she was smiling, too.

"Of course I do. You brought the house down." At the beginning of their junior year all the drama majors were asked to perform a five-minute monologue for the incoming freshmen. Gael picked a scene from *Chronicle of a Death Foretold* by Gabriel García Márquez, and controversially decided to do it in the original Spanish. Perla remembered being in the front row, feeling jittery with nerves for him. Not because she didn't think he'd nail it, but because it felt important. "You were magical that night."

She turned to look at him, remembering the not-quite boy, but not full-grown man he'd been then. How he'd had people on the edge of their seats as he acted out the scene. Magnetic as he moved around the stage, and there hadn't been a single person who wasn't riveted by his presence. She remembered thinking, *He's going to bring our culture to the world. He'll be one of the precious few who get to do that.* And now he really would, and this time she wouldn't just get to see him; she'd be there working with him.

On impulse she reached for her phone, remembering she kept a ton of old videos on an app. After a few taps she had it. She connected her phone to the car's Bluetooth, hit Play and instantly the car was filled with Gael's impassioned voice as he performed García Márquez. His eyes widened almost comically as he realized what he was listening to.

"You still have this?" he asked, struggling to keep his attention on the road. "This isn't fair. I have to focus on the road and can't properly react to the magnificence of twenty-one-year-old me!" She laughed, certain he was only partly teasing, because this man had a lot of wonderful qualities, but humility about his acting skills was not one of them. And even that she'd always loved about him. That he knew the gift he had and tirelessly worked to hone it, to learn how to wield it better.

"You've always been so humble," she joked and leaned in to kiss him as the sound of his voice filled the car. They listened to the clip until it was over, and she was surprised to feel her tear ducts tingling at the crescendo.

"I'm glad you're doing this," she said as she reached for his hand.

"*We're* doing this," he countered, and she heard the scratchiness of emotion in his voice, too, as her own heart bounced in her chest like a rubber ball. For a second, he took his eyes off the road and turned to her. The certainty in his gaze seemed to cauterize any doubt she had about his intentions. They *would* do this, together.

"Are you sure you don't need to get back? Veronica only gets you for a few more days before you have to go on your press tour," Perla asked distractedly as Gael kissed his way down from her collarbone to the swell of her breasts.

After a quick stop at her place so she could repack, they'd come to his apartment. They'd barely gotten in the door before he took her in his arms and started ravaging her.

"My mother is ecstatic that I've escorted my girlfriend up to the city and will be even more ecstatic when I get back tomorrow and let her know when she gets to see you again."

Perla's insides hardly knew what was happening to them anymore. From hour to hour she was awash in emotions. And even if she was certain that Gael's intentions to keep things going between them were sincere, she wasn't so far gone she didn't know they had a challenge ahead of them. She lived in Manhattan and even if he had an apartment here, too, he spent most of his time in LA. Not to mention all the traveling he did for work. Hell, last year he spent most of his time filming in Croatia. To his chagrin she slid out of his arms and got enough distance to have an actual conversation.

"Nope. I keep letting you hypnotize me with your mouth, but we need to talk," she declared as seriously as she could manage, given that he was chasing her around his well-appointed living room with Frankenstein arms and whispering "give us a kiss, love"—in an admittedly pretty decent British accent. "I'm not letting you promise your mother anything on my behalf until we discuss exactly how we're going to do this. We both have busy lives and melding them won't be easy." The last bit sobered Gael up. He leaned against the breakfast counter dividing the kitchen from the rest of the room and raised an eyebrow.

"I want this to work," he told her as if it was all it took.

"It's not just up to us," she said, her arms across her chest, trying to stay strong, because right now with him looking at her like that, he could probably talk her into anything. "Your uncle is not happy about the project, and he's not the type to—"

He didn't even let her finish. "I'll handle Manolo. Don't worry about him. I promise," he said with such confidence, she couldn't not believe him. "Why don't I go down and get some stuff to make you dinner. It is Christmas, after all." He hiked a thumb over his shoulder at the glass cabinet holding floor-to-ceiling rows of wine. "Why don't you pick something for us to drink, and by the time you get comfortable I'll be back with ingredients for asopao de camarones."

"Fine, bribe me with my favorite food," she said, trying and failing to not sound utterly besotted. He brought her into his arms, and she went, even if she knew the conversation he kept deflecting absolutely needed to happen.

The real world would not stay at bay for much longer. But it was Christmas and this man wanted to feed her and then make love to her before she had to leave him, and she was going to take this gift she'd been given.

Seventeen

"Are you back already?" Perla looked up from the book she'd been reading and jumped off the couch when she saw Gael's uncle standing just a few yards away. Something about the way he ran his eyes over her made her want to cover herself up, even when she was wearing leggings and a sweater that practically reached her chin.

"Manolo," she said, trying to infuse as much lightness as possible into the name as she stood rooted to the spot by the couch.

"Perla," he said, not even attempting a friendly tone. She'd never liked Manolo. He always seemed to be annoyed by her mere presence, like he wished he could vanish her on sight. Seeing that kind of naked loathing directed at her was disorienting after two days of warmth and affection from Gael's family.

"Feliz Navidad. Gael's out right now," she told the older man, attempting to at least get him to say something.

"I'm not here to see my nephew." He smiled coldly. "I

wanted a word with you," he told her as he moved farther inside the apartment. Gael had purchased his two-bedroom in the iconic Calabria building a few years earlier and even though it was tastefully renovated, it was not very big. "I assumed you'd be here." The menace in his voice made a shiver run up her spine. "I know my nephew well enough to predict how these things go with him and his lady friends."

Perla felt a wave of nausea at the way he said *lady friends*, but she was not letting Manolo get to her. She and Gael had been together long enough for her to get to know his uncle. He'd always been callous when he was unhappy.

With only a few steps he was practically in front of her and it seemed to Perla that he was taking up all the space in the room. She moved so that the large sectional leather couch acted as a barrier between them. She wasn't going to give him the satisfaction of seeing her cower, though, so she crossed her arms and tipped her chin up.

"How can I help you? If you want to discuss the details of the contract, you'll need to talk to our attorneys. I only get the talent to sign on—what they actually *sign* is out of my jurisdiction," she said, trying for a joke, but landing with a thud.

"He won't care what he gets," Manolo scoffed and the way he furrowed his brows, with an almost piratical slant, reminded her of Gael. Manolo was his father's younger brother, after all. He had the same bronzed skin as her lover, and that imposing size. "Gael is taking this role to get you back. That boy could never think straight whenever you were involved. Did you know he almost threw away his career for you?"

"What?" she asked, her heart accelerating with every word that came out of Manolo's mouth.

"He kept turning jobs down because he was constantly having to deal with you and your drama. He almost declined that show with Shapiro after you called him crying about your mother bullying you at some party on a yacht or some other nonsense." The series directed by Arnold Shapiro had been Gael's breakout role. It premiered only six months after their college graduation. And that night on the yacht had been one of the most humiliating of her life. Someone asked her about Gael in front of her mother and Carmelina had laughed out loud and said, "He's probably with his real girlfriend."

Manolo's cruel laugh snatched Perla out of the awful memory, but the twisted anger in his face didn't make her feel much better. "I had to beg him to take the part, and when he realized the chance he'd almost blown because of you, he finally saw that you would end his career before he'd even started."

"I never asked him—"

He kept yelling, like she hadn't even opened her mouth. "You don't understand the sacrifices we all made for Gael to get where he is. The multiple jobs his mother and I had to take to help him and Gabi with tuition."

"I know that—"

"What could you possibly know about struggling to make ends meet?" he sneered, making shame roil inside her. "You were born with a silver spoon in your mouth, and then you caught your showpiece. That was all he was going to be to your family if he'd stayed with you. A pretty boy you brought to parties." Manolo glowered as Perla tried to muster up something to say. "You don't think I know what your mother said about him? You don't think she called me up to demand I keep Gael in check because he didn't have the pedigree to date a Sambrano?"

"She did what?" Perla asked, amazed that her mother's disgusting behavior still managed to surprise her.

Manolo let out another one of those chilly laughs. "Oh,

yeah, and to think he almost threw everything away for you, just so your mother could look at him like he was trash when you brought him home. Our family is not like yours, Perla. There is no trust fund to fall back on. Gael has people depending on him."

"I didn't know my mother had done that. I'm sorry," she said numbly, head spinning.

"Oh, your mother did more than that." The smile on his face was pure ice. "Your mother had one of her lawyers call me up and offer me money to get Gael away from you."

"What?" she heard herself say, and she had to lean on the back of the couch just to keep from sinking to the ground.

"It was a nice chunk of change, too," he said casually. "But I'm not for sale and neither is Gael. In this family we work for what we have, and if we have to make hard decisions in the process, then that is what we do. When you were trying to play house with Gael he was building a career to help himself and his family, and you put that in jeopardy." That was a jab, but she could scarcely feel it. The shame and humiliation from what her mother had done made her feel like she'd been coated in slime.

"You've been back on the scene for days and he's already being reckless. His mother's medical bills cost him hundreds of thousands of dollars already and there will mostly likely be more. That mansion he bought her needs to be paid off by working. He can't afford to turn down roles so he can chase after you. He's taking this role and turning down a good opportunity because he feels guilty, not because it's what his career needs. He's giving up millions for you. That has consequences. My reputation and Gael's will take a hit for this."

"But he said he hadn't committed to anything," Perla said in a daze. But Manolo was right; she knew how things were in Hollywood. It didn't take much for an actor to get a reputation for "being flaky" and soon offers started drying up. Latinx actors could not afford to be seen as unreliable. Manolo was an ass, but he wasn't wrong.

"You've always been that boy's weakness. He almost sank himself once before to keep you and he'll do it again. Are you willing to live with that, Perla?"

This hurt, so much she couldn't get air in her lungs, but she could not deny the truth in what he was saying. Hell, an hour ago she'd been wondering how she and Gael could even make their relationship work. She should've stuck to the plan. She should've let everything end when she left the Hamptons, but once again her desire for Gael had made her lie to herself, and this time at least she could walk away with some dignity. She knew he'd be hurt, but this was for the best. Eventually, he'd understand.

"Okay," she told Manolo. She moved like a sleepwalker to the spot next to the doorway where her small suitcase was still sitting. She grabbed her coat and her purse and moved to the door. "I think I'm going to go back to my place. I'll call my sister and tell her we'll have to go with another actor."

"This is for the best, Perla," Manolo called after her as she shut the door behind her. She had no one to blame for this but herself. And now she'd have to clean up the mess she'd made.

"Did you open a bottle already? Because I found the Albariño you liked at dinner last night." Gael walked into his apartment and almost dropped the two bags of food he was carrying when he found his uncle on his couch with a glass of Scotch in his hand.

"Where's Perla, Tio?" he asked as he put down the bags and went to the hallway leading to the bedrooms. "Babe?"

"She's gone, mijo."

Gael whipped his head back to look at his uncle, sure he'd misheard. Gone? Where would she go? He'd left her reading a book not even an hour ago.

"Gone where?" he asked suspiciously. Something was very wrong, and he suspected it had everything to do with the fact that Manolo was sitting in his apartment in Manhattan and not at the house in Sagaponack.

"What is going on, Manolo?" he asked, not even attempting to tamp down the anger that was already bubbling up. "I thought you were going to the Hamptons."

"I had to come and fix this." He said it like barging into Gael's uninvited was a big fucking imposition. "I knew you wouldn't do it, not again."

"Fix what? What the hell are you talking about, Manolo?"

His uncle let out a long-suffering sigh, because apparently explaining how he'd run off Perla from the apartment was a big chore.

"I told her the truth. That *The Liberator and His Love* is not a good move for your career. That your mother's illness has and will continue to cost a fortune and you have your whole family depending on you." He gave him that wise fatherly look that always made Gael's blood boil. "We've been here before. I know you care for the girl, but they're not like us. Remember what her mother tried to do."

There it was, the reminder that Carmelina Sambrano had tried to blackmail Manolo to keep Gael away from Perla, and he'd turned it down. One of the many things his uncle used as currency to remind Gael what a saint he was. He'd always thought his uncle pushed him out of love, out of wanting what was best for him, but now he saw that this was all manipulation. "Gael, deep down you know I'm right, son."

"Don't call me son!" he yelled, stepping up to his uncle

so that he was only inches away from his face. He didn't even try to check his fury. If Manolo was man enough to come into his house and do this, then he could deal with the consequences. "The only person in this world that has a right to call me that is Veronica Montez."

Manolo's eyes widened as if finally realizing that he had not played his cards right.

For a moment Gael thought of a time-lapse video he'd seen of a lake icing over. That was how his anger felt now, like it was filling him from head to toe.

"How did I not see what you've been doing?" Gael asked, shaking with rage. "This has never been about me and my happiness. It's about you keeping the golden calf as fat as possible."

"How could you say that? After all I've done—"

"Enough!" Gael roared, cutting Manolo's falsehoods off. He was so close to doing something he'd regret. He was fighting to get himself under control when his phone rang. He almost let it go to voice mail, but decided against it in case it was Perla. When he fished it out of his pocket he saw it was his sister and answered anyway, hoping Gabi would distract him from punching his uncle in the face.

"Is Perla with you?"

"No. She's gone, thanks to Manolo," he growled as his uncle stood up. His sister sounded frantic, her voice so loud Manolo heard her, and when the man made a move to come closer, Gael held up a hand. If his uncle got too close he wouldn't be responsible for what he did. He'd been raised to respect his elders, but his mother had also taught him that people needed to earn that respect. In the last few minutes, he'd lost every ounce he'd ever had for Manolo.

"Dammit, Gael, are you listening to me?" Gabi's loud voice brought Gael back to the moment, and what she said sank in. "Can you say that again?" he asked, feeling like his mind might shatter from the blind rage he was feeling.

"Bro, I did a little digging around and it looks like this project Tio has been trying to talk you into is with Baxter Jones."

Baxter Jones, the Hollywood mogul currently under investigation for dozens of allegations of sexual assault. Gael would rather lose his career than work with that man. "What are you talking about? I saw the name of the production company. It's not him."

His sister exhaled and when she spoke, her voice was wooden. "That's the thing. Apparently, he's set up this one as a front so people don't connect it to him, but it's his money. And, G, my friend said Manolo took a kickback from them in exchange for a guarantee that you would join the project. That's why he's been so pressed about you taking the Sambrano project instead. He took a bribe from them."

"I'll call you back."

"Wait! We're on our way to you."

"You're what! Gabriela, for fuck's sake."

"Mami had a bad feeling when Tio said he couldn't come out today, and you know how she gets. She wouldn't stop fussing until I agreed to drive her over to make sure everything was okay. We'll stay at my place."

"Fine. I have to go. I need to take care of this." Fury boiled over in Gael until he shook with it. He slammed the phone on the breakfast counter so hard he was sure he'd shattered the screen.

"You," he garbled out as he stalked toward his uncle, "associated my name with a sexual predator. You chased away the woman I love for money?" Gael looked at his uncle, and it was like he was seeing him for the first time. He was older now in his fifties, but he still was a big man, imposing. Manolo was used to getting his way, of cajoling and pushing boundaries until he obtained the results he wanted. And over the years Gael had let his uncle sway him just to keep the peace, but this time he had gone too far. "This was never about my career, was it?" he demanded as he fought for control. "You just wanted money. It's not enough that you've made millions off me, but now you're taking kickbacks and whoring me out to work for a literal monster. Do you know what working with Baxter would do to my career, Manolo?" Gael knew he was screaming; he probably looked terrifying, but control was beyond him. The betrayal and the panic of having lost Perla again was driving a rage in him that he'd never felt before.

"I did it for you," Manolo pleaded, his eyes wide with fear. But Gael knew he wasn't what scared his uncle. What scared Manolo was knowing he was about to lose access to his money. Still, he tried.

"You were never going to stay with that girl. You know how we are. The Montez men are no good to women. Per—"

"Don't," Gael barked, blood roaring in his ears. "Don't you dare even say her name," he said as he jabbed a finger in the direction of his uncle. "And do not pretend for a second this has anything to do with me or Perla. You did this all for yourself, just like my father used his tired excuses to justify his own selfishness. You have been dangling the help you gave my mother over my head for too long, and you know what?" Gael bared his teeth as he got so close to his uncle he could see the man's jaw trembling. "I think I've more than paid back what we owed you. I'm going to go look for Perla now, and when I come back you better not be here."

Manolo stumbled as he tried and failed to act like everything was fine. "Sure, I'll just let you sort things out and we can talk in a couple of days."

Gael was already grabbing his keys from the hallway table when he answered his uncle. "No, you don't understand, Manolo. I can't have someone who I don't trust managing my career. You're fired."

With that, Gael stepped out of his apartment and got in the elevator, sick with the fear that he may have lost her for good this time. He'd suspected it from the first moment he saw her getting out of that SUV, he'd been almost sure when he'd danced with her in his mother's living room, but now he was certain. He'd never stopped loving Perla; his heart had been frozen these past six years. Life, success, fame washing over him while he walked around numb. Because he didn't have the one person in his life who made him stop and look around. The person who made him want to live for himself. And just when he'd gotten her back, she had slipped from his fingers again.

Eighteen

"Come in," Perla called when she heard a soft knock on her bedroom door. Well, bedroom didn't exactly do the space justice; it was more like a luxury suite. Her sister and her fiancé had purchased this villa in Punta Cana a year ago and it was magnificent. It was a ten-thousand-square-foot home done in a minimalist design. Glass and metal covered the facade of the house, so that you could take in the majestic Caribbean Sea from wherever you were standing. Perla's room was done in white and corals, and everything seemed to blend in with the views.

"You're up," her sister, Esmeralda, said as she stepped into the room. It was barely 7 a.m. but Perla hadn't been able to get a lot of sleep.

"Only just." Perla smiled instinctively as she saw her sister. "I was admiring the view. I can't believe the curtains are able to block all this sunlight," Perla said as she looked at the swaying palm trees beyond her balcony.

"There are pocket doors in the wall that slide out when

you hit the button for the blackout curtains. It cost a fortune," she laughed as she came over to the bed and put her arm around Perla's shoulder. "But you know Rodrigo. He wanted the best. And the best was a house where you could see the ocean from every room." Her sister turned to look at Perla, her eyes brimming with a kindness that almost broke her. "How are you *really* doing?"

"I'm not fully sure yet," Perla sighed and closed her eyes as she tried to gather her thoughts. The past eighteen hours had been terrible, but she at least had landed in a place where everyone welcomed her with open arms. She'd left Gael's apartment and gone to the parking garage where they'd left her car and sat in it for what felt like hours. And then she started driving. She'd ended up at JFK. She'd bought a first-class ticket on the next flight to Punta Cana and sat in the airport for four hours, waiting. Gael had attempted to call her, leaving her multiple messages begging her to talk to him. He'd told her in those messages that he was sorry for what Manolo had said. That it was not how he felt. He pleaded with her to let him come to her.

But she hadn't responded to a single one. Eventually, after she got ahold of Esmeralda and told her she'd arrive late in the evening instead of the next morning, she powered off her phone. She'd kept it off until she opened her eyes a few minutes before Esmeralda had knocked on her door, but there had been no more calls from Gael. Maybe he realized his uncle was right and decided she was still a liability, after all.

"I'm not sure if Gael will be doing the Rios project anymore," she confessed. "I'm sorry, Esmeralda. It's all my fault."

Perla braced herself for her sister's reaction. Esmeralda had never been anything but supportive of her, but this was a major fumble. And it was all because Perla had not been able to keep her feelings out of the situation. She'd lied to herself about faking the relationship with Gael. She hadn't been pretending for a second. From the moment she'd seen him he'd gotten right under her skin. Like he always did. And now she'd messed up in her first big project for the studio.

"First of all, nothing is your fault," Esmeralda assured Perla. Her sister's eyes were so kind. There wasn't a semblance of anger or even slight frustration as she spoke. "Second, there's no problem. Jimena in legal texted this morning to say that Gael's new manager emailed last night saying they were reviewing and would send the contract back promptly."

"His *new* manager?" Perla asked, surprised.

"Yes," Esme said brightly as she gave Perla another squeeze. "Looks like his sister, Gabriela, is in that role now. As far as Jimena was concerned, Mr. Montez seems very committed to everything related to this project and whatever he promised you." Perla's head snapped up to look at her sister. Something in the way Esmeralda said the last part made her heart kick up in her chest.

"Did they say why they were still interested? As far as I know this was not financially as good an offer as the other he was considering," Perla said in a subdued tone.

"I didn't get a lot of details, but Gael is no dummy, and from what Jimena told me, neither is his sister. But they have not even hinted at pulling out."

Perla's head felt like it was spinning. She was certain that Gael would come back to his place, find her gone and decide it was all for the best. That he'd side with Manolo and go with the project that would make him more money. But he...hadn't.

"I didn't think he'd take it," she told Esmeralda, her gaze on the cerulean waters in the distance.

"Can I ask you something?"

Perla rolled her eyes at her sister's question, then nodded.

"Would you take a second chance on him?"

There was no point in even asking who the *him* was. There had only ever been one *him* where she was concerned. And she wished that the answer to that question took her longer to figure out. That was a door she should never again want to see open. The agony of losing him the first time should have made her hesitate, and yet the only word on her tongue was *yes*.

"Gael is too much of a professional to back out of a commitment, but that doesn't mean he has any intention of carrying on with me." And even saying that felt like a betrayal, because he'd told her he did. She'd had to leave, there was no way she could stay in that apartment with Manolo, after the things he'd said, but she couldn't deny that she wondered if she should've picked up the phone when Gael called, heard him out.

Her sister looked at her and shook her head sadly. "You know what was the biggest lesson I learned last year when Rodrigo and I were at each other's throats for the CEO position?"

"That my mother and brother are horrible people?" Esme clicked her tongue at that and reached for her hand.

"I learned that when life gives you a path forward you have two choices: get on it with all your old baggage dragging you down, or you can leave that stuff behind and walk into your fresh start with a lighter load. And you know what's the best part of shedding some of that deadweight?"

"What?" Perla asked, even if she suspected she knew the answer.

"That you'll have room for a companion." Before she could even fully let Esme's words sink in, a clear image of her walking hand in hand with Gael appeared in her mind like a memory.

"You know what?" Esme asked, breaking Perla out of her thoughts. "I think we should do a sleepover on the yacht. Just the two of us."

"You do?" Perla wasn't exactly surprised; the yacht had been a wedding present Rodrigo and Esme had gotten each other. They would spend their honeymoon on it a few months from now. Even if Perla wasn't in the mood, Esmeralda's excitement was infectious, and she could use a day or two focusing on something other than her mixed-up emotions.

"Let's do it," she said with as much enthusiasm as she could manage, which admittedly was not a whole lot.

"Excellent." Esme clapped in excitement. "We'll head over there before dinner. My mom has plans for a beach day and would kill me if I steal you from her and the tias."

Perla didn't believe for a second that Esme was put out about spending time with her mother and aunts. Esmeralda adored those women and she took every chance she got to pamper them. "We'll give them the morning and after-noon. We can party like rock stars in the evening," she told her with a wink. "I'll have the chef make us some treats."

As she watched her older sister walk away already talk-ing into her phone, Perla wished she could muster up more enthusiasm, but all she wanted was to curl up in her bed and cry. Losing Gael a second time hurt as much as she'd known it would.

"So what's your plan again?" Gabi was leaning against the door frame, watching him frantically pack a bag.

"I am going to grovel and let her know I made the big-gest mistake of my life when I let Manolo convince me she was a liability all those years ago. And then I'll do whatever it takes to convince her that I would give up everything for her, including my career."

"Okay, I like the basics of that plan, but how do you know she wants you there?" his twin sister asked as she pulled her phone out of her pocket. "Do you even have a flight secured?"

"Yes, Gabriela," Gael snapped as he zipped his small bag. "I called the crew and they have the jet ready at the Westchester airport. We fly out in a couple of hours. And I've been in touch with Esmeralda."

"Sambrano?" Gabi inquired, obviously surprised.

"Yes, you're not the only one who can call people. I reached out to her when I couldn't find Perla. We've been talking and she told me that she wouldn't tell me where they were until she was sure Perla wanted to see me. But she texted and said she thought Perla would be up for talking to me. So I'm flying down there."

"And what are you telling her once you get there, son?" His mother challenged him as she shuffled into his bedroom, because his sister, his mother and his grandmother were all in his house. Not one of them, as they promised they would, had left him alone. They'd stayed with him all day and watched him pace his apartment when he couldn't find Perla. They'd all reminded him a thousand times that he deserved to be happy. That Perla loved him, too. That all wasn't lost. It had been good to have them there.

Gael turned to his mother. She still looked frail wrapped in his robe, but he knew the steel that hid in those brown eyes. Manolo had helped with money, that was true, but his mother had raised him in every way that counted.

"I'm going to tell her I love her, Mami," he stated and felt the truth of those words settle in him. "I just hope I deserve her."

His mother walked up to him and placed her hands on

either side of his face. "I want you to hear me. Your father was who he was, and no matter what you think that means, I want you to remember that you're half mine. I raised you and you're a good man. The best." She poked his chest, and he let out a yelp, making her laugh. "Believe that, mijo."

He wondered how his mother had known that it was exactly what he needed to hear. For so long he'd believed there was something in him that would eventually break Perla's heart. And there had been. But it wasn't a curse. It was his own insecurity. It was him letting his past dictate his present. He was done with that.

"I believe it, Ma," he assured her.

"Good," his mother told him as she kissed him on the cheek. "Now, go get your girl, mijo. We'll be here waiting for you both when you get back."

Nineteen

"Here we are. We have a slip on the end. We needed the extra space because we fancy," Esme said with a waggle of her eyebrows as she maneuvered the car in the parking lot of the marina. "I'm excited about this and you look great," her sister said, gesturing at Perla's black maxi dress and her silver sandals. She had to admit it was very nice to switch from snowy New York to beach weather.

"I'm looking forward to taking my mind off..." She didn't even know where to start. It would be impossible to not think about Gael. He was ever present in her mind. It was like she thought about him even when she didn't. Everything she saw, heard, smelled somehow reminded her of him. Or reminded her that she missed him, that she'd almost had him and she'd lost him again. Since those initial attempts to reach her, he hadn't called, not even once. She wished it didn't hurt like it did. She'd tried so hard to convince herself she was past this. And she knew she wasn't the same insecure, lonely girl who had fallen for Gael.

She was different now, stronger. She knew that. She *felt* that. It just so happened that this new version of her loved him, too. She couldn't deny that fact any more than she could deny her own name. That man had always felt like he'd been made for her. Even when she felt inconsequential and undesirable, he looked at her like she was all he could see. And one didn't forget being wanted like that.

"Perlita, did you hear me?" Her sister's voice jolted her out of her thoughts, and she realized she'd been sitting there staring out the windshield.

"Sorry," she said, more than a little embarrassed. "My mind keeps drifting."

"Pobrecita," Esmeralda clucked like a mother hen, and leaned to pat her cheek. "It'll be okay. I promise." Perla tried her best to smile at her sister's optimism, but knew she likely looked more like she was in pain. "Here, why don't you head over to the boat. I just need to make a call. I'll be right behind you," Esme said as she tapped something on her phone.

Perla laughed at her sister calling a fifteen-million-dollar yacht a *boat*.

"Your boat has a gym, five staterooms and a swimming pool, but okay, sis."

Esme grinned at that. "*Our* boat, Perlita. Rodrigo and I want our family to enjoy it, and you're family."

Perla felt a stone lodge in her throat as tears filled her eyes. It was such a small thing to say, probably just out of politeness, but it meant so much. She'd needed to hear it. It's not like she'd never been on a yacht. Her father's was in a berth in a marina in Florida. But she was no longer welcome to use that. Her mother had been more than clear. Not that she'd miss it; there were too many bad memories attached to it. Like so many things connected to her mother.

"Go, the crew is expecting you. It's right at the end of the dock." Perla noticed that Esme was looking a little frazzled as she read the message that had just come in on her phone and wondered if something was wrong.

"Are you sure? I can wait for you."

Her sister beamed at her as she nodded. "I'm sure. Rodrigo just wanted to get some details about the honeymoon. You know how he is." Esme winked, and Perla laughed. Rodrigo was devoted to Esmeralda. The man worshipped the ground her sister walked on. She couldn't even be jealous of what they had. It was too pure. That didn't mean that she didn't feel a pang of yearning in her chest at the reminder that she'd never have that. Gael's career would always come first.

"Okay, I'll see you there," she told her sister after she opened the car door. She grabbed her purse and her hat as her sister gestured in the direction she should go.

"That way, and don't worry about the bags. One of the crew will get them and bring them aboard."

Perla took a moment to take in the ocean breeze and the beauty of the place. She'd always had a loose and complicated connection to her father's homeland. But now it felt like she was turning a new page here, too. As she made her way up the dock, she spotted the yacht. It wasn't exactly easy to miss. It was sleek and imposing, the biggest vessel on the dock. Perla noticed a man on the bridge headed toward the walkway. He looked…no. Perla stopped in her tracks, sure that her eyes were playing tricks on her. It couldn't be. She was still about fifty yards away and the sun was setting. It was probably the crew member coming to get their bags.

But the moment she saw him step on the walkway, she knew it was him.

"What?" she exclaimed as she turned around. Her sister, that traitor, was standing by the door of her Cayenne, grinning from ear to ear. "Did you do this?" Perla yelled, too spooked to turn back around and face him. Her heart had given up on pounding and was now doing triple somersaults in her chest. She felt like she wanted to run, then scream, then pass out.

Esme just shook her head and pointed at something over Perla's shoulder. "He did it! I just helped. Go get your man, Perlita!"

She felt him before he said a word. His presence big and undeniable at her back. It has always been like that with him. She could sense Gael in a room before she ever laid eyes on him. Like her entire being was attuned to his presence.

"Can you turn around, baby?" She could feel the warmth of him all the way down her body, and after taking one long and deep breath she moved to face him.

"You're here," she breathed out, taking him in, larger than life, almost too beautiful to be real. Her fallen angel. The man who had never stopped owning her heart.

She could see the emotions displayed all over his face. The way his eyes scanned over her. As if reassuring himself that she was really there. The way he gnawed on his bottom lip made her want to reach for him.

"I'm so sorry, mi amor," he told her as their eyes locked. "I wish I could go back and erase everything that I've ever done or allowed someone else to do to hurt you."

"You don't need—"

"No, please," he pleaded, taking her in his arms. "Please let me say this. I *need* to say this. There hasn't been a moment in the last six years that I didn't feel that something essential was gone from me. I didn't have the tools to deserve you back then, and I probably don't have all that I need now, but I swear to you. Perla, if you let me, I will spend the rest of my life striving to be the man you need."

Without a word she jumped so that her legs were wrapped around his waist. She pressed her forehead to his and breathed in the scent of him. That thing that was uniquely him and that she *always* craved. "I never wanted perfection, Gael. All I ever wanted was you." His breath hitched at her words and in the background she was pretty sure she heard her older sister whooping in delight.

"We're making a scene," she muttered as she hid her face in his neck.

"What good is being a movie star if I can't give the woman I love a fairy-tale ending?" Gael asked in a teasing voice.

"I don't need a fairy tale, Gael," she told him as she looked into his eyes.

"What if I want to give it to you anyway?" he asked as he turned to walk them up to the awaiting yacht, and Perla thought she might actually have a chance to get everything she ever wanted, and she was finally ready to let herself believe she deserved all of it.

Epilogue

"Are you ready for this, mi vida?" Gael asked as he looked out the window of their Escalade while they waited their turn in the long line of cars dropping off a good portion of Hollywood's A-list at the evening's red-carpet event.

"I am absolutely ready," she assured him, brushing a kiss on his cheek before leaning in to look at the crowd outside. Right beyond the car she could see the throng of paparazzi and journalists waiting as couples dressed in their awards-season finery stepped out of limousines and SUVs, posing for the cameras. Tonight Gael was up for a best actor nomination for his performance of Francisco Rios, and the series *The Liberator and His Love* had garnered over ten nominations. Their small project about the life and love of the Puerto Rican liberator had turned out to be an enormous financial and critical success. And now she got to walk out into the spotlight hand in hand with the man of her dreams—with her future husband.

Perla smiled as she lifted her left hand where a beautiful vintage Van Cleef & Arpels engagement ring sat on her finger. Gael had proposed over Thanksgiving at his Hamptons home surrounded by his family and her sister. Perla grinned, remembering how she'd gasped when he'd shown her the ring. A platinum band with a perfect black pearl at the center surrounded by a halo of ten old-cut diamonds. It was delicate and elegant, and perfect for her. Just like he was. Just like their life together was.

"We're here, Mr. Montez, Miss Sambrano." The low voice of their driver brought her attention back to the moment. Gael tugged on her right hand and winked as he looked down at her other hand, which was still suspended in the air.

"It's showtime, baby."

Perla took a deep breath and grabbed the clutch bag that matched her gown. Late January in LA meant sunny weather with a bite, but she would have to brave the few minutes on the red carpet with her shoulders completely bare. Anything for fashion. She'd gone with a vintage Charles James clover gown in gold, and on her ears and neck she had a few hundred thousand dollars' worth of sapphires, courtesy of Bulgari. To Perla's absolute delight, her jewelry matched Gael's custom Tom Ford tux. He looked devastatingly handsome, as always.

He'd gotten a haircut to play his part as Rios and decided he would keep the style. His brown hair was cut close to the scalp on the side and back and longer on the top. It suited him, although who was she kidding? The man looked good in everything, and she was not going to pinch herself again. This really was her life, and she deserved all of it. Including the absolutely perfect man with whom she was about to walk the red carpet.

"Let's do this," she declared, already moving. As Gael

helped her down from the car, she smiled at the cameras frantically flashing in her face.

What a difference two years made.

Well, two years and a month if you wanted to get specific. After Gael had come to the DR and they'd decided to give each other another chance, time had gone by in a flash. They both had their demanding jobs, and blending all that took time. But they'd managed to prioritize the life they were building together and Perla had never been happier. They were both bicoastal now and making it work, and they'd even been seeing a couple's therapist for the past year, which had helped them understand each other better. Perla could talk about how her family dynamics had impacted her, and Gael was able to open up regarding the wounds his father's abandonment had left in him. It was wild to think that by now they'd been together as long as they had their first time around. And no, it wasn't always easy, but this time they were building a solid foundation, and she knew that they could weather any storm.

"Can we see the ring, Miss Sambrano?" called the throng of photographers as Gael guided her up the long red carpet. She'd been to awards shows before, but never one of this caliber, and *never* like this. Not with one of the biggest stars in Hollywood by her side and her heart full to the brim with happiness. And definitely not when a show she was a producer on was predicted to sweep the awards season.

Perla lifted her hand in front of her chest and immediately a flurry of camera flashes started bursting in her direction. Gael wrapped his arm around her waist and pressed a kiss to her ear. "You're a trouper, baby."

"It's no hardship to brag that the sexiest man alive according to six different magazines just put a ring on it," she said, inciting a bark of laughter from her fiancé. They kept walking until they were stopped by one of the show hosts who were standing around intercepting celebrities to ask them about their clothes.

"Gael Montez!" beckoned a Latina in a teal mermaid gown Perla recognized from a competing network. There were people walking in all directions and if you even blinked, you ran the chance of missing a Hollywood living legend passing by.

"Hey, Sandra," Gael said, leaning in for a kiss, then gestured to Perla with a smile. "My fiancée."

"Of course, Miss Sambrano, congratulations on the engagement," she cried as she tried to commandeer a corner for all three of them to stand. "I'd heard you'd be wearing vintage Charles James today," Sandra exclaimed and made a bowing motion in front of Perla's gown. "Exquisite," the woman exclaimed, as she looked at the camera. "All the folks at home, behold the Latinx Power Couple of the moment, Perla Sambrano and Gael Montez." Sandra actually clapped as if they were worthy of a standing ovation.

Perla's stomach fluttered slightly, her nerves getting to her a bit as she took in the moment. And as if he could sense her discomfort, Gael brought Perla closer, pressing her to his side. "How are you feeling for tonight, Gael?" Sandra asked, then turned to Perla. "It could be a big one for you both."

Gael's smile was almost beatific as he looked down at Perla, taking his time before answering the reporter's question. Someday her heart would stop pounding in her chest whenever he looked at her like that, but today there was no helping it. He bent down to brush a kiss to her cheek before he turned his attention on the expectant woman who was looking at them with obvious delight.

"I'm honored for the nomination and immensely proud to be a part of this production. I became an actor with the hope that I could someday get to play a role like this one. To Boricuas, Francisco Rios is more than a legend. He represents the bravery and dignity of our island, and I will always be grateful to the love of my life for convincing me to take the role of a lifetime. But I have to say, I'm already walking in feeling like a winner knowing I get to spend my future with this woman." Perla struggled between almost swooning at Gael's words and blinking furiously in an effort to hold back tears.

"Gael!" she wailed. "You promised you wouldn't make me cry!" That got a laugh from Sandra and the few others who had gathered to watch Gael Montez be interviewed.

"It's true," he told her as he softly kissed her forehead.

"There you have it, folks," Sandra said with a bow as they got ready to move on. "True love at the awards tonight. We wish Mr. Montez and Miss Sambrano the best of luck tonight and for the wedding."

Within moments they were walking the last yards of the red carpet and heading into the foyer of the theater. As soon as they were past security, Gael pulled her into a little alcove where she could catch her breath.

"Are you all right?" he asked as he ran his hands in soothing circles over her back.

She nodded with her head pressed to his chest. "I'm good, even though you made me cry."

She heard the rumble of his laugh, but stayed right where she was, safe and warm in Gael's arms. The only place in the world where she felt completely at ease. "I was only telling the truth. The nomination is an honor, but no matter what I will go home with the greatest treasure I could ever ask for."

"I'm already marrying you," she said, feigning an annoyance that was a sharp contrast to the swarm of butterflies in her stomach.

"Look at me, baby." His fingers gently nudging her chin until their eyes were locked on each other. "Thank you."

"For what?" she asked breathlessly.

He smiled, shaking his head like she had asked the silliest of questions, and bent down to kiss her. It was a small brushing of lips, but she felt the depth and strength of his love even in that minimal contact. "Thank you for giving me the chance to make you happy."

"I love you," she whispered, certain in their love and the life of happiness that awaited before them.

* * * * *

THE STAKES
OF FAKING IT

JOANNE ROCK

For the dreamers. I'm rooting for you!

One

The outdoor audience in Brooklyn Bridge Park held its collective breath as the last scene in the *A Streetcar Named Desire* reboot rolled to its inevitable conclusion. Tana Blackstone was playing against type in her role as Blanche DuBois, even in this version's younger and grittier twenty-first-century retelling. But that didn't stop her from nailing her final line as the doomed femme fatale.

"I've always depended on the kindness of strangers." Tana batted her lashes at the actor playing the doctor character whose job it was to cart poor Blanche off to a psychiatric hospital.

Wrapping her hand around the actor's arm, Tana walked off stage right with him while the other players concluded the scene. The production had been months in the making in the small temporary venue, as they'd waited for the pandemic to ease enough that audiences would come out for performances.

Tana had been lucky to be tapped for this one considering her limited professional résumé. But too many other talented actresses had either left the city or taken alternate work during the Broadway shutdown. She'd been close to having to bail out of the profession when this job offer arrived.

"Brava," her colleague, an older man with shaggy white eyebrows and a grizzled beard, whispered to her a moment later as the audience burst into thunderous applause. "Well done, Tana."

"Thanks." She tugged on the short, tight skirt her part called for since this version of Blanche was a burned-out club kid with a predilection for prescription painkillers. "It was a fun show."

They pivoted to take their curtain calls for their small but appreciative outdoor audience. The show wasn't Broadway quality, but it'd been well directed, and the fans had obviously missed theater as much as the actors had during the pandemic.

Waiting her turn to take her bows, Tana cheered for the rest of the cast. She was so new to the city that she'd never had the chance to even try out for a Broadway show, so she couldn't "miss it" exactly. Still, she would have liked to see how she'd fare in a big audition.

She might have gotten her performing experience unconventionally as the offspring of professional grifters, but she'd been acting for as long as she could remember. At five years old, she pranced around wealthy neighborhoods with stray dogs her father cleaned up to sell as pedigreed pooches. Tana had cried her eyes out every time she lost one of her temporary "pets" to the scheme, but she'd learned to identify kindness in potential pet families really quickly so at least she'd consoled herself that the animals were going to better homes. By the age of ten, she could have won Tony Awards for her recurring role of "lost girl" so her mother could pick-pocket people who stopped to help, another job she'd resented bitterly, but her parents had threatened to put her into foster care if she didn't comply. She'd been just frightened enough of the possibility to wade through another demoralizing day.

The moment she turned eighteen, she'd told her dad she was done with cons and using her acting skills for his personal gain. If only she'd escaped the life a little sooner than that last summer between high school and college. Instead, she'd unwittingly tangled herself in the middle of one of her dad's biggest scams while doing nothing more than living under his roof. In the end, her father had swindled a widow out of her ranchlands at the same time the widow's son stole Tana's heart.

These days, she confined her performances to the theater. As she stepped downstage to take her bows for her role as Blanche, she told herself that she was finally where she belonged. The theater world was her new family. The outdoor audience full of young families seated on picnic blankets with strollers in tow paid her for her work because they wanted to see her act, not because they were getting separated from their wallets by sleight of hand. Finally, she had something to offer others rather than just taking. A few whistles and calls of "brava!" made her heart smile.

Lifting her fingers to her lips, she blew kisses into the crowd, soaking up their joy for a few more seconds as her gaze roved the groups of people breaking up on the lawn. Then her eye stuttered to a stop on a man standing alone in the center of the lower orchestra seats—aka, the stretch of grass between the front of the stage and a bicycle path.

He was a tall, athletic figure dressed in dark jeans and vintage T-shirt, a black jacket hugging broad shoulders as he put a Stetson back on his head. The man's mahogany-colored hair and olive skin made the women around him look twice. Or maybe it was his pale gray eyes, or the dark shadow along the sculpted jaw.

Her knees turned to water at the sight of him, but not because he was an outrageously good-looking man.

No. She felt faint because Chase Serrano was a ghost from the past she thought she'd never face again.

"Tana!" one of her coactors whispered from behind, pulling Tana from her musing, reminding her she was hogging the spotlight, albeit unwittingly.

Whoops.

Heart pounding wildly, she scuttled off the stage, brain working overtime to puzzle out what just happened. Deaf to the atmosphere of happy celebration around her, she wound her way through clusters of colleagues toward a trailer parked behind the stage. She needed to get out of here, away from the apparition she'd just seen in the audience.

Because how could it possibly be Chase Serrano, the very same rancher who'd once captured her heart? The one whose widowed mom lost his inheritance by signing it over to con man Joe Blackstone? Tana's dear old dad.

She raced down the steps that led away from the staging area, then jogged to the cramped trailer where the female cast members could dress and store their bags during the performances. The security guard, a tall former roller derby queen, nodded to Tana before opening the door to admit her.

"I hope you're not going to take off before we go out for drinks," Lorraine said, peering into the dimly lit trailer while Tana riffled through a stack of sweaters and lightweight jackets to find her satchel.

"I can't tonight." Tana pulled off her jet-black wig, then yanked the ponytail holder from her own brown hair that had been hidden beneath. The ends were normally dyed pink, but she noticed the cotton-candy color was fading as she ran her fingers through the strands. "Sorry, Lorraine. Maybe next time."

She checked her appearance one last time in the mirror. Not that she was trying to look good. If anything, she hoped her altered appearance would ensure she wouldn't be recognized if that had really been Chase in the audience. Yanking a wipe out of a packet in her purse, she scrubbed the towelette over her face to remove a layer of stage makeup, all the while wondering how Chase had found her.

And even more concerning, what could he possibly want with her? She'd already left Nevada to begin her arts degree in a small town north of New York City by the time Chase's mom married her dad and all hell broke loose on the ranch. She'd assumed Chase had been in Idaho where he would have been starting his finance program. But he could have been living most anywhere when he sent her that final cruel text accusing her of being part of the con and using her virginity as "misdirection," so Chase missed the signs of what was happening with his mom.

"You don't need to be sorry, sweetie," Lorraine said, her New Jersey accent coming through. "I'll still be having myself a fine time." She polished her long red fingernails on her T-shirt, chuckling softly. "Tonight's the night I make a move on Stella."

Megan, the actress who played Tana's sister in the play, was one of the sweetest cast members, but she had about as much discernment in partners as Stella Kowalski.

"Really?" Shimmying off her skirt, Tana peered out the trailer's only window, looking for the man she thought she'd seen. But there were no signs of a Stetson anywhere. "Good luck. If Megan's smart, she'll see that you're worth ten of the players she's been dating."

She let go of the window blind and pulled on her denim cutoffs, not even bothering to layer the leggings she would have normally worn underneath.

Time was of the essence.

Heading toward the door again, she paused at Lorraine's narrow-eyed look where the other woman still leaned into the Airstream.

"Is everything okay?" Lorraine asked, scrutinizing Tana's face. "You look like a woman with trouble on her heels."

"Just hoping to avoid someone from the audience," Tana admitted, more concerned with a speedy exit than protecting her secret. "If anyone asks for me—I don't care if it's Scorsese himself—I'd be grateful if you say you don't know anything, okay?"

Frowning, Lorraine leaned back to give her room to pass. "Sure thing, honey. I can get someone to escort you to the train station—"

Tana was already rushing by her, head swiveling as she searched the crowd on Pier One for signs of the black jacket and mahogany-colored hair beneath the rim of a cowboy hat. "Thanks. And I'll be fine. See you Wednesday."

She berated herself for not bringing a hat today as she hitched her satchel higher on her shoulder and navigated the pedestrian traffic at an inconspicuous pace. There'd been a time in her life when she wouldn't have left the house without a slouchy, wide-brimmed hat in her backpack, but she hadn't needed to blend into the background for a long time. Still, the old tricks returned now. Stick to the middle of a group. Don't move too quickly. Head down.

She was just debating whether or not to drop down into the closest subway station when a familiar voice spoke next to her ear.

"Hello, Hustler."

Her stomach sank.

She should have kept walking. Instead, she stopped short as abruptly as if he'd lassoed her the way he used to do with running calves. She stumbled just enough to make the man beside her catch her elbow in one strong hand.

Too late to run now. Tana had no choice but to brazen it out. Steeling herself, she looked up into the light gray eyes of the only man she'd ever bared her soul to.

A man she'd lived to bitterly regret.

"Hello, Chase."

Chase Serrano willed himself to loosen his grip on Tana Thorpe. No. Make that Tana Blackstone. He should have gotten used to the fact that he'd known her by an alias all those years ago.

Everything about her had been a lie.

She'd been an artful creation of male fantasy, from her wide-eyed interest in ranch life to her breathless admission of virginity. And while that last bit had technically been true, a discovery he'd made the night of her eighteenth birthday, Chase had to assume her innocence had been calculatingly bestowed where it would do the most good for her family's confidence games.

He'd done all the research he could on Joe Blackstone and his family once he'd learned the true identity of "Joe Thorpe." The man had married his mother and promptly sold off the family ranch that had been in Chase's mother's name at the time. The Blackstone patriarch was creative in his scams, sometimes involving his daughter, Tana, and his then-legal wife, Alicia, Tana's absentee mother who'd since divorced him. Joe had been married at least three other times under false names.

Had Tana continued the family business?

Chase released her slender arm. He didn't think he could stop glaring at her, however. There was simply no other way to look at a woman who'd helped swindle him out of his birthright. Around them, dozens of park-goers headed toward the subway station as twilight fell, while bicyclists and runners darted by. A few dog walkers, their pets sporting light-up leashes and collars.

Despite the bustle, Chase's world had narrowed to the thief in front of him. She was petite and delicately made, her features so fine they looked like they belonged on a fairy-tale princess. She had high cheekbones, full, rosy lips and chocolate-brown eyes. She looked different now with the bright pink ends on the glossy brown waves he remembered from eight years ago, however. There were new tattoos on her wrists and a diamond stud winking on one side of her nose, too. Even her clothes were a far cry from the simple T-shirts and jeans she'd favored that long-ago summer. Now she wore cutoffs with a heavy belt covered in spikes that hugged narrow hips. A pair of black combat boots were so scuffed he wondered if they'd actually seen combat. Her white T-shirt had a graphic of a spider on a dizzying Escher-like background. He knew the wild outfit wasn't part of the show she'd just been in, because he'd watched the whole thing.

And he hadn't been the least bit surprised that she was a talented actress. She'd been playing a role every second they'd spent together.

Too bad the anger he still harbored about that didn't keep him from noticing this woman was still undeniably appealing.

Damn it.

"We need to talk." He pointed in the direction of One Hotel, on the opposite end of Pier One from where they were standing. "My hotel is over there."

Her eyebrow lifted. "No hotels on the first date, thanks. How did you find me?"

"Does it matter?" He refused to let her commandeer this conversation. He'd done the legwork to find her, and he wasn't leaving until she'd committed to his plan. "If you don't mind discussing your criminal past in the middle of a public park, that's fine. But we'd have more privacy if we sat in a quiet corner of the hotel's rooftop lounge."

Her cheeks flushed briefly at his words, but she still gave him a tight smile.

"There's nothing you can say to me that can't be said on a park bench." She thumbed to the right, indicating a vacant spot under the trees. "I can give you five minutes before I need to leave for my next appointment."

Without waiting for his answer, she marched toward the bench. The park lights were on now, illuminating the ground around the base of the tree, but the seating area itself remained dim. Swinging her satchel to the ground, Tana dropped onto the wooden slats and crossed her legs before hooking her hands around one knee. She looked at him expectantly.

This wasn't exactly the way he'd envisioned this interview playing out, but so be it. She wanted to talk in a park, then he would lay it all on the line right here.

"You're going to help me." He lowered himself onto the bench beside her.

"How kind of me." She looked up into the tree overhead as if lost in thought while she listened.

He wondered briefly if she avoided looking at him for another reason. Did she not want to face the past? Or could she feel any remorse about what she'd done?

"We both know you owe me more than you can ever repay, so I want to make it clear I'm not asking for your help. I'm demanding it."

That got her attention. Her brown eyes flickered over him.

"I don't know where my father is anymore, so if that's what you want to know, you're bound to be disappointed. My mother couldn't even find him to notify him of their divorce."

"That's not what I'm here for." Although he found it interesting she assumed he cared about that. Did she know that he'd regained Cloverfield Ranch? Remade his father's fortune twice over? "The police will deal with him if he ever resurfaces."

"How's your mom?" she asked suddenly, nibbling the corner of her lip as if she wanted to take the question back.

"Better off without your father in her life," he informed her coldly. "I moved her out of Nevada immediately after her fake husband disappeared so she wouldn't be surrounded by bad memories of her phony family."

Tana's lashes lowered at the jab. Not that he thought her capable of shame. But he hadn't intended to make this meeting an airing of grievances. Tana Blackstone's day of reckoning wouldn't be about that. She might have escaped legal charges in the hustle that stole his inheritance, since she'd been the one to notify the police about her dad using a fake name while living in Nevada. And from a police perspective, she hadn't materially participated in the land scam.

But that didn't mean she was not guilty.

"Good." Her soft answer was almost lost in the shrill whistle of a bicyclist on a nearby path.

A small dog off the leash darted out of the cyclist's way, the harried owner running behind.

Chase remembered well the feeling of never catching up. Thankfully, those days were almost behind him now. Reclaiming his father's fortune had gone a long way toward soothing some of the fury the Blackstones had left in their wake.

Now he just needed one last missing piece to restore his birthright.

"I know you're under a time constraint, so I'll come right to the point."

She shifted to face him more fully. Alert. Curious.

He continued, glad for the excuse to be as succinct as possible. The quicker she agreed to his terms, the better. "I've spent the better part of the last eight years recovering what your father stole from my family. The money, of course. But more importantly—to me—the land."

"You were able to buy back Cloverfield?" Tana's brown eyes widened as she toyed with a heavy silver bangle on her wrist.

The gesture reminded him of the way she'd played her character on stage, the nervous gestures that had made Blanche DuBois seem so fragile. Did Tana think she could pretend to be anyone other than the cold-hearted con he knew her to be?

"Offering far more than it was worth helped my cause," he said drily, failing to keep the old bitterness in check. "I thought the score was settled once I reclaimed the ranch."

"But that's not enough for you." She leaned against the back of the bench, but still eyed him warily.

Behind her, the lights of Manhattan on the other side of the East River made a bright backdrop.

"It might have been enough, if the parcel of land had been the same one my father meant for me to have once I turned twenty-one."

Her forehead wrinkled as she scrunched her nose. The diamond stud refracted the light, twinkling in the growing darkness. "I don't understand. I thought my dad sold the whole thing to a horse breeder from Tennessee?"

"I did, too. I was so confident of that, I allowed an agent to handle the deal for me." Chase had been overseas on business, preferring to avoid his old hometown full of bad memories. He had an ongoing dispute with a powerful neighbor who'd taken advantage of the upheaval in the Serrano household that summer. Another score he still needed to settle. "It wasn't until I visited the property myself last winter that I realized a small portion of the original parcel was not included in the sale."

"I don't understand. Why would he sell most of the ranch but not all of it? Who has the rest?"

He studied her now, from the cadence of her voice to the expression in her eyes, looking for a tell that would betray her. He'd read a lot about swindles and the con artists who pulled them, educating himself on how he'd been screwed out of his fortune. But despite his studies, he couldn't spot any hint that she already knew what he was about to tell her.

"That's the amusing part of all this," Chase pressed on. "It turns out the land has been held in trust for you."

A beat of silence followed his news.

"That's impossible." She shivered slightly and wrapped her arms around herself. "I assure you, I don't own any land. Not in Nevada, and not anywhere else. Look at the tax rolls and see for yourself."

"It's been controlled by a trust for the last eight years. They've paid the taxes consistently." It had taken him months to hunt down the information since the title currently belonged to a shell company.

Technically, he probably shouldn't have been able to trace the trust back to her, because those holding companies were well paid for their discretion. But he'd spared no expense to obtain the proof he required.

She shook her head and held out her arms, shrugging her shoulders. "Do you really think I'd be living on ramen noodles and popcorn in this most expensive of all cities if I could have sold off some mystery piece of property for income? I'm still paying back loans to a state school, Chase."

He had researched enough to know this was true. But then, he wasn't so naive as to believe the daughter of a successful con man didn't know a thing or two about hiding what she didn't want other people to see.

"I assure you, the trust is for you. I don't know why you haven't been contacted by them if you were really unaware of this, but it's yours to claim legally at any time."

"Great. If you care to share the contact information, I'll go cash in. Obviously, the land is yours in the first place, so I'll sign it over to you." She reached for her satchel and passed him a card with her contact information. Then she made a move to stand. "I really do need to go—"

After shoving her card in his pocket, he rested a hand on her knee. He'd just meant to catch her attention so she stayed put, but the momentary brush of her bare thigh under his palm was enough to send sparks through him.

"Wait. That's not all." He let go of her again, noting the way she covered the spot he'd touched with one hand. "I need you to go to Nevada with me to sort out the paperwork."

"Why?" Frowning, she shook her head. "You just told me you had an agent buy your land for you. Why do I need to go in person for this?"

"This is more complicated." Which was the truth. But he had other reasons for wanting her to return to his hometown with him. Plans far bigger than he was ready to share today.

"I can't leave New York. I have a life here. I'm doing a show—"

"First of all, I've already checked the performance schedule, and you don't have a show at the time I need your help. And second, you owe me." He let the weight of that reminder settle around her narrow shoulders. "You and your father robbed my mother, Tana. There's no other word for it."

"That's not true." She chewed a fingernail for a second before ripping it away from her mouth. "I didn't rob anyone. I just had the misfortune of still living under my father's roof that summer."

"A misfortune for us both, then," he reminded her softly, not letting her off the hook. "Since you served as my distraction while your father took everything my mom owned."

She pursed her lips and took a moment before answering, her brown eyes shooting daggers.

"For the record, my purpose was never to distract you. And assuming I can take the time off for a trip, when would I need to go?" She shouldered her bag and stood.

He rose, too, keeping his tone conversational. Easy. Preparing her for the bigger request.

"This weekend. We need to fly out on Friday evening."

"As in three days from now?"

He nodded. "Yes. Your play isn't running thanks to the book festival on the pier."

He'd done his homework, and he wouldn't let her off the hook.

"I don't understand—"

"I didn't understand when you disappeared from my life forever, either. But that didn't change the fact."

Hesitating, she looked away from him, as if scanning the horizon might provide answers. Then, she nodded.

"Fine. I'll make it work." She tucked a few strands of brown and pink hair behind one ear, her feet already shuffling in place as if she couldn't wait to sprint away. "Just message me the details and I can meet you at the airport."

Relieved, he felt one of the knots in his chest unkink a bit. He needed her help, and he'd known going into this meeting that she could very well refuse him.

"I know where you live. I'll send a car. But Tana?" His heart thudded at the knowledge that he was so close to recovering his family legacy.

Close to having the vengeance he craved on the Blackstones.

"Yes?" Impatience threaded through her voice and body language, shoulders stiff and feet shifting.

Maybe it was wrong to take pleasure from her discomfort. But he'd lost too much at her hands to care. If anything, he savored the moment to extract one last thing.

"You'll be traveling as my fiancée."

Two

A stress headache pounded behind Tana's right eye. She felt her heartbeat pulse there, causing a tic. Normally, she was skilled at hiding her emotions and showing the world only what she wanted them to see. But an encounter with Chase Serrano blew that all to hell and back.

Bad enough he'd sought her out in the first place after eight years of believing the worst about her. But now she knew he'd been investigating her background, making himself familiar with her life and—no doubt—her lack of accomplishments in the years she'd been struggling to find direction. He wanted to drag her back to the setting of their affair where she'd experienced gut-wrenching betrayals.

Her father had conned the family of the guy she'd fallen for. The guy she'd fallen for blamed her for it all. Then her mother had washed her hands of the whole thing, choosing to divorce Joe Blackstone in absentia

while telling Tana she'd rather not associate with anyone who would narc on her own father.

Why on earth would Chase want to go back to the
site of the implosion while she wore his ring? As if
their relationship wasn't colossally screwed-up enough.

"You can't be serious." She jammed her fingers into
her hair near her scalp, massaging the front of her head
in an effort to relieve the thumping pressure.

It wasn't fair that he looked so good while taking
a wrecking ball to her carefully constructed life. His
broad shoulders blocked her view of Manhattan. All she
could see was the vee of his chest tapering to narrow
hips. Muscular thighs hugged by dark denim.

Realizing she was staring, she tipped her chin up
again, only to catch him smirking, well aware of where
her gaze had drifted.

"Quite serious. It's a nonnegotiable point." He
checked the oversize watch on one wrist, the rose-gold
face glinting briefly in the landscape lights where she
spotted the Patek Philippe name below the date. "Can
I walk you where you need to go next? I don't want to
detain you further."

"How kind of you," she drawled, glancing around the
pier at the evening crowd. She didn't need a babysitter
to walk her own neighborhood, but she also wanted to
be home as quickly as possible after this craptastic day.
"I'm going this way."

Grateful to be moving so she could work off some of
the nervous energy from this encounter, Tana led him
up Furman Street toward Old Fulton. They walked in
silence so long that she wondered what his game was.

"Don't you think you owe your would-be fiancée
some explanation for this bizarre request?" she asked
finally, keeping her focus on the sidewalk. Pedestrian

traffic was lighter away from the park, but she was grateful for any distraction from Chase's probing gray eyes. "Why on earth would you want to fake an engagement with me?"

Even as the words tumbled from her mouth, however, a possible explanation rose to top of her mind. She halted under the trees of Cadman Plaza Park, near the stone steps to one of the entrances.

"What?" he asked, halting a step ahead of her and turning to read her expression.

"Don't tell me you think a public engagement will bring my father out of hiding." She spun the ring on her thumb, agitated and restless.

Joe Blackstone had fled the country eight years ago, and she hadn't heard from him since. A couple of times, blank postcards had arrived from exotic locales with no signatures, just strings of numbers that meant nothing to her. She knew they were from him.

Even that had ended once she finished her stint at college.

But he hadn't called. Hadn't emailed. Hadn't written.

"Probably not," Chase admitted slowly. "But if nothing else, your dad will hear about it." His voice turned low and gritty. "He'll know I've taken back what he stole from me."

For the briefest moment, she saw past the anger in Chase's eyes to the hurt of betrayal. But then he turned on his heel and continued walking.

Which was strange, since he'd volunteered to accompany *her*. But oh well. She followed him since he was going the direction she was headed anyhow. Her chest ached with the memories of the way her father had sold Chase's family lands right out from under him. It had happened too fast, while she'd been away at her student orientation in the small-town college outside New York City. By the time she learned of his betrayal, her dad was long gone.

She had no way of taking out her fury on him for hurting someone she loved. Of course, that relationship had taken a nosedive immediately afterward, with Chase convinced she'd been in on the con.

She'd tried to warn him, hadn't she? She'd advised him ahead of time that her father was not to be trusted. But since she could only guess what her dad might do, she hadn't been able to be specific about what to watch out for. Especially when her parents' old threats of foster care had morphed into threats of sending her to juvie for the role Tana had played in their past schemes. She'd just wanted to hang on until she turned eighteen and went to college, where she could finally have some freedom and a safe place to live far away from them. Her head throbbed harder, and she squeezed both temples at the same time.

"I can't believe you're doing this," she murmured, mostly to herself, as they neared the Korean War Veterans Plaza.

"Your father likes games. He'll appreciate this one." The steel threading through his tone made her glance over at him.

His jaw flexed as he stared straight ahead. Even so, he pulled her against him when a reckless bicyclist whizzed past on the sidewalk where he did not belong.

Momentarily squeezed to his side, Tana relived a hundred memories of being in this man's arms in an instant. She inhaled the woodsy and musky scent that catapulted her back to his truck bed in the moonlight, a bonfire just outside the open tailgate. His warm palm curved around her hip recalled the way he'd steered her where he wanted her that first unforgettable time together. She'd visited him in the barn he'd been converting to a bunkhouse, and somehow they'd ended up tangled together...

She straightened away from him, cheeks hot. The memories of her happiness were too much to take right now. She'd left that person and that life far behind. Better to focus on the present. And his frustrating reasons for a fake engagement.

"So this is all a game to you?" With a tug on her shirt, she resumed their brisk pace. She still felt off-stride, however, and knew it had everything to do with Chase's presence beside her.

"You and your father made my life a game." He stopped as they reached a crosswalk, then turned to face her. His gray eyes were serious under the light of the streetlamp. "And I won't forget that."

She swallowed past the lump in her throat that was all guilt, even though she hadn't been the one to set Chase up. She should have known her father was making a big score, but she hadn't been part of the scam since she'd chosen to be done with that life. At the time, she'd believed her father was just trying to convince widow Margot Serrano to invest in some bogus business. She'd warned Chase about that, in fact, telling him to watch out for his mother's finances on the pretense that she didn't trust her dad's financial savvy.

Little did she know her father had his eye on a bigger prize, eloping with Margot after Tana left for school, and selling the ranch as part of their plan to "travel the world." Except then her dad emptied their joint bank account and got a flight for himself in secret, leaving Chase's mother waiting for him at the airport, her bags packed for a Paris trip that never happened. Or so she'd gleaned from the news coverage of the police report on the crime when Chase brought the cops into the case. She'd understood then why Chase hadn't returned her calls. Understood he must hate her.

Especially when she'd received one last ugly text from him, accusing her of using seduction to distract him from what was happening between his mother and her dad. They'd never spoken again until today.

"It was never a game for me," she said finally, knowing he wouldn't believe her but needing to put it out there. "I don't blame you for hating me for what my father stole, but I had no idea what he was planning since I told him I'd report him to the authorities the moment I turned eighteen. He kept me in the dark those last few months."

He held her gaze for a moment longer, then gave a rueful shake of his head, a bitter smile playing about his lips.

"So you say." He crossed the street, hastening his pace. After a moment, he glanced back at her. "Are you headed back to your place?"

She missed a step. Then rushed to keep up with him. "I forgot that you already mentioned you know where I live."

"Yes. You didn't think I just accidentally happened to find you at your performance in the park today, did you?" He shoved his hands in his jacket pockets, slowing down to wait for her. "I looked you up when I discovered you owned a piece of Cloverfield."

It wouldn't have been difficult to locate her, even without a private eye. Her name had been in some prominent New York news outlets when she'd won a coveted spot in her Brooklyn brownstone, a sponsored residence for women seeking careers in artistic professions. Tana had submitted a clip of her acting, but she'd since discovered a love for the production end, as well.

As they passed Brooklyn Borough Hall, they traversed a wide pedestrian path lined on either side with trees and old-fashioned streetlamps that cast a golden glow on the late-summer evening.

"Have you been in New York long?" she asked, wondering exactly how much he knew about her.

"In the city? No. But I bought a house in the Hamptons last year, so I've spent a few months there."

She did a double take, trying to picture the man she'd once known mingling with the East Coast elite. "The Hamptons? Since when do cowboys take homes in towns known for their social cachet filled with beautiful people?"

"Since I had to earn back a small fortune to regain my father's legacy. You recall I was studying finance in school?" At her nod, he continued, "I parlayed that into investing. Access to some of the country's wealthiest families has been good for business."

"But…the Hamptons?" She recalled the weeks she'd spent with him on the ranch when they'd spent hours riding. "It's hard for me to picture you spending a day where you're not on the back of a horse."

She peered up at him in his dark Stetson, the hat shadowing his clear gray eyes. Their gazes met for a moment, memories flooding back of those long trips they'd taken into the mountains. He'd shown her the things he loved about the dramatic Humboldt Range in northern Nevada, and she'd fallen for both the man and the place. She looked away first, clearing her dry throat.

"I purchased a house with stables," he admitted a moment later, pulling her gaze back to him. "But I bought the property as an investment, as well. I'll keep it until I can turn a nice profit on a sale."

They walked in silence a little longer, crossing onto Fulton Street before he spoke again. "What about you? Are you going to tell me what you're really doing in New York?"

"What do you mean? You know what I'm doing. I'm acting in a play and trying to build a career. The same as I've always wanted." Except now she also wanted to work behind a camera, too.

"Come on. We both know that's not true."

She stiffened at his tone, the bitterness returning as they passed a food cart selling halal food, the scents of coriander and cumin tingeing the air.

"I assure you it is. But since you're anxious to remind me that I'm not a good person, why don't you tell me what you think I'm doing in New York?"

A bus left a nearby stop, the diesel fumes making her cough through a haze.

"I read enough about the Blackstones to know you're in the family business." Chase's jaw flexed as he made the damning announcement. "That means you must be working a con."

Chase could see the dark cloud descend on Tana's pretty features, her brow furrowing as she scowled.

That was just as well.

He'd reached for the comment to resurrect a barrier after she'd kindled memories of their summer together. He'd enjoyed sharing his love of horseback riding with her, especially when she'd gravitated to it so naturally. But then, everything between them had felt easy, as if it had been destined.

Little did he know at the time that it only felt that way

because con artists specialized in answering a need. They gained the trust of a mark, falling into the carefully set trap of the con.

And he'd fallen for it. For her.

Eight years hadn't erased the anger he had about that. So he'd be damned if he'd fall for Tana Blackstone's pretty smiles now. He knew better.

If there was still an attraction between them, then *he* would be the one to leverage it, not her. He wasn't getting played again.

Now, walking beside Fort Greene Park, they neared her building before she finally responded to his jab.

"My family doesn't dictate my work or my life choices." She clamped her hands into fists at her side, her stiff posture making her look as tough as her boots and studded belt suggested. "The only con I'm running now is the engagement *you* proposed."

They passed a group of about twenty step dancers working on their moves underneath the lights in a paved area of the park. The rhythmic stomp of their feet reminded him of line dancing.

Another pastime he'd introduced Tana to. Or thought he had.

Hell, she could have been born line dancing and horseback riding for all he knew.

Tension cranked through his forehead, and he resisted the urge to vise-grip his temples. "Maybe you should give me some pointers then, since you're the expert in deception." He slanted a glance her way, wondering how those painted-doll features of hers could hide such a shady side. "How are we going to pull this off?"

She exhaled a huff, and he swore he could almost see her breathing flames. "Fine. You want to know?"

She made a sharp turn down South Portland Avenue,

stopping abruptly in front of the brownstone where she lived. When he'd hired a private investigator to track her down, Chase had researched Tana's life thoroughly enough to know the basics.

Her talents as an actress had won her the spot in the building. And he recalled that she currently shared the brownstone with two other women—a fashion stylist and a makeup artist.

He slowed to a stop after her, taking her measure. "I do."

Dropping her bag on the stoop, she leaned against the stone balustrade and glared at him.

"First, we need to consider our target." She brandished her index fingers, as if preparing to count off the steps. "Who's the mark in this case? Who are we trying to convince?"

"You're on a need-to-know basis for that." He had more than one mark in mind, but he couldn't help but hope that hearing of Tana's engagement to Chase would bring her father out of hiding.

She'd been right about that.

"Then we're already going into this without being prepared enough. It'll be on you if we can't pull this off." She stood with her hands on her hips. She was at least a half foot shorter than him but still ready to go toe-to-toe with him.

He fought the contrary urge to stroke her hair, wanting to sift the pink ends through his fingers.

"Maybe we should move on to the next tip for a successful con," he suggested in an easy tone, folding his arms as he leaned back against the opposite balustrade. "I understand that I'm responsible for messing up the first one."

"Fine. Second is that we both have to play our roles."

She flashed two fingers, her middle one glinting with silver bands. "It doesn't matter how good an actress I am. If you're not playing your part, we'll never convince anyone we're a couple."

"You don't need to worry about me." He'd manage his business, the same way he always had. A relentless work ethic and good investment strategy had taken him from just barely getting by after Joe Blackstone sold off Cloverfield, to a second house in the Hamptons that supplemented his primary residence in Nevada. "I'll do my part."

She shook her head while a group of skateboarders wheeled past, their shouts and board tricks distracting them both for a moment before she spoke again.

"That's not even close to good enough. The best actress in the world can't do a believable scene for two by herself. You need to have your head in the role." She spouted the advice as if she were teaching a class on survival in the desert and the stakes were life and death.

But then, maybe that was how her father had taught her. He'd never thought much about what her life had been like before she'd helped deceive his family, but Chase felt a momentary curiosity before reminding himself he didn't want to empathize with this woman.

"I said, I'll do my part." Shoving away from the balustrade, he stepped closer to her. "I know how to make it believable."

Her brown eyes tracked his movements, her breath going shallow as he neared.

Yeah, he'd have to be dead not to notice the signs of her attraction. He still wrestled with his own.

"We don't even know each other anymore," she argued, her head tipping back a little to maintain eye contact.

His blood surged as he continued to close the distance, even while something in the depths of his brain warned him to step away.

"We probably never did." His gaze roamed her face from her widening eyes to the tight pucker of her frown. "But we should still know enough about each other to convince the world we're a couple."

His attention narrowed to her lips. He couldn't deny that he wanted a chance to relax that frown. Maybe make the rest of her loosen up, too.

"Impossible." She shook her head in denial, but her voice sounded breathless.

"Then let's start by convincing ourselves." He'd dreamed of touching her so many times over the years. Kissing her. Tasting her.

Of course, the dreams started with torrid encounters and ended with him extracting revenge.

Taking back his lands and his pride.

"The last thing you want to do is believe your own con," she retorted softly, her melted-chocolate eyes dipping to his mouth.

"Then we'll have to walk that line carefully, won't we?" He cupped her chin in hand and pressed his thumb into her lower lip, rubbing the spot back and forth gently.

Like a lover.

Her eyelids fluttered.

He felt a sense of victory, causing a rush of adrenaline to surge through his system. That victory came at a cost, though, because she wasn't the only one affected by their nearness. It wasn't easy to stop himself from skimming his fingers into her hair and tugging her closer for a long, thorough taste.

But he couldn't allow Tana Blackstone to get the best of him this time, so he stepped back after a moment.

"Yes, we will," he answered his own question aloud, more than satisfied with what he'd learned here today. "I'll text you the travel plans tomorrow so you can make any needed arrangements for the weekend we're away."

She reached behind her to steady herself on the balustrade before taking a step away from him.

"I need to be back in town for a show rehearsal on Monday." Tana peered at the doors to the brownstone before darting up the steps, grabbing her satchel on the way.

"You will be," he assured her, already looking forward to their next encounter.

And not just because she'd be signing over that property to him.

"Good." She gave a nod as she reached for the door, then stared back down at him. "And for what it's worth, *you* should be the one rehearsing before this weekend."

"Me? Is that right?"

"Definitely." She arched a brow at him, her tone derisive. "I didn't buy into that almost-kiss for a second."

He didn't have to hide a smile at her blatant lie, because before he knew it, she'd disappeared into the brownstone with a loud bang of the front door.

Three

Tana had barely crossed the threshold into the foyer when her friends rushed toward her from the adjoining great room.

"You've been holding out on us," her friend Sable Cordero accused in her southern Louisiana drawl, folding her arms in a way that drew attention to her baby bump. The hint of belly was a reminder that the fashion stylist would be moving out of the brownstone soon to begin her new life with her boss at the design house where she worked.

The stunning brunette had been engaged for four weeks, waiting to wed her baby daddy until the renovations on their nearby brownstone were completed. Even now, Sable spent her nights with him, but Tana had been happy her friend still passed as much time with her former roommates as she did.

"Seriously. Who is the hot cowboy?" Blair Westcott, a blue-eyed, platinum-blonde makeup artist who appeared to have descended from Vikings, took up the conversation as she planted her hands on her hips.

She wore faded jeans and a pink sweatshirt with the name of an upstate hospital facility emblazoned on the front, a place where she spent most of her weekends visiting her cancer warrior mom.

Tana had little in common with either of her roommates other than a fierce desire to make it in their respective competitive fields. They'd all gravitated to New York in the hope they could distinguish themselves in a place that could make or break talented people. Sable and Blair had come to her first show when she'd been cast in *A Streetcar Named Desire*, and they'd cheered the loudest. She loved that about her friends.

Even when they were being ridiculously nosy.

"It's not like that," she told them flatly, allowing her bag to fall to the limestone floor as a wave of exhaustion hit her.

Seeing Chase again may have had her senses buzzing, but now she felt faint as she thought about what she'd just agreed to. Had she really said she'd go to Nevada with him? As his fiancée?

"Oh?" Sable circled her, narrowing her hazel eyes as she studied Tana. "Flushed cheeks. Aura of frazzled agitation. Breathing too fast. I'd say you're showing all the symptoms of something intriguing happening between you and the cowboy."

"Sable and I were just sitting by the front window, drinking a pregnant-mother-approved tea blend and minding our own business, when a man strolled up Portland Avenue like a gunslinger out of an old Western." Blair fanned herself with one hand. "Did you see the shoulders on that man?"

Tana felt her cheeks heat more, even though she had no reason to feel anything about any of this, damn it.

"Aren't you two supposed to be in committed relationships?" She raised both arms in exasperation and marched past them to drop into one of the easy chairs near the front windows. She made a point of lowering the blinds so the view to the street was shut out. "What do you care what he looks like?"

Her friends followed her into the great room, the scent of popcorn drifting up from the kitchen telling her that there'd been a recent batch made. Her stomach growled, reminding her that she would have normally gone out to dinner by now with her castmates.

"I fell in love, Tana," Blair explained patiently, referring to the new man in her life. She dropped down onto one rolled arm of Tana's chair. "I didn't lose my senses. So how do you know him? Details, please."

Sable sat on the other chair arm so that Tana was bracketed by her friends. Their presence comforted her even as they tried to drag answers out of her. The realization of how much she'd grown to rely on these women in the short time they'd known one another had her chest tightening unexpectedly.

Growing up, friends were a luxury she couldn't afford because of her family's lifestyle. They'd never remained in one place for too long, so there'd been no opportunities to forge deeper connections. And even if there had been time, she couldn't confide anything about herself, not when she'd been part of a criminal enterprise. From a very young age, she'd known that her family wasn't like other people's.

So having Sable and Blair poking her for answers because they loved her? Maybe it wasn't so bad. She just didn't know how to tell them the story without revealing a criminal past…something she really wasn't ready to share.

"Okay." She huffed out a long breath and sat straighter in the chair, scooting up to sit on the edge. "Here's the deal. Chase Serrano was my first everything. First love. First boyfriend. First heartbreak…you get the idea. Basically, I screwed up with him, he hated me for it, I moved away, and we never spoke again until today."

There was a beat of silence, making her look up at her friends' faces to see their reactions.

Blair frowned, her blond eyebrows knit together. Sable reared back like she couldn't understand what Tana had said.

"You are a colossal failure at storytelling," Sable announced. "Shouldn't the ability to hold an audience be part of an actor's gift?"

Blair turned on the arm of the chair so that she faced Tana fully. "You don't want to tell us what happened in the past. That's okay." She lounged sideways, leaning an elbow into the chair back as if there would be lots more talking to come. "Just tell us what happened today."

Sable mirrored the posture, propping herself on her elbow and resting her dark head on her palm. "Right. How did he find you after hating you for so long? Or maybe more importantly, *why* did he want to find you?"

"And did he ride a horse into Brooklyn Bridge Park at any time?" Blair wanted to know.

Tana slumped back in the easy chair again, so that their heads were all just inches apart for this conversation. She was the one clearly in the hot seat, but she still found herself wishing she had her video camera rolling to record the moment. She could imagine exactly how she'd block the scene to have all three faces in the shot.

She'd have proof on film that she had friends. Good friends who believed in her.

Closing her eyes, she allowed herself to mentally record what was happening. Somehow, the trick made it easier to talk.

"Picture this. Me on stage, delivering my final killer line as Blanche DuBois. I walk off, all smiles and sunshine. Then I return for the bows and I see him, front and center in the lower orchestra seats." She didn't bother to explain where that was in a theater. Her friends had helped her rehearse enough times that they knew more than they ever wanted to about the theater world. "The sexiest man I've ever met, Stetson and all, glaring at me like he's come to dole out vengeance for my…past transgressions."

She couldn't bring herself to share her past with them. Couldn't jeopardize the good opinions they had of her.

"Oh. Shivers," Blair said softly.

"I take back what I said about your storytelling," Sable added from Tana's other side. "What did you do?"

"Duh. I ran off stage as fast as possible and thought I made a clean getaway." Tana wondered if he'd seen her the whole time. He'd probably clocked the Airstream trailer before he even watched the show. "Then suddenly there he was, walking me home because he came to New York specifically for me. To…settle an old score."

She forced her eyes open, knowing she couldn't just dream away the reality of what had transpired between them. Her gaze flipped from Blair's face to Sable's. Both women were watching her intently.

Both cared.

Her belly tightened at the thought of them finding out about her past. All the ways she'd hurt and disappointed people by being a Blackstone.

"What does that mean for you?" Sable asked. "Can you help this guy—Chase—with whatever it is that he wants?"

"Sure I can." She shoved to her feet, knowing that she couldn't afford to confide much more than that today. With any luck, she'd go to Nevada, sign over the land, and that would be the end of it. No harm, no foul. Her friends never had to know what she'd done to deserve Chase's anger. "I just have to fly to Nevada with him this weekend and pretend I'm his fiancée."

Jaws dropped.

When her friends recovered, the questions commenced.

"Is it to get a matchmaking mother off his back?" Sable proposed. "In the books I read, that's usually the reason someone wants to have a fake engagement."

Blair didn't give Tana time to answer before she pitched another possibility. "Or maybe he needs a fiancée to secure an inheritance from a rich relative. That's pretty old-school, but people can attach all kinds of crazy caveats to their wills."

"Honestly, I'm not sure." Tana knew he had an ulterior motive. He'd admitted to more than one. But she was at a disadvantage with him because she hadn't kept tabs on him over the years and didn't know much about how his life had changed. She needed to address that lack of knowledge before she saw him again and get busy with some research. "But I owe him a favor after the way things ended between us. So if he needs me to be a pretend fiancée, so be it. I'll be back in time for show rehearsal on Monday, and that's all that matters."

Her friends lobbied energetically for more details, but in the end, she convinced them to make dinner with her and drop the discussion for now. Grateful for the reprieve, she soaked up the time with them, knowing the whole while that her days of living outside the shadow of her past were numbered.

Midway through the flight from New York to the airport in Elko, Nevada, Chase studied his lone traveling companion from across the aisle of a friend's private plane.

He'd sent Tana the flight details two days ago, and she'd texted him back a single word of acknowledgment, making him wary that she'd back out of their agreement. But sure enough, she'd shown up on time in the car he'd sent for her to begin their cross-country venture. After choosing a spot on the eight-seat Gulfstream, she'd withdrawn a tablet from her lone bag and directed her attention to the screen.

Chase had let her be, reading her back-off vibe loud and clear, even without the ominous new tattoos designed to look like superhero bangles on her wrists. He'd been surprised to see the fresh ink at first, until he realized on closer inspection—okay, maybe he hadn't ignored her after all—that her tattoos were henna. Those that he'd noticed three days ago had faded a little. The bangles she'd added were darker. All of them looked hand-drawn, making him curious if she did them herself.

Making him even more curious to know if she had additional designs elsewhere on her body.

Dragging his thoughts from such tempting speculation, he continued to take her in. She'd refreshed the pink strands in her glossy brown hair since he'd seen her last. She'd ditched the clunky combat boots in favor of pink high-top sneakers completely covered with silver spikes. Combined with her black skinny jeans and a worn T-shirt from a West Coast Day of the Dead festival, she'd clearly dressed to send a message.

But he refused to allow himself to be distracted by something so superficial. The first time he'd met Tana, she'd turned his head so thoroughly he had missed what was happening right under his nose in his mother's life. If he'd learned one thing eight years ago, it was not to fall for misdirection. When a con artist drew your attention to what was in the right hand, you'd damned well better look at what was in the left.

With that in mind, he steeled himself for conversation. Now that they neared their weekend destination, he needed to outline a few ground rules to keep things on track. He was in charge of how things shook down at Cloverfield this time.

Chase reached into his jacket to produce the ring box he'd stashed when a photo on Tana's tablet screen caught his eye.

A picture of him.

"You're googling me?" he found himself asking in spite of his efforts not to let her distract him.

Tana didn't even glance his way. She kept her head down, attention ostensibly focused on the screen, though her hair hid her features from view.

"Just trying to even the odds," she murmured offhandedly, trailing a finger over the tablet to scroll down a page. She wore a delicate chain around her wrist that connected to a second chain around her middle finger. The jewelry had one silver charm of an eye that lay flat on the back of her hand. "You know everything about me since we parted, but I know nothing about you. This consumer education website you put together, for example, is all news to me."

Chase forced his gaze away from her to stare out

the plane window. Thin wisps of clouds seem to cling to the aircraft.

"Since I gained no satisfaction from mounting a civil suit against your missing father, I thought I'd at least warn other vulnerable people about the kinds of scam artists out there." His research on the subject had been appalling. "It's disheartening to learn how many ways people avoid honest labor by cheating their neighbors."

A beat of silence followed his words. But when Tana spoke again, she didn't bother arguing with him.

"And it looks like your ex-girlfriend is getting married this weekend." Tana recrossed her legs in a way that put one pink-sneakered foot in the aisle between them. "How is Ashley, anyway?"

Irritation flared in Chase, both at the mention of the other woman's name and at the reminder that Tana had once known so much about him. He'd confided in her about his complicated relationship with the daughter of the richest man in the northern half of the state. Ashley Carmichael was a spoiled daddy's girl, used to having her own way. She'd taken it poorly when Chase had broken things off to be with Tana. So, too, had her powerful father. Warren Carmichael had swindled him at cards when Chase was at his lowest point in life. And the bastard had continued doing everything he could to sabotage Chase's business interests ever since.

So Chase had been more than a little surprised to receive an invitation to his former girlfriend's nuptials.

"You'll find out soon enough." He reached into his pocket again, ready to put the next step of his plan in motion. "But you'll need this first."

He thrust the ring box across the aisle to her, setting it on top of her tablet without touching her. After the almost-kiss in front of her brownstone earlier in the week, he knew his resistance to this woman's touch was not as strong as he would have preferred.

She swung surprised eyes toward him. "I hope you're not suggesting there's a visit with your horrible ex-girlfriend in my future."

He arched an eyebrow. Letting her put the pieces together for herself.

Her jaw dropped open a moment later.

"Oh. My. God." Tana gripped the ring box in one fist without opening it. Without taking her fathomless brown gaze off him. "*Please* do not tell me that you dragged me all the way across the country to attend Ashley Freaking Carmichael's wedding with you."

"You're perfectly dressed for it, actually." In a week full of vengeance schemes and righting the wrongs of his past, Chase could hardly be blamed for taking whatever pleasure he could out of the situation. And the vision of Tana in her new tough-girl incarnation on his arm this weekend was definitely cause for a grin. "I'd take great personal satisfaction if you show up to the reception in studded pink high tops."

She scowled hard at him, banging the ring box against her tablet like a gavel. "You asked me to straighten out the land deal, not mince around some society princess's bridezilla nightmare."

"You don't need to mince," he assured her, unexpectedly glad to have someone on his arm tomorrow who would dread the company as much as him. "And you knew that I had more than one reason for asking you to pose as my fiancée. This is one of them."

She huffed out a long breath, her glare fading by degrees, replaced by a fleeting look of genuine worry.

That expression, however brief, stirred apprehension. He might want to settle a debt with Tana for her deceit, but at the moment, it occurred to him he didn't want to cause the kind of pain he'd just glimpsed.

A moment later, her face cleared. "Fine. But I'm not going to play Cinderella for you to dress me up in fancy clothes when I don't want to attend this thing in the first place."

"And you call yourself an actress?" he teased. "But no worries. I don't think I'd know how to carry over your aesthetic into formalwear anyhow."

Once again, she didn't take the bait, making him aware that by being petty, he revealed too much of his own bitterness. Even now, after he'd schooled himself on the tactics of con artists, he'd forgotten one of the most important rules: keep personal feelings out of it.

The woman next to him sure did.

"I can play a role for you, Chase." The seriousness in her tone had him reevaluating her. No matter what message her new look sent to the world, there was an extremely clever, clearheaded woman beneath the facade. "But I need to understand the objective first."

"No." He refused to bring her into his plans. "I can't trust you with that. It's enough that you're by my side tomorrow. I want Warren Carmichael to think we're a couple, and that we've been back together for months."

She nodded. "I can do that. But I need some particulars so we keep our stories straight. How did we meet up again?"

Her keen attention reminded him of old times. When he'd taught her how to ride, she hadn't just jumped on the back of a horse. She'd taken time to learn how to care for an animal. How to saddle it properly and speak soothingly to it.

Out of the blue, he suddenly recalled that he'd remarked on her attention to those details. She'd told him that she'd had so few possessions in life that it had taught her to be respectful with the things she had, and anything she cared for even temporarily. For a long time, he'd dismissed everything she'd said to him during that summer as lies. But now he wondered if that had been true.

Or was her concern about his goal this weekend just another smokescreen?

"Let's keep it simple. How about we say that I met you at a play you were doing?" He wasn't worried about a cover story since he didn't plan to stick around the wedding for long. He just wanted to make an appearance to put Warren Carmichael on notice.

The plane bumped along an air pocket, causing Chase to reach across the aisle on instinct. His hand landed on her forearm before he recalled what a bad idea it was to touch her.

Already, his fingers flexed automatically, seeking more of her smooth skin before he hauled his hand away again.

She glanced down at her arm where his fingers had been just a moment before. Then she shook her head.

"*Streetcar* is my first real show, though, and it only started four weeks ago. How about we say I looked you up at your office downtown after I read about you online? I sought you out to apologize for the past and we—you know." Her eyes found his, heat flickering in their depths. "Reconnected."

The temperature spiked between them as memories flooded his brain. They'd shared hot, passionate nights that lasted into the next day. Their affair had been all-consuming. It took him several moments to get his tongue unstuck enough to answer her.

"Yeah. We'll go with that." His voice rasped with

the remembered attraction. He needed to move the conversation away from those dangerous thoughts. "You should put the ring on. We'll be landing soon."

He didn't even watch as she cracked open the lid on the box, the hinges making a soft sound. Chase closed his eyes for the landing, reminding himself this weekend was not about the connection he still felt with Tana Blackstone.

It wasn't about remembering how soft her lips were when she kissed him. Or how fully she surrendered herself to him in his arms. Or how he'd never found any other woman to match her. None of his relationships since her had compared, and how messed up was that when his relationship with Tana hadn't even been real?

He was simply bringing her to Nevada to help him recover the rest of what she'd stolen from him. Once that was done, he'd make the most of the engagement to lure her father back to American soil to finally face legal and civil charges.

Then he could walk away for good.

Four

An hour later, seated in Chase's Ford pickup truck that was so big she'd practically needed a stepladder to haul herself into it, Tana stared down at the breathtaking engagement ring on her finger. The late-day sun shot prisms of light off the facets as they approached Cloverfield Ranch.

Chase had passed the ring to her with such a total lack of ceremony—slapping the box onto her tablet back on the plane—that she hadn't been sure how to react. Especially when she'd seen the cushion-cut double halo ring with pink diamonds in platinum. It was a description she would have never called up from her personal knowledge, but a quick photo sent in a group text to Sable and Blair had revealed the details, set off with dozens of exclamation points and heart emojis.

Tana only knew it was gorgeous. And for the life of her, she couldn't understand why Chase would put her in possession of something so valuable when he clearly thought she was little better than a common thief. Maybe he was trying to trap her into bolting with the thing, then have her arrested.

With a sigh, she returned to the view of the dramatic Humboldt Range outside the pickup's windshield as they neared their destination.

Her fingers twitched over her bag with the need to find her camcorder and capture what she saw, but how would that look to her surly and silent travel companion? No doubt he'd accuse her of wanting to commemorate a con or something equally dire, which hurt more than it should. In truth, she simply wished to hold this image in her mind, the soaring mountains serving as a backdrop to green hillsides dotted with grazing brown cows. The colors were so rich it looked like someone had turned on a filter to enhance them. Something about the expansive vistas made her want to take deep, healing breaths, as if the air alone could soothe a soul.

Foolishness, really, considering this was the site of one of her father's worst crimes. She should feel uneasy, perhaps, sensing that Chase grew more agitated the closer they came to Cloverfield. Yet all she felt at the moment was a satisfied sense that she hadn't dreamed how stunning this place had been. In the intervening years, she'd sometimes wondered if she'd only imagined the magnetic draw of it, her vision too influenced by how happy she'd been during the brief months she'd spent here.

But she hadn't dreamed it. The remote corner of northern Nevada where Cloverfield sat remained the most spectacularly beautiful place she'd ever seen.

"Anything look familiar yet?" Chase's voice called her from her musing as he downshifted before the turn-off to a private road.

If Tana's friends had thought he looked like a Western gunslinger when they saw him three days ago, she wondered what they'd say if they spotted him now. Dressed in dark jeans that clung to strong thighs, Chase wore boots and a fitted Western shirt in a shade of gray that made his eyes look almost silver. He hadn't worn his black Stetson on the plane, but it went on his head the moment they'd stepped on the tarmac, and it remained there now, shading those stormy eyes. The Patek Philippe watch he'd worn in the city had been replaced with a sturdy-looking vintage piece with a thick leather strap.

"Of course I recognize the area." Attempting to keep her tone neutral, she wasn't ready to let him see all the ways this drive had already affected her when she hadn't worked out her emotions for herself yet. No matter what her father had done here, this was the place where Tana had known more happiness than any other. "The cabin Dad rented that summer is up here on the left."

Her stomach tightened, preparing for a barb about her father. She understood Chase's anger. He was entitled to it. She just wished he didn't color her with the same brush as her felon parent. Chase would never understand how hard she'd worked to separate herself from the past.

"Not anymore, it isn't." He slowed the truck for the rougher road they now traveled. "The first thing I did when I bought back the land was raze the building."

She blinked at the harshness of the sentence for a house that was—after all—an inanimate object and not responsible for her father's crime. A moment later, the spot where the cabin should have stood came into view. The old horseshoe driveway remained, along with the western juniper tree that used to shade the front bedroom that had once been hers.

But the small log structure was gone. In its place, a handful of work vehicles were parked in the shade of the juniper. A dump truck and utility van were flanked by pickups with beds full of orange cones, shovels and a couple of wheelbarrows.

"I'm surprised you could tear it down. I was under the impression it was historic." She knew much of the ranch dated from the 1800s, including the stone-block home where Chase's mother had lived.

"It's not as old as it looks. I just had to pull a permit to take it down, and the appraiser's office confirmed the structure was more recent." Chase shifted again, one knuckle grazing her knee. "Less than a century old."

The warmth of his hand against the denim sent a bolt of reaction through her thigh, tickling her in places that had gone a long, long time without tickling of any kind.

This was going to be a rough weekend if she couldn't rein that in.

She crossed her legs. Tightly.

"So you didn't destroy any history, you just tore down something perfectly good to make way for something fancier. Sounds like the Hamptons are wearing off on you."

His chuckle surprised her. "As it happened, I made a nice chunk of change selling the reclaimed wood from the cabin. There's a good market for wood that looks like it has a history even if it doesn't."

"Sort of like me." She propped an elbow on the truck door and kept her gaze trained outside. Away from her ex-lover and the appealing sound of his laughter. "I may appear to have a suspect past when I'm actually just the offspring of criminals. Looks can be deceiving, you know."

When he didn't answer at first, she assumed he

wasn't going to reply. But after passing an equipment barn and what used to be the foreman's house, Chase finally cleared his throat.

"I am aware of that." He glanced over at her, the weight of his stare making the fine hairs on the back of her neck stand up even though she kept her attention fixed outside. "Logically, I understand you can't be held responsible for your father's actions."

"And yet you blame me." She hadn't expected him to have some big epiphany about her this weekend, but she couldn't help feeling frustrated that he wanted to remind her at every turn that he held the past against her. "Considering we have to get through a wedding tomorrow as a couple, it might help build the illusion of romance if you quit reminding me I'm the root of all your misfortune."

"Right. Agreed." The sincerity in his voice had her turning her head to look at him.

Sure enough, he appeared almost…chastened?

"Really?" She shifted on the seat as the main house came into sight. "You think I'm right?"

Parking the vehicle, Chase switched off the ignition and gave her his undivided attention.

"I took your advice to heart when we spoke that evening outside your brownstone. You said I needed to prepare for my role, and I plan to do just that."

"Well then. That's good." She smoothed a nervous hand through her hair, unsure how to respond. She'd been so busy bracing for confrontational Chase that she suddenly had no clue how to cope with cooperative Chase.

"You said we should practice being a couple," he reminded her, moving one long arm to rest along the back of her seat.

Not touching her. But the nearness of his hand, the *potential* for touching, sent a little shock wave through her system.

"I—don't think that's what I said." Memories of the almost-kiss loomed large in her brain.

That moment had started out like this one. They'd been face-to-face then, too. Her knees had gone weak that day when he cupped her chin, tilting her face up to his. Embarrassingly, she'd about chewed her bottom lip raw that night in an unconscious effort to taste him where he'd touched her.

"Maybe you said we should *rehearse* our role as a couple," he clarified, pushing up the brim of his Stetson a fraction with the passing of his thumb over his forehead. "Either way, the implication was clear."

Her heart thumped so loudly she suspected she'd missed approximately every other word out of his mouth. In New York, she deflected men as easily as breathing, with a prickly vibe built into everything about her appearance and manner. But the skill eluded her with Chase, as if her body refused to transmit the don't-touch signals she sent to everyone else.

It was annoying.

"What implication?" She stared, wide-eyed, at him.

"That we should get comfortable around each other." He reached across the truck cab to lay his palm on her knee. The warm weight anchored her to the spot even as it kicked her pulse into a staccato beat.

She might have protested the casual way he touched her—deftly setting fire to her senses even as he seemed unaffected—except her tongue remained glued to the roof of her mouth.

"You had a good point about that," he continued, his

thumb sliding back and forth along the seam of denim just inside her knee.

A caress that should not have been so damned potent. *Focus.*

"Are you regarding this as rehearsal?" she finally managed, glancing down at his wandering hand. "Because I'm not sure winding me up is the same thing as making me feel comfortable around you."

His thumb went still as his gray eyes darkened.

"I look forward to hearing all about the difference after we get settled." His voice smoked along her senses before he eased back.

Then, after opening the driver's-side door, he exited the vehicle, leaving her hot and bothered as well as confused. She hated not knowing his endgame for this engagement, but she couldn't deny that being around him again aroused her.

That was dangerous for her peace of mind.

So when he opened the passenger door to help her down, Tana was careful to let go of his hand the moment her feet hit the ground. She might be a good actress, but if Chase kept touching her this weekend, she couldn't possibly pretend to be unaffected.

Everything about having Tana back at Cloverfield Ranch felt surreal.

Chase wandered the exposed stone hallways of his historic birthplace while he waited for her to unpack and settle into the guest room. He'd only brought her into his childhood home a couple of times when they'd been dating that long-ago summer. He'd lived in the bunkhouse he was remodeling, for one thing. Only his mother had resided in the main house. Besides, Chase and Tana had spent more time horseback riding or hiking. Occasionally, they'd attended bonfires and picnics with other locals close to their own age.

But he'd made dinner for both Tana and his mother once in this house. Tana had stayed afterward to help him clean up, and then they'd slow-danced around the firepit in the backyard. Another time, Tana had brought his mother wildflowers she'd picked on one of their hikes, and Chase had been convinced his then-girlfriend would be in his life for years to come.

A doorknob turned in the room down the hallway, wrenching him from memories he didn't want to revisit now.

Tana peeked out the doorway, a scowl furrowing her forehead. "Hey, Serrano. I thought I said I wasn't going to play Cinderella this weekend."

He'd known she would give him flak about the evening wear he'd stocked in the wardrobe for her since he hadn't warned her about the wedding. He pretended interest in the view out the gabled window at the far end of the corridor, keeping his tone easy.

"Suit yourself if you want to wear the high tops," he told her blandly. "Or else I can drive you into downtown Elko tomorrow to see what you can purchase off the rack. Though, keep in mind, they may not have the selection you're used to in New York."

He turned toward her while she made a garbled sound of exasperation, vanishing into the room as she continued to speak.

"You realize every outfit in here looks straight out of the cartoon princess collection?" She reappeared on the threshold of the door, thrusting out a gold gown on a padded hanger. "Look at this."

The garment was beautiful by any standards. A handmade designer original. He wouldn't know how to describe it, but the layers of beaded tulle and the floral embroidery spoke of careful craftsmanship.

"Is it the wrong size?" He slowly walked toward her, trying to get his bearings in the conversation. All the while, he kept thinking about how lovely she looked with her hair piled on top of her head, a pair of cat-eye glasses on her nose, the frames a pink leopard print. "I fail to see what's wrong with it."

"What's wrong?" She clutched the waist to her slender middle and stared down at the effect of the gown pressed to her body. "I'll look entirely too precious for anyone to believe I'm not playing a part."

He stopped just shy of the door frame, the whitewashed guest room already bearing a hint of her citrus and amber fragrance even though she'd cracked the windows overlooking the backyard, letting the scent of fresh-cut hay into the room. Behind her, he saw the contents of her dark leather overnight bag spilled on the white duvet, a few T-shirts tangled with jeans and a black lace lingerie set that had him mentally undressing her so he could imagine it on her.

"I see what you mean," he forced himself to say past a dry throat. "Maybe you can accessorize with a spiked collar and boots."

Her gaze flew to his, her dark eyes assessing him through the funky glasses. She frowned for a moment, then huffed out a long sigh.

"Sorry for being an ingrate. The gowns are beautiful and I'm sure I'll find something suitable for the wedding." She backed deeper into the room before opening the door of the rustic cypress wardrobe and hanging the dress inside.

She withdrew a pink dress and held it up for inspection.

"Wait a minute. What just happened there?" He

dragged his gaze from the lingerie—how had it returned to the black lace without his permission?—and watched Tana. "You went from railing at me over the gowns to thanking me."

"I'm practicing what I preach." She padded over to the bed and laid down the gown to study it, her bare feet with pink toenails a curiously intimate sight. "I'm letting you see more sides of my personality so you're comfortable with me tomorrow when we have to be a couple in public. I do have an agreeable side, you know."

He wasn't sure how much to believe her anymore between her acting skills, her past as a grifter and her vaguely hostile attitude toward him. An attitude he was no doubt responsible for inciting.

But now that he was close to achieving the first of his objectives in the form of attending the wedding with Tana, Chase was prepared to cultivate a facade of romance and passion with her.

Not that they'd be sticking around the reception long enough to show it off. But why not reap some pleasure during this time together since the attraction between them was—to his surprise and confusion—still very much alive.

"I appreciate that." He stepped over the threshold into the guest room while she straightened the tangle of other clothes still cluttering the bed. "Both the agreeable aspect and the effort required to bring it to the fore."

His heart slugged heavily against the inside of his chest at his proximity to her. He stopped near the foot of the old-fashioned wrought-iron bedstead, his gaze dropping to the curve of her neck bared by the way she'd pinned her hair in a twist.

She'd changed into an oversize lounge T-shirt while she unpacked, the ivory boatneck collar slipping off one shoulder. There was something vulnerable-looking about the back of a neck. Something that made him want to step behind her and shield her. Right before he kissed the spot.

He breathed in the fresh air drifting through the cracked window in an attempt to cool himself down.

"If you don't love the clothes, you should take it up with your roommate," he found himself saying, fingers reaching through the wrought iron to smooth a silk ruffle hem on the pink gown that lay discarded there, one of six he'd requested so that she had a choice of wardrobe for the wedding.

"Excuse me?" She swung to face him, planting her fists on her hips.

"I read the articles about how you won the spot in your apartment, and there were profiles of your roommates online. One makeup artist. One fashion stylist." No doubt he'd read more about Tana Blackstone than was strictly necessary.

He shouldn't have found her movements after she left Nevada so interesting, but his curiosity had been avid. And now that he stood before the woman herself—as intrigued by her as ever—he had to ask himself if he'd craved this meeting with her as much as he craved vengeance.

"Blair and Sable," she murmured, half to herself. Then, lifting an eyebrow, she cocked her head to one side. "You spoke to them?"

"I messaged with the stylist and asked if I could hire her services to assist with a wardrobe for you this weekend. She seemed very enthusiastic."

Her eyes narrowed. "Are you telling me she knew I was attending a wedding before I did?"

"She did. She commented that she's been dreaming

of dressing you. Her exact words." He'd trusted her friend to at least know Tana's sizes, but Sable Cordero had proven keenly efficient at her job, sending shoes and accessories along with the outfits from a handful of fashion houses, including the designer she worked for.

"That explains a lot," she muttered drily as she re-folded a T-shirt, the engagement ring he'd given her casting sparkles in the sunlight. "I'll remember who to blame when I show up at the reception looking like Elsa. Now, if only I knew who I'm putting on the fian-cée show for."

He ground his teeth at the thought of seeing his local nemesis. But the time had come to share the target with her.

"Ashley's father. Warren Carmichael." Briefly, he outlined how the man had tied up thousands of Chase's acres in a baseless land dispute, contesting grazing per-mits and bringing the federal Bureau of Land Manage-ment down on Chase's head. "I've spent a small fortune on legal fees already, but Warren seems determined to undermine me as often as possible."

While he spoke, Tana had given up all pretense of organizing her clothes. She looked up at him now with thoughtful brown eyes. "So how will it help to have me as your fiancée?"

"Remember the piece of land that you're signing over to me?" He wondered if Joe Blackstone had any idea how valuable that particular piece of property was. If he had, wouldn't he have clued in his daughter some-how in the intervening years?

Suspicion simmered in the back of his mind even while he battled a fierce attraction to the woman be-side him. He remembered how her eyelashes had flut-tered when he'd touched her knee in the truck earlier, and knew that the chemistry between them was a caress away from igniting again.

"Of course I do." She nodded, full lips pursed.

"About half of it is at the center of the dispute between Warren and me. He's had an investigator trying to discover the identity of the owner for as long as I have. I just found you sooner."

She shook her head, the hair twisted at the back of her head wobbling with the motion. "I still don't see how it makes any earthly difference if we're engaged since I volunteered to sign it all over to you in the first place."

Maybe it was because they'd been standing next to a bed this whole time, but her declaration sent a surge of longing through him. Something about her willingness to do what he wanted sparked the latent attraction until it blazed up his spine.

"Warren will stop at nothing to win the personal war against me." He resented everything about Chase, from the time he'd broken things off with Warren's daughter, to the audacity of Chase's bid to regain lands Warren had run roughshod over for a decade, grazing his cattle illegally. "That could mean he would harass you in ways I can't predict. Our engagement sends a message up front that you're under my protection. Also that I've already won this round."

He'd edged closer to her while he spoke, more than ready to test the authenticity of their connection before they put it on public display.

"Ah. How very caveman of you. I'm a symbolic prize, then." She licked her upper lip as he neared her, a quick, nervous swipe.

Or was that anticipation?

"To the victor belong the spoils." He wasn't sure why

he said it when he hadn't planned to rile her up. He just wanted to kiss that spot she'd licked.

But getting under her skin let him see more of her character. She revealed more about herself when he baited her.

"I'll certainly be dressed like a hapless war prize if I wear one of the dresses Sable chose." She fingered a loose lock of hair that trailed along her neck, not sounding terribly upset about the role he wanted her to play. "But I draw the line at being carried off and ravished."

"I never suggested any such thing," he reminded her, reaching to take the lock of hair from her fingers so he could repeat the action. He smoothed the strands between his thumb and forefinger, rubbing the silky length. "Although I find it gratifying your mind went there. I was thinking more along the lines of a kiss than a full-on ravishing. But I could be persuaded."

The fire in her eyes leaped as she tipped her head up to look at him. A vein in her neck throbbed with a fast-pounding pulse and he wanted nothing so much as to cover that spot with his lips. To feel the warmth of her on his tongue.

"Is this another game for you? Trying to make me feel some of the old draw between us?"

They were so close now he could feel her soft exhales on his knuckles where he toyed with her glossy dark hair.

"This is no game. I want to kiss you, Tana. So very much."

She gripped the shoulders of his shirt, tugging him closer still. "Then for crying out loud, please hurry up."

Five

Tana didn't wait for an answer.

One second she was talking to Chase beside the bed in the guest room. The next she propelled herself up against him, flying into his arms to press her mouth to his.

Heat rushed through her limbs, circled her chest, pooled deep in her belly as their lips met. The past merged with the present; her best memories all included this man and the kind of kisses he'd taught her during one unforgettable summer.

She'd never gotten him out of her head. They'd been so young, but he'd been the first to kiss her like she was a woman. The first to show her the wonder of her own body. She'd gone on to compare every man to him afterward, and no one had come close to matching the heat and passion he inspired.

He did not disappoint now, either.

While she arched into him with an urgency that

surely communicated how much she wanted him, Chase seemed to channel all his energies on delivering the perfect mating of mouths. His tongue stroked over her lips in a way that had her trembling, partly because the memories of that first kiss were still so potent.

But also because Chase at twenty-six years old was a different sensory experience than Chase at eighteen. The lithe grace of youth had hardened into steely muscle that flexed and shifted against her as he moved. The gentle scrape of his jaw—cleanly shaven when she'd first met him this morning—was shadowed with bristles when she ran a hand along his face.

His lips were as gentle as ever, though. His tongue every bit as sensual, teasing hers into a dance that slowly set her on fire through a delicious give-and-take. Stroking. Licking. Sucking lightly.

She gripped his shoulders through the cotton button-down, needing an anchor when she feared she might float away on a tide of longing.

Longing for heat. Connection. A moment when she felt like she could be herself and not have to put up a facade...

At that thought, her blood chilled. She forced herself back a step, breaking the kiss. Shattering the moment.

"What are we doing?"

The words were wheezed out from burning lungs. Possibly she'd forgotten to breathe while Chase kissed her.

Coming back to herself, she took in his gray eyes, still a little molten. Other than that, she saw no sign of the inferno that had just scorched her inside and out.

"I think we were preparing ourselves for tomorrow." He backed up a step, scratching his thumb along his forehead while he seemed to contemplate her.

Her heart still galloped too fast. Her lips tingled where his mouth had met hers. The urge to touch the spot was almost overwhelming, but she managed to turn her attention back to the task of organizing her things.

She needed to keep her hands busy to prevent herself from touching Chase again.

"Did we learn anything useful?" she asked, shaking out a folded shirt so she could fold it again.

"Only that we won't have to fake the sparks between us." He backed up another step, nearing the door. "That part comes naturally enough."

She swung her head toward him to gauge his expression. He appeared sincere if a bit rueful.

Yeah. She related.

Without answering, she returned to her task, giving her full attention to relocating her underwear to a dresser drawer.

He paused at the threshold of her door. "I'll leave you to get settled. The groom in the stable will help you if you'd like to ride later. Dinner is at seven."

"Thank you. A ride sounds nice actually." She hadn't been on horseback since she left Cloverfield, and she'd missed it.

Or maybe she just missed anything that she used to do with Chase Serrano and the fleeting, fragile happiness she'd once felt with him.

Should she invite him to ride with her? She opened her mouth to frame the question, but her companion had already gone.

The hallway outside her room remained silent, but Tana's nerves were jangled as she recalled the way that kiss had made her feel. Chase was the only man who'd ever quieted her insides to the point where she didn't feel like an imposter in life.

Sadly, he only wanted her for her ability to play a role. And she would be wise to remember that.

Dressed in his wedding guest finery the next afternoon, Chase extended his hand to help Tana from the hired Land Rover in front of Briar Creek Ranch, home of his local nemesis.

"This is a private residence?" Her brown eyes were wide as she took in everything from the valet service implemented for the special occasion to the scale of the main ranch house near the pristine barn built solely as a special events venue.

"Believe it or not, yes. This is a working cattle ranch, but Warren Carmichael purposely overbuilt the place so he could always host his political cronies." Chase's gaze swept over Tana in her cream silk gown printed with big roses, a small train attached to the fitted sheath.

Her pink pumps and square clutch were equally elegant, but he'd noticed she wore a thin band of cream-colored leather strapped around one wrist that featured tiny gold spikes. The piece was so narrow it blended with a collection of more traditional chains encircling the same wrist. How well her friend must know Tana to have sent the accessory that was a throwback to the style she normally embraced.

She looked so stunning, in fact, he sort of wished she'd gone with the jeans and high tops. Although considering how many times he'd relived the kiss they shared the night before, he suspected he would have found her appealing no matter what.

"Clearly he's done well for himself," Tana observed. "I've seen luxury venues in Las Vegas that weren't this elaborate." She allowed him to tuck her hand into his elbow for the walk down the red carpet that led from the valet stand toward the nearby barn, where the huge doors were thrown open to guests.

Mellow country music sounded inside the barn, the strains of a fiddle blending with the crooning of a female singer as guests began arriving for the reception. On the hill outside the barn, Chase could see liveried waitstaff passing hors d'oeuvres and trays of champagne to guests milling around. He smoothed a hand down the lapel of his classic black Tom Ford tuxedo as he leaned closer to Tana to speak more quietly.

"Warren has sealed more than one deal favorable to his land by inviting key local figures to the ranch for weekends spent shooting and playing cards." Chase warded off the old fury about one card game in particular while he tracked the guests mingling under a juniper tree off to one side of the barn. He needed to mentally prepare himself for whatever Carmichael had up his sleeve today.

Their enmity had never been a secret over the last eight and a half years, so Chase couldn't be sure why Warren had invited him in the first place. Unless Ashley just wanted to flaunt her marriage to some rich dude. Not that Chase cared.

Beside him, Tana stiffened. "Cards? I hope you know I don't play." She made a small sound of disgust. "Not anymore, at least."

Chase didn't plan to address that statement at the moment, clearly a jab to get a reaction from him, maybe even start an argument that would let her off the hook as his date. She was by his side today, and that was enough. He wouldn't push her about the role he hoped she'd play in the rest of his agenda.

Especially not when he couldn't stop thinking about how she'd tasted when he kissed her.

They'd just reached the perimeter of the festivities when a shrill female gasp sounded a few feet away.

"Tana Thorpe? Is that really you?"

Chase's blood cooled at the sound of his ex-girlfriend's voice. Turning, he spotted the bride as she peeled away from her new groom and walked toward them, the skirt of her two-piece wedding gown billowing around her while the crop top showed off a band of bare skin. She'd dispensed with her bouquet of peach roses along with her pleasant veneer, openly scowling at Tana.

"Tana Blackstone, actually," Chase's date answered in a sweeter voice than he'd ever heard issue from her mouth. He almost did a double take, but managed to restrain himself while she extended a hand toward the other woman. "Congratulations on your marriage, Ashley."

Ashley Carmichael did not take Tana's hand. "Blackstone, of course. How could I forget the name of the woman who duped Chase?"

Ashley's gaze swept over him, still hostile after all these years. She was accustomed to having whatever—and whomever—she chose, so Chase's defection had wounded her pride.

He would have responded, but Tana seemed determined to keep the other woman's focus on her.

"I assure you my heart was broken far more than Chase's," Tana confided like they were longtime besties. "But that's so long in the past, and I want you to know you're one of the loveliest brides I've ever seen."

Surprise made Ashley's blue eyes track back and forth between them, clearly wary. But in the end, she patted the blond updo at the back of her head, where it had been interwoven with tiny white flowers.

"The gown was custom-made for me," she informed them, apparently taking the compliment at face value. "I insisted on the three-dimensional floral embroidery in the bodice and the Chantilly lace in the skirt." She swayed a little, as if for effect, making the skirt layers shift around her legs.

Impatient and wanting to put the confrontation with her father behind him, Chase was about to ask after him when Tana murmured encouraging comments about the gown.

"It suits you perfectly. I love the big bow tied with the excess fabric on the back of the bodice." Tana turned her melting-chocolate eyes up to him, smiling as she laid her left hand on his shoulder in a way that put her engagement ring on display. "I only hope my gown is half as pretty when Chase and I get married."

The bride's silence was so pronounced he had no choice but to shift his attention away from Tana to observe the other woman. Ashley's face had gone pale, her lips set in a hard, thin line.

"You have some nerve, Chase Serrano." The bride skewered him with one look, her raised voice attracting some attention from other members of the bridal party still posing for photos in front of a split rail fence along the edge of a picturesque field. "You're going to marry *her*?"

Her tone was so openly venomous Chase found himself wrapping a protective arm around Tana.

"I am. Thanks again for inviting us, Ashley. We'll let you return to your other guests." Without waiting for an answer, he tugged Tana away, hurrying her into the dim interior of the barn.

Peach and white roses clung to every surface. Arrangements swathed the rafters, circled the freestanding candelabra, and wreathed the mounted elk's head over the huge stone fireplace. A fire was already burning in preparation for the cooling evening temperatures.

The band played in a far corner of the room, the dance floor empty save an older couple circling slowly. The sight of the white-haired pair, laughing at some private joke while they danced, gave Chase a pang over how lightly he'd been treating the idea of marriage.

"I'm ready for a performance critique." Tana stopped near the seating chart and ran an idle finger over the tables. She appeared lost in thought over the table arrangements while she prodded him in a low voice. "How did I do? Is that the kind of thing you were expecting?"

The down-to-business tone shouldn't have surprised him anymore since he'd long known about her efficiency and willingness to work hard. But after the way she'd maneuvered Ashley so effortlessly, he found it hard to believe she would require feedback.

"You were exceptional." Palming the small of her back through the silk dress, he guided her toward their seats at table twelve, a round one in the back of the room.

He felt her startle a bit as she peered up at him.

Was that disbelief he read in her eyes?

"What? You don't believe me?" he asked as they reached the spots with their place cards.

She set her purse and thin shawl on a chair, the movement exposing an intricate crown and a small pair of wings tattooed between her shoulder blades. Unlike those he'd seen on her arms and neck before, this appeared permanent. When she straightened, the ink disappeared under her pink-streaked brown hair.

There was no point in taking a seat since the cocktail hour was still underway.

"I do. I'm just unaccustomed to words of approval." Lingering by the chair, she shrugged one shoulder in a gesture that appeared far from careless. "My dad perpetually found fault with me. I sold a character too hard, or I didn't sell it enough."

Anger leaped along Chase's nerves at the mention of the man, especially in this new context as antagonist to Tana.

"It hardly matters what a felon has to say about you or your talents," he bit out.

"When your father is the felon, it does. I may hate his crimes, but he was still the person who taught me how to make a peanut butter and jelly sandwich and tie my own shoes since my mother lacked any maternal instincts." Tana gave another awkward shrug, her delicate clavicle tilting with the movement and drawing his attention to the expanse of flawless skin above the bodice of her strapless gown. "Should we go take a photo in front of the rose wall?"

He recognized her obvious attempt to change the topic, yet he was inclined to let it pass until he had more time to mull over her difficult relationship with her family.

Whatever else might be an act with Tana, Chase believed those mixed feelings were real enough. The fact that she'd avoided any trouble with the law in the years since he'd known her spoke of a commitment to a more honest life. And his private investigator corroborated the idea of Alicia Blackstone not having much use for her only daughter. The guy had found very little evidence of phone calls or visits between the pair.

"As you wish. You should send a photo to Sable so she can see you in that gown." He wouldn't mind a copy of the image himself, because he had the feeling once

Tana signed over the piece of land to him, she would do her best to vanish from his life.

Of course, he would need her help for one more weekend.

His fingers shifted on her back as he walked with her toward the backdrop of flowers arranged for commemorative photos of the day, his fingers slipping lower to curve around her hip before he remembered himself.

How oddly natural it felt to touch her. To pull her close.

Her words from yesterday had played in an endless loop when he'd closed his eyes to go to sleep last night. *Please hurry up.*

No doubt she'd craved that kiss as much as him. And yet she'd been the one to pull away, as if she'd recalled some pressing reason why they couldn't indulge the attraction. He'd give his left arm to know what that was.

Now, waiting in a short line of couples who would pose in front of the floral wall beneath an elk antler archway, Chase used the time to get to know her better. The more he understood her, the better chance he had of getting past her boundaries. So that the next time he kissed her, she wouldn't want to pull away.

"I have a question for you." Angling toward her, he spoke the words into the top of her hair as they stood side by side. He hadn't let her go yet, more than content to hold her against him under the pretext of their engagement.

"That sounds ominous." She peered up at him. "Anytime you preface a question with a warning, it can't be good."

The lavishly decorated barn was filling with more guests, and the country band began playing more upbeat tunes. The older dancing couple gave way to a handful of two-stepping pairs. Chase made a mental note to ask Tana to dance since the need to have her in his arms that way simmered like a fever in his blood.

"You mentioned you don't play cards anymore," he began, shifting his head lower, so it remained close to her ear. "May I ask why not?"

He'd watched her play a few hands with his friends at a long-ago party and had been mesmerized by the way she handled the cards. No doubt that should have been a clue about her past. But after taking the first few hands, she'd folded early and walked away from the game. She hadn't even taken her winnings, which had caused a bit of a stir among the group, even though they'd only been playing for imported beers.

"How can you question why?" Frowning up at him, she folded her arms in a defiant position. "I told you I left that life behind, Chase. I never ran scams for the love of it. It was the family business, and I would have been abandoned to foster care or sent to juvie if I didn't comply."

He couldn't miss the tension vibrating through her words. He felt it humming in her skin like electricity.

Should he believe her? Even as he framed the thought in his mind, he knew that he did. She'd been a convenient scapegoat when her father left the country, especially when Chase had felt far more personally betrayed by her. Or, if he were being completely honest, he'd felt foolish about falling for her.

"I'm sorry." He flagged down a waiter passing by with a tray of champagne flutes and took two, handing one to Tana. "I've spent so much time thinking about the wrongs that were done to me, I never considered how difficult it might have been for you."

Her arms relaxed as she accepted the drink, though

her gaze remained wary as she lifted the glass to her lips and took a small sip.

"I was fed, clothed and loved—after a fashion. The moral compass I was given was obviously faulty, but I've worked hard to correct it. That's why I don't play cards anymore." She took another sip as they moved ahead in the line of people waiting for a photo.

The couple in front of them finished their pictures, and an attendant who managed the cameras waved Chase and Tana forward. They set their drinks on a table for that purpose, and for a moment, the activity gave him a chance to consider her words. Consider *her*. Tana Blackstone had surprised him in every possible way since he'd found her in Brooklyn Bridge Park. She was a different woman from the one he'd known eight years ago. Prickly and wary, yes. But also thoughtful and compassionate. She'd put effort into reforming her life once she'd left Nevada, and she'd done it without any help from her crooked family.

There was a lot to admire in that.

So as they wrapped their arms around each other for a photo in front of the peach and cream-colored roses, Chase allowed himself to simply enjoy the feel of her against his body. She was petite but fierce. She brandished her strength of character the same way she liked to flash the decorative spikes she favored.

And he was beginning to feel a few pangs of regret that he'd roped her into his plans for revenge. Especially when the next phase involved asking Tana to return to the poker table one last time.

After they finished their photo, the attendant encouraged them to input their email addresses on a small device so the images would be sent to them. Once they finished, Chase drew Tana toward their table again, but he took the long route behind one of the eight-foot-tall candelabra so he could say one more thing to her privately before they took their seats.

"For what it's worth, it's obvious to me that you've put a lot of distance between yourself and your family." He finished his champagne in a long swallow and set aside the glass to direct his full attention on her.

The surprised expression on her face made him all the more sorry that he hadn't told her sooner.

"You don't have to say that. I'm going to help you secure your land either way." The candlelight made her pale skin glow, bringing out the hint of a flush in her cheeks.

"I wouldn't say it if I didn't mean it," he said simply. "I wish I hadn't—"

Chase stopped himself abruptly as he glimpsed a gray-haired man in a flashy tuxedo rushing toward them, his hand-tooled leather boots clomping loudly across the barn floor.

"What is it?" Tana glanced over her shoulder, no doubt to see what had claimed his regard.

Wariness strained his shoulders, and he curled a steadying arm around the woman next to him.

"Brace yourself. Our host looks like he's coming over to greet us personally."

Six

Tana may have leaned into Chase's strength a little. How could she not take comfort from him when the father of the bride was stalking toward them, nostrils flaring like a charging bull?

Built like a boxer with a square face and thick neck, Warren Carmichael appeared out of sync with the ranching way of life. Tana couldn't envision him working his land with his scrupulously slicked-back hair and pale skin that didn't see much sun. His tuxedo and leather boots were both decorative to the point of being almost fussy. He wore a rodeo buckle beneath his open jacket, yet he sported cufflinks on a shirt that looked custom tailored.

Tana, who'd never shaken the habit of sizing up people quickly, pegged him as someone you didn't want to cross.

Their host raised his voice to be heard even before

he reached them. "When Ashley told me who you'd brought here tonight as your guest, I had to come see for myself."

Dark, beady eyes fixed on her, and a chill shivered over her skin.

"This is the same girl who turned your head away from my Ashley?" he continued, coming to an abrupt stop just inches from her while the wedding party started to file into the barn from outdoors to find their seats.

People were bound to overhear.

"I'm Tana Blackstone, and I'm twenty-six, Mr. Carmichael. Hardly a girl." Tana offered him her hand to shake. "You have a beautiful home."

The man, like his daughter earlier, ignored the friendly offering. Instead, he swung his head toward Chase.

"She's the landowner, isn't she?" He jutted his chin, everything about his posture aggressive. "I spent a small fortune to find out who was behind that trust, but you knew all along, didn't you?"

For a moment, Chase imagined what Warren would have done with that information if he'd discovered the truth first. Would he have confronted Tana? Attempted to trick her into signing over the land to him?

Could he have gone so far as to threaten her? Just the possibility made Chase want to rake the vision out of his eyes.

"No need to make a scene, Warren," Chase admonished the other man, trying to hold on to his cool. "You wouldn't want to upstage the bride on her special day."

The man frowned, but he did take a step back, the thought of upsetting his daughter clearly making an impact. For a moment, Tana couldn't help but think of her own father, who'd never felt protective of her. She'd simply been a useful tool in his scamming operations.

"The police might be interested to know that she's had it all this time." Warren spoke to Chase, but he eyed her. "She got off without any charges eight years ago, but if she benefited from her father's scam—"

"She didn't." Chase's arm was like an iron band around her waist, as if he wanted to be sure his enemy couldn't wrench her away.

It felt oddly comforting. She warmed where he touched her. And perhaps somewhat at his defense of her as well, even if he was just playing a role.

Still, the old guilt about her family returned, a heavy weight on her shoulders that felt all too familiar. She'd tried so hard to put the past behind her, but how could she when there were so many people still reeling from the consequences of her dad's schemes? How could she not blame herself for failing to turn him in sooner?

"According to her, maybe," the rich rancher scoffed. "But these Blackstones make a living off of being good liars."

The confrontation was attracting attention now that more of the wedding guests were taking their seats. Heads swiveled toward her and Chase while Warren Carmichael steamed.

Still, Chase's touch anchored her through the encounter, his heat and strength both communicating that—in this, at least—he was on her side. That she was in no danger. It was a small thing, perhaps, but she'd been left to wriggle out of risky situations enough times on her own that she could appreciate having someone stand by her.

"I'll thank you to keep a civil tongue in your head in regard to my future wife," Chase answered quietly, lifting her left hand to kiss just above the knuckles. The gesture made her engagement ring catch the glow of the closest candelabra, sending rainbow fractals dancing.

If the Carmichael patriarch had been angry before, he grew livid now. His face flushed dark red. He pushed one finger against Chase's chest, ignoring her completely.

"Your wife? In other words, you're locking down that property either way through marriage. You son of a—"

"We're leaving," Chase announced, cutting the man off as he pushed aside the offending finger. "Give Ashley our best."

Leaving? Before they even took their seats for the meal, when this event had been their whole reason for this charade?

Too surprised to know how to react, Tana was glad that Chase retrieved her bag and shawl for her before he led her toward the barn doors. The room had grown quiet, the argument having attracted all eyes by this time.

Gripping her short train in one hand to make walking easier, she hurried to keep pace with Chase's long stride. She held on to his upper arm, the muscle thick and hard beneath his jacket. She could hardly complain that they were leaving an event she'd wanted no part of from the beginning. Yet that relief was tempered by a growing awareness that this had likely been Chase's goal all along—to create a spectacle with his enemy and put the other man on alert about the land. In public. There were easily a hundred witnesses to the altercation.

Every bit of her training as a con artist told her that scene had been carefully choreographed for someone's benefit.

Warren Carmichael's? Or was Chase trying to hook someone else? And for what reason?

By the time they reached the valet stand and stepped into the back of their hired vehicle, Tana had a whole lot of questions simmering, ready for Chase to answer.

"Are you pleased with how that went?" She flipped the silk train free so it pooled on the floorboards near her feet.

No matter that she'd protested to Chase about the wardrobe being too precious, there was no denying every gown was stunning. When she'd been a girl, her parents had used her wide-eyed, fragile looks to help rope in marks. So after she'd moved to New York and claimed her life as her own, she'd gravitated toward anything that might make her look like a gang member. Superficial as it sounded, people responded to those clothes. They were more wary around someone wreathed in leather and spikes.

Which was exactly what Tana wanted. No one could accuse her of tricking them if she never let anyone too close to her in the first place. The clothes were a first line of defense. Her costume. But she couldn't deny this ultrafeminine gown was beautiful to look at, and it made her feel beautiful to wear it. She just needed to be careful that she didn't start believing the message the dress sent out. Because she wasn't fragile.

And she was far from innocent.

Chase leaned back in the seat beside her while the hired car headed toward Cloverfield Ranch. "I'm very pleased with how it went. I assume you didn't mind leaving early?"

"Of course not. I just wish you'd told me that you wanted to make a scene. I might have been more willing to participate."

"We hardly crashed it." He frowned, as if he hadn't thought about it that way. "They'll go on to have dinner and dancing, with free drinks all night."

"And they will be talking about us the whole time, speculating on the argument and starting new rumors." She traced the outline of one of the pink roses on her skirt. "If you would share your endgame with me, maybe I'd be more help in whatever con you're running."

Chase double-checked the partition that separated the back seat from the driver of the chauffeured Land Rover. The return drive to Cloverfield was short enough, but who knew how much more provocative the conversation might get from here? Thankfully, the tinted glass had been fully raised. Chase preferred not to have the residents of this small ranching community gossiping about this conversation.

"Fooling people into thinking we're engaged isn't a con game. It's a simple deception. Misdirection." He spat out the last word with particular bitterness, recalling how easily he'd been misdirected from Joe Blackstone's real intentions toward Cloverfield Ranch.

"You're fooling people with a purpose. Intention." She stabbed a fingernail into the leather seat between them as they turned onto the main road. "I'm asking you to share it with me. Don't I deserve that much for flying out here to be a part of this charade in the first place?"

As she spoke, a tendril of pink-tipped hair slid forward in front of her shoulder, calling to his fingers. He tightened his hands into fists to avoid the temptation to test the texture and see if it was as soft as he remembered.

He'd been hard-pressed the night before to stay away

from her, knowing she was under his roof. He hadn't joined her for dinner or riding after that kiss they'd shared, certain he was too keyed up to keep things platonic. The fact was, he wanted her with an urgency he hadn't experienced in any of the eight years that had passed since they'd first met.

"I'm not sure," he answered carefully, watching the foothills of the Humboldt Range flash past the windows while they headed toward Cloverfield Ranch. "I thought I deserved your help after the role you played in the scheme to defraud my family. I don't know that I owe you any explanations."

She cast her gaze heavenward. Not a full eye roll, but close.

"Suit yourself. If you feel comfortable dragging me back to Nevada to expose me to the unreasonable anger of a man I've never even met before, then I will trust your judgment. But the sooner I can sign your papers and go home, the better." She leaned forward in her seat, as if she would leap from the vehicle as soon as the car stopped in front of the ranch house.

Seeing the tension thrumming through her, visible in everything from her stiff shoulders to the death grip on her clutch purse, Chase felt another pang of regret about what he'd asked of her. He hadn't anticipated the level of Warren Carmichael's fury, and he sure hadn't wanted it directed toward Tana.

"I hope you know I would never allow him anywhere near you." He had no choice but to reach for her, his hand falling on the soft skin of her upper back. She deserved his reassurance, even if he found it nearly impossible not to pull her closer. "That really was one of my primary goals in the engagement. Warren Carmichael hates me. But he won't threaten you if he thinks we're together."

The rigid set of her body eased a fraction. She glanced at him over her shoulder.

"You won't be there to stand guard once I'm back in New York." Her dark eyes held his for a moment before sliding away again. "I'm just hoping that signing over those lands ends whatever enmity he has toward me."

Unease troubled his conscience since he needed her to extend her fiancée role just a bit longer after the weekend ended.

She must have read the conflict in his features because she rounded on him as the hired car halted in front of Cloverfield Ranch.

"What? Does Warren Carmichael pose a threat I should be aware of?" The concern in her eyes—worry he'd put there—was a call to action to his scruples.

"Let's talk about it while we ride." He could tell he'd caught her off guard by the way her eyebrows shot up. "We have bonus free time since we didn't stay for the reception. We can talk on horseback."

How many afternoons had they ridden together that memorable summer? She'd loved being on horseback, and he'd loved seeing her there. Knowing that he'd introduced her to something that brought her joy had filled his chest with pride—up until he'd found out about her father's schemes.

Now he wondered if he'd overestimated the role she played back then. Either way, the desire to be with her that way again—riding side by side instead of the verbal sparring—was almost all-consuming.

"All right. I'll go riding with you." She allowed him to exit the vehicle and help her from it. They stood together on the stone walkway that led to the historic main house. "But I expect answers this time, Chase. I want to know the undercurrents between you and Warren, and why he's angry with me."

He nodded, knowing what she asked was both fair and reasonable. Also, he would have agreed to most anything to have this time with her on horseback again. It felt so right he could almost believe that all of his plotting and scheming to find her again and return her to Nevada had been to arrange this moment.

Of course it wasn't. But being with her here again felt that inevitable.

"I'll tell you everything. Can you meet me at the stables in fifteen minutes?"

"Certainly. As an actress, I can do a costume change in sixty seconds when I have to." She pivoted on one pink heel, her train trailing behind her, and headed into the house.

An hour later, Tana was dressed in jeans and boots once again and seated on a sorrel mare named Shasta. Beside her, Chase rode a tall buckskin gelding called Harley as they threaded their way through the foothills of the Humboldt Range. It had been unnerving to see how quickly she'd fallen into their old rhythms of readying their mounts. He'd led the animals to the crossties while she'd gathered tack. He'd helped her with the saddles even though she'd been managing just fine on her own. And when it was time to mount, he'd held her stirrup for her.

Such a small thing. Just twisting the metal ring so she had a better angle to mount.

And it had catapulted her backward like her own personal time machine.

Even now that they'd been riding for at least a quarter of an hour, she couldn't quite shake the mingling of past and present. How many times had they ridden this way, talking and laughing, sharing their dreams?

And if they found their rhythm together so easily on horseback, how quickly might they fall into sync in bed? The idea caused a shiver before she shut it down.

Those thoughts were foolishness. Distractions from her real mission here, which was to find out what Chase was planning, how it involved her and how she could settle the debt she owed him so she could walk away guilt-free.

She was about to begin an interrogation to that effect when he spoke first.

"I'd never guess you hadn't ridden in eight years." He glanced over at her as they kept a slow pace through a steep section of their old riding path. "You took to it again easily enough."

"You were a good teacher," she told him honestly. "Plus riding was a joy for me."

An escape. For those hours she was with Chase, she could almost forget her roots. Forget the fear that her father might be planning a scheme that could shake the foundations right out from under Chase and his mother.

She'd been so naive. So hopeful that she was free from her dad's scams for good.

"Did you take any of the horses out yesterday?" He shifted in the saddle to avoid a low-hanging branch on his side of the path. The trees were still sparse this close to the ranch, but they would become more numerous the higher they climbed.

"I did not. I realize I could have asked for a recommendation from one of the hands for which animal to saddle, but—" It wouldn't have felt the same without Chase. "I was tired."

She kept her focus on the path ahead, afraid her eyes would give away her real thoughts. Something stirred inside her the longer she spent with this man. Something she'd been sure was long dead.

"All the more reason I'm glad we escaped the wedding reception early, then. How are you liking Shasta?"

Tana bent over the mare's neck to stroke her, murmuring encouraging words to the animal. "She's perfect."

She felt the weight of Chase's gaze on her, but still couldn't bring herself to meet his eyes. The familiarity of this ride was breaking down her barriers faster than she could rearm herself.

"So, I promised you answers about Warren Carmichael," Chase began, catching her off guard with the abrupt shift in conversation. "I wasn't sure how much you knew about your father's relationship with him and was waiting to see how the two of you reacted to each other today. But it seems obvious to me now that you've never met him."

She swung on him, all her attention narrowing to this new twist in her understanding of the past.

"Never. And I had no idea Dad spent time with Ashley's father." Her mind raced, searching for memories of that summer. "Between how much time you and I spent together and how often my dad took trips to see my mother in Las Vegas—"

She cut herself off, realizing her misconception. Her mother had taken a condo close to the Strip that summer, and Tana had been under the impression her mom was spearheading the bigger con. Tana thought maybe her dad was providing support somehow by keeping himself away from her, when all along it was her father who had lured the bigger mark. That summer had been the beginning of the end to their marriage, though Tana hadn't realized it at the time. After Joe Blackstone disappeared, Alicia Blackstone moved on without a second glance back at her ex-husband or her daughter, either. Tana had honored her mom's self-imposed solitude in Las Vegas, especially after her mother remarried and hadn't even invited Tana to the wedding.

Chase waited a moment for her to continue, their mounts picking their way along the narrowing path. When Tana didn't say anything more, Chase spoke again.

"Maybe he didn't take as many trips to Vegas as you thought. He organized some high-stakes local poker games, reeling in wealthy visitors to Warren's ranch. And, of course, Warren himself."

Missing pieces of an old puzzle fell rapidly together. Her father hadn't simply been conning Chase's mom while he'd been living at Cloverfield. He'd put his card sharp skills to work on the side, luring players to the table with higher and higher stakes, letting them feel comfortable that they could beat him, until the bets turned huge. That's when her father had struck, his true poker prowess coming out to beat the others when it counted.

"Dad took Warren deep. That's why Ashley's father holds a grudge." Her knee brushed against Chase's as their mounts shifted for room on the trail.

Awareness of him tripped through her veins. Involuntarily, she tightened her hold on Shasta's reins before forcing herself to relax again.

"Afterward, Carmichael told anyone who would listen that Joe Blackstone was a cheat. It was the only way he could save face in front of his friends who also lost a lot of money to your dad." At a fork in the trail, Chase steered his horse to the left, a route that opened up to a wide meadow between the hills.

Grateful for the sway of Shasta's steps that soothed her fraying nerves, Tana couldn't help filtering Chase's words through what she knew of her father since she'd spent all her formative years being party to his schemes. More often than not, her dad didn't cheat to win at cards. He had a keen intellect for the game and a natural feel for it that could have made him a ranked player if he chose to pursue the tournament route.

She'd suggested it to him more than once, never understanding why he'd turn down a legitimate way of making money. Her dad had tried to explain that it wasn't about money for him. It was about the thrill of the win. The rush that came from a successful con.

"That explains why Warren Carmichael hates my father. But I'm not sure I understand what he has against me." Her face burned at the memory of the man calling her out in front of a reception hall full of wedding guests.

"You know that land your dad put in a trust for you?" Chase asked, slowing Harley's pace until the horse stopped in his tracks.

Tana followed suit, reining in Shasta beneath the shade of a juniper tree.

"The one I'm signing over to you? Of course." She would have already done it if Chase had given her the paperwork. Settling the issue with that land was the main reason she'd traveled to Nevada.

"Apparently that plot isn't made up solely of lands that used to be in the Cloverfield Ranch parcel." Chase's gray eyes locked on hers, his voice stirring her senses even as she feared the rest of what he would say. "There are forty prime acres with river access that belonged to Warren Carmichael before your dad won them in a hand of poker."

Anger and resentment churned as this latest revelation rattled through her. Her father was at fault, without question. But didn't Warren Carmichael have some accountability for the loss, too? He'd gambled.

"There's my answer," she returned tightly, knowing that the joy of the ride was gone for the day. "Now it just remains for me to know if you want me to sign over that portion of the land to you, too? Or should I make restitution to Warren Carmichael for being foolish enough to bet his property?"

Too agitated to wait for his response, Tana nudged her horse forward. Breaking into a run, Shasta seemed as eager to put the conversation behind her as Tana was.

Still, as hard as the horse's hooves pounded the burnished meadow grasses, Tana knew they wouldn't outrun the trouble brewing.

Seven

Keeping his horse at an easy walk, Chase watched Tana's figure grow smaller in the distance, understanding she needed space.

For now, at least.

Hell, he didn't blame her for wanting to run from him. He'd deliberately blindsided her with the wedding and the meeting with Warren Carmichael, needing to see her reaction firsthand. He'd wanted to gauge for himself how much she knew about her father's side-hustle activities while he'd been in Nevada.

Having witnessed her surprise and confusion, Chase now believed she knew nothing about the poker games her dad had organized. The realization weighed uncomfortably on his shoulders, making him wonder what else he'd misjudged about her.

Tipping his head back, Chase watched a turkey vulture circling low overhead, silently riding the dry late-summer wind. He forced himself to take a deep breath and reconsider what he knew about Tana's part in her father's shady dealings.

Was it possible she hadn't known her dad had come to town to scam Chase's mom?

A week ago, he would have laughed at the idea. But considering her surprise about the trust her father had set up, and how readily she'd agreed to sign over the lands to Chase, he was beginning to question his former assumptions. Hadn't she tried to warn him not to trust her dad?

She'd been emphatic about that, but at the time, he'd thought she worried too much and had dismissed her concerns out of hand. That was on him.

Now, following the flight of the turkey vulture as it disappeared behind a rise, Chase pinched the bridge of his nose to counteract the tension headache that had Tana's name written all over it. No matter what Tana knew or didn't know, he owed her more courtesy than he'd extended so far.

Right? Or was he making excuses for how much he wanted to touch her? Taste her?

The need for her hadn't abated a bit in the years they'd been apart. If anything, she intrigued him more than ever. So if there was any chance that she hadn't been part of the setup to defraud his mom, Chase would learn the truth.

Which was why, after giving Tana a few minutes to run off her frustration, he nudged his mount faster to overtake her.

There was only one spot she would be heading for. One place they'd ridden to over and over again that summer together. She was too smart a rider to venture anyplace but a well-known destination.

And yeah, thinking about the things they'd done in

the remote privacy of that old cabin already had his blood simmering in his veins. Was she remembering them, too?

Minutes later, the original homestead on the historic Cloverfield Ranch came into view. A small wooden structure with a humbly stacked stone chimney, the building had long been abandoned as a residence, but it made for a good hunting cabin. Shasta stood nearby, grazing in the shade along a shallow creek bed.

At first, he didn't see Tana. But a moment later, as he guided Harley closer to the mare, he spotted her on the other side of the creek. She sat with her back against the smooth gray bark of a mountain alder tree, fingers sifting through some fallen leaves before pulling out a flat rock.

She must have heard him approach, yet she said nothing as she skimmed the stone along the surface of the creek water, being careful to aim away from where the horses were tied.

He allowed himself a moment to drink in the sight of her there in a place full of happy memories that all contained her. They'd had bonfires here, sharing their dreams over a stolen beer or two. They'd danced in the moonlight. He'd kissed her against the very tree where she now sat.

Then, of course, inside the shelter of that cabin, he'd discovered endless ways to give her pleasure. His entire sexual education had happened with her. No one else had quite measured up to her, and he needed to find out if he had some sort of euphoric recall. If he could just be with her again, maybe he could loosen the bond of the memories of the past. Then he could move forward.

Just thinking about the possibility tantalized him now as he slid off his mount and ground-tied his horse.

"You found your way back here." He made the obvious observation as he crossed the creek on a series of jutting rocks, his brain too full of hot memories to attempt more thoughtful conversation.

She glanced up at him, the pink tips of her brown hair brushing along the logo for her theater company emblazoned on her black T-shirt. She wore faded jeans today with no holes and no fishnet stockings beneath them. Even her black boots were practical. Not a stud or spike in sight.

Because she felt more comfortable here, back at Cloverfield Ranch with him? He dismissed the idea as soon as it formed, knowing that couldn't be the case. She'd just dressed for expediency. End of story.

"I took the only trail I remembered." She sifted through pine needles and came up with another stone. She studied it for a moment before tossing it with a side-arm throw. "We rode this way often enough."

His steps slowed as he neared her, his heart thudding heavily at the mention of what they'd shared here.

"Yes, we did." His voice deepened, his blood firing hotter.

Memories of their kiss the night before returned with a vengeance. She'd poured all of herself into that kiss up until the second she'd pulled away. He'd felt the heat. The passion. She'd singed his senses then, and every moment that they'd been together since then.

Now her dark gaze flickered up to his, latching on to it and holding steady.

"You said last night that we didn't have to fake the sparks between us." Her voice sounded as thick with desire as his. Unsteadily, she laid one hand against the alder tree and pushed herself to stand. "That attraction came naturally enough."

Even in the deep shade of the tree, he could see the leap of heat reflected in her eyes.

"I remember." His hands ached to touch her. Pull her close. Relive a thousand memories. "I said as much right after the kiss you ended."

He emphasized that last part, needing to remind her.

"Did you mean it?" Her gaze narrowed, almost as if she could ferret out his secrets if she studied him long enough. "That is, are you still attracted? Even now?"

"Hell, yes." How could she doubt it? Soon enough, she'd see for herself. "Come closer and I'll prove it."

She reached to tuck a strand of hair behind her ear, but he was pretty sure she did it to hide a shiver of desire. Her fingers had trembled for an instant.

"I only ended the kiss because I was afraid—" She jammed her hands into her pockets, hissing out a frustrated sigh. "I didn't like the idea of being the only one still feeling some of the old…feelings."

The admission surprised him. Although maybe it shouldn't, since her boldness was something he'd always admired about her. She spoke her mind and went after what she wanted. But then again, maybe she was only referring to attraction when she referred to the old emotions. Probably so.

He didn't want to mislead her by implying they were dealing with more than just physical desire. But then again, wasn't he experiencing a whole lot that wasn't precisely about sex?

He shut that thought down fast.

"You're not alone in any of that." He answered without considering the wisdom of honesty. He only knew he wasn't letting this moment get away from him if there was any chance Tana wanted the same thing as him. "Believe me, attraction wasn't on my personal agenda when I looked you up again. But here we are."

She gave a slow nod as the birds overhead chirped a cheerful chorus. "Here we are."

He waited, taking her measure in the swirling heat between them, not wishing to spook her.

Finally, he edged closer. Close enough to breathe in the clean scent of her skin. Close enough to track the patterns of light and shadow in her face from the sunlight filtering through the trees.

"Now that you know the sparks are one hundred percent mutual, what would you think about trying another kiss?"

The small stand of nearby trees seemed to lean in to hear her answer, the entire clearing holding its breath with anticipation. Only the creek babbled on, and one of the horses snuffled on the other side of the stream.

"I'd like that, Chase." Her chin notched higher, pupils widening with heat. "But you should know I won't be the one to end this one."

Tana knew she'd raised the stakes too soon.

If this had been a poker game, you didn't do that unless you were confident in your hand. And did she have any reason to be confident in what was happening between her and Chase? No. None.

But her father had always told her that her biggest weakness at the poker table was her lack of appreciation for measuring the odds ahead of time and working out all the probabilities.

Even realizing she was guilty of that same mistake now, Tana couldn't find it in her heart to care about the consequences. Not when Chase stepped so close his feet bracketed hers. His big hands clasped her waist, warming her skin right through the cotton of her T-shirt. His gray eyes seemed to see past all her smoke and mirrors to the woman she was beneath.

He knew her past. All the worst parts of her.

Yet somehow, miraculously, he seemed to want her every bit as much as she still craved him.

"I won't be ending this kiss, either," he promised, the words wrapping around her more seductively than any embrace. "Not unless you tell me to."

Her heart pounded so loudly he must have heard it. The sound filled her ears even as her fingers walked up his chest to rest on his broad shoulders. "Do your worst, cowboy."

In spite of her taunting, Chase brushed the softest of kisses over her lips. Testing. Teasing.

Her bravado melted underneath the skillful seduction, her whole world narrowing to the play of his mouth over hers. Nipping. Licking. Sucking.

Every stroke of his tongue stoked the fire inside her, making her ache and squirm in his arms, desperate for more. For everything. Especially since she could feel the rock-hard length of him pressing against her belly.

Edging back, she gasped his name.

"Chase. Please." She cupped his bristled jaw in her hand, her fingers tracing his cheekbone. "I need more."

His growl of satisfaction rumbled right through her. "Me, too. Are you okay with the cabin?"

A thrill shot through her at the prospect. This was happening. Her and Chase Serrano. After all these years.

Despite all the reasons that it was probably a really bad idea, Tana couldn't wait another minute.

"You could take me against this tree, and I'd ask for more."

His gray eyes went molten silver.

"Don't tempt me." He spun on his heel and led her toward the cabin, his long strides necessitating that she double-step through the dried pine needles and fallen leaves.

If she wasn't so thoroughly turned on she might have laughed at the picture she must make, practically sprinting back to this man's bed in spite of everything that had happened between them.

Reaching the cabin, he nudged the door open and pulled her inside after him. Despite the rustic exterior, the interior was clean and well maintained, if sparsely furnished.

She guessed a cleaning crew must make regular rounds here since Chase didn't live in Nevada full-time. The scent of pine and lemon polish pervaded the space. They headed toward the lone bed, only breaking their kiss long enough for him to pry open the cupboard so he could reach past the linens and towels to withdraw a silky blanket and flannel sleeping bag.

A smile tugged at her lips as the past merged with the present. She'd forgotten that detail about being with him here in the past. They'd laid down a sleeping bag on the bed to explore one another's bodies, camping out here until just before dawn, then riding home, sweetly sore but well sated.

A surge of nostalgia threatened to haul her into the past where old hurts lay, so she purposely stomped it back down. Instead, she took the heavy flannel from him, needing an activity.

Her breasts brushed his arm as she moved, sending a jolt of electric heat through her.

"Here. I can help." She unzipped the insulated bag

and laid it out on the queen-size mattress that took up almost the whole bedroom.

When she finished, she realized Chase had been watching her closely. Studying her, almost.

"You're nervous." It wasn't a question.

Her pulse sped faster as she smoothed the fabric over the bed. "It's been a long time since I—" She licked her lips. "Was with someone."

Years, actually.

She'd been with exactly two other people besides Chase. The first had been a disaster from start to finish, never to be repeated. The second had been a boyfriend she'd cared about, but the sex had never come close to what she remembered with Chase. Both of those had been a long time ago; her focus had been on work and not romance for the last few years.

Now Chase dropped the soft quilt he'd been carrying and wound his arms around her.

"Don't worry. It's like riding a horse." A wicked smile curved his lips. "You don't forget."

Welcome laughter bubbled freely from her, banishing her nerves.

"That's excellent news." She twined her arms around his neck, arching her back so her hips met his. "Will you show me?"

The hungry sound that emerged from the back of his throat heightened her senses as the last of her reservations fell away.

"I've been thinking about little else since that kiss last night," he admitted before his mouth claimed hers.

She tipped her face up to his, offering him more. Everything.

Each stroke of his tongue drugged her, her knees turning liquid under her. Her hold on his neck tightened, his body the only thing anchoring her in a world going up in flames.

This was what she remembered. Fire. Passion. A connection so strong that she didn't have to think about how to proceed or worry about what he thought of her. They were too busy setting each other ablaze.

She tunneled her hands under his shirt, eager palms splaying over his abs to trace the ridges and valleys. The lean athletic frame of his youth had filled out to hard-muscled perfection.

She had to see for herself. Breaking the kiss, she lifted the tail of his shirt higher, then sucked in a breath at the sight of him. Jeans riding low on his hips, Chase had a body that was the stuff of fantasy. With a fingertip, she followed the valley along his obliques before dragging her knuckle along the denim waistband, his breathing growing harsh in her ear as she touched him.

Pausing at the button, she worked it free with some effort, the fabric straining to contain him. She would have moved to the rest of the buttons, but he captured her hands in one of his.

"Let me." His voice rasped against her ear. "It's been too long for me, too. I'm not sure I have enough restraint to survive those fingers working me over like that."

Her gaze shifted to his as she tried to hide her surprise. She wouldn't have guessed this man of potent sexuality would take any downtime, assuming he must have his pick of women to bring home.

Still, the idea pleased her far more than it should. Why should she care who he slept with?

But Chase was already stripping off his jeans and stepping out of them, distracting her from her thoughts and putting all her focus right back on him. He peeled off his shirt next, leaving him wearing nothing besides his boxers.

"Oh." She reached for him again, but he sidestepped her, gathering her wrists in one hand.

"Your turn, Tana." He hooked a finger in the neckline of her T-shirt and tugged it lightly. "Do you want to do the undressing, or do you want me to?"

"Your hands would feel better than mine," she confessed, already yanking the hem of her shirt from her pants. "But I'll be faster."

She kept her eyes on him while she toed off her boots and shimmied out of her jeans. His gaze tracked her every movement, and the only sound was the old cabin creaking gently in the late-summer wind.

When she slid a bra strap off one shoulder, Chase stopped her, his hand curving, holding, caressing.

"Wait." He stepped closer, the warmth of his body heating hers even before they touched. "Efficiency be damned. I can't let you have all the fun."

When she released the black satin strap, Chase's fingers slid beneath it, grazing her shoulder. At the same time, his hips nudged hers, the impressive erection pressing into her belly.

Biting back a gasp, she felt her eyelids flutter closed, the better to concentrate on all the new sensations bombarding her.

"Chase." She hummed the name to herself, wanting to soak up everything he had to offer. His pine-and-musk scent. His heat.

His strength.

"I'm going to take the best care of you, Tana." He breathed the sensual promise in her ear. "Relax and let me."

The huff of his breath near her temple gave her goose

bumps. She gripped his shoulders, balancing herself on her toes as she swayed still closer to him.

"Yes. I want you to." She didn't recognize her voice or the sentiment behind it. Since when did she hand over control to anyone? For any reason.

But she didn't want to worry about that now. She just held on tighter while he peeled down the satin fabric and exposed a nipple to the cool air. A moment later, he lowered his head to kiss her there, his tongue playing back and forth across the tight peak.

Pleasure rippled through her, her whole body hungry for more. She pressed her hips to him, seeking pressure. Needing him.

He understood, too. Because a moment later, he'd removed her bra and lifted her against him before laying her on the bed. She shivered at the sight of him looming over her. Ready for her.

Except…an unhappy thought occurred to her.

"I don't have condoms." She bolted upright, guessing Chase wouldn't be able to magically produce some from the small bathroom in the hunting cabin.

Provisions were limited here.

"I picked some up last night." Leaning down, he retrieved his jeans and pulled a foil packet from the pocket. "After that kiss, I figured it couldn't hurt to—"

She kissed him. Hard.

Grateful for the presumption that would let them be together. She didn't know how she'd gone from ignoring the unwise attraction last week to exploring every facet of it today, but she knew there was no turning back now. She needed this.

Him.

"You're a very smart man," she praised him, plucking the packet from his fingers to tear it open. "Thank you for this."

He watched her as he lowered his boxers. "You're not the only one who benefits, believe me."

Her heart rate quickened, her attention captivated. Distracted, she fumbled the condom, dropping it on the bed.

Luckily, Chase was ready to finish the job. He rolled the prophylactic in place before gripping her thighs and dragging her to the edge of the bed to put her in the best position for...

"Oh. Chase." Tana wrapped her legs around his waist as he pressed his way inside her.

For a moment, they remained still. Locked together. Breathing each other in after so many years apart.

Then the heat began to build even before he moved. And when he did, easing partway out and entering her all over again, she almost wept at how good it felt. How good *he* felt.

She hadn't dreamed this. Hadn't inflated her sense of how amazing they'd been together. If anything, this was even better.

The realization both gratified and daunted her.

Sure, she'd been right, and that was nice. But Chase Serrano was only in her life very temporarily. So she needed to enjoy every second of this before he was gone again for good.

"Are you with me?" he asked, pausing to comb his fingers through her hair, sifting through the strands and kissing his way along her jaw. "You looked like you disappeared for a second."

"Just wondering how it could feel this way when we haven't seen each other in so long. When there's so much…unsettled between us." She regretted mentioning it as soon as she'd said the words.

Sex should be simple. Physical.

She had no wish to discuss the emotional side of their unorthodox, renewed relationship.

"I don't know." His voice was grave, his eyes never leaving hers as he reached between their bodies to stroke between her legs. "But you're welcome to stay in my bed until you have the answers you're looking for."

Her breath caught at the way he touched her, his fingers teasing her higher while he slid into her, again and again.

Heart pounding faster, she felt the orgasm building. Needed the release it offered. Her eyes closed while she let the sensations tighten and coil, ready to spring.

She was holding her breath, anticipating, when Chase spoke softly in her ear.

"Would you like that, Tana?"

Visions of lingering here, in bed with him, while they pleasured each other day and night only made her release hit harder. Sweet shock waves reverberated through her, blinding her to everything but what she was feeling.

She tightened her hold on his hips with her legs, her body arching hard into his.

She hadn't even come down from that high when she felt Chase still. When he found his own release, the pulsing of it pushed her toward a second orgasm, a brief, sweet shadow of the first.

It left her wrung out and spent, still wondering how she could have such an incredible connection to a man who didn't trust her. A man still withholding secrets of his own.

When he lay down beside her in the aftermath, dragging the second blanket over their cooling bodies, Tana didn't know where to begin untangling all the messy emotions she had as far as Chase was concerned. For now, she just breathed in the scent of Chase and sex, telling herself she'd sign over the deed to the property tomorrow and fly home to Brooklyn.

Maybe then, back in the safe haven of her shared apartment building with her girlfriends, she'd be able to work through the complicated knot of everything she didn't want to feel.

But even as she burrowed into the crook of Chase's arms, she knew that was naive thinking. No matter how much they connected in bed, she had to remember that he'd requested a fake engagement with her for more than one reason. And she had the feeling he'd only just begun to reveal the depths of whatever revenge he had in mind for Tana.

Eight

Night had fallen before Chase convinced himself they needed to return to the main ranch house.

But damn, he still didn't want to leave the bed he shared with Tana. The last few hours with her in the cabin had been like stepping into the best part of his past, returning to a time when he hadn't thought of anything beyond her.

Of course, that had been foolish of him back then. He'd like to think he knew better now. This time, he could enjoy the incredible connection they shared without giving her his heart or his trust.

Moonlight shone through the thin glass windowpanes and onto the queen-size bed, the air beginning to cool now that the sun had set, since the old homestead had only a fireplace to regulate the temperature. The pale light illuminated Tana's face where she lay in profile facing him, her bare shoulders showing no evidence of the henna tattoos that had been there the day before. He didn't think they were easy to scrub off.

The thought provided just the excuse he needed to delay returning to the main ranch house for a few more minutes at least.

"I noticed the tattoos were gone today," he observed, grazing a fingertip along her collarbone and over her shoulder before trailing down one slender arm.

"All but one." She didn't glance up at him, her attention focused on tracing the plaid pattern in the flannel blanket beneath them.

"The crown and wings." He remembered seeing them on her back earlier.

Her finger stilled. She glanced up at him.

"Those are the only real ones I have. I don't mind them being permanent because I don't see them as often. But I like changing what I wear on my arms since I look at them every day." She returned to her idle tracing.

Deciding to circle back to the wings, he asked the other question that tugged at him.

"Where did you learn to draw like that? All the henna work was so detailed." If she'd possessed that kind of artistic talent when they'd known each other, she'd never shared it with him.

"Practice. Lots of practice." For a moment, it seemed as if that was all she'd say about it. But then she drew in a deep breath and continued. "I'm not sure how much you read about my family, but I was born in Flushing, Queens. Close to an Indian neighborhood."

He'd read everything he could find about her in those months after her father's scam. Then he'd learned even more from the private investigator who'd ultimately found her in Brooklyn. That had still left big gaps in his knowledge about her since her father had often used aliases that he'd shared with his wife and daughter.

"I remember. You left the city when you were still young." He'd read that her dad had run afoul of the Russian mob and moved to the West Coast. Tana would have been about ten years old.

She propped herself up on one elbow, giving him her full attention.

"Right. I was sad to go because it meant I had to leave the neighbor who'd been my sitter when my parents were…busy." A frown curved her lips before she spoke again. "Kalyani ran a beauty shop out of her apartment, and she was especially known for her henna work."

"She taught you?" He remembered how detailed Tana's drawings were with their elaborate shading and intricate designs.

"No. But I watched her work often enough. Sometimes brides would be there for eight hours while Kalyani applied the designs." She smiled to herself. "I'd beg her to draw on me, but she never did."

He waited, curious about her friend since Tana had already spoken more about this woman than she ever had about her parents.

"But before I left Queens, she drew me a crown that she said belonged to Kali, a fierce protector goddess. Under the crown, she drew angel wings, and she told me those were for my guardian angel to keep me safe wherever I went." Her smile wobbled a little. "I'm sure she knew I would be facing a tougher life once I left her."

Chase nodded, understanding. "You started working more for your father after that."

"I felt I had no choice," she said shortly. Then her voice softened again as she continued. "Anyway, I saved the paper with her sketch for years. During college, I took the drawing to a tattoo parlor to have the design permanently inked."

Empathy for all she hadn't said—the dangers she'd faced under the roof of criminal parents—crowded his chest. Picturing her as a ten-year-old kid couldn't help but shift his perspective a bit. No way she'd chosen crime at that age.

"I'm sorry you didn't have a protector." He cupped her face in his palm, realizing this time with her was doing more than shift his perspective.

He was starting to care all over again.

The thought startled him so much his hand slid away from her cheek. Perhaps some of his dismay showed on his face because she reared away from him, levering up on her pillow.

"We should get back," she blurted suddenly, her eyes darting to look anywhere but at him.

Damn it.

Had he revealed his thoughts somehow? He blinked, as if that could help erase whatever had been reflected on his face or in his eyes.

"Tana—"

She shook her head, already scrambling off the bed. "I'll need time to shower before our meeting with the attorney and the notary."

He studied her a moment, wondering if he'd offended her. He pinched his temple, wishing he could rewind the last couple of minutes so that they could talk through things instead of retreating to their old standoff of mistrust. Could she blame him for not trusting her after the con her father pulled? She said she didn't have a choice. But why hadn't she turned to Chase for help if she really wanted to get out from under her family's thumb?

Why hadn't she chosen him?

But the moment for that conversation had passed, and maybe it was just as well. He had business to attend to.

"Right. My lawyer should be arriving at the ranch house soon with the documents to sign over the deed." Chase pushed off the bed to retrieve his clothes.

This wasn't how he'd wanted their time together to end, but then again, he hadn't thought beyond the need to be with her again. To see if the chemistry were still as potent as he'd remembered. Now that he knew it was even hotter? He didn't have any idea how to handle that. Tonight, he just needed to move forward with their paperwork and reclaim his lands.

That would at least finalize their business at Cloverfield. Later, he'd see about using their engagement to lure her father out of hiding.

Because no matter what feelings he was starting to have for Tana, Chase wouldn't abandon his plans for revenge on her father anytime soon.

Back at Cloverfield Ranch, Tana had retreated to her room as quickly as possible, needing some breathing room after what had happened between her and Chase.

Ducking into the lavish marble shower stall, she tried to wash away the fear that she'd made a huge mistake by sleeping with her host. Soaping her sensitized skin, she was torn between berating herself and reliving every single detail of their time together. In slow motion.

His touch had transported her back in time to the happiest summer of her life. His kiss had stirred all the same sensual energy, filling her with a heat that no other man had ever summoned.

It was unfair, given that he'd only wanted a fake engagement to further his own schemes. Schemes she didn't fully understand yet.

As she worked the citrus-scented shampoo into a lather, Tana thought back to the way Chase had set her up to confront Warren Carmichael. He'd said he wanted to see for himself if she knew Warren, apparently not trusting her word. But why was that important to him? Did he think Warren and her father had colluded somehow to defraud Chase? She knew nothing about the poker games her father had organized while he'd lived in Nevada.

When her scrubbing didn't coax any answers to the surface of her brain, she tipped her head into the hot water designed to fall like a rain shower from the ceiling as steam rolled up and around her. Somehow, the poker games of her father's past were important to Chase. But why would Chase care if her dad had taken Warren Carmichael deep at the card table?

Chase had an agenda he hadn't shared with her yet. Maybe he never would. The idea stung since she already knew she would forever associate this trip with the hours spent in his bed. No doubt it had meant more to her than him. She'd read the retreat in his expression during her misguided attempt to share something about her past with him. He hadn't wanted to get to know her beyond what they'd enjoyed physically.

Which was fine. She understood, even if there had been a moment when she'd felt a twinge of hurt at how fast he'd pulled away. Especially when she'd tried to share something of herself with him. Something real.

But he wasn't interested in the woman beneath her armor now any more than when they'd been in their teens. He'd brought her here to play a role, and she'd done that. Once she signed over the lands to him, she would consider their fake engagement over, and she'd never see Chase Serrano again. And while the idea already hurt, Tana knew it was the only way to keep her heart safe.

Chase shouldn't have been surprised when Tana strutted into the library wearing the silver-studded high-top sneakers and ripped jeans with black tights under them. Her vintage Sex Pistols T-shirt would have cemented his understanding of her mood, but she'd taken it a step further by inserting a splashy green stud in her nose piercing and stenciling a henna snake on the back of her left hand.

If it had been just the two of them in the room, he might have laughed out loud at the way she'd drawn the snake's open jaws positioned around her engagement diamond, as if it were about to swallow the ring whole.

But Chase's attorney and a local notary were already seated at the walnut desk in the corner, their four chairs drawn around it to ease the signing process.

The notary, an older woman who worked at an area bank, appeared to hide a smirk as she peered over her half-glasses at Tana striding toward the group. Chase's lawyer, a friend from college, followed Tana's every movement with an interest he didn't disguise well enough for Chase's liking.

Maybe that was what drove Chase to his feet to meet her midway across the library floor. He couldn't help the need to loop a possessive arm around her.

Had it only been a couple of hours since he'd had her naked beneath him? It already felt like years. And he needed her again.

Lowering his head to kiss her on the cheek, he had

the chance to speak softly to her. "Was it something I said that brought on the wardrobe change?"

"I'm sure I don't know what you mean," she said in an innocent voice that borrowed heavily from her Blanche DuBois character.

Her clean, citrusy scent made him want to taste her. His hand tightened on her waist for a moment before he turned to the others.

"Sharon, Hunter, this is my fiancée, Tana Blackstone. Tana, meet Sharon Eckert and Hunter Randolph." Chase shot his lawyer a level gaze, making sure the guy got the message.

Or he would have, if Hunter had ever torn his attention from Tana.

Chase felt a scowl settle on his brow, but at least Hunter skipped small talk in favor of business, quickly explaining the paperwork as Chase and Tana took their seats. Knowing already what he was asking her to sign, Chase took the next few minutes to observe Tana more closely.

She looked as delectable in her jeans and tennis shoes as she did in the gown she'd worn to the wedding, her beauty transcending whatever she wore. Both those sides of her were so different from his favorite aspect of her, though: the simple, pared down woman who'd joined him on horseback.

For those hours at least, she hadn't bothered to hide behind a role.

And he'd been foolish enough to close the door on that tenuous connection he'd formed with her.

"Chase?"

His friend's voice called him out of his musing. He realized three sets of eyes were all turned his way.

Clearly he'd missed something while he'd been contemplating Tana.

Her jaw tightened, full lips pursing.

"Sorry?" Leaning forward, Chase refocused on the task at hand.

Hunter slid a document across the polished wood surface of the desk. "Your fiancée would like to know if she'll be signing over the former Carmichael property to you in this deed. Did you explain to her how that works?"

Of course he hadn't. He'd been too busy undressing her.

Tasting her. Satisfying her the best way he knew how.

Judging from the daggers in her brown eyes right now, however, he realized he should have set aside time to do more than that this afternoon. But she'd been upset when she first learned that her father had won a parcel of land that had once belonged to Carmichael in a card game. Tana had ridden away from him and they'd never returned to that conversation, or the plans he had for that particular piece of land that Tana now owned. Chase didn't want her to sign that part of the property over to him.

He needed her to keep ownership of that portion of the parcel her father had put in trust for her. Temporarily, at least, until Chase had the chance to enact the rest of his plan for revenge.

"Hunter, Sharon, will you excuse us for a moment?" Chase didn't think either of them would mind since he was paying them well to make a house call on a Saturday.

And a moment later, he had Tana all to himself in the library. The door snicked closed behind the others as they departed, sealing Chase and Tana in privacy.

Before he could speak, however, she surged from her chair, slapping a hand on the desk as she stood.

"What the hell are you doing?"

Anger whipped through her as she stared into Chase's gray eyes.

Not just because he hadn't bothered to explain half of his schemes to her. Also because their time together had changed exactly nothing between them, and she was fast regretting giving her body to a man who couldn't bolt from her bed fast enough.

He had the audacity to nod, as if she'd made some obvious observation of little concern. "It's very simple, actually—"

"Don't." She pointed a finger at him, her abandoned chair rolling back. "You don't get to mansplain this to me now when you've been deliberately evasive all weekend about what I'm doing here."

"I didn't know how much I could trust you."

"That's why you took off my clothes rather than talk to me?" She shoved away from the desk to storm around the library, a book-laden man cave from another century.

The whole place screamed wealth, from the humidor holding some of the world's best cigars to the bottles of Macallan and Chivas on the bar cart. Rare old volumes graced the bookshelves. It was a world she'd seen many times while she'd been an unwilling part of her father's schemes. And she had no desire to return to it. Whatever she possessed now, she owned because of her hard work.

"That's not fair," Chase said quietly, still seated at his desk while she walked off some of her agitation. "I thought we both wanted to be there. Very much."

She pivoted to face him, needing to see his features to gauge his sincerity. He sat with fingers steepled, studying her. She held her silence, though, determined to wait him out.

"I will allow," he continued, "that I should have made time to discuss this with you in detail. But the chemistry that kicks in sometimes between us…you have to admit it's potent. Distracting." His brow knitted, as if he couldn't possibly account for their connection. "It threw me."

"Explain that to me," she demanded, not backing down now. "What do you mean it 'threw you'?" Her heart did a little leap at his words even as she told herself that was ridiculous.

More time with Chase could only lead to heartache and disaster when she *knew* he wanted vengeance on her family.

"Tana, you know perfectly what it means. You were there with me. Today stirred old memories. For a little while, it felt like old times, and we both know that's dangerous terrain." His jaw muscle flexed. "You don't want to revisit the past any more than I do."

She bit back a half dozen retorts to that loaded statement.

"We're getting off track," she said finally, determined to finish signing the papers as soon as she understood the language of the documents that required her signature. "Just tell me what's happening with Warren Carmichael's land. Why isn't it included in the real estate transfer that I'm signing over to you?"

There'd been separate paperwork for those forty acres, and Chase's lawyer had told her not to sign it yet. Confused, she'd asked for clarification, and that had held up the whole meeting.

Did Chase want the land to be returned to the Carmichael family? She was fine with that, given that her father had obtained it in a card game. But she didn't understand why she couldn't sign and be done with it tonight.

What was Chase planning? What had he been hiding from her?

Rising from his seat, Chase came toward her. Each footstep made her heart race faster. She should not want him this much. But her body did not understand the message.

When he reached her, his hands slid around her elbows. His fingers pressing gently into the tender skin there. Amazing how an elbow could become an erogenous zone when Chase was involved.

"Warren wants that land badly. I'd like you to hold on to it to entice him into a high-stakes poker game next weekend at my house in the Hamptons."

Her heart sank to the floor. No, lower. Chase had far bigger schemes afoot than she'd ever guessed.

"I don't gamble." She hadn't touched cards since she turned eighteen.

She would not. Memories of past games—grown men losing their life savings on the turn of the cards—sickened her.

"You wouldn't be playing with your own money. You'd use the land as your buy-in." Chase's hands never left her. He touched her so gently when his words ate into her skin like acid.

"It doesn't matter. I. Don't. Play." Turning away from him, she folded her arms tight. How many times had she fought this battle with her father? And lost. He'd been an expert in coercion, using his manipulative tactics on his own daughter to ensure she kept dealing cards.

Her gut roiled. "I told you I left that life for good, and I meant it."

"You left the con game. This isn't a con. It's a perfectly legal poker game, the same as they play in casinos all over the country."

"You sound exactly like my father." He'd made the same argument to her plenty of times.

If Chase took offense, he didn't show it. "I'm not asking you to do anything against the law, and you know it."

She thrust her hands over her head in exasperation. "So go find the closest riverboat with gaming tables and have a blast, but leave me out of it."

In the silence that followed, she heard the soft ticking of a grandfather clock, the moon chasing the sun across the sky on the antique face. Tana stared at it, wishing the sun would win soon so she could be back in Brooklyn where she belonged, far from Cloverfield Ranch and her father's misdeeds that wouldn't stop haunting her.

"I'm not good enough to beat him."

She shook her head, not sure how to argue the point. She couldn't take on Chase's plan for vengeance for him. Even if it wasn't illegal, it was still unethical to play a game with such stacked odds. And yes, she'd been an excellent player once upon a time. It had brought her no joy. Only pain.

After a long moment, Chase continued.

"I need to even the score with Warren for two reasons," he admitted, his gray eyes weary. "First, because he dragged me into a game right after my mother lost her land, telling me it was a chance to win something back." His voice had never sounded so bitter.

"Oh, Chase." She knew how that story ended. Emotional players never won. The cards didn't care if you were angry. Or desperate. If anything, they were all the crueler to people who were on the verge of losing everything. "How could he? And what did you even have left that he wanted?"

"A cash inheritance from my dad." He moved toward the bar cart, opened a heavy crystal decanter and poured two fingers' worth of dark amber liquid into a rocks glass. "Your father hadn't taken that from me. Just the land."

He downed half the drink while Tana's stomach knotted with a fresh pain. She'd thought she felt sick before. But this new development made her dizzy with anger.

Her dad might not have taken Chase's last savings directly, but he had stirred the fever for high-stakes poker in the area. That gambling fever led to the kind of game that must have lured Chase to risk his money.

"Bastard," she said softly, even though she knew her father was far worse than Warren. "I'm so sorry."

For a long moment, Chase said nothing. He sipped the second half of the drink more slowly while the clock ticked down their time together. Tomorrow they'd return to New York first thing in the morning. Although if Chase had his way, Tana would be seeing him in the Hamptons next weekend for a poker game.

Not that she'd be playing. Finally, when Chase didn't seem inclined to say anything more, Tana spoke. Dared to ask the question that circled around her head.

"What's the second reason you want to face Warren at the card table? You said there were two."

Setting his drink down, Chase faced her.

An unhappy premonition settled inside her, making her dread his next words.

"I think you already know." His level look chilled her even before he continued. "A card game with an aggressive, reckless player like Warren Carmichael is sure to draw your father out of hiding."

Nine

Two days after returning to New York, Tana cursed the high heels she'd worn to today's afternoon audition. She'd managed to channel the pain of pinched toes into a kick-ass audition for a small role in a soap opera. But as she walked from the subway station back to her apartment, the blisters proved too much.

Every step lodged the back of her shoe deeper into the broken skin on her heel, a sting that wouldn't have hurt as much if she thought she had a snowball's chance of getting the soap opera part she'd tried out for. But she'd guessed from the high percentage of models at the casting call that the show was more interested in a pretty face than killer acting skills.

With *Streetcar* nearing the close of its four-week run, Tana was staring at potential unemployment again soon if she didn't nail a new acting gig. The prospect weighed heavily on her, as did her looming bills. Yet the stress of being jobless seemed like a dance party compared to the far greater stress of the poker game at Chase's house in Southampton slated for Saturday night. She knew he would be promoting the game up and down the eastern seaboard, hoping to draw her father out of hiding. She wasn't sure what upset her more about that. The possibility of facing her dad again after all these years? Or might there be some actual worry about her dad being arrested after all this time?

Of course not. She wanted justice for Chase. Her father deserved the jail time. But there were risks to an old con coming out of hiding. There were more dangerous enemies to Joe Blackstone than the police. And even after all his crimes, she didn't want him to be hurt.

Then, there were worries for herself, too. Eight years ago, her skills had been top-notch, even when she didn't cheat. But she wouldn't employ the old tricks anymore. Not when she'd striven so hard to live honestly since she'd turned eighteen.

It hurt that Chase had asked her to play. She hadn't realized until then how much she hoped he would see her differently now. See the woman she'd tried so hard to become. But she was only useful to him as a part of her old life. A crook's daughter.

"Ow. Ow. Ow." Hobbling up the steps to the brownstone, Tana could hear rock music vibrating through the front door as she approached.

Normally, the sounds of female laughter and electric guitar would have her smiling after a hard day, since it meant girl time with her favorite people in the world, Sable and Blair. But tonight she had the feeling her roomies were waiting to ambush her. Blair had cornered her multiple times since Tana returned home

Sunday, bombarding her with questions about what had happened with Chase.

Tana's hand hovered on the front door handle. She wasn't sure if she was ready to face them.

A loud burst of laughter from inside made up her mind, however. She had friends—genuine, sweet friends—for the first time. She'd been so isolated growing up, never allowed to get attached to anyone since her family had moved so often. No way would she run from a chance to enjoy the bond with Sable and Blair.

Not when she desperately needed the counsel of wiser heads than hers. Hauling open the door, she called into the building.

"Honey, I'm home!" She yanked off her offending shoes and left them on the welcome mat. As much as she would have enjoyed hurling them across the room, she needed to take them to a consignment shop. Maybe she could get credit toward a better-fitting pair.

A happy squeal sounded from downstairs in the kitchen, accompanied by Blair's voice shouting, "You're just in time for Mont Blanc chocolate pavlova!"

The scent of chocolate and something nutty floated up the sweeping mahogany staircase along with Blair's words.

"I have no idea what that is, but it smells amazing." Dropping her backpack on the marble console table, Tana hurried barefoot down the staircase connecting the entry-level parlor with the kitchen on the garden floor.

Inside the all-white kitchen, Sable sat on a granite countertop slathering whipped cream on a confection that looked like a meringue-covered cake on a layer of chocolate mousse while Blair finished washing a mixing bowl at the sink.

"Don't ask me what it is." Sable grinned up at Tana

as she entered, pausing in her work to wink. She wore a pink T-shirt that said We're Hungry with a red graphic heart over her baby bump. "I just co-opted the frosting duty so I could lick the spoon."

"Guys, come on. Don't you watch any baking shows?" Blair asked, blond ponytail swinging as she opened a cabinet to pull out glasses, setting three on the white-and-gray-flecked granite. "A pavlova is a meringue-based dessert, and I made this one chocolate. And the Mont Blanc part refers to the chestnut puree topped with whipped cream."

Tana washed her hands, hip-bumping Blair a hello. "You should be blogging this, you know? That's a work of art over there."

"If I start blogging about baking, then it might feel like work. And as it is, baking is my outlet." Blair pulled off the purple apron that had been covering a denim skirt and slouchy gray sweater that drooped off one shoulder. "Baking is also my way to bribe my friends into sharing details about their trips with mysterious rich ranchers."

Drying her hands, Tana shook her head. "No need to bribe. I'm going to freely surrender all the dirt be-cause I have no clue what I'm doing, and I need advice."

Blair and Sable exchanged meaningful looks, but Tana didn't bother trying to interpret it. She was too stressed about everything that had happened over the weekend, from her potential return to the poker table, to her very probable heartbreak at the hands of Chase Serrano.

Sable snapped off the volume on the music and slid off the countertop, landing on the tile floor in her ten-nis shoes. "Right. Everyone, report to the girlfriend war room, aka the dining table. We're going to scarf down sweets and figure this out."

Despite the hurt in her heart and the broken blisters on her heels, Tana couldn't help a small smile at the way her friends marched double time to address her crisis. Her eyes might have stung a little bit, too, because it had been a long time since she had people to look out for her.

Minutes later, they were seated around the antique plank table in the big white wingbacks that served as dining chairs. Bottles of sparkling cider and seltzer rested on a silver platter in the center of the table. Sable filled crystal glasses while Blair served thick slices of the pavlova on stoneware plates.

In as few words as possible, Tana outlined everything. Her grifter past. Her last summer under her father's roof before she went to college. Falling for Chase and the collapse of their relationship thanks to her father's betrayal after she left town. And oh God, what were her friends going to think of her after learning the things she'd done?

"Wait a minute." Blair's fork clattered to her dish as she called a halt to Tana's recap. "Just to clarify, your dad tricked the mother into letting him sell Chase's land while you were already in New York?"

"Right. I had to be in New Paltz in early August that year. My dad married Chase's mother, quietly sold the ranch and then went off the grid a few weeks later." She'd honestly thought everything would be fine in northern Nevada. She'd assumed her father would relocate to Vegas to help her mom with whatever scam she was working there.

So she'd been blindsided to hear what happened. Both her parents had disappeared after Joe Blackstone failed to meet Margot Serrano at the airport for their supposed Paris trip.

Sable lifted her glass to mime a toast toward Blair. "Good point. Chase can only blame Tana so much when she wasn't even in the same state as her dad when he committed the crime."

Blair nodded, picking up her fork again to spear a bite of dessert. "Plus Tana tried to warn Chase to keep an eye on her dad. If she were out of the loop on her father's activities, she couldn't know when or how he planned to strike next." Reaching over to Tana, she squeezed her wrist. "Sorry to interrupt. You were saying that Chase texted you afterward and that's how you found out what your dad did?"

"Yes. I went to the police and told them everything I knew." It hadn't been much, since he'd quit discussing his plans with her after she said she was leaving for good once she turned eighteen. "Giving them more about my dad's background at least resulted in bigamy charges. Not that he ever faced them in court since he'd already disappeared."

"Does Chase know you cooperated with law enforcement?" Sable narrowed hazel eyes at her across the table.

Tana shrugged, swirling her fork through her dessert. "Hard to say. He had a private investigator find me, so I imagine he knows quite a bit about my past."

"I hope he knows more about your present, which is what matters." Blair bristled as she spoke, her back straightening. "Your choices as an adult have been exemplary. You're not defined by your parents."

The indignation in her voice soothed Tana as much as the words. That her friends believed only good things of her was sweeter than any pavlova.

"Thank you for that. But I'm not sure it will be an exemplary choice to go play poker in the Hamptons, acting as bait for one high roller and one fugitive who happens to be my father." Bad enough she'd be breaking her personal vow never to touch the cards again. She knew that would risk her peace of mind.

But what about the risk to her heart sure to come by engaging in this one last favor for Chase? While he saw her as his ticket to revenge, she couldn't help but see him as much, much more.

Their time together in Nevada had stoked too many old feelings to life again.

Across the table, Sable drummed short pink fingernails against the polished surface, a rhythmic sound like a horse's trot.

When she stopped, she looked back and forth between Tana and Blair. "So take us with you."

Tana stared at her in shock. "I don't follow."

"You're worried about your choices and the stress of this game." Sable met Tana's gaze. "You said it was a party, so why not bring your friends? We can be your on-site sounding board, and we'll have your back."

Blair was already humming affirmative noises while Tana grappled with the idea. Yes, it sounded wonderful to have her friends nearby in a scary situation. But it also sounded awful to have these women—friends she loved and respected—witness the seedy past she yearned to forget.

"I don't know—" she began.

"I do!" Blair protested, banging a palm on the table for emphasis and making her plate jump just a little. "You're not in this alone anymore. You have friends. And friends stick together."

"That's right." Sable nodded slowly. "Who was there

for me when I was terrified I lost my baby?" Her hand curled protectively around her belly at just the thought of the scare she'd had early in her pregnancy. It had all been fine, though. Her baby was healthy and developing right on track as she passed the twenty-week mark. "You both were there, making sure I was okay, telling me I could raise this baby even if things didn't work out with Roman." A blissful smile curved her lips. "Which they did."

Blair nodded, winding her ponytail around her fist, and then letting it go again. "And who helped me raise the money for my mother's cancer treatments with the most moving, heartfelt video ever?"

Tana's heart softened at the memory of the footage she'd put together to help fund Amber Westcott's chemotherapy. It had felt good to use her talents behind the camera for such a worthy cause.

"But my situation is so different—"

"We're going," Sable announced, "even if I have to get the party details directly from the hot cowboy."

Blair lifted her glass of sparkling water. "All for one, and one for all, right?"

Sable raised her tumbler and clinked it against Blair's as they both turned expectant gazes her way.

Unused to displays of affection, Tana felt a little awkward at the love. But since she returned it in full measure, she took a deep breath and brought her drink to the center of the table.

"My dad used to say, 'play the hand your dealt like it's the one you wanted.'" She blinked away the emotions threatening to spill from her eyes. "Ladies, thank you for making this hand suck a whole lot less."

They drank to it, sealing the bargain. Tana still wasn't sure how she was going to get through the weekend with Chase when her emotions were so raw. At least her friends had faith in her in spite of her shady past. The confidence boost that gave her made her feel stronger. More ready to face the world she swore she'd left behind forever.

Even if she still had no idea how she was going to resist the man she was falling for all over again.

Three thousand feet in the air, Chase stared down at the gridlock on the Long Island Expressway, grateful for the helicopter service that would take him and Tana directly to Southampton.

"Do you always travel this way when you visit your house in the Hamptons?" she asked from the seat beside him. She smoothed a hand over the shoulder harness of her safety belt, her engagement ring winking in the late-afternoon sun.

She looked different today. She'd rinsed the pink ends from her hair, returning to her natural glossy brown. Her dress and heeled leather boots were both black, but there were no studs in sight. A henna tattoo of a peacock wound around her wrist, the feathers spreading all the way up her forearm. The snake was gone, and so was the stud in her nose. She looked beautiful, but Chase realized he'd grown to enjoy the quirky statements she made with her appearance.

He hoped the lack of spikes in her wardrobe didn't mean she was anxious about the weekend. He already second-guessed himself for asking her to participate in the card game, since it had obviously troubled her. Now that he'd had time to see how much she'd turned her life around after leaving Nevada, he appreciated why she didn't want to be pulled back into that world. And he hated the idea that he was no better than her father, asking her to play another role. But he failed to see how else he could ensure he could lure her father and Warren Carmichael to a card table. Chase had come too far in his quest for revenge to turn around now. The quest had been his objective for eight years.

For now, he refocused on her question as they neared their destination, the chopper humming eastward.

"If I'm going out for a weekend, yes. The traffic is always worse then."

She nibbled her lower lip in a way that made him want to take a bite, too. "I hope my friends make the trip without any trouble tomorrow."

Chase couldn't stop a grin at the memory of her text request for extra party invitations.

"I'm glad you'll have support," he told her honestly, even if a part of him wished she would rely on him for that. Did she think he wouldn't protect her every moment she was under his roof?

He knew that she was only taking part in this weekend for his sake. That alone would have stirred a sense of loyalty even if he hadn't already felt protective of her after what they'd shared at the old homestead on Cloverfield Ranch.

"It might be more than just Sable and Blair who make the trip," she warned him, flicking her thumbnail over the band of the engagement ring as they began their descent. "Some of my castmates expressed interest in coming."

"Really?" He thought back to her performance in the park, surprised she would have mentioned the party to her colleagues. He'd always envisioned Tana as a bit of a loner. "Wasn't today your final show?"

"Yes, it was my farewell to Blanche DuBois." Her smile was tight. Polite. "I got a commercial for next week, but that will only be a day or two of filming. I was thinking about pursuing work on the other side of the camera since I'll have some time on my hands."

Reaching to the floor of the aircraft, she retrieved a satchel-style handbag and pulled a sleek-looking camera from it, brandishing the heavy lens before stuffing the device back in the well-worn bag. The sight of it reminded him that she truly had never profited from her father's scams. She'd worked hard to carve out an honest life for herself since parting from Joe Blackstone's influence.

"While I'm sorry to hear your production ended, I'm glad you've got new options. And of course your cast-mates are welcome tomorrow night." He tried to shuffle what he knew about Tana to incorporate these new facets.

The filmmaking aspirations. A wealth of friends eager to support her. He'd read about her admission into the brownstone that was a rent-controlled haven for aspiring women artists. She'd impressed some extremely important people with her talent in order to land the spot.

The thought gave him another dose of guilt about what he was asking her to do this weekend.

"Thank you." She opened her mouth to say something else, but just then the helicopter touched down with a jarring motion.

Reflexively, she reached for him, her hand gripping his knee. The denim didn't begin to dull the sensation of her touch. He'd missed it, craved it all week long.

Without taking time to question the wisdom of responding, he covered her fingers with his, trapping her palm against his leg. The chopper came to rest, the blades slowing their rotation while Chase and Tana stared at each other.

Her breaths came quicker, her pupils going dark as her tongue darted along her upper lip. He tracked the movement, his heart thundering in his chest, urging him to act on the heat sparking between them.

"You know why I wanted you to come here with me tonight, the day before the game." It wasn't a question.

He turned her hand over and then cupped it between both of his. In his peripheral vision, he could see the pilot's door opening on the helicopter, but Chase refused to rush this moment with Tana.

"I thought maybe you wanted to go over the layout of the card room. Discuss strategies—"

"No, not at all." His fingers threaded between hers, fitting their hands together. "We can do those things. But I wanted you here tonight to spend time with you. To be with you somewhere nicer than a sleeping bag in a cabin with no central heating."

The quick intake of breath was almost silent, a tiny gasp of surprise or—he hoped—pleasure.

"I liked the cabin," she protested mildly.

The answer pleased the hell out of him, since he'd been content there, too. If anything, it had felt inevitable returning to a place where they'd passed a lot of good hours together long ago.

"You'll like the bed here even more," he promised. "Assuming you want to spend the night in mine."

She shifted in her seat, crossing her legs in a way that made him hope she was feeling the same needy ache that had plagued him all week.

"Why would we do that when—after this game— you'll be returning to your life at Cloverfield and I…" She cast dark eyes toward the roof of the chopper, as if searching for answers anywhere but with him. "I won't be with you?"

He'd known, of course, that this weekend would bring an end to their time together. She'd been extremely accommodating to sign over his lands to him. And now she was helping him entice Warren Carmichael to the card table, and possibly her criminal father, too.

But he had no illusions about a future together. He was deeply attracted, but how could he ever trust her after the way things ended the first time, no matter how much she'd changed? What's more, how would she ever trust him given that he was the one dragging her back into a world she'd worked hard to leave behind? The guilt he'd wrestled all week threatened to ruin all his carefully laid plans. He just needed to focus on seeing this through.

"Isn't that enough reason? If this weekend is all we have, why wouldn't we enjoy it together?" He lifted his free hand to cup her face, tilting it so he could see her better. He stroked his thumb along her cheekbone, imagining having her all to himself for the rest of the night.

For a moment, he thought a shadow of doubt crossed her eyes. But then it was gone, replaced with heat and hunger.

"Okay." Turning her face into his hand, she dragged her teeth along his palm before nipping the base of his thumb. "I'd rather lose myself in the connection we have than waste another second thinking about what tomorrow will bring." Then she reached for her seat belt and clicked the button to unfasten the restraint. "Let's go."

Ten

On the short car ride from the helipad landing to Chase's Southampton home, Tana's body hummed with anticipation. She leaned into the feeling, needing him now more than ever when her fears about tomorrow bubbled so close to the surface.

Chase's touch guaranteed she wouldn't be able to think about anything else but him, and she craved that kind of forgetting. Her heartbeat was a rapid knocking inside her rib cage, every pulse urging her closer as they sat side by side in the back of the chauffeured luxury sedan he'd hired for the trip.

As they drove past a double-gated entrance into a giant horseshoe driveway, however, some of the flushed excitement dissipated. The sleek Mercedes rolled to a stop in front of a palatial gray cedar mansion flanked by complementary buildings that looked like a pool house and guest cottage. Tana felt the full depth of being out of her element. The disparity between her life and Chase's hadn't been quite as apparent on Cloverfield Ranch. But here, in this elegant and lushly landscaped home in one of the world's most exclusive neighborhoods, Tana understood the sort of wealth Chase had amassed in the years they'd been apart.

She hadn't even realized that Chase had exited the vehicle until he pulled open her door himself. He reached a hand in to help her out while the driver removed their bags from the trunk.

For a moment, she hesitated, looking into Chase's gray eyes for a hint of the man she'd fallen for eight years ago. The rancher who'd taught her to ride a horse. The lover who'd claimed her innocence and taught her about pleasure. She needed him now, not the slick billionaire bent on revenge.

"Is everything okay?" he asked, his brow furrowing at whatever he saw reflected in her gaze. His hand dropped to her knee, where he brushed a reassuring touch.

The warmth of his fingers penetrating her knit cotton dress stirred the attraction back to life. Or maybe it was the tenderness in his eyes that suggested he cared how she was feeling. She seized on that, gripping his hand in hers.

Steering it, briefly, higher on her leg. She never broke eye contact, letting him see the way that touch sizzled through her.

His nostrils flared and his chest expanded.

"More than okay," she returned, swiveling on the seat to exit the vehicle. "Just ready to hold you accountable for what you promised me once we arrived."

Chase made quick work of tugging her to her feet, his strong arms banding around her waist. In one motion, he drew her against him so she could feel the hot brand of the erection hidden beneath the gray sport jacket he'd worn with his jeans.

Lowering his mouth to her ear, he spoke softly. "I'm very ready to make good on the promise."

The edge in his voice alone would have made her tremble with need. But the feel of him against her only made it worse, and Tana fought to hold back a hungry whimper.

Chase released her for a quick exchange with the driver, then took her hand to guide her up the wide stone steps and onto a narrow veranda running the length of the gray cedar exterior. After punching in a code on the security system, he opened the front door, then ushered Tana inside a foyer with a sweeping split staircase before admitting the driver carrying their bags.

Between the staircases, Tana could see through the foyer into a library with high coffered ceilings and two fireplaces. There was a formal dining room off to her right and a living area to the left. With white walls and dark wood floors, the house had a minimalist aesthetic that allowed the beautiful architecture to shine.

She swallowed past the swell of nerves, just as she heard the front door close again.

The driver had departed. Leaving them very much alone.

"Hey." Chase stood in front of her again, tilting her chin up, his big body blocking her view of his wealthy world and all the complications that came with it. "Are you still with me?"

She lifted her hands to his chest, smoothing them over the white cotton shirt beneath his jacket, splaying her fingers wide to feel as much of him as possible.

"I am right here with you. Yes," she murmured, gaze

dropping to the shirt buttons as she began unfastening the top one.

"Tana." He breathed her name out like a curse or maybe a prayer, stretching the syllables. "What are you doing to me?"

His hands settled around her hips, drawing her to him before his broad palms wandered lower, slowing as they reached the hem of her dress midthigh. There, he fisted the fabric, drawing it tight around her and making her very aware of what he would soon uncover.

Heat thrummed in her belly. Her nipples tightened to hard points.

She licked her dry lips before she could speak. "I hope I'm doing the same thing to you that you're doing to me. You're setting me on fire. Turning me inside out."

"Damn right." He chafed the fabric of her hem back and forth across her thighs for a moment before letting it go. "Come with me."

Abruptly, he let go of her dress to lead her up one side of the massive staircase. Her legs wobbled a little; she was drunk on her hunger for him and the knowledge that tonight would be the last night they spent together.

After another moment, they were in a luxurious master suite with a private terrace on one side and a sky-lighted bathroom on the other. While Chase closed the door, she stepped deeper into the room onto the soft gray rug that covered the dark wood floors. The white walls were blank slates save the large windows overlooking the grounds, tall trees all around preventing her from seeing any neighboring houses.

But then her time for gawking was over when Chase's strong forearm curled around her waist to draw her back against him. Air rushed from her lungs at the contact. Her spine arched, hips rocking closer still.

"Did you miss me this week?" she asked before she thought better of it, her voice a breathless wisp of sound.

"You tell me. Does it feel like I missed you?" He lifted her against him, notching his erection between her thighs.

"Yesss," she hissed the final sound between clenched teeth. She squirmed restlessly, needing more of him.

His palm covered her breast, squeezing. Molding. "Good. Then you'll understand why I can't wait any longer to have you."

Sensation sparked everywhere they touched, sending ripples of pleasure to every nerve ending in her body.

"I can't wait, either." She strained against his grip, but only to turn around so she could see him. "I want to undress you."

He lowered her to the floor, loosening his hold so that she could face him. Before she could go to work on his shirt buttons, however, he lowered his head and covered her lips with his for a drugging kiss.

She forgot everything else, sinking into the feel of his tongue mating with hers. He stroked and explored, conquered and claimed. She clung to him, her fingers fisting around his lapels while he had his way with her mouth.

By the time he let her up for air she was boneless and quivering. Her lashes fluttered, and she slowly raked open her eyes to see Chase stripping off his clothes, his hand at his fly.

She made a mewling sound, half needy, half pleased. His gray eyes flickered to hers, twin silver flames warming her everywhere.

In an instant, she slipped off her leather boots to stand barefoot on the soft carpet, toes curling into the deep pile. As Chase studied her with primal male hunger etched in every feature, Tana reached for the hem of her black knit dress and lifted it up slowly. Slowly.

By the time she shimmed it up and over her head, Chase was naked and inches from her, his hands landing on her bare ribs to stroke over her body.

"Baby, you're so beautiful," he breathed against her temple, his palms moving to cup her breasts. "I need to see every part of you."

"But I'm ready for you *now*," she confided, smoothing her hands over the hot planes of his hard chest. "You can look while you're inside me."

Restraint slipping fast, Chase had to bite his tongue to keep from laying Tana on the bed and driving deep, over and over. How did this woman get under his skin so fast? Like she belonged there.

Like she'd never left after the first time he'd fallen for her.

He clamped down that thought hard. Because he needed to focus on *her*.

Didn't matter what he was feeling right now. He'd promised her a night to forget everything else but this sizzling connection, and he'd be damned if he didn't deliver.

So as much as he wanted to bury himself in her, he would gladly delay his own gratification to make sure she got off as many times as possible tonight. He wanted to see her reach her peak again and again, and to know that he was the man responsible for taking her there.

"I'm dying to be inside you, too, but I'm going to make it worth your while to wait a little longer, okay?" He snaked an arm around her narrow waist, holding her steady while he dipped the other hand into the satin waistband of tiny black panties. "Trust me?"

She sucked in a gasp as he grazed his fingers over the swollen bud between her legs, but she nodded agreement. He felt the movement where she tucked his head against his chest.

"Good. I think you're already close, don't you?" He teased slow circles around her sex, listening to her breathing quicken, feeling her breasts rise and fall faster. What a privilege to see her this way. To be the one holding her tonight.

His gaze narrowed to her face, watching the flush of color in her cheeks deepen.

Her fingers crept higher on his shoulders as she anchored herself. He quickened his rhythm, knowing her well. Remembering what she needed.

He watched as her lips formed soundless pleas, sensing the tension build as she tilted her hips. And then...

"Oh, Chase." Her body arched hard against him as she ground down into his hand, taking what she wanted. Her throaty cry raked his ears.

The satisfaction of seeing her come apart, feeling her sex pulse and flutter against his hand as he slowed his movements, was almost as good as any release of his own. He wanted to beat his chest with pride at making her come, taking pleasure in knowing he could give that to her. Instead, he kissed her, slow and deep, as he walked her over to the king-size bed in the center of the room.

"I can't wait anymore," she told him as he lifted her up onto the mattress, laying her gently down in the middle. "No more delaying."

A smile pulled at his lips as he raked her panties down her legs. He got a condom from the nightstand before he covered her with his body.

"Was the last delay so bad?" With one knee, he spread

her wider while he unfastened the hooks on her bra with his hand.

"Well, no, actually." Tana slipped her arms around his neck, fingers toying with the hair at the base of his neck in a way that sent shivers down his spine. "I'm not complaining. It's just that—"

He rolled on the condom, his knuckles brushing the slick heat between her thighs as he worked it in place. She'd caught her lip between her teeth at the contact.

"No more delaying," he promised, lifting her arms up over her head.

He meant to pin them there, but as his hand spanned her wrists, the glitter of pink diamonds in her engagement ring caught the light. The satisfaction of seeing the ring there—his ring—was even more potent than what he'd felt over teasing her to release.

The knowledge that she would be giving it back to him tomorrow…

Shutting down the wrongness of that thought, Chase redoubled his focus on her. He edged his way inside her, letting the silky heat of her tight body ease the frustration. With every inch he claimed, the ache of impending loss receded.

When he bottomed out, fully seated inside her, he dropped his forehead to hers.

Bliss.

Utter. Absolute.

He breathed in the citrusy scent of her skin, reveling in how right it felt to be with her this way. When the squeeze in his chest came, a small fissure that threatened to break wide, he knew he needed to move.

Releasing her hands, he started driving his hips into hers. Deeper. Faster. She locked her limber thighs around his waist, meeting every thrust.

The heat built. Raged out of control. Burned over both of them. He would have let it consume them, but he'd promised himself he would make sure she found her peak again before he reached his.

He placed his hands on either side of her shoulders, finding purchase on the bed as he dragged his body over hers slowly, angling himself in a way that provided more friction where she needed it. Sweat popped along his brow as he held himself back, knowing he could get her there, wanting to feel her pulse all around him.

Her fingers scrabbled along his shoulders, nails lightly scoring his spine while her head tossed back and forth. He wanted to bury his face in the silky dark mane of her hair, but he knew she was close.

He nipped her earlobe and then licked it. "No more delays, baby." He threw the words from earlier back at her. "Come for me."

She flew apart so hard, so fast, he didn't have enough time to watch her. The squeeze of her feminine muscles shattered the last of his restraint, shoving him over the edge into his own release. Waves of pleasure pummeled him, dragging him down and holding him under.

For long moments he let the sensations wash over him, his breath huffing between them like billows. At last, arms damn near weakened from the rush, he lay down beside her and waited until the world righted.

In the quiet aftermath, he felt her snuggle against him, her silky hair blanketing his chest as she found a place for herself there. He managed to flip one side of the duvet over them, enough to cover them as their bodies cooled.

Her left hand lay beside her cheek, the platinum band of her ring a reminder of the pretense he'd forced on her.

The fake engagement she hadn't asked for but had undertaken because she felt guilty for her father's actions.

In the stillness of feeling her breathing sync up with his, Chase could admit to himself that had been wrong of him. She had no reason to feel guilty for an act she hadn't committed. A crime she hadn't known her father was planning.

She'd been his scapegoat. A way to avoid placing the blame where it belonged on her father's shoulders. And, yes, on Chase's shoulders too, to a certain extent. He hadn't heeded her warnings about her father, after all. He'd refused to see what was happening all around him that summer, too consumed with falling for Tana to recognize how thoroughly his mother had been ensnared by a con man.

Then, afterward, his bitterness about Tana had blinded him to how Warren took advantage of him, too.

"Don't think about it," Tana said quietly, her words puffing warmly along his chest.

"How do you know what I'm thinking?" He squeezed his eyes closed at the same time his hand cupped her hip. He just couldn't stop wishing he'd thought of some other way to right the wrongs of the past that didn't involve her.

"It's going to be fine." She kissed the place over his heart before settling against him again. "You've never seen me play in a high-stakes game, but I'm good."

Anger at himself bubbled up again. He turned toward her enough to see her, unseating her from the position she'd been in so they faced each other on the bed.

"What if I told you I've changed my mind?" His heart drummed faster at the idea.

"We both know it's too late." Her dark eyes were impossible to read. The light in the room had become dim as the sun lowered in the sky, and there were no lights on in the master suite. "Warren is already flying in for the game, and if my father has heard about the high-stakes poker happening here tomorrow, it's not like we have any way to reach him to tell him it's called off now."

Chase swallowed hard, wondering what the hell he'd been thinking to choose revenge over...what? He didn't know if he could trust Tana any more now than he ever had.

Just because he'd stopped blaming her for the past didn't mean he'd suddenly be able to trust again. After all, maybe he hadn't just blamed her for her father's crime. Maybe he blamed her for the way things ended between them. For him alone at school in Idaho when he got the news that Joe Blackstone had tricked his mother into marriage in order to rob the family of its land.

It was only natural for Chase to think he'd been tricked into a false relationship, too.

"Maybe it is too late," he admitted finally, the idea dropping on him like a stone. "But we could still host the game without having you play."

"And miss the chance to win back some of the inheritance that Warren stole from you after my father sold off your lands?" She shook her head. "No way. You've worked too hard for this moment to give up on it now."

The vehemence in her words caught him off guard.

He studied her face. "You really want to help me recover it, don't you?"

"I know you might find it tough to believe, but after the life I've lived, Chase, it hurts me more than most people to see someone cheated."

"Even though I've done well for myself in spite of what happened?" Rolling onto his back, he huffed out a sigh. "I noticed your expression when you first saw this house. You're aware that I'm not hurting for the money."

She levered up on her elbow so she could peer down into his face. "Because you worked your tail off to re-cover what you lost. *No one* deserves to be cheated."

Her dark hair spilled onto his chest while she made her fierce claim. He gathered up some of it and stroked his palm over the length.

"So we won't call off the game." He wanted to kiss her again. To show her how much it meant to him that she was on his side even though it meant going against her own father. Even though it meant opening up her past for others to see. "But I want you to promise me something."

She laid her hands on his chest and then propped her chin in the middle of them. One dark eyebrow arched. "What kind of promise?"

"I know you've gone eight years living your life hon-estly." He wasn't going to mess that up. Not for any-thing. "I want you to promise that—even if it looks like you're going to lose to Warren—you won't cheat for my sake. I don't want you to throw away your long streak of living honestly for me."

Her full lips drew together in a frown. Even in the dim light, he could have sworn a chill came into her eyes.

"You still don't trust me?"

"It's not about trust. It's about how hard you've worked to build a different life." He was proud of her for that. "You've achieved so much."

Her gaze narrowed. "It hasn't been hard work not to cheat people. It actually comes very easily to me to be honest."

"Of course I know that now. And I don't want you to think that I'm asking you to do anything different than you've done for eight years." He didn't understand why he'd offended her, but he could feel her pulling back even as they lay there together. "Either you win at cards or you don't, but there's no need to stack the odds in your favor."

Tana dragged a throw blanket from the far end of the bed and wrapped it around herself as she moved to sit on the edge of the mattress. It wasn't lost on him that she was pulling away, closing herself off.

"Fine. I promise not to cheat." She slid off the bed and moved in the direction of the bathroom, tossing her hair over her shoulder. "For now, we should eat. All the sex made me ravenous."

She closed the bathroom door behind her before he could respond. Something was off in her response. Was she offended that he'd asked her not to employ the old tricks of her days in a con artist family?

Maybe it would have made her play easier. Less stressful.

Then again, he understood she hadn't wanted to play in the first place. Perhaps she was frustrated that he wanted to dictate how she approached a game she hadn't wanted to be in to start with.

Rising from the bed, he tried not to dwell on it. His plans were in place. She'd told him not to cancel. And he still had a whole night in front of him with Tana before he confronted the men who'd wronged him.

Or at least one of them, if her father didn't show up.

Chase would use every minute of the time they had left to show her he believed in her, to make up for the hurt he'd caused. He just hoped that would be enough to help them through whatever tomorrow brought.

Eleven

Staring into the dressing room mirror the next afternoon, Tana leaned on the marble countertop of the elegant vanity table to slick on her eyeliner, flicking the end to create a cat's eye. Her stomach was full of butterflies. With so much riding on tonight, it took all her theater training in tackling nerves to keep her hand from shaking.

She'd spent far more time on her appearance today than normal, knowing that—like Yogi Berra had famously said of baseball—poker was 90 percent mental. That meant she needed time to get her head focused before the other players began arriving. That seemed easiest to do while locked in the master suite dressing area, far from Chase and all the confusing feelings that last night had unearthed.

Remembering their time together threatened to tumble all the precarious barriers she'd erected around her heart. It had been more than just phenomenal sex.

There'd been a synchronicity, an anticipation of each other's needs. And afterward, there'd been the long hours of holding each other. Sharing the happy memories of their past instead of only the bad ones, both of them determined to savor the moment for however long they could.

Switching to the other eye and running the black makeup over her lash line, Tana just wished that they'd never had the conversation about cheating at cards. A conversation in which he'd asked her not to cheat, which felt to her like an implication that she might have otherwise. It had hurt. Especially after the night they'd shared.

Flinching slightly at the memory, she messed up the cat's eye, smudging the line at the end close to her temple.

"Damn it." She set down the brush and searched her makeup bag for remover to clean up the mistake.

Hadn't she told herself not to think about Chase? About his lack of trust in her? Her stomach knotted. She knew tonight would be the end of things between them. He'd take back his ring after she helped him win the money Warren had swindled from him. She would return the land her father had won from Warren. Balance would be restored in Cloverfield. Then, she and Chase would go their separate ways for good, and she'd tell herself that it was okay since he still didn't trust her anyway.

Even though she was doing all of this for him.

So maybe it wasn't just her stomach that was in knots. Her heart felt like it was being yanked in two different directions, too.

Rubbing a cotton swab dotted with makeup remover over the black blotch, Tana heard a knock on the bed-

room door. Nerves stretched thin, she didn't move from
the dressing table. She didn't trust her knees to hold up.

"Chase, I told you. I need to focus." In theory, she
was giving herself a pep talk about playing poker again.
Remembering all the old wisdom her dad had taught
her from an early age.

*A pair of balls beats every other hand, sweetheart.
Remember the power of bluffing.*

Or, *play the man, not the hand.*

She could spout the maxims for hours. If only she
could concentrate on them and not Chase.

"It's not the hot cowboy, girlfriend. Let us in!" a dis-
tinctly feminine voice called through the door.

Relief flooded through her at the sound of Sable's
thick Southern drawl. Tossing aside the makeup tools,
Tana rushed to the door and unbolted it. As she swung
open the barrier, her friends swarmed in. Blair carried
her professional cosmetics kit that looked like a heavy
silver tackle box. Sable had black garment bags with
Zayn Designs printed on the side in gold lettering.

Tana glanced into the hallway behind them, but the
landing was empty. She could hear the catering staff
downstairs in the kitchen, however. No doubt Chase's
work crews had arrived to transform the great room into
a card room, while the caterers would be arranging the
hors d'oeuvres and drinks appropriate for an exclusive
party of high rollers.

Locking the door behind them, she turned to see
Blair settling the makeup kit on the vanity and Sable
hanging the garment bags in the huge closet that opened
off the bathroom. They were dressed casually in jeans
and T-shirts, but Tana guessed their gowns for later
were contained in the garment bags.

Blair, who wore a pink blazer over her white T-shirt,

turned to hug her. "The cavalry is here, hon. I can finish your makeup for you."

Tana squeezed her friend back, breathing in the rose and vanilla scent of her long blond hair, which fell in loose curls to her shoulders. Tana might not be used to hugging, but she needed the love today. Desperately.

"Thank you. I was turning my cat's eye into a black eye." She let go of her friend, so grateful for the distraction.

And the friendship.

Blair bent her knees to see Tana's face better, angling her own underneath. "I can turn it into a smoky eye. It'll be gorgeous."

Before Blair had finished the assessment, Sable was by Tana's side, sliding an arm around her waist.

"And wait until you see what you're wearing. You're going to die." Her drawl drew out the last word into an extra syllable as she tipped her dark head onto Tana's shoulder. "I needed to dress you two extra sexy tonight since this baby bump is forcing me into muumuus and caftans."

"Oh, please," Tana retorted as Blair drew her back into the chair at the vanity table. "You were buying maternity clothes ten seconds after that pregnancy test and you know it."

"Okay. Guilty." Sable smiled as she moved to unzip one of the garment bags. "It's more fun to think about pregnancy outfits when you still have a waist." She wrenched off the bag with a flourish. "But what do you think of this?"

The red silk gown she'd revealed was breathtaking. The halter neck had plunging décolletage and a floor-length hem. The lines were clean and simple, uninterrupted by flounce or ribbon so the attention would be on the feminine form beneath the fabric. And before Tana could wonder what the back looked like, Sable spun the hanger to show off the way the dress would appear backless once it was on, the fabric ending just below the waist.

Speechless, Tana could only stare from one amazing friend to the other.

Sable didn't appear to need words, however. She winked at Tana.

"I know, right? You thought the gowns I sent you for that wedding were too much of a fairy princess vibe. So this time I went with more of a queen of diamonds look." Then, pulling out a shoebox from the bottom of the open garment bag, she tugged off the top. "Even the shoes are hot-to-trot red."

Overcome by the gestures, Tana felt herself relax the tiniest bit for the first time all day. Yes, tonight was going to be difficult. Scary.

But she'd have a new kind of armor to wear as she entered the card room.

Better yet, she'd have her friends at her side.

Exhaling a deep breath, Tana let Blair tip her chin up into the light she'd repositioned in order to work on Tana's face.

"Okay, I'd better get busy," she murmured half to herself, sweeping Tana's hair into a clip to keep it out of the way. Then, opening her makeup kit to lift the accordion-style trays inside, Blair continued, "When we first were at the door, you said you had to focus. You mean on the game?"

Behind them, Sable kicked off her shoes and paired her phone with a speaker near the bed, filling the room with guitar-heavy rock music. It was the kind of thing they'd always played on their Friday nights together in the brownstone. And even that small nod to their friend-ship helped Tana relax a little more.

She would enjoy this time with her friends because their days together in the Brooklyn apartment were numbered. Sable spent fewer and fewer evenings with them as her job and fiancé vied for her time. Plus, she needed to prepare for her baby. Blair was planning a future with Lucas Deschamps, heir to a cosmetics em-pire and her former boss.

As for Tana, she wouldn't be able to afford even the rent-controlled apartment much longer if another act-ing gig didn't come through. Who knew how many more moments she'd have like this with her friends? Because while she'd treasure them for life, the days as roommates were special.

"Yes. I've been trying to remember everything I know about poker so I can psych myself up to play." She watched Blair choose an eyeshadow palette and a brush.

"Would it help you to have quiet to think? Or did you want to talk through strategy out loud?" Blair swirled the narrow brush in a metallic gray powder.

Tana closed her eyes in preparation for the makeup, grateful for the friend time. Soaking it up like healing medicine for her nerves.

"I'd love to talk it out." She felt safe here, in the company of these ladies who trusted her. Who didn't feel the need to warn her not to cheat. "For starters, I've just been thinking through all the things my dad used to say. Not that it was such great wisdom, but it helps take me back to a time when I played every night. When it felt easy."

Blair hummed, half to the beat of the song and half in response to Tana. "Like what? Know when to hold 'em? And know when to fold 'em?"

Tana laughed, a little more unease floating away. "Sort of. For one thing, he used to say, 'Tana, if you're staring at your cards, you're not watching the other players look at theirs. Read the game. Read the players.'"

And for the next hour, she dug deep to remember all the things she'd buried eight years ago. About her father. About poker. About the games they'd played together back when he'd had fun showing off his card-playing protégé. Surprisingly, it wasn't all bad. There'd been some good memories in the awful ones. A few nights where they'd pulled Robin Hood–style wins at the table, beating rich whales who treated the cocktail waitresses like crap. Then Tana and her dad had tipped those waitresses with almost all the winnings, walking out of the card room with little more money in their pockets than what would buy them a big breakfast.

She talked and reminisced, remembering the old game rhythms, not realizing how much time was passing. Until, suddenly, she was standing in front of a full-length mirror letting Sable zip her into the sexiest dress Tana had ever worn in her life.

The red silk caressed without clinging, following the lines of her body like it had been made for her. Blair fastened the halter neck tighter, making sure Tana wouldn't fall out of it. But there was no room for underthings.

Still, the dress was a layer of confidence. For years she'd worn spikes and an abundance of eye makeup, daring the world to judge her for her past. But this was a different kind of costume. A look that said she was a woman comfortable in her own skin. Between the red silk on her body and the exquisite makeup on her face that made her look...well, *queenly*, Tana felt like a new woman.

Bold. Ready.

She would not resort to any card tricks tonight. But she absolutely had to win. Only then would she be able to walk away from Chase with her head held high, knowing she'd done everything in her power to right her father's wrongs.

Tana might not be able to save her heart from breaking. But she would heal an old wound and—just maybe—forgive herself in the process.

Chase roamed the Hamptons house shortly before game time, double-checking his preparations as guests began arriving for the cocktail hour. There were plenty of locals and a few business associates who weren't there for poker, preferring to mingle and—in some cases—preview the house that Chase had renovated and would be putting on the market soon.

Those guests were in the conservatory overlooking the grounds. The night was warm enough that there was an outdoor bar set up near the pool house.

But Chase was more interested in the living area that had been set up as a card room.

Spotting the professional dealer he'd brought in for the evening, he paused to ask, "Do you have everything you need?"

"Yes, sir. Thank you," the silver-haired gentleman replied, glancing up from his open box of cards and chips. He wore a bow tie and vest over his shirtsleeves, and a gold signet ring flashing on his pinkie as he shuffled cards on the black cloth playing surface in the middle of the antique mahogany table. "I'll be ready at game time."

Chase nodded his thanks, looking over the ten leather-upholstered chairs—enough for the dealer, seven confirmed players, and two empty seats to accommodate possible guests who'd failed to RSVP.

Joe Blackstone, for instance, could still show.

Or, for all Chase knew, Tana's missing father could be using an alias and had already confirmed a spot. The man had certainly employed fake identities in the past. Still, Chase had checked the backgrounds of the confirmed players and felt confident none of them was Joe.

He'd wanted to show the list to Tana, but she'd retreated from him completely today. He shouldn't have extracted the promise about not cheating. He understood why that unsettled her. Had he really needed it? He'd told himself that he was beyond the mistrust. Especially since their night together had been unforgettable, every moment of it seared into his memory forever. But this morning, she'd insisted she needed quiet to mentally prepare for the game, the coolness suggesting she hadn't forgotten about his lack of faith in her. She'd locked the door to the master suite, only admitting her girlfriends who'd arrived that afternoon.

So he'd been forced to wrestle all over again with the idea that he should call off this game. Haul her back to his bed and tell her she didn't need to recover what he'd lost eight years ago. He didn't blame her, so he couldn't possibly ask her to do any more to help him recover the last of his inheritance.

It was money that had ceased to matter, other than in principle. So why was he still moving forward? Why undermine the small amount of trust he thought they'd rebuilt? Unless his confidence in her wasn't as solid as he thought.

"Damn it." He pounded his fist on the bar, making a huge arrangement of purple irises jump in their sleek white vase.

"Pregame jitters?" a seductive feminine voice asked from behind him.

Whirling around, he faced the woman he'd been missing all day. A stunning vision in red tonight, Tana rivaled any Hollywood star in beauty and elegance. Soft waves framed her face, a jeweled clip on one side winking in the light of the chandelier. A hint of glitter just under her brow bone and red lipstick were fanciful touches, along with the diamond drop earrings swinging against her dark hair.

But the dress she wore…no, it was her gorgeous body inside the dramatic dress that would have every jaw dropping tonight. The red silk halter plunged deep between her breasts, showing a hint of the high, subtle curve of each. Skinny straps tied the thin fabric around her neck, making it look like a good breeze might blow the whole thing off her.

"No one at that table will have their mind on poker tonight. Not while you're wearing that dress," he growled quietly as he pulled her to him, needing to feel her. Reassure himself that he still had the right to touch her.

But for how much longer? a contrary part of his brain wanted to know.

"That would be an amazing advantage, but I'm not sure I'll be able to distract anyone else as thoroughly as I seem to have distracted you." She edged back a step, peering up into his face. "Is everything all right? You sounded upset a moment ago."

Now that he'd recovered—mostly—from the sight of her in that dress, Chase noticed the tension in her bare shoulders. The hint of anxiety in her dark eyes.

"I'm fine. Just still wondering if this is a mistake." He took her hand now that he was no longer touching the rest of her. His fingers skimmed over the ring on her finger, wishing things were different between them.

That they'd met under different circumstances. "I don't want to subject you to something that's going to cause you more stress."

"At this point, I'm counting on a win to be healing for me. For both of us. You'll see that I'm not a cheat." She withdrew her fingers from his. Straightening the jewelry, she pivoted to look out over the card room. Away from him. "Besides, we're so close to achieving everything you wanted when you first approached me at the play. I'm not giving up before we close the deal."

Her cool words felt like they'd come from a stranger, even though she was giving him what he'd wanted. And, as gorgeous as she was beside him right now, he missed the way she sparred with him. The tattoos and spikes. The pink in her hair.

He'd turned her into this remote beauty tonight by asking her to play a role she'd never wanted.

"Tana—"

"There's Warren." She pointed to the rancher entering the card room, his slick blue suit paired with elaborately stitched leather cowboy boots. "And I think I see a few faces from my play behind him. I should say hello."

Damn it.

Chase nodded stiffly, knowing he couldn't escape Warren Carmichael if he wanted to as the man charged toward him across the great room.

"We'll talk later," Chase reminded her. "You've avoided me all day, but I need to speak with you after the game."

He wasn't ready to let her go tonight. He didn't know what that meant, or how they could spend more time together. But after the night they'd shared, he hungered to explore the option.

"Of course." Her smile showed no teeth. With a brief

nod, she seemed to float through the growing crowd toward her arriving friends.

And Chase knew he'd just seen her poker face. It boded well for the game table, since he didn't have a chance in hell of reading her and he'd doubt anyone else would be able to, either.

But as for what it meant for them? He wondered if she'd already retreated so far from him there'd be no winning her back.

Her father wasn't coming.

Tana's thoughts turned more and more to that realization as the evening wore on. She'd lost track of how many hands had been played so far, but she'd started off the evening in the button seat—an advantageous position since she was able to place her bet last—and she'd won a significant hand the second time she held that position.

By now, the table had shrunk to four players, and she had a good feel for her opponents. Warren's play had not impressed her, but she knew better than to underestimate him. So far, she'd played with the cash that Chase had staked for the game, but she knew the time would come when she'd need to put the deed to Warren's former lands on the table.

He'd raised frequently, sometimes unwisely, no doubt in an effort to make her put the paperwork in the pot. But she wouldn't be goaded into playing that game. She wanted to recoup Chase's lost cash inheritance every bit as much as Warren longed for the return of the property he'd lost to her father long ago.

And where was Chase?

She risked a quick glance up from the table, missing his presence in the room. He'd sat at the bar across from her for the first hour or so, visiting with her girl-friends until Sable and Blair had disappeared out onto the patio. But Chase had lingered at least a few hands afterward, though the spot was vacant now. Even more telling, she didn't *feel* him nearby. How funny was it that, just days after seeing him again, she could already sense him when he was close?

Her chest ached at the thought of breaking that con-nection for good. Far more than the other, surprise ache of not seeing her dad tonight. She'd put him out of her mind for years, knowing he was a bad influence. A criminal. But a therapist at her college had once told her that it wasn't a crime to have love in her heart even for people who hurt her. She could feel those emotions without letting them hurt her again.

And yeah, in spite of everything, there'd been a piece of her that had wanted to see him again. Or rather, there was a piece of her that hoped her father would want to see *her*. Which, clearly, he did not.

Now, folding a weak hand, Tana bided her time until the dealer called for a short break in the action. Once the hand finished, the pot going to the quiet older woman named Odina at the far end of the table, Tana stood to stretch her legs. The real work would begin in the sec-ond half of the evening when play was elevated.

All the remaining players had taken one another's measures. Odina, the stoic older lady, played a conser-vative but effective game. Warren, the hothead rancher, played with more reserve than Tana had anticipated, but he still made aggressive plays that could bite him in the end. Then there was Tana and a jovial Eastern European man named Cyrilo who spoke with such a thick accent that Tana had briefly wondered if it could be her dad in disguise—changing his voice along with his appearance.

But that thought had been fleeting, given he was at least three inches taller than her father, a symptom of how much she'd secretly hoped her dad might make an appearance after all this time.

Frankly, it ticked her off that she'd given him so much thought when he didn't care if he ever atoned for his crimes. Or atoned for being a sorry excuse for a father.

Tana picked up speed as she neared the doors out to the patio where she hoped to find Blair and Sable, or some of her friends from the *Streetcar* performance. The security guard, Lorraine, had brought Megan, the actress who'd played Stella. They were dating now, and it had been so kind of them to support her. She wanted to see them before the inevitable heartbreak that awaited her at the end of the evening when Chase took back his ring.

"Tana?" The unfamiliar voice behind her stopped her just short of the open French doors.

Turning, she saw Odina a few steps behind her. The older woman had her head down as she seemed to be digging in her oversize handbag. With her neutral-colored pantsuit and dark, blunt haircut, Odina was the kind of player who would have been easy to underestimate. The clothes were a great misdirection now that she thought about it. Smarter than Tana's fiery red dress actually, even though she wouldn't trade Sable's generous fashion help for anything.

"Did you lose something?" Tana asked, taking a step back into the corridor that she thought led to a guest bathroom and maybe a home gym.

"Just looking for my denture glue. I'm so embarrassed." The woman peered up from her handbag, holding a set of false teeth in her hand.

Something about the woman's face seemed off. Or familiar somehow. But she didn't want to stare when Odina had just said she was embarrassed.

"Erm. You think it's in your bag?" she suggested helpfully, trying to pull her gaze away from how the lack of the false teeth changed the shape of the woman's mouth.

Even her cheeks looked different…

"Took you long enough to recognize me," Odina said, her voice utterly altered. Masculine. And yes, very familiar now.

Her father.

Much thinner. With different colored hair and eyes, and maybe some cheek plumpers in his mouth.

But what had thrown her the most was that she'd never thought to look for him in a feminine disguise.

"Oh my God." Tana covered her mouth to prevent an outburst, not quite sure what her next move should be.

Scream? Call Chase?

Or take this break in the game to ask her dad where the hell he'd been for eight years?

"Come on." Her father took her wrist in a grip that was far from feeble and pulled her down the hall. "We need to talk before the next hand."

Twelve

Chase had searched for Tana during the break, but didn't find her. Then, before the game resumed, Warren Carmichael had dragged him into a conversation. So Chase was only able to watch as the players reconvened around the table, the group whittled down to just four competitors and the dealer.

An hour into the next tense round of poker play, a glass appeared in Chase's vision.

"You look like you could use a drink." The speaker, Roman Zayn, held his own beverage in his other hand. Beside him stood Lucas Deschamps.

Chase had met the two men briefly when they arrived a couple of hours ago. They were the respective partners of Tana's friends Sable and Blair. Chase knew them both by reputation since his own investments required a relentless eye on the business world. Fashion and cosmetics weren't areas of particular familiarity for Chase, coming from ranching. But as the personal luxury goods market was worth almost $300 billion worldwide, he certainly knew their companies.

"Is it that obvious?" Chase asked quietly, in deference to the ongoing game. He accepted the glass, recognizing the pecan and caramel scents of a top-shelf bourbon. He took a sip appreciatively, confirming his guess.

The drink provided a pleasant burn but didn't come close to easing the tension that had settled thick in the card room nearby. The bar was far enough from the action that they could speak here, although in general, the conversation grew more muted in the great room as the stakes rose at the poker table. The party outside remained in full swing, however, the music and laughter from the pool deck area still audible over the sounds of the bartender mixing drinks and the dealer narrating the game.

Roman, the owner of a fashion label and the soon-to-be father of Sable Cordero's baby, was built like a soccer fullback, all shoulder and muscle. With dark hair and eyes, he slouched into the corner seat at the bar. "More than obvious. You looked ready to grind your molars to dust."

Lucas Deschamps dropped into the seat on Chase's other side, his height and lean form all casual grace. He looked like he'd been to plenty of parties in the Hamptons in his time, his tailored navy jacket and relaxed air in keeping with his wealthy East Coast upbringing. "I've never understood this game. Care to interpret what's happening over there? Tana looks like she's holding her own."

Tana's name on another man's lips snagged Chase's attention sharply away from the woman and toward the speaker.

"You know her, then? I mean, aside from just a nodding acquaintance as Blair's roommate?" Chase took another sip of the bourbon, feeling it safe to look away from the game since Tana wasn't betting. The older woman, Odina, looked like she was going all in on this hand, though.

The pot was already hefty.

"I'll say." Lucas's smile was wry as he plucked a cherry from the bartender's stash and tossed it in his mouth. "She was Blair's personal security team while I was trying to court her. At the end, I was lucky to get past Tana to see Blair after I screwed up and fired her."

Chase lifted an eyebrow at Lucas while the next player—the Eastern European guy with a thick accent—deliberated his bet. "You fired your girlfriend?"

"Well, no. But that's how Tana saw it, and she didn't let me forget it." Lucas stretched long legs in front of him, Italian loafers toeing the carpet. "She made me bring my A game to winning back Blair, that's for sure."

Chase smiled with satisfaction to hear it. "She's not someone to mess with," he agreed, his chest swelling with pride.

On his other side, Roman leaned closer to confide, "Tana convinced Sable that they could raise my child in the brownstone—without me—and told her to take her time deciding if I was the right choice for her."

While Chase wanted to inform him that it sounded like wise advice to any expectant mother, the shadow of fear that lurked in the back of the big guy's eyes told Chase how much the idea of being separated from his child had shaken him.

"I'm glad it worked out for you," he told the other man sincerely, his admiration for Tana growing still more. "Congratulations to you and Sable."

"Thank you." Roman managed to touch his glass to Chase's almost soundlessly before he glanced up at the poker table. "Hey, what did Tana just add to the pot?"

Jerking his attention back to the game, Chase saw a piece of paper on top of the pile of chips.

She'd bet the deed to the lands Warren wanted.

Chase's gaze went to Warren Carmichael, recognizing the greed in the other man's eyes at the same time the dealer nodded, seeming to accept Tana's bet. "Player three raises with property assigned a cash value of fifty thousand."

The lands were worth more than that. Especially to Warren, who used the acreage to move his cattle from one section of his ranch to another. But they'd wanted Warren to take this bet when Tana made it.

Had she chosen the right hand to dangle the carrot?

Heart in his throat while he waited to see if his old enemy would take the bait, Chase's gaze slid around to the others at the table. Cyrilo, the Eastern European high roller, had folded. Odina, the older woman, had gone all in.

And as Chase's eye was about to skim past the petite woman's black bob, he noticed the way the lady glanced up at Tana.

A quick, furtive moment of eye contact.

Or had she winked?

His instincts twitched uneasily, spine tingling with new awareness. What was he missing here? Chase glanced around the room, confident someone else must have seen the exchange if it had actually happened. There were plenty of observers.

Yet who else here knew Tana's history besides him?

Chase could hardly pay attention to Warren's next move, though he knew his nemesis was over a barrel.

He'd either have to fold and lose everything he'd put into the pot already, or match Tana's bet to stay in the hand.

And even though this was the moment Chase had been waiting for—a revenge scenario he'd long dreamed about—he realized in the moment it didn't matter at all. Hell, he'd rather have lost all the money and the land, too, if it meant he'd never put Tana in a scenario where she could have been tempted to—

No.

His heart pounded harder. She'd promised him she wouldn't cheat, and he trusted her. She wasn't the same woman he'd known eight years ago, and he'd witnessed firsthand how hard she'd worked to turn her life around. Besides, she didn't know the older woman who'd winked at her.

Did she?

Chase must have missed something—Warren going all in—while Chase's old demons whispered in his ear. Because a moment later, the dealer was announcing the winner of the hand—Tana—while the room erupted into applause.

"That was amazing," Lucas acknowledged on his left side. "She had a royal flush the whole time."

On Chase's other side, Roman gave a wolf whistle before clapping Chase on the shoulder. "Nicely done. Congrats, man. Your girl is a poker champion."

Trying to shake off the uneasy feeling, Chase's attention fixed on Tana again. She was acknowledging congratulations from Cyrilo while Warren walked away from the table in disgust. Still, Tana's dark eyes sought Chase's as the dealer called for another break.

Why didn't Tana look happier? She'd just won the biggest pot of the night, worth over a million thanks to the no-limit stakes. Enough to refund the cash inheritance Warren had taken from him.

Yet Chase saw only worry etched on her pretty features.

"Excuse me," he muttered to his companions, charging toward her to find out what was wrong.

Shouldn't she be pleased? Or maybe she simply hadn't wanted the evening to end either, since they'd planned to go separate ways after tonight.

Of course, he'd hoped to renegotiate. He just needed to tell her about the feelings stirring inside him.

"Congratulations, Tana." He greeted her with a kiss on the cheek, appreciating the comfort that came with wrapping an arm around her narrow waist.

But then he realized she was shaking like a leaf.

"Chase." Her voice was low and urgent in his ear. "We have to go outside. Follow Odina."

Rearing back, he tried to compute what she'd just said. Tried to figure out why she was trembling.

"Odina?" Had the other woman cheated somehow? Maybe that was what the wink had been about. "What about her?"

His attention was already spanning the room, searching for the older lady.

"It's my father," Tana confided in the softest of whispers, jabbing a pin into all of Chase's overinflated hopes about her. "In disguise."

Just that fast, she'd gutted him.

Chase hadn't been wrong about the look exchanged between Tana and her ex-con parent. She'd cheated her way to the bitterest of victories.

Tana felt Chase stiffen beside her, but he followed her out to the pool patio where she'd seen her father retreat.

Her dad was sick—dying of pancreatic cancer—and probably shouldn't have been out at all. He'd lost a tremendous amount of weight, but he'd promised her he just wanted to sit in on the hand to see his daughter compete one last time at the game he'd taught her.

What was she supposed to say?

Still, she knew Chase would be angry. But she also trusted that he would understand when her father turned himself in as he'd promised to once the other guests left for the evening. Her father didn't want to taint her evening or the victory that—even two hours ago in their private reunion—her dad knew she would have. He'd had total faith in her ability to pull it off fairly.

Now, Joe waited for them out on the beach, the waves of the Atlantic audible as Tana skirted the pool house that marked the edge of Chase's party.

"Where are we going?" Chase hooked an arm in her elbow, hauling her to a stop just before her feet hit the sand.

They stood on the flagstone path that wound between the tennis courts and the beach. The late-summer wind blew stronger here, with fewer trees to block it. She gripped the skirt of her silk dress to keep it from flying up.

"My dad's out on the beach, waiting for the party to end." She had so much to tell him. Her brain had been so fixated on the game and winning back what Warren Carmichael had stolen from Chase that she hadn't really let herself process the news that her father was back. That he was terminally ill. "He's turning himself in, Chase."

"And you *believe* him?" The sharp edge in his voice cut straight through all the tender and raw emotions of the night. The whole day.

The last week and a half.

Gripping the gown tighter, she willed herself to stay strong against those feelings for fear they'd knock her right down.

"Yes. I do. He had no other reason to come here tonight, other than to see me one last time—"

Chase's bark of cynical laughter cut her off and sliced through her. "He hid out for eight years, never contacting you. Never showing his face. But suddenly he wants to see you on the night when there's a no-limits game he thinks he has a shot of winning?" He shook his head. "Excuse me if I'm skeptical."

His disbelief hurt, but she understood. Steeling herself, she hoped Chase could still separate his feelings for her criminal father versus his feelings for her. After all, the time she'd spent with Chase over the last ten days must have meant something to him.

He might not love her, the way she now realized she'd never stopped loving him. But he must care for her.

"I know you have every reason to doubt him, but I hope you won't doubt me." She wanted him to know why her dad had left the Nevada lands in trust for her. What he'd hidden there. She'd learned a lot in her conversation with her father. But first she needed Chase to listen.

The muscle in his jaw worked back and forth as he seemed to consider this, the Atlantic wind tousling his hair, brushing strands in his eyes. The fissure in her chest split open wider at how long it took him to speak again.

"I wish I didn't have reason to doubt you," he said finally, his gray eyes dark. Flat.

She couldn't blame it on the night sky, either. There was a full moon that lit his expression well.

"W-what do you mean?" Her voice wobbled. No amount of spikes and studs, tattoos and piercings would have been enough to ward off the pain his hard voice was inflicting.

"I mean, I saw the look you and your father exchanged across the poker table right before that last bet. It seemed off when I thought it was an old woman winking at you. But now that I know it was your father…" He shook his head, his expression grave as he seemed to size her up and find her wanting. "I thought you weren't going to resort to the old tactics. Collusion is still cheating."

The thin ice she'd been skating on with him all week broke right under her feet. A new, frigid chill surrounded her, dragging her under. Tana welcomed that cold, praying it would keep her numb enough to walk away from Chase Serrano before he saw how he'd just devastated her.

She'd need her guardian angel, though, to pull it off. She kept the thought of those protective wings in mind as she reached for the engagement ring on her finger and took it off.

"How. Dare. You." She articulated the words carefully between shivers so he wouldn't hear her devastation. She was proud of how she'd managed it. Reaching for Chase's hand, she slammed the jewelry into his palm and closed his fingers around it. "Take this. Take your land. Take your winnings. I never want to see you again."

"Tana, wait." Chase might have reached for her. She thought she felt his fingers brush her shoulder.

But she was keeping the numbness around her like a protective shawl, her sole focus on finding her father so she could say goodbye. She'd have to tell Chase the rest of the news in a letter. Registered mail, so he couldn't ignore it.

Because one thing was certain. She would not be speaking to him again. She didn't want him to see the love he'd just crushed to pieces under his boot.

Thirteen

Chase didn't know how much time had passed when he opened the fist containing the engagement ring. He stood rooted to the spot where Tana had left him, her words circling around his head, berating him.

Telling him over and over again how badly he'd misjudged her.

What had he just done?

The Atlantic wind blew harder, stirring grains of sand off the beach to pelt his face. The moment he'd uttered the word *collusion* he'd witnessed the blood drain from Tana's lovely face. In the moonlight, that had meant she'd turned three shades paler. Even her lips had gone slack with shock.

Immediately, he'd realized he'd blown it. He'd let his fears get the best of him. Instead of hearing her out, he'd taken the offensive, scared of being fooled again.

Tana had been facing down her own fears for his sake, sitting at that poker table tonight even though she hadn't wanted to ever play again. But he'd been so hell-bent on a revenge that it hadn't mattered he'd put her in that position anyway.

Then, when she'd needed him to conquer his own fears, what had he done? He'd lashed out like a coward, believing the worst.

Loss hollowed out his insides.

The sounds of the party—dance music and laughter—reminded him he had a responsibility to his guests back at the house. But he couldn't bring himself to care. Instead, his gaze went out to the beach. In the moonlight he could see the figure of Tana. Beside her, the outline of another person.

Her father?

He noticed Tana had just walked away from the other figure, and the rest of the beach was empty. Tana moved farther away from the party, heading in the direction of a public parking lot for beach access. Chase longed to intercept her, hating the idea of her wandering around Southampton after midnight.

But he knew she'd meant it when she told him she never wanted to see him again. He might not be able to change her mind about that, but if he hoped to have any chance of an audience with her again, he guessed tonight was not the time to press the issue.

Stuffing down his fear at that possibility, he directed his footsteps toward the other person on the beach instead.

Sand slid into his dress shoes, but he ignored the grit to focus on the man dressed in a woman's pantsuit. This was Joe Blackstone? While he'd never been a big man, the guy had lost at least fifty pounds. But as Chase closed the distance, he could see the figure had ditched the black wig to reveal thin gray wisps of hair blowing to one side. He'd taken off his shoes, his pants rolled up just below the knee as he checked a phone screen.

"Joe?" Chase asked as he neared, the wind apparently masking the sound of his approach.

The light on the phone screen went off and Tana's father pivoted toward him.

"Chase." The older man gave a nod of acknowledgment, his face expressionless. "I was just checking on the status of my ride. The local cops agreed to pick me up when I told them I'm wanted in Nevada."

In the moonlight, Chase could see he must have removed some of his makeup from his Odina disguise. His cheekbones had fallen, too, as if they'd been plumped by some artificial means. Even the teeth were different.

"You're really turning yourself in?" Chase couldn't believe that of Joe Blackstone, not even once Chase realized that—of course—Tana had not cheated. "I assumed you just told that to Tana."

The con man shook his head. "I'm done lying to her. To everyone. Five years of Gamblers Anonymous has taught me better habits."

"Yet you gambled tonight," Chase couldn't help but point out, still not sure he believed anything from the man who'd duped his mother. Broken her heart.

"I told Tana why. I knew this game was your way of luring me out of hiding, and it was high time I paid the price for what I did to you and your mom. I don't mind serving the time for that now, but I couldn't resist the chance to see my girl play at the top of her game tonight." Joe flashed a hint of white teeth in a smile.

She shouldn't have been playing at all, Chase thought to himself, hating that he'd asked her to. Hating that he hadn't just enjoyed the gift of being with her while he'd had the chance.

Joe tipped his face into the wind, folding his arms across his chest. "She was magnificent. I know I shouldn't be so proud that I gave her a skill some consider a vice. But she could compete at the highest levels. Make a fortune in tournament play if she chose."

Seeing the expression on the other man's face put the wink he'd seen at the poker table into context. Joe hadn't been signaling his daughter for some kind of collusion during the game. He'd simply been proud of her.

Chase's heart sank a little farther.

"I'm surprised she left you to wait out here alone," he observed, turning to peer in the direction he'd seen her wander. Eyes hungry for a sign of her.

"I wouldn't let her stay." Stuffing his hands in the pockets of the pantsuit jacket, Joe faced Chase again. "She washed her hands of my life even before she turned eighteen. And once that girl makes up her mind about something, she doesn't change it."

Chase felt like her father was beating the last of Chase's hopes to death. He rubbed his hand over his chest, wishing he were with Tana now. He needed to at least be sure she got home safely.

"Did you see if someone picked her up?" Chase withdrew his phone, ready to text one of her girlfriends.

"A couple of her theater friends were meeting her." Joe stopped, turning his head. The sound of a distant siren rode the breeze. "Look, my time is almost up, so I'm going to tell you what I told Tana. I've only got a year or so to live at most, so I realize the jail time I'm facing isn't adequate to pay my debt to you or society."

Alarm rattled through him. "What do you mean a year to live?"

But Joe shook his head as if he preferred not to answer. "Listen, Chase. I tried to send Tana a couple postcards with the coordinates on that land I left her, but she didn't realize what they meant. I buried some of my winnings there. Half is for her that I won fair and square off of blowhards like Carmichael. But the other half is money I owe to people I conned. It's all written down."

The words came fast even though Chase had a whole host of questions. But the sound of the sirens was growing closer.

"Are you saying you never took anyone's money? That you buried it all?" Chase wondered if the guy had ever even left the country or if he'd been in disguises since going off the grid eight years ago.

"I took a little," he admitted, wincing as if he had a sudden pain in his side. But he straightened up again. "But it was never about the money for me. It was about the thrill. A game that hurt too many people."

"Like my mother," Chase reminded him bitterly. "I got back the lands, but I couldn't fix the way you hurt her."

"I will never forgive myself for hurting Margot. Regret for that—for what I did to her—is what got me into group therapy." He turned to face the public parking area as the police cars pulled in, headlights illuminating his face. "I really did want to leave the country with her. Tana's mother had already kicked me to the curb. But I couldn't let Margot tie herself to me."

In the swirl of blue and red lights, Chase could see how haggard the other man looked as he lifted his hands above his head.

Regret sighed through him for a hundred ways he'd screwed up tonight. For the first time ever, he felt the smallest twinge of empathy for Joe Blackstone. It wasn't a good feeling to know you'd messed up, possibly beyond repair, and hurt someone you cared about.

Because whether or not Joe had ever really cared for Chase's mom, Chase believed he cared for Tana. The grifter had proven it to him tonight by turning himself in. By the obvious pride he'd taken in watching her play. By the way he'd tried to make up for some of his wrongs.

Maybe that was why he found himself telling him, "For what it's worth, my mother forgave you a long time ago."

Chase wasn't sure he'd ever extend the same grace to the man. But he didn't mind giving him this small gift. It was true enough.

Two police officers neared them now. Chase prepared to explain who he was, but for now he held his hands in the air, too, just to be safe.

Joe Blackstone met his gaze in the moonlight. "Thank you for that. And good luck winning my girl back. She's hurt and she's angry. But she loved you eight years ago. If you're lucky and she still does, maybe you've got a shot."

Chase would gamble everything he had on the smallest chance the old man was right.

Walking home from another audition late the next Friday afternoon, Tana did not take her studded high-top tennis shoes for granted. They were comfortable for one thing, unlike last week's high heels.

And they'd been on her feet for her second callback for the soap opera. She hadn't gotten the bit part intended for a pretty face that she'd tried out for the week before. But the casting director had liked her reading and had asked her to try out for a new character on the show. A tough, streetwise woman raised by derelicts who triumphed over her past to open a bar in Port Henry, where the show was set. And the stars had aligned for the reading, apparently, because she got that part.

Yet even as Tana knew she should be on cloud nine over the professional victory, she felt more fragile than ever in the wake of Chase's accusation. A week apart hadn't soothed the burn of that wound in the least.

Of course, she shouldn't have been surprised that he didn't trust her. His request before the game that she not cheat showed her how much the past was still on his mind. How much he still viewed her as her father's daughter. It was like eight years of good behavior meant nothing.

Now, turning the corner in front of Fort Greene Park, she wondered if she even wanted to go home, where her roommates would doubtless want to celebrate her new role. Sable was moving out tomorrow for good, so she'd promised to sleep over one last time. No way would Tana miss out on that.

So why did she contemplate walking back to the park so she could cry in private on a park bench for a few hours? Her numbness cloak had worn off as soon as she'd left the Hamptons last weekend.

Instead of indulging the crying spree the way she wanted, she picked her head up as she reached her stoop.

Only to find Chase Serrano seated there. A black Stetson shaded his eyes, his denim-clad knees sprawled to either side of him.

Her heartbeat went into triple time while her brain counseled her to retreat. Fast.

But did tough, streetwise women run and hide at the first sign of trouble? She tried to think like her new character, bar owner Liberty Montgomery. For once, she was grateful for the chance to play the role of someone else around Chase.

"I think you have the wrong address," she informed him, fisting her hands on her hips. Willing her eyes not to fill with tears…or her heart to fill with hope. "Because I'm sure I told you we wouldn't be seeing each other again."

She wouldn't allow him to hurt her again. So her best defense was a good offense.

Except he didn't look offended. He looked like he hadn't slept either, the purple shadows under his eyes matching the ones she'd been seeing in the mirror all week on her own face.

"Tana, I'm so sorry." His words were quieter than she would have expected. Humble.

He spun something in his hands, worrying it back and forth in an agitated motion.

A sparkle from the object made her look closer. Her heart seized. It was the engagement ring she'd slammed into his palm at the party.

She told herself that even feisty Liberty Montgomery would have had her interest piqued. She looked at him levelly, grateful he was seated.

"For what exactly?" she asked.

An unhappy smile ghosted over his features. "How much time do you have?"

Around them, the street was quiet. There were a couple of teenage girls sharing a pair of earbuds, each engrossed in a phone screen. A package delivery carrier ran up to a house across the street.

She waited. "I'm listening."

His hands went still. "For taking for granted the time we had together. For using it to pursue a revenge scheme that didn't matter to me. For asking you to play that cursed game in the first place." He shook his head, gaze falling to the concrete steps briefly before meeting her eyes again. "But most of all? I regret letting my fears speak for me that night on the beach instead of listening to my gut and everything I knew about you."

The sadness etched in his features spoke to her as much as his words. Seeing that regret for herself softened something inside her. Made her want to hear more.

Taking a chance, she dismissed her Liberty character and ventured closer to Chase. She leaned a hip on the stone balustrade.

"You mean about accusing me of cheating?" Even now, a phantom pain came with the word. "You realize the dread of being associated with dishonesty is what drove me to cut ties with my dad in the first place, right? I didn't want that to taint the person I needed to become. But you insisted on seeing me that way."

"I didn't. I *don't* see you that way." He pivoted the ring back and forth, catching the light with the familiar stones. "If I'd used logic, Tana, I would have known the truth right away. You've shown me in a hundred ways that you're not the person I was afraid you were eight years ago. But I was scared of finding out I'd been deceived again, and I let my mouth run with the fears instead of listening."

She'd protected herself for so long, afraid of letting herself get too close to anyone, that she'd almost lost out on the chance to make the friends she had now. Friends who were—she could see out of the corner of her eye—sneaking peeks at them out the front window even now.

What if she took a chance with Chase, the same way she had with her girlfriends? It was easier with Blair and Sable. They'd lavished her with love so readily. But she knew that—if it worked—the payoff with Chase would be even greater. So she cracked open some of her pain, sharing it with him so he understood it.

"Whatever the cause, Chase, it hurt me so much to find out we were right back where we were at the beginning. As if the time we'd spent together meant nothing to you." She held herself very still, feeling vulnerable. Wary.

"I would do anything to undo that, Tana. Anything." His silver eyes were bright and flinty at the same time. Emotional, but determined. "But since I can't go back and change that night, I can lay the whole world at your feet and hope you try to forgive me."

Hope wound through her, even as she cautioned herself not to be wooed by words.

"What do you mean?" She didn't care about material things. But she couldn't deny she was curious. What woman wouldn't be at that kind of declaration?

"I'm asking you to spend time with me and let me show you how deeply I care about you. How much I love you." He juggled the ring to one hand and reached for hers with the other. "I've missed you for eight years. I didn't know how much until we spent time together again. But having you at my side in Cloverfield felt so right, I think I knew then that you're the only woman for me."

Her heart expanded. A deep breath filled her lungs in a way that made her think she hadn't really breathed for a whole week. It felt glorious. Happy. Hopeful.

"Chase." She couldn't think quite what else to say, so she just squeezed his strong hand, letting herself get lost in that molten silver stare and allowing the feeling of love to wrap her up. "It felt really right for me, too. When we were back at Cloverfield again." Then, as the words started to come, she found more. "I loved you from that first night we were together eight years ago," she admitted, letting go of her most closely guarded secret. "Don't let the clothes fool you. I might be more romantic than both my roommates combined."

A moment later, she was in Chase's strong arms, her head tucked against his chest and her hip tucked into his lap. He stroked her back with one broad palm and kissed the top of her hair with the other.

"Tana, I love you so much. I promise you're never going to regret being with me," he vowed before lifting her chin to look into her eyes. "You know the real reason I wanted you to be my pretend fiancée?"

In her peripheral vision, she saw the curtains at the front window flutter. But her attention remained on the pink diamonds that covered the engagement ring he held in front of her again.

"I kept asking you," she reminded him softly, biting her lip against the new surge of hopes that were wildly romantic. Foolish, even. "I never understood why we needed to pretend."

"I think the reason I could never come up with a very good answer is because I never wanted it to be fake." He stroked her hair off her temple, tucking it behind her ear. "I know you might not be ready to make that kind of commitment yet, but we could call it a promise ring—"

"As in you promise to propose one day?" She tried to imagine what life would be like with Chase Serrano in it every day.

A shiver ran over her at the idea of being in his arms. In his bed. But she also liked the idea of going horseback riding with him. Sharing her dreams with him. Filming him and their life together.

"That is absolutely what I'm promising. I just know I want you to have it back, whether you put it on your finger today or not."

Her heart leaped. She already knew her answer. She leaned closer to kiss him, letting her lips glide over his slowly. Thoroughly.

This time, she could hear feminine squeals right through the front room window. She drew back on a laugh and saw that Chase's smile matched hers.

"I'm glad someone else is enjoying this, Tana, because facing you and knowing you had every reason to turn me down is the scariest thing I've ever done." Brandishing the ring once more, lifting it high enough that anyone in the peanut gallery would be able to see it, he held it above Tana's hand. "Would you like to wear it now?"

Joy filled her whole being. She couldn't remember ever feeling a smile so big. "I'd like to if you say the promise that goes with it."

His gaze went a shade darker as he stared into her eyes.

"Tana Blackstone, I promise you all my love and all my trust." The hand on her back rubbed lightly, as if he could make the words sink in with his touch. "And I also promise that when the time is right, and we've mapped out a life that will make you the happiest, I will ask you to be my wife."

Moisture gathered in the corners of her eyes. She didn't bother to blink it away, ready to let him see how much he affected her. How much she returned all those feelings.

"Yes, please, Chase Serrano. I love you. I forgive you. And I can't wait to say yes."

When the ring slid on her finger, Tana felt like her whole life slid into place. She had a job. A future with a man she loved. A happy final night with her girlfriends to celebrate her good fortune and theirs.

And most of all, she had a love she could count on forever.

Epilogue

One month later

Tana's finger hovered over the button on her phone that would almost empty her bank account. She made sure she had input the correct routing number for the money's destination.

Seated at a small dressing table in her room inside the Brooklyn brownstone, she had a few minutes to finish the financial transaction that would disperse the last of her father's gambling winnings. She'd been stunned when she and Chase had flown to Cloverfield to dig up the buried money and log book her father had kept from his poker heyday. Sure enough, there was a thorough accounting for two years' worth of his games and a list of everyone who'd lost money to him through trickery. Tana had a hard time finding a couple of the people on the list, but it had been rewarding labor to restore money to people who'd thought it had been lost for good.

Of course, there'd been a few players who'd still been angry with her father. But even the most bitter of Joe's victims had been appeased to hear he was serving time behind bars. One woman had even cried on the phone over the news and had sworn she would write to him.

"Are you sure about this?" Chase's low rumble from behind Tana preceded a kiss on the top of her head. He squeezed her shoulders, the scent of his aftershave making her long to lean back against him. "That's a lot of money you're giving away."

Refocusing on the numbers on her screen, Tana didn't need to think twice about the amount. The left-over funds in her father's buried lockbox had been fairly won, but that didn't mean she wanted any of it. Walking away from that life meant she had no intention of keeping a penny from his card sharp days. Besides, with the earnings from her regular work as an actress now that she had a steady role, finances were no longer an ever-present concern for Tana.

"Positive." She stabbed the send button with her finger and watched a confirmation number for the transaction appear on the screen. A sense of calm relief filled her to know the money had been given to a worthy cause. "I told my dad what I planned to do with the money and he really liked knowing it was supporting my friend's non-profit startup." Setting the device aside, she rose to her feet, turning so she could wind her arms around Chase's neck. "Now Blair can take her beauty program on the road in a customized cargo van that advertises her care services for cancer patients."

Tana and Sable had helped Blair launch the program when they saw how much time Blair devoted to offering free beauty services to people going through chemo-therapy alongside her mother. Blair's mom had a hopeful prognosis now, but Blair continued to be passionate about the community of underserved people who were often too tired or discouraged for self-nurturing. Tana had been enthusiastic about the project from the beginning. And now, seeing her dad's decline in health due to pancreatic cancer, it felt all the more fitting to channel his winnings this way.

"Have I mentioned that I am so proud of who you are?" Chase asked, cupping her face in his hands as his gray eyes peered down into hers.

Happiness swelled inside her, the way it always seemed to when he was around. In the last four weeks, they'd found an easy rhythm to being together. He'd taken a suite at a hotel close to the Brooklyn pier where her performance of *A Streetcar Named Desire* had been, close enough to her brownstone that they could see each other daily. They'd spent two weekends at his house in Southampton so they could go horseback riding, but they talked about spending next summer at Cloverfield so they could ride every day. The nice thing about working on a soap opera was that she'd have a few months off before they began shooting again in the fall.

Maybe then she'd work on some ideas she had for producing. Now that her life had calmed down, she found herself reaching for her video camera more and more often.

When she wasn't reaching for Chase, at least.

"You may have mentioned it." She smiled up at him, mesmerized by the look in his eyes that told her how much he loved her. How much he trusted her. "But I don't think I'll ever get tired of hearing it."

She'd spent so long trying to recalibrate her ethics after her childhood that it still thrilled her to hear that Chase saw her in such a strongly positive light. His faith in her had her reaching for her spikes less and less often. But she still liked sketching the occasional monster on her wrists in henna. She'd done a dragon with lacy wings two nights ago and she'd toyed with the idea of turning him into a cartoon character. How fun would it be to create a kids' show for her first production?

"You're an amazing woman, Tana Blackstone." He spoke into her hairline as he kissed her, pressing the words into her skin for emphasis. "You inspire me to be a better person, and I can't believe I'm the fortunate one who gets to have you by my side."

She hummed something inarticulate in answer, her whole life vibrating along a new, happy chord. Pressing herself tighter against him, she let the feel of hard muscle and warm man tempt her to lead him toward her bed.

Until a shout sounded from downstairs.

"Tana, let's go!" Blair called from the next floor down. She and Lucas were moving in together soon, but they were taking their time to find the perfect place, and Tana had appreciated the bonus weeks with her friend. "You know Sable will strangle us if we're not on time for the courtroom vows!"

Chase leaned away from her, chuckling softly as his hold on her eased. "Guess we'd better get going."

"Right." Tana retrieved her phone and a small, beaded bag for the low-key nuptials that would tie Sable to Roman, her baby's father, until after their child's birth. There would be a beach wedding next summer, but the two of them wanted to make their marriage official today. Tana was honored to have been asked. Blair and Lucas would join Tana and Chase to witness the event before a catered dinner at the brownstone for old times' sake. "Never keep a pregnant woman waiting."

Chase kept one of her hands in his and he tugged on it briefly as they reached the top of the staircase.

"I can't wait until it's our turn." He lifted her ring finger to her lips and kissed the spot just above her engagement diamond.

Her pulse sped, the way it always did when he was near. Especially when he said things like that.

"I bet it will happen sooner than you think, if you play your cards right." With a wink, she brushed past him to head down the stairs, more than ready to celebrate happily-ever-afters with the people she loved most in the world.

* * * * *

COMING SOON!

We really hope you enjoyed reading this book.
If you're looking for more romance, be sure to
head to the shops when new books are
available on

Thursday 11th November

To see which titles are coming soon, please visit

millsandboon.co.uk/nextmonth

LET'S TALK
Romance

For exclusive extracts, competitions
and special offers, find us online.

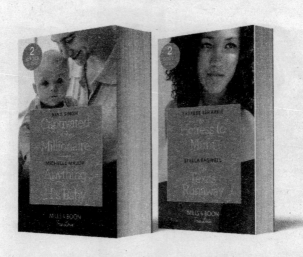

MILLS & BOON
MEDICAL
Pulse-Racing Passion

Set your pulse racing with dedicated, delectable doctors in the high-pressure world of medicine, where emotions run high and passion, comfort and love are the best medicine.

MILLS & BOON
MODERN
Power and Passion

Prepare to be swept off your feet by sophisticated, sexy and seductive heroes, in some of the world's most glamourous and romantic locations, where power and passion collide.

MILLS & BOON
Desire

Indulge in secrets and scandal, intense drama and plenty of sizzling hot action with powerful and passionate heroes who have it all: wealth, status, good looks…everything but the right woman.